Praise for the Broma

"Nothing about Adams's novel i⸻⸻⸻⸻ᵘⁿⁱˢ catchy
premise with surprising wisdom and specificity."

—The New York Times Book Review

"*The Bromance Book Club* is a gloriously tongue-in-cheek celebration of all the things that make romance so entertaining."

—Entertainment Weekly

"A fun, sexy, and heartfelt love story that's equal parts romance
and bromance." —*Kirkus Reviews*

"Sweet and funny and emotional. I zoomed through this one
Sunday, totally compelled by the romance (and the bromance!). I'm
so looking forward to seeing more of this book club."

—New York Times bestselling author Nalini Singh

"*The Bromance Book Club* is a delight!" —Alexa Martin

Isn't It
Bromantic?

LYSSA KAY ADAMS

JOVE

New York

A JOVE BOOK
Published by Berkley
An imprint of Penguin Random House LLC
penguinrandomhouse.com

Library of Congress Cataloging-in-Publication Data

Names: Adams, Lyssa Kay, author.
Title: Isn't it bromantic? / Lyssa Kay Adams.
Description: First edition. I New York: Jove, 2021. I Series:
The Bromance Book Club; 4
Identifiers: LCCN 2020058550 (print) I LCCN 2020058551 (ebook) I
ISBN 9780593332771 (trade paperback) I ISBN 9780593332788 (ebook)
Subjects: GSAFD: Love stories.
Classification: LCC PS3601.D385 I86 2021 (print) I
LCC PS3601.D385 (ebook) I DDC 813/.6—dc23
LC record available at https://lccn.loc.gov/2020058550
LC ebook record available at https://lccn.loc.gov/2020058551

First Edition: July 2021

Printed in the United States of America
2nd Printing

Book design by Elke Sigal

To my daughter
You're the light of my life

THE BACKSTORY

Six months ago

It's all fun and games until someone shits their pants.

And for once, Vlad Konnikov wasn't the culprit.

Luckily, however, he knew what to do. Because Vlad—a.k.a. the Russian, as his friends called him, since he was, in fact, Russian—had an unfortunate history of gastrointestinal catastrophes for which he'd only recently gotten a diagnosis. Now the man with an official gluten allergy and occasional irritable bowel symptoms never left the house without an emergency kit.

And *this* was definitely an emergency.

Vlad grabbed his bag from his hotel room five stories above the ballroom where he was a groomsman in his friend's wedding and then raced back to the mezzanine floor. He found another groomsman guarding the door to the main bathroom.

"He is still bad?" Vlad asked, his heavy accent more pronounced than usual because he was out of breath and slightly tipsy. It was a wedding, after all, and his stomach be damned, he was Russian. Russians drank at weddings.

"Bad," said Colton Wheeler, fellow groomsman and a country music star. "We're talking full machine gunner." Colton held up his hands to mimic the handles of the weapon and made a rapid *pffft-pffft-pffft* noise. "I wouldn't go in there yet if I were you."

"I have to. He is the best man. He must give the speech."

"Unless he's giving it from the toilet, I don't see it happening anytime soon."

The sound of dress shoes slapping on tile floor brought Vlad about-face. The groom, Braden Mack, slid to a stop. "Where the fuck is my brother?"

Colton hooked his thumb over his shoulder with a grimace.

"Still?" Mack wiped his hands over his head and then cursed, realizing he'd probably just messed up his hair. Mack was very particular about his hair. "Jesus, what'd he eat?"

Vlad shrugged. "Probably cheese."

Cheese used to be Vlad's nemesis, too, until he realized it wasn't. He'd just been eating the wrong kinds of cheese and the wrong things with cheese. Now, he had a strict diet and daily medicine and could eat as much cheese as he wanted as long as he was careful. He was officially a new man.

"I know what to do," Vlad said. He opened his emergency bag, pulled out a box of peppermint tea bags, and handed them to Colton. "Fast. Go ask the hotel staff to make a mug of tea with these."

Colton studied the box. "Seriously?"

"Just go." He shook his shoulders and stretched his neck. "Okay. I am ready. I am going in."

Colton held up his hands in surrender. "It's your nose."

"I'll go with you," Mack said, tugging down on the jacket to his tuxedo. "He's my brother. I can handle it. I grew up with that little shit."

"Big shit," Colton said, moving aside, hands still raised. "Trust me. Big shit."

The heavy door creaked as Vlad pushed it open. "Liam?" he asked gently, approaching the row of stalls like a hostage negotiator closing in on his suspect. "It is Vlad. Mack and I are here."

"Go away," came the groaned response.

Vlad pointed silently to the last stall. Mack nodded, grimacing as he inched closer.

"How's it going in there, man?" Mack asked.

Liam answered with another groan. Mack smothered a laugh behind his hand.

"Leave him alone," Vlad whispered. "It is very not fun to have a stomach problem. Not funny like you think."

"You're right, man," Mack said, straightening. "We've made fun of you too much for that. I'm glad you're feeling better." Mack patted Vlad's stomach through his tuxedo shirt. He lifted an eyebrow and backed up. "Damn, dude. You're hiding some steel under there."

"I am a professional athlete," Vlad said, shoving Mack's hand away. "What did you think I had under there?"

Vlad was a defenseman for the Nashville professional hockey team, which is how he'd managed to meet and befriend this crew of star-studded degenerates. Colton was by far the most famous, but the entire crew was a who's who of Nashville's movers and shakers. Vlad wasn't even the only professional athlete in the wedding. Three others—Gavin Scott, Yan Feliciano, and Del Hicks—were members of the Nashville Major League Baseball team, and Malcolm James played football for the local NFL team. In the six years since Vlad had immigrated to America to play hockey, these guys had grown to be the best friends of his life, and Mack was the glue that had brought them all together through the Bromance Book Club. Together, they read romance novels written by women to learn how to be better men. This group, these men, the books—they had changed Vlad's life. He was not going to let Mack down by allowing his brother to miss the most important toast of the night.

"I can't believe this," Liam moaned from inside the stall. He followed it with a noise that made Mack reel back in horror. "What am I going to do?"

Vlad stood in solidarity on the other side of the stall door. For years, he'd been known among his friends as the man most likely to clog their pipes. A reputation he was happy to put behind him. No one understood what it was like to be at constant war with your own body. Yeah, yeah, nothing funnier than an ill-timed fart, unless you're the one doing it. Nothing quite like the panic of being in a public place and suddenly having your insides seize up in warning with nary a public bathroom in sight. "I can help," he said simply.

"You don't have to stay in here," Liam said. "In fact, I'd kinda rather you didn't."

"Friends do not let friends suffer bad bowels alone."

"They do, actually," Liam moaned. "Just go."

"You are the groom's brother. The best man. You have to give the toast."

"I can't." He made a noise that proved it.

Vlad winced in empathy. He opened his emergency kit and pulled out a vial of essential oils. He slid it under the stall door. "Rub some of this on your belly."

"It's my goddamned asshole that hurts!"

"This will ease cramping," Vlad said. "Trust me."

Next, Vlad pulled out a packet of fast-acting Imodium capsules and slid it under the stall door. "Take two of these now. They will not work immediately, but they will help."

A shiny black-shoed toe dragged the packet out of sight. "Thanks, man."

Lastly, Vlad pulled out a brand-new package of men's underwear. He slid those under the stall. "Just in case," he said, standing.

The door swung open, and Colton walked in, mug in his outstretched hand and a napkin tied around his face like a mask. "Here's your peppermint poop tea."

Vlad scowled and took the mug from Colton's hands. "Liam," he said calmly. "I am leaving some tea on the counter for you to drink. It will soothe your gut."

"Mack," Liam groaned. "What am I going to do about the toast?"

"You can give it later, if you feel up to it."

"Yeah, about that," Colton said, his voice muffled through the napkin. "Liv is outside. She wants to know what's up."

Mack and Vlad tensed in unison. Liv was Mack's bride—an amazing, badass woman who scared the shit out of every man in the group. Mostly Liam, apparently.

Mack clapped his hands on either side of Vlad's shoulders. "You feel like giving a toast?"

Vlad's stomach seized. "M-me?"

"I can't think of anyone I'd rather have fill in for my brother, man."

"I—I haven't written anything," he said, voice thick as tears turned his vision blurry. It was the other thing he was known for in the group—spontaneous displays of emotion. It was the Russian in him. He couldn't help it, and there was no medicine or diagnosis that could cure it. He cried at weddings, books, songs, commercials, cute animals. But this? Giving a toast at Mack's wedding? He'd never make it through.

Mack looped his hand around the back of Vlad's neck and squeezed. "I'd be honored to have you say whatever comes to mind. No one has a heart like you."

Vlad wiped a tear away. "I am the one who is honored."

Liam squeezed out a noise that brought an abrupt end to the tender moment.

"Maybe we should continue this outside," Mack suggested.

Vlad nodded, and Mack called out to Liam, "We'll be back to check on you later, okay?"

"Love you, big brother," Liam groaned.

"Love you too—"

Another noise sent them scurrying for the door.

Outside, Liv was pacing in her wedding gown, arms crossed. "Finally," she said, throwing her hands up. "I was about to come in there. Is he okay?"

"He will be," Vlad said, "but not for a while."

Mack patted his back. "Vlad is going to give the first toast so we can keep things moving."

Liv's face softened into the kind of smile that he knew was the reason Mack fell in love with her. Beneath her tough exterior, she was as soft as a baby chick. She hugged her arms around Vlad's chest. "I'm going to cry."

"So am I," he said, squeezing her back.

"I hate crying," she said.

"I know you do. I will cry for us both."

Mack tugged her away and plopped a heavy kiss on her up-turned lips. "Let's get this party started."

Back in the ballroom, the DJ made a quick announcement that there was going to be a minor change in the night's festivities. Everyone accepted a flute of champagne from the serving staff who wandered through the crowd, and then Vlad took the microphone.

He scanned the room, and a different kind of emotion washed over him, one he'd become too familiar with lately. *Envy.* His best friends nuzzled their wives and girlfriends as they waited for him to impart a bit of wisdom for the new couple, but Vlad had none to give. He was a fraud. He'd joined the book club because Mack had said "the manuals," as they called the romance novels they read, would help him be the best husband he could be to his wife, Elena, but, of course, he had failed.

Because his marriage had never been real.

And though he hated deceiving his friends, the idea of telling them after all this time that Elena had only married him to find a way out of Russia and to attend university in America was too humiliating to consider.

He'd learned one important thing, however, from the manuals. He'd learned that he deserved more than this one-sided relationship. He wanted love. He wanted a family. He wanted the grand gesture and the happy ever after. So, one month ago, he'd finally taken a step toward a new story for his life. He'd done the scariest thing he'd ever done. Scarier than his decision to leave Russian professional hockey to play for the NHL. Scarier than his hasty proposal to Elena. Scarier than his decision to let her leave him for school in Chicago after they'd moved to Nashville.

One month ago, he'd mustered every lesson he'd learned from

the manuals and told Elena that when she was done with school next spring, he wanted them to have a real marriage.

He had hoped she would throw her arms around him and kiss him. Tell him she had loved him all along and just never knew how to tell him. Instead, she'd just quietly told him she needed time to think about what he'd said. And though that broke his heart, he felt more hopeful than he had in a long time. He'd finally done something to push beyond the state of limbo he'd been living in for nearly six years.

"My friends," he finally started. Everyone quieted and turned their smiles his way. "I am Russian—"

"No shit?" one of his friends shouted.

He held up his hand appreciatively. "I am Russian, so I will not make it through this without crying. I must warn you of that. When I came to America, I did not know what to expect, and the first few months were . . . they were lonely."

He looked to his right, where Liv and Mack had their arms around each other as they listened to him speak. "But then I met Mack. He is very, how do I say this, annoying."

A collective burst of laughter filled the ballroom.

"That is not what I mean. Confident is what I mean. He is very confident. I myself was not."

This time, the crowd said, "Aww," together.

"Mack was the first person who made me feel like leaving my country and coming here was a good idea. He was my first friend in America and my best. But he was really, really bad with women, you know."

More laughter.

"He was, as Americans say, all talk. Big confidence but no

game, like, like the sportswriters who say they play hockey better than us, but then they get on skates and break their faces."

He looked at Mack again in time to see Liv kiss his cheek as the crowd roared with laughter. Mack was scowling playfully in his direction.

"But Mack, he was lonely too. He never found the right woman, until he met Liv. And we all knew the first time they met, we knew, she was going to be the one for him because she did not like him at first. She thought he was annoying. And I do not mean confident. *Annoying.*"

Liv laughed and buried her face in the crook of Mack's shoulder. Vlad smiled as he watched Mack drop his lips to the top her head.

"It has been the honor of my life—"

Vlad stopped and cleared his throat, and the crowd once again let out an *aww*. Vlad sniffed. "It has been the honor of my life to be part of Mack's life and to watch him become an even better man than he already was because of Liv." Vlad wiped away a tear. "I love you both so much."

Liv peeked out from Mack's shoulder, her eyes glistening with tears.

Vlad raised his glass, and everyone in the room followed. "I know you will be happy together forever, even when Mack is annoying. Thank you for letting me be part of this. So as we say in Russia, *Zhelayu vam oboim more schast'ya.* Wishing the both of you all the happiness in the world."

Vlad sipped his champagne as applause erupted and everyone drank. Mack and Liv walked over to him and hugged him together.

"Jesus, man," Mack said, weepy. "I love you too."

Liv kissed his cheek. "The only thing that could have made any of this better is if Elena could be here with you."

A tear dripped down his cheek, and Vlad hoped his friends thought it was from the emotion of the toast and not because of the mention of the woman they'd never even met.

"No more crying," he said, forcing laughter into his voice. "This is a party."

Mack grinned down at Liv. "I have a surprise for you."

Yes! Vlad had been most looking forward to this part. He and the other groomsmen had been practicing for weeks to perform a surprise dance routine at the reception. Vlad knew he was big and goofy-looking, but he loved to dance. Wiping the tears from his cheeks, he pointed at the DJ to let him know it was time to start the music. The rest of the groomsmen pulled Vlad and Mack on the dance floor, and as the guests hooted with laughter, they thoroughly humiliated themselves for Liv, the love of Mack's life.

When it was over, Vlad watched the other guys return to the arms of their wives and girlfriends. Fighting jealousy again, he walked to the bar for a glass of water. Colton, who was double-fisting a whiskey and a beer, started to speak to him but stopped mid-sentence. The noise he made was pure *hot woman, right ahead*. Vlad turned around to see who had caught Colton's attention. A tall woman in a long red dress with brown hair swept over one shoulder stood regally in the doorway. She was, indeed, gorgeous. She was . . . holy shit.

Vlad coughed as everything stopped.

Time. Motion. His heart.

His vision narrowed as if he were following the puck on the ice. Colors faded. Noises silenced. The milling crowd disappeared into the periphery until all he could see was her.

Elena.

A whiskey-clenching hand passed back and forth in front of his vision. "Yo, dude. You're a married man, remember?"

"Yes, I remember." Vlad's heart pounded and his knees went weak. "And that is my wife."

Colton snorted and then stopped himself. "Holy shit, dude. Are you serious?"

His chest fizzed and buzzed with anxious joy, as if the bubbles from the champagne had risen again. Was this her answer? Was this her way of telling him she'd made a decision? Elena's eyes found his from across the ballroom. Vlad opened his mouth, but nothing came out. He tried to go to her, but his feet wouldn't move.

Without warning, Elena spun around and walked back out.

A wave of déjà vu washed over him. Only a few months after she joined him in America, he watched her sling a backpack over her shoulder and disappear into a security line at the airport for a flight to Chicago. His heart had begged him to go after her, to tell her to please stay with him, but his mama—always the romantic—had told him it would take time.

"Be patient with her. 'I let a captive bird go winging . . . '"

Vlad forlornly finished the stanza of the poem. "'To greet the radiant spring's rebirth.'"

"She needs time, Vlad. If she needs to go away to find herself, to find her rebirth, you have to let her. She will find her way back to you."

Had she finally found her way back to him? Vlad broke free of the shackles of indecision and forced his feet to move. The hallway outside the ballroom was crowded with wedding guests and sloppy drunks who'd just returned from a night of honky-tonking. He spotted Elena about fifty feet ahead, walking so fast it might have just been easier for her to break into a jog.

He raised his voice above the din of conversations and laughter. "Elena, wait."

She kept walking, so he broke into a jog and switched to their native Russian as he caught up to her. "Elena, please stop. Where are you going?"

She stopped so quickly that she skidded and nearly toppled over in her high heels. Her long red dress swirled around her legs. On instinct, he shot out his hands to steady her, wrapping his fingers gently around her bare elbows.

"Be careful," he whispered, his voice a low rasp because the shock of touching her had stolen all the air from his lungs.

She slowly turned around, and with regret, he let his hands fall away. She radiated heat and smelled like comfort. "I can't believe you're here," he said, still speaking Russian, because that's what they did. They always used their native language with each other. "You look so beautiful."

Elena shook her head and refused to meet his gaze. "I'm sorry. I should have called. I shouldn't have surprised you like this."

He reached again for her elbows. "This is the best surprise of my life."

Her eyes darted left and then right. Anywhere but at him. "Vlad, maybe I should just wait for you at home. I don't want to interrupt—"

"You're not interrupting. I want you here."

She bit her lip and hugged her torso.

"Hey," he said. He took a bold chance of caressing the underside of her chin to encourage her to look at him. "Are you nervous to meet my friends? You don't need to be. They will love you. I promise. They've wanted to meet you for so long."

"Vlad, you don't understand. I thought . . . I thought this

would make it easier. I thought I could come here, and we could meet on friendly terms and it would be easier this way. But then I heard your speech, and I saw you with them, and I—I don't belong here. I'm not part of this. I never was." Her voice shook, and her lip began to tremble.

And suddenly, reality was like a hard hit on the ice. Cold and jarring. His stomach pitched as he put an extra foot of distance between them. "Elena, what—what are you doing here?"

"I'm sorry . . ." She barely got the words out. "I'm going back to Russia."

CHAPTER ONE

Six months later

In another era, the neglected building on the south bank of the Cumberland River might have been quaint and inviting. Happy, even. But no more.

Empty, broken flower boxes hung beneath windows that had been painted black and boarded up from the inside. The thin scraps of what had once been red-and-white awnings flapped in the humid June breeze, clinging to the building's past like ghosts who whispered of the dangers that awaited. Only fools would willingly fail to heed their warning, but Vlad had already proven himself a fool. And even as his mind berated his body for its weakness, his skin prickled in anticipation of the sweet relief he knew he would find once he knocked on the door.

The man sitting next to him in the passenger seat of his car berated him for another reason entirely. "Let me get this straight," Colton said, adding some whiny twang to his voice. "I don't hear from you for three months, and when you finally call, it's for this? So we can sit here while you mutter to yourself in Russian?"

"It has not been three months," Vlad protested. It had actually been four.

In the first several weeks after Mack's wedding—after Elena told him she was leaving and wanted to end their marriage—Vlad deluded himself that he could still be part of the book club. But every minute with the guys was more painful than the last. Their happiness was salt to a wound, and when he finally told them that he and Elena were getting a divorce, their earnest offers to help were even worse. He couldn't stand to spend one more minute making up excuses and lies. Couldn't stand to watch his friends live the life he always dreamed of, knowing he would never have the same. Couldn't stand to be reminded that his belief that he could build a real marriage with Elena was nothing more than a delusional fantasy. The manuals had filled him with nothing but false hope that Elena could ever see him as the romance hero of her dreams. That she could ever love him like the romance heroine of his. He knew the truth now. Happy ever afters were for other men.

All Vlad had left was hockey.

And now, for first time in twenty-five years, the Nashville Vipers had made it to the conference finals of the Stanley Cup playoffs. One more win, and they'd be in the championship series. Vlad had never hit harder, skated better, or scored more goals than he had in the past six months.

He couldn't risk losing now. What would be left of his life?

"I curse the day I told you about this place," Colton said. "I thought I was doing you a favor, cheering you up and shit. I didn't know you'd become an addict."

Vlad clenched the steering wheel. "I'm not an addict."

"Really? Then what the fuck are we doing here?"

"I need it. For the game tonight. *I need it.*" Even to Vlad, his voice sounded small and weak, powerless to the pull of his desire.

"No, you don't. It's a dumb superstition."

"I swore the last time that I would never come again, and look what happened. We lost the game."

"So that's why you finally called me? So I can get you back in with my membership?"

Vlad stared ahead at the gloomy façade. "Since I started coming here, I have played like a beast. I cannot risk it again."

"This is the last time, Vlad," Colton said, throwing open his door. "I'm not coming here again with you."

Vlad followed closely behind as Colton marched toward the door of the building, his feet crunching on gravel and shattered glass.

"I mean it," Colton said, spinning and poking Vlad in the chest. "You can't just disappear on us for months and then call me up for a favor like nothing ever happened. The guys and I deserve better than that."

The weight of regret and guilt tugged Vlad's gaze to the dirty, broken concrete beneath his feet. "I know. You are right. I am sorry."

"We miss you, man. And we're worried about you. I know the divorce is hitting you hard, but that's what we're here for. To help you fix things."

"There is nothing to fix," Vlad said, meeting Colton's gaze again. "I told you before. She is leaving, and there is nothing I can do to stop her."

"How do you know if you won't let us try?"

"Enough!" Vlad barked.

Colton blinked, shock coloring his expression at the unfamiliar bite to Vlad's tone. He never raised his voice with his friends. Never.

Vlad swore under his breath and dragged his hand across the whiskers that had already begun to sprout along his jaw even though he'd shaved just a few hours ago. "I know you are trying to help, but Elena has made her decision. She is going back to Russia to be a journalist like her father. There is nothing I can do about that."

Colton regarded him silently for a moment before acknowledging Vlad's words with a simple nod. Then he turned around and resumed walking.

A single window in the center of the door was blocked by a small wooden shutter. Colton knocked three times in quick succession and then twice more. A moment passed, and someone from inside knocked once. Colton followed with two more knocks. The shutter slid open, and a pair of dark eyes peered out.

"Coin," a voice said.

Colton held up the round silver disc that proved his membership in this clandestine club. The shutter closed with a snap and was followed by the sound of heavy locks turning. The door opened, bringing a burst of cold air and a sour smell.

Colton slipped into the darkness, Vlad closely behind. As soon as they were inside, the door slammed shut behind them.

"Back again so soon?" The stern voice that demanded their coins now mocked them. Vlad clenched a fist, but Colton stepped between them.

"Our money no good for you or something?" Colton snapped.

The man, a scrawny little cuss who made up for his slight build with an attitude that would've gotten him knocked on his ass on the ice, just smirked and pointed. "Wait inside. He'll be with you shortly."

Vlad and Colton walked down a short hallway that ended with a slight ramp, where a thick black tarp hung low to the ground.

Vlad pushed the curtain aside. When he walked through, bright lights automatically turned on, momentarily blinding him. But after blinking a couple of times, he adjusted to the light, and his mouth began to water.

The inner room was as sterile and pristine as the outer entryway was disgusting and dirty. Stainless-steel refrigerators lined an entire wall, and matching countertops were lined up classroom-style through the center of the room.

Atop each table, a line of platters displayed the source of his weakness. The names were scribbled on tiny chalkboards, an alphabetic smorgasbord of the world's greatest delights. *Ädelost. Burrata. Fontina. Passendale.*

Cheese.

So much cheese. Cheese from everywhere in the world, made from original recipes without the fillers and artificial flavors and preservatives that could irritate his stomach. Cheese that he couldn't get anywhere else. Underground, black-market cheese that tortured his dreams as darkly as the memory of what Elena said to him before bursting into tears. *I'm sorry. I can't give you what you want.*

Only one person could give him what he wanted anymore. A tall, dangerous man who now smirked darkly at him from across the shiny room. "Knew you'd be back."

So did Vlad. Deep down, he always knew he'd be back because this was all he had left. Hockey and this dirty, secret cheese shop.

He should have known better than to tempt Fate.

Of all the mistakes Elena Konnikova had made in her life, and there had been so, so many, this would probably count among the top five.

Because *this*—meeting a source in the middle of the night without telling anyone where she would be—was exactly how her father had disappeared.

But what choice did she have? She was running out of time. She would graduate from the Medill School of Journalism at Northwestern University in less than a month, and after that, she would return to Russia. This might be her last chance. So if a creepy, abandoned building was the only place her source felt safe meeting her, then that is where Elena would meet her.

Go where they're comfortable. It was one of the many lessons Elena had learned from her father. Indirectly, of course. He never taught her anything on purpose, because he never wanted her to follow in his journalism footsteps. But if that's what he'd wanted, he shouldn't have been so good at his job.

There was a time when Elena would have been happy to oblige him. A time when she made some hasty decisions that created a ripple effect until it eventually caused a tsunami of damage to people she cared about most. But time had clarified things. Opened her eyes to something that pain and selfishness had blinded her to.

Her father was a hero.

And all that pain and selfishness that had once driven her to flee both the country and the profession that had stolen her father from her had been replaced by a determination to make things right. Though Elena could never change the mistake she'd made the night he disappeared or any of the mistakes she'd made since then, she owed it to everyone to attempt to try to undo whatever damage she'd inflicted. And she was going to start by finishing the story that had most likely gotten her father killed. It wouldn't bring him back, but it would at least give his disappearance, and everything that happened afterward, some kind of meaning.

Now, finally, after years of frustration and of working in secret, Elena had the one thing her father apparently never did.

An inside source.

The decaying Chicago warehouse where they were supposed to meet was four blocks away from where Elena had the Uber driver stop. *Make it hard for people to follow you.* Another lesson she'd learned from her father. Maybe he was paranoid, but he had to be as a journalist in Russia, where reporters who refused to trot out state propaganda sometimes mysteriously fell out of windows. Or vanished from train stations in the middle of the night, like him.

Elena kept her head down as she walked along the cracked sidewalk. Half the streetlamps were broken, casting her steps in alternating dark and light shadows. Gravel scattered across shards of glass and pockmarked concrete in the alley behind the warehouse where honest blue-collar workers once earned a decent living making car parts before greedy corporations shuttered the plant and sent the jobs overseas. Nearly every window in the four-story brick structure was now shattered as surely as the promise of a better life. Americans liked to tell themselves that in their land of the free, nothing but hard work was needed to succeed, but places like this proved otherwise. There were oligarchs here, too, just like in Russia. No matter what flag they flew on their front porch, men with money would always care more about their own fortunes than the lives of the people who actually did the work.

Shivering in the late-night chill, Elena pulled her phone from her pocket to check the time. It was five minutes after eleven. Marta was late. Concern inched its way up Elena's spine. Marta's boss kept all of his employees on a tight leash. If Marta didn't show up by midnight for her job as a waitress at the strip club, he wouldn't hesitate to fire her or worse. And Elena had learned enough to know how bad *or worse* could be. Marta's boss was a monster, just like all the others. But Marta had had enough. She didn't just want out. She wanted to make him pay. Elena was going to make sure he did, and not just for Marta and all the other women he'd victimized, but for her father too.

It had taken years for Elena to figure out what he'd been investigating when he disappeared—a sex-trafficking ring run by a notorious but mysterious Russian mob boss who was known only as Strazh. In English, it translated to *guardian*, but there was nothing noble or protective about him. Among his many criminal enterprises, he was rumored to be involved in a chain of strip clubs in America that were nothing but fronts for luring desperate young women from Russia and Ukraine with promises of big money and lavish lifestyles. But when they arrived, the women found themselves trapped in a nightmare.

It was clear from the notes her father left behind that he'd gotten close to unmasking Strazh's real identity. And they'd killed him for it.

A skittering noise made Elena whip around. Marta had appeared out of nowhere. She wore a dark green hoodie high over her hair and a threadbare pair of jeans.

"I was worried," Elena breathed, speaking quietly in Russian. "I thought you'd changed your mind or—"

Marta rushed forward. "I don't have much time."

"I know. You're sure they didn't follow you?"

Marta nodded quickly and shoved her hand into her coat pocket. Her every motion was a frantic display of anxiety and fear, but the look in her eyes was resolute and determined. She handed Elena a tiny scrap of paper that looked like the torn edge of a pastry bag, the kind you'd get at a coffee shop with a bagel or muffin. A four-digit number and a name were scribbled hastily in pencil.

Nikolei 1122. Elena looked up. "What is this?"

"I don't know." Marta's eyes darted around as if looking for *them*. "I overheard him say it on the phone last night. I wouldn't have thought anything of it, but he—" Marta swallowed deeply.

"He what?" Elena prodded.

"He got very mad when he realized I had heard him. He grabbed my arm and shoved me and told me to get back to work."

Bile stung the back of her throat. This was what Elena feared most—that someone else would get hurt. "You're not safe, Marta. You have to let me help you get out of here."

"And go where?"

They'd had this argument a thousand times. "A shelter. The FBI. Anywhere would be safer."

Marta shook her head, much more slowly this time, as if the weight of reality had turned her muscles to lead. "Not until this is over."

"But I'm not going to be here much longer. A few months at the most. As soon as my divorce is final, my visa will be invalid. What happens when I go back to Russia?"

Marta turned away. "I have to go."

"Wait." Elena gripped Marta's arm to try to keep her from walking away. "Promise me you'll be careful."

Marta paused, her face frozen in a hard mask of resolution. "You too." Then she turned around and ran down the alley.

Elena watched her go, once again feeling a connection to her father that had never been there before. The spark of excitement for this new piece of the puzzle flickered against a cold breeze of fear for Marta's safety. Was this how her father felt all the time? Elena understood so much about him now that used to make her so angry—his long hours, his frequent absences, and most of all, his secrecy. She now knew why he would never tell her what he was working on. He wanted to protect her. She'd kept Vlad in the dark about this for the same reason. She didn't want him to get hurt.

She'd already hurt him too much.

Several minutes after Marta left, Elena walked five blocks to a bar where she called for another Uber. It was midnight by the time she got home. Elena unlocked the door to her studio apartment and quickly locked it again behind her. After toeing off her shoes at the door, she donned her house slippers and walked the five short steps to her tiny kitchen. She filled her kettle with water and then set it on the two-burner stove. A few minutes later, she carried a steaming mug of tea to her cluttered desk, which was wedged next to a futon that doubled as a couch and a bed. She could have had a larger apartment; Vlad had offered to pay for something much more lavish several times over the years. But she could never bring herself to accept the offer. She didn't want to be any more of a burden on him than she already was.

But that, too, was a mistake she had vowed to correct. Elena tried to block out all the voices of recrimination in her head as she dug into the pile of notes and documents she'd been able to compile. She'd arranged everything chronologically—something else she'd learned from her father. Just start at the beginning and build the timeline. When gaps appeared, you knew where to focus your research. The problem was, there were still more gaps than not in the information. And this information Marta had given her tonight was no different. Just one more clue. One more unanswered question that would lead to more questions. And time truly was running out.

Once she went back to Russia and got a job at a newspaper there, she wouldn't have the same freedom to work on this. Literally.

The sudden shriek of her phone sent her heart into her throat. She answered it without checking who it was because only Marta called this late, and it couldn't be good. "Marta? What's wrong?"

"Um, Elena?"

Elena pulled the phone from her ear and looked at the number on the screen. Josh Bierman. Confusion tugged her eyebrows together. He was the family contact for Vlad's hockey team. Why would he be calling her?

She returned the phone to her ear. "Yes, yes, this is Elena."

"It's Josh Bierman. I'm sorry it took so long to call, but I wanted to make sure I had the best information. He's being looked at by the trainers and the team doctor, so—"

Elena shook her head. "Wait. Slow down. What are you talking about?"

"Vlad." Josh paused. "Weren't you watching the game?"

Guilt infused her blood like poison. She hadn't been following Vlad's team. She knew they were doing well, that they were pretty far into the playoffs, but she didn't know details. She didn't even know what city he was in. "No. I— No. What happened?"

"Vlad got hurt in the first period."

She heard the words, but they didn't make sense. Or maybe that was just her brain's way of not accepting the news. "How—how bad?"

"We've stabilized him for now, and then he'll be taken to Nashville Orthopedic Hospital. I can get you a chartered flight out of Midway Airport at two thirty a.m., and you can meet us there."

Her brain finally caught up. "A *hospital*?"

Most professional teams in America had on-site medical units that rivaled emergency rooms, which said as much about the state of American health care as anything. They only sent players to hospitals for bad injuries.

"We're going to wait for the doctor to see him before making any predictions."

"How. Bad." She barely got the words out over her clenched jaw.

Josh's voice was resigned. "He broke his tibia. He's going to need surgery."

Bile choked the back of her throat as she whipped around, found the remote to her TV, and clicked it on. "What channel was the game on?"

"Elena—"

"I have to see."

"Don't do that to yourself."

She found a sports network, and as if the broadcast crew knew she was there, they broke into a replay of Vlad's injury. She watched as he went after the puck toward the wall, battled for a second with a player from the other team, and then it happened. A freak accident, the commentator said. Vlad's pants somehow got tangled with the stick of the other player, so when he turned to skate, he lost the edge and went down, his leg wrenched beneath him in an awkward, unnatural way.

There was a split second of anguished surprise on his face, and then he dropped to the ice. The play continued around him as if no one realized he'd been injured. And why would they? Vlad never got hurt. He tried to stand, but his leg gave out, and he fell again. A hush fell over the crowd as they began to realize he was down and not getting up, that he was pounding the ice and yelling to his teammates, his face twisted in an expression of someone in agony.

"Oh my God," Elena breathed, her hand fluttering to her

mouth. She had to grab the back of her desk chair to keep from losing her balance.

"Elena," Josh said gently. "I promise you, he is being taken care of. All you have to worry about is getting here."

"Does . . ." She stopped. There were a million questions behind that one word. *Does he know you're calling me? Does he want me there?* And then another question. Did the team even know yet that they were getting a divorce? They had to know. Her visa was linked to Vlad's and had been arranged through their immigration attorneys. Once the divorce was final, she would be deported. But if they knew, why were they sending for her?

Josh let out a frustrated sigh, and this time, his voice took a hard turn. "Look, Elena. I don't know what's going on with you two. I've never understood your marriage, but it's not my business. All I know is that he's scared, and he's going to need someone to hold his hand and to take care of him. Someone who really knows him, someone he trusts. I can't get his parents here in time. That leaves you. So are you going to get on that plane, or not?"

He was right. Vlad shouldn't have to go through this alone. Vlad had wonderful friends, but this was different. And maybe it was selfish, but suddenly the answer was staring her in the face. How could she ever pay him back? How could she ensure that they parted as friends?

This. She could do this.

She was going to take care of him.

Elena straightened and swallowed away her doubts. "I am on my way."

CHAPTER TWO

At just before four thirty a.m., Elena walked into the dark, empty lobby of the hospital and approached the lone security guard sitting at the half-moon reception desk. Her heavy backpack full of all her story research and her laptop dug into a large knot on her shoulder, and her arm throbbed as she dragged her small suitcase behind her. She'd packed quickly, focusing more on getting all of her notes than clothes. She wasn't even sure if she remembered to grab pajamas.

"I'm here to see a patient."

The guard—a youngish woman with a hard edge to her—barely looked up when Elena spoke. "Visiting hours don't start until seven."

"But it's my husband. I just got in."

The woman glanced up finally. "Name?"

"Vlad Konnikov."

The woman snorted and rolled her eyes. "Nice try."

"Excuse me?"

"You're the tenth fan who has tried to get in here to see him."

Elena had barely registered that bit of information when she heard an out-of-breath voice behind her. "Elena, hi, sorry."

Josh Bierman jogged to the desk in a disheveled dress shirt and jeans. He waved at the guard. "It's okay. This one is actually his wife."

Elena wanted to nurture the small flame of resentment that she'd been dismissed as just another puck bunny, but what right did she have to feel slighted? She hadn't even been watching the game. She'd never been a real hockey wife and never would be.

Josh reached for her things. "Let me take those from you."

Elena clung to the backpack. "I—I'll carry this."

Josh nodded and took the handle of the suitcase from her. "He's on the fourth floor. The elevator is around the corner up here."

"How is he?"

"He's in recovery."

"Did you call his parents?"

Josh hit the button for the elevator. "Talked to his dad about an hour ago."

It would be late afternoon in Omsk, the Siberian town where she and Vlad had grown up and where Vlad's parents still lived. Elena had spent countless hours as a child and teenager in their home to escape the emptiness and the silence of her own.

As they exited the elevator, Elena tugged her backpack higher on her shoulder and followed Josh down the hallway. Their sneakers squeaked on the linoleum floor, a chirping chorus to the drumbeat of her suitcase's wheels. Josh settled his hand gently on her back and guided her around a corner. Two automatic doors whooshed open at their approach. Inside, a nurses' station sat at the center of a star-shaped intersection of hallways. A man in blue scrubs sat behind the tall counter, studying a computer screen. He glanced up briefly and then nodded in recognition at Josh.

"He's in room 414," Josh said in a hushed tone. "It's a VIP room, so there is a couch you can lie down on until he wakes up, if you want."

Her heart thudded erratically at the assumed intimacy in the suggestion. Just because Josh knew their marriage was unusual didn't mean he knew the whole story. It was their little secret. What would people think if they knew that after six years of marriage, husband and wife had kissed exactly once? Just a chaste brush of lips after saying their vows.

Josh stopped outside the door to his room and moved aside to make room for Elena. She wrapped her hand around the knob but didn't turn it.

"He'll play again, right?" Her voice shook.

"Not this season."

"But what about next season?"

Josh got the kind of expression that people use when they want to break bad news gently. "I think you should wait to talk to the doctor."

No. Elena was done waiting, and Vlad had spent enough time waiting for her.

She hoisted her backpack high on her shoulder and opened the door. Josh set her suitcase just inside the door and then raised his eyebrows to ask if that was okay. Elena nodded, whispered, "Thank you," and waited for him to back out of the room before shutting the door. With a quiet click, she was alone, finally, with her pounding heart and her soon-to-be ex-husband.

She lowered her backpack to the floor and slowly turned around, allowing her eyes to land on the farthest object in the room—a large window with a view of the city that probably would have been beautiful in any other circumstance. Josh wasn't lying. This was a VIP suite, three times the size of a mere mortal's room and more hotel suite than medical unit. Built-in cabinets along the walls hid all medical equipment from view, and beneath the window, a full-size couch faced two plush chairs.

Elena sucked in a breath, held it for a beat, and then turned her eyes to the center of the room. And there, like a felled giant, was Vlad. Flat on his back in an oversize bed. All the air in her lungs evacuated in a shaky puff. His six-foot-four frame somehow managed to look small with his broken leg wrapped in an Aircast and held aloft by a harness attached to the ceiling.

His face was tilted in her direction, his eyes closed and lips parted. Along his jaw was a thick layer of whiskers that probably would have taken other men a week to grow. For Vlad, it was likely just a day's worth of growth. A thin white blanket covered his good leg and . . . Elena gulped. Very little else. It stopped just below his belly button, leaving bare to her gaze a hard, flat stomach and a broad, defined chest covered by more dark hair.

The room seemed to shrink in half as she inched forward. She realized that someone had at least attempted to dress him in a hospital gown, the kind that tied in the front. But at some point in the night, the ties had come undone, and the two sides had fallen open. He was essentially naked under that blanket.

Elena cautiously approached the side of the bed, where the arm had been raised presumably to keep him from falling out in his sleep. His chest rose and fell in a deep rhythm, accentuating the valley between his pecs. It was voyeuristic, the way she stared at him, but this was the first time she'd seen her own husband shirtless in years.

Elena shut her eyes and pressed her hands against her closed lids until spots danced in her vision. This was wrong and inappropriate. Vlad was hurt and had no idea she was even there. *And* they were getting a divorce. The least she could do was give him the dignity of not ogling over his naked body while he slept.

Elena peeled her hands from her face and gingerly picked up the edge of the blanket so she could tug it higher. When she gently draped it across his chest, he stirred and turned his head in the other direction on the pillow. Elena froze, hands hovering atop his body. She stayed that way until his breathing resumed its heavy rhythm.

Easing out a breath of her own, she backed away from the bed, turned around, and tiptoed back to where she'd left her things. She toed off her shoes, picked up her suitcase and backpack, and carried them to the seating area. The cushion creaked when she sat down, and once again she froze, breath locked in her lungs. She watched him as he stirred again, this time letting out a small moan as he rolled his head back and forth twice on the pillow.

Elena leaped up and quickly walked back to the bed. Was he in pain? Was he having a nightmare? His head rolled again in her direction, and his breathing picked up. Beneath his closed eyelids, his eyes moved rapidly. Elena reached out her hand and, after a moment of hesitation and second-guessing, lowered it to his forehead. She smoothed his thick hair back.

"It's okay, Vlad," she whispered in Russian.

He relaxed beneath her touch, so she repeated the gesture and the words. But instead of falling back to sleep the second time, his eyes opened. They were glassy and red, but he appeared neither confused nor surprised by her presence. He held her gaze, blinking slowly, before saying, "My leg is broken."

Elena ran her fingers through his hair again. "I know. But everything is going to be okay."

"I can't lose hockey. I can't lose that too."

The pain on his face combined with that one word—*too*—broke her heart in half. This beautiful man deserved so much better than her. "You're not going to. You are going to heal stronger than ever. Just go back to sleep for now."

"Don't want to," he said, but it was a losing battle. His eyelids were dropping again. "Don't want you to go."

"I'll still be here when you wake up," she said, but she had no idea if he'd heard her.

He'd already fallen back asleep.

"Vlad."

He didn't want to wake up. The dream had been too good this time, too vivid. He could almost feel her hands on him and hear her voice reassuring him that everything would be okay. This time, she'd promised to stay, and he wanted to stay too, stay in that place where she was touching him.

"Vlad, can you hear me?"

Light and sound broke through the weightless haze, and with a groan, he opened his eyes. Morning sunshine cast a long, bright streak onto the floor. He squinted at the silhouette of a woman next to his bed. A moment of hope surged that maybe he'd manifested Elena into existence, but when the woman stepped out of the glare, he saw that she wore blue scrubs and a nurse's badge. His hope went as numb as his broken leg. Whatever they'd given him last night after carting him off the ice had yet to wear off.

"Good morning," she said. "Can you tell me how your pain is?"

"Fine," he rasped. His mouth was fuzzy and sour, and his throat felt like he'd swallowed sand.

"How about some water?" the nurse offered, handing him a disposable cup with a lid and a straw.

Vlad lifted his head from the pillow to accept a long, much-needed drink. "Thank you."

After returning the cup to the table next to his bed, she did something on an iPad before smiling down at him again. "Dr. Lorenzo will be in soon to discuss the procedure. Your wife should be back in just a minute. She was exhausted from sitting up all night, so I sent her down to get some coffee—"

Vlad's brain was sluggish, so it took him a second to catch up to what she said. "My what?"

The nurse looked up from her iPad. "Your wife? Elena?"

"M-my wife is not here."

The nurse's smile turned amused. "You don't remember her getting in last night?"

Vlad shook his head as his heart began to pound. No, that was a dream. Wasn't it? But the wisp of a memory pulled his eyes toward the couch by the window. On the floor was a suitcase and a backpack. *Her* backpack.

Everything is going to be okay.

The sound of the door brought his gaze in the other direction. He rose up on his elbows as she walked in with a to-go cup of coffee, her fist pressed against a wide yawn. Her hair was pulled back in a loose ponytail, and she wore a large sweatshirt with the word *MEDILL* emblazoned across her chest.

She stopped short when she saw him, and the yawn became a gentle smile. "You're awake," she said in English.

Vlad coughed against his dry throat. "You are really here?"

The nurse laughed and looked at Elena. "He doesn't remember much about last night. I was just telling him that the surgeon will be in in a few minutes. Do you need anything until then?"

The question was directed at him, but Vlad was still staring at Elena. She answered for him with a quiet, "No, thank you."

The nurse left a moment later, and when the door clicked shut, it was as loud as an air horn announcing to the world that they were alone. Vlad tried twice to speak but failed both times as she inched toward his bed. He still didn't trust that he was actually awake. This could all just be a hallucination to distract him from the nightmare of his reality. Maybe his mind was playing tricks on him by dangling the illusion of the only thing he wanted more than hockey.

"Are you okay?" Elena set down her coffee next to his water and then rested her hands on the arm of his bed. "Can I do anything?"

He licked his dry lips as he reclined again. "How did you get here?"

"Josh got me a flight."

Josh had said that he would call Vlad's family. He hadn't said anything about calling Elena. "I don't understand. Why are you here?"

The brusqueness of the question, which was more a product of his shock than his intent, made her lips part in surprise. "Josh thought—I mean, we didn't want you to be alone."

That was the last thing he needed. Her pity. "I'm sorry he bothered you. You didn't have to come."

Her mouth fell open again. "He didn't bother me. I thought—"

"Where's my phone?"

She started again at his tone. "I—I don't know. I think they put your stuff in the closet."

"I need to check my messages."

"I'm sure anyone who texted you will understand if you haven't responded yet."

"My parents—"

"I can call and update them."

"I need to do it. My mom will get her hopes up."

"She should. You're going to be fine."

He dragged a frustrated hand down his jaw. "About *us*, Elena. If she knows you're here, she'll get her hopes up about us. So just . . . just let me handle my own family."

She reacted as if he'd reached across the arm of the bed and smacked her. Her eyes pinched at the corners as her lips tightened. "You're right. I'm sorry. Let me find your phone, and I will step out so you can call them."

She immediately turned away from him, giving him a chance to mentally punch his own face. That had been cruel. His parents were the only family she had left, and just because he and Elena were getting a divorce didn't mean she was being exiled from them.

"I didn't mean that," he said, trying to make his voice convey sincerity.

She pulled open the door to the closet next to the bathroom. "They put all your things in here, I think." Elena crouched and pulled his overstuffed duffel bag from the floor of the closet. "Do you mind if I go through this?"

"Elena, please, I'm trying to apologize."

"For what?" She opened the zipper and started digging through the clothes he'd worn to the arena before the game and all the other things they'd pulled from his locker.

"They're your family too."

"Not for long, though, right?" She retrieved his phone and tugged the white charging cord out from the bottom of the bag. It was wrapped around a sock. "Found it."

She shoved everything back in the bag, shut the closet door, and then returned to his side. She wouldn't look at him as she plugged the phone into an outlet attached to the arm of the bed. "It will probably take a second to charge up."

Her arms came around her torso in a pose he once found defensive, standoffish. Now it made her look small and insecure.

"Elena, look at me."

She plastered a fake smile on her face as she raised her gaze to his.

"They will always be your family. Always."

Her chin lifted and lowered in a single, noncommittal nod.

The phone screen blared white as it came back to life. Vlad punched in his passcode and then sighed heavily when he saw the number of notifications he'd missed. More than three hundred texts had come in overnight. Probably half were from the Bros alone. Another surge of guilt soured his mood even more.

The door swung open. A tall woman walked in wearing scrubs and a white doctor's coat. Behind her was a familiar face from the team—head trainer Madison Keff. Both women paused to pump hand sanitizer into their palms from the dispenser on the wall before advancing farther into the room.

The doctor approached his bed with a wide smile. "Good to see you awake, Vlad." She extended her hand to Elena. "I'm Dr. Celia Lorenzo. You must be Mrs. Konnikov."

"Konnikova," Elena corrected.

At the doctor's look of confusion, Elena clarified. "Women in Russia often feminize the last name when they marry."

It was an old tradition, and some people didn't even do it anymore. But his mother had done it, and so had Elena's when she'd married Elena's father. So Elena had decided to do it too. At the time, it had meant something to Vlad. It meant she thought their marriage was special. Now he knew better. And the last thing he needed besides her pity was a reminder of how naive he'd once been.

Madison strode forward next, hand outstretched to Elena. "We haven't met before. I'm Madison Keff, the head trainer."

Elena shook hands with both women. "Where is the coach?"

"Coach . . . ?" Madison asked.

"Yes. The coach of the team. Why is he not here?"

"Because he's on the road," Vlad said, failing to keep the annoyance from his voice. "They left this morning for the next game in the series."

Because they'd lost last night. If they'd won, his team would already be on their way to the Stanley Cup. They had to win tonight, or it was over. But no matter what, Vlad would not be there.

Dr. Lorenzo, either because she was efficient or because she sensed a growing tension, interjected. "Let's go over the surgery."

Madison turned on the wall-mounted TV, did something on her iPad, and then the TV screen came alive with a still image from the game. It was the moment just before the fall. Vlad didn't need to see it to relive it. He would never forget the moment his career flashed before his eyes. There was a pop followed by a searing pain, and then his vision blurred as he fell to the ice. He might have cried out, but all he could hear was the sound of his own frantic heartbeat. The game went on, but time stopped for him as he tried and failed to get back up.

A hush fell over the crowd, and officials finally paused the game. Trainers raced out. Crouched beside him. Asked him questions as they tried to locate the source of the injury.

He'd seen it play out a hundred times to a hundred different players over the course of his career, but now it was him. It was his turn to wonder if this was it. Had his entire career just ended in a split-second mistake?

They splinted him on the ice and carted him off on a stretcher. It was a blur after that. At some point, they'd peeled off his pads and cut off his pants. Thankfully, they gave him a shot of a powerful painkiller almost immediately, numbing him all the way to his toes. Then they moved him to the X-ray room, followed up with an MRI, and walked back in with a look that told him it was as bad as he'd feared. His brain could only grasp key words and phrases over the rush of blood in his ears and the pounding of his heart.

Broken tibia.

A clean break, but he would need surgery.

And then they loaded him into an ambulance and brought him here, Nashville Orthopedic Hospital. He was rushed into surgery before he could even fully process what was happening.

And then he'd had the dream about Elena. She'd lulled him into a peaceful state with her gentle touch, her voice, her reassurances. Only now he knew it wasn't a dream. She was really here. But instead of making him feel better, it made him feel worse.

The doctor approached the screen and pointed with a pen. "We think the initial break from the fall itself was probably small," she explained. "But when you stood, you likely displaced the bone further."

The video began. In slow motion, Vlad watched himself try to stand before falling back to the ice, face twisted in agony. "So, I made it worse," he said.

"Yes, but also no." Dr. Lorenzo turned away from the TV. "Ironically, your recovery would have been a lot longer with the simple fracture. We would have had to cast you and let the bone heal on its own with almost no weight-bearing activity for twelve weeks. With this kind of break, we place a metal rod into the bone to hold it in place. Believe it or not, this means you'll be up walking and rehabbing a lot sooner."

Dr. Lorenzo checked her watch. "I have to prep for another surgery. I'll check back in before I head out for the day."

Vlad didn't even wait for the door to close before he looked at Madison. "When will I play again?"

"You know I can't tell you that yet."

"Please, Madison. Give me an idea of how long I will be off the ice."

She pursed her lips and exhaled a reluctant sigh. "If you were an average person, it would be a year before you could return to normal activity." Madison held up her hand at the look on his face. "But you are not average. You're a professional athlete in top physical condition who will have access to round-the-clock care, nutritional support, and a detailed rehabilitation plan."

"So how long?"

"Our goal is to get you back on skates by October."

Vlad let his head fall against the pillows. Four months off the ice. He pressed his fist to his forehead. How could this be happening?

"But there is a lot that happens between now and then," Madison said. "Most people with this kind of break wouldn't be allowed to put any weight on their leg for at least a month. You? We expect you to stand for a few minutes every day starting next week."

"What happens next?" Elena asked in a voice that managed to be both quiet and determined. She had inched closer to his side as she spoke. As much as it pained him to admit, there was something comforting about her presence and her journalistic skill for pushing through the panic of the situation to ask the important questions.

"He'll stay here again tonight," Madison said. "Barring any complications, he should be able to go home tomorrow."

Elena made a noise. "Tomorrow? You can't send him home tomorrow!"

"We'll make sure he has everything he needs," Madison said.

"But this was major surgery. What if something goes wrong?"

"Elena," Vlad said, trying to redirect her attention, because the look on her face was the same one she'd given him when he was sixteen and had the boneheaded idea to jump into the frozen Om River.

"The trainers will be in contact every day," Madison said with a patient smile. "Probably more than Vlad would like. We'll equip the house with mobility assistance and training tools, and he'll have a detailed rehab plan. If you have any questions—"

"Of course I have questions! Can he go up and down stairs? Can he get his leg wet? How often does his bandage need to be changed? Does he need to ice it? Will he get painkillers? What if he falls down?"

Madison smiled again. "I know how worried you must be. But all of those questions will be answered, I assure you. Trust us to do our jobs, okay?" She nodded without waiting for a response and turned her attention to Vlad. "One thing I do need right now is access to the house. The team needs to deliver several things before you can go home tomorrow."

"One of my neighbors has a key to the house. She can unlock the door for you."

"That will work. Let her know we'll be there this afternoon." Madison folded the iPad against her stomach and winced, as if her next words were going to hurt. "I don't mean to pry, Elena, but I need to know if we should hire someone to take care of Vlad for a while or if you are planning to stay—"

"She's leaving."

"I'm staying."

Vlad dragged his gaze from Madison's confused and uncomfortable expression to gape at Elena. He switched to Russian. "What—what did you say?"

Elena held his stare. "I'm going to stay and take care of you."

"*Why?*" He hadn't meant to sound so incredulous, but he was.

"Because you need me," she said. At his answering silence, she blinked rapidly and shrugged. "I mean, you need *someone*."

Madison cleared her throat. She didn't speak Russian, but she obviously understood tone of voice. Her own conveyed a desire to get out of there as quickly as possible. "Why don't I leave you two alone to discuss things, and you can let me know what you decide tomorrow?"

Vlad spared her barely a glance as she ducked out of the room. As soon as she was gone, Vlad ran a hand over his hair. "Elena, what are you doing?"

"You need someone to take care of you."

"The team can hire someone to help."

"But they don't have to, and why would you want a stranger? I can cook for you and—"

He cut her off before she painted too tempting a picture. "What about your classes?"

"They're over. I defended my thesis last week."

Vlad's lips opened and closed twice as he searched for something, anything to change her mind. Anything short of *I need you to go*, because that would be just as cruel as what he'd said about his family. He didn't want to hurt her. He just wanted to protect himself from getting hurt. And that's what would happen if she stayed. "It's going to be a lot of work. I don't want to be a burden on you."

Her lips thinned in annoyance. "You're injured, Vlad. Taking care of you is not a burden."

"Elena—"

She held up her hand. "Look, I know we haven't talked in a long time, and things have not been good between us, and I hate it. I don't want us to be enemies. I want to do this for you. I owe you at least this much."

His eyebrows tugged together. "Owe me? What are you talking about?"

"You've done so much for me, and someday I hope I can pay you back for my tuition and everything else, but for now this is what I can do."

He jolted as if she'd nailed him in the nuts. "When have I ever asked you to pay me back?"

"Never, but only because it would never occur to you. So let me do this for you. *Please*." She blanched suddenly and backed away from the bed, arms once again wrapped protectively around her chest. "I mean, unless . . . unless you don't want me here."

Want her there? He'd been *wanting* for as long as he could remember. Longing for a moment just like this—her, next to him, promising to stay. But he never wanted it like this. He didn't want her there temporarily, and he definitely didn't want her there because she felt obligated.

"Oh," she breathed. "I see." Her arms now hung loosely at her sides, and her eyes were wide with the surprised betrayal of someone who'd just been sucker punched.

Her crestfallen expression cleaved him in half. "I'm just not sure it's a good idea, Elena."

"Right," she said, forcing a smile on her face. "No, of course. I—I understand." She turned quickly, her sneakers squeaking on the floor, and she crossed the room to where she'd left her things by the couch.

"Elena, I'm sorry—"

She crouched to zip up her backpack. "Why? It's my fault. I put you in an awkward position. I shouldn't have come without talking to you first."

"What are you doing?" Because it looked like she was getting ready to leave right that second, and dammit, he didn't want that either.

"You have a lot to deal with, obviously," she said slowly, as if choosing her words carefully. "Maybe it would be easier if I just go unlock the house instead of you trying to track down your neighbor. I still have a key. And then I can stay at a hotel tonight before heading back to Chicago tomorrow."

"You don't have to stay at a damn hotel," he growled. "You have a bedroom."

Elena stood, swung her backpack over her shoulder, and extended the handle on her suitcase. The wheels made a *click-click* noise against the floor as she crossed the room before pausing at the end of his bed. "If you need anything from the house, do you want me to have someone from the team bring it over?"

A familiar panic seized his chest. "Are you leaving? You don't have to go right now, Elena."

"Or I can bring stuff to you tomorrow. I can stop by before I go to the airport to say—" Her words got stuck on something in her throat that she had to cough to clear. "To say goodbye."

The door to his room swung open once again before he could respond. He bit off his words with a scowl at whomever had the bad luck to interrupt right now. The team's media manager poked his head around the corner. "Can I come in?"

Elena held Vlad's gaze for a split second before greeting the unwanted visitor. "Yes. Come in."

The media manager looked back and forth between them, finally catching up to the drama apparently unfolding in front of him. "Um, I can come back."

"Can you please give us a minute?" Vlad asked.

"No need," Elena said, her voice clipped and her lips thin. "I was just leaving."

She walked toward the door without looking back.

"Elena, wait—" Vlad tried to sit up as he called her name, but the tightness in his leg sent him flinging back with an *argh*.

The door clicked shut with quiet finality.

CHAPTER THREE

"Where y'all from?"

Elena looked out the window from the back seat of the Uber she'd called to pick her up from the hospital. "Chicago."

The driver, an older man with salt-and-pepper hair and a kind smile, laughed. "No, I mean originally. Your accent."

Not a week had gone by since she'd come to America that she didn't get asked that. Some days she was willing to offer details, but today wasn't one of those days. "Russia," she answered plainly.

"I thought so. I thought maybe Ukraine or somewhere in that region. What part of Russia?"

"Moscow," she lied, because no one ever knew where Omsk was, and when she explained that it was part of Siberia, they always wanted to know how cold it was, and she just didn't have the energy for that kind of small talk right now.

"Cool," the man said. "What brings you to Nashville?"

"Just visiting a friend in the hospital."

"Hope everything is okay."

She smiled because it was the polite American thing to do. "Yes. He is going to be fine."

The driver must have finally caught on to her reluctance to converse, because he turned up the radio and settled into his driving. Elena returned her attention to the passing scenery. She didn't recognize much of it. In the few months she lived with Vlad after they got married, they'd rarely gone out together beyond the borders of the suburb where he lived.

But when the Uber driver took the exit, things started to look more familiar. Big trees and wide lawns on twisty-turny streets protected the rich and famous from the riffraff that might wander in without permission. When she joined Vlad in America—her visa was delayed, so she didn't join him until a few weeks after they were married—she had expected a nice house because he was a professional athlete. Everyone knew that American athletes made a lot of money, and he'd already been playing here for a year. But when he'd pulled into his long, tree-lined driveway and she saw his soaring brick house for the first time, her mouth dropped open, her voice reduced to a useless squeak. A girl from Omsk could never imagine such grandeur.

The effect was different this time when the Uber driver pulled in. The magic was gone.

"Wow," the driver said. "Nice place. Is your friend famous or something?"

It was a safe assumption. Nashville's suburbs were home to the world's biggest country music stars. "He's done well for himself," Elena offered, opening her own door.

The driver got out and went around to the back to get her suitcase. He set it on the paved driveway, and Elena thanked him as she hoisted her backpack on her shoulder. As the driver pulled away, she tipped him on the app and then climbed the cement steps to the small front porch. The door was black and flanked by two long windowpanes. The first time she'd come here, she'd been afraid to look inside as Vlad unlocked the door. Her stomach had churned and twisted as he opened the door and stepped aside for her to go in first. Her shoes had echoed on the glossy floor in the cavernous entryway, but his were a soft, gentle thud as he came up behind her.

"Welcome home." His voice was a honey glaze, warm and sweet and soft.

In her peripheral vision, she saw him lift his hand as if to touch her. She moved away.

Elena shook off the memory and pushed open the door. Not much had changed. The same decorative table that had been there before was still there, still a deposit for loose change and mail and other odds and ends from his pockets at the end of the day. Pulling her suitcase behind her, Elena walked toward the wide staircase that bisected the entryway. Ahead was the kitchen. To the left was a large living room with a fireplace and a wall of bookshelves. To the right was a dining room with French doors leading to a covered patio. Her first night there all those years ago, he'd ordered takeout and set it out on the patio with candles. She'd taken her plate and eaten in her room.

"Who the hell are you?"

Elena let out a startled shriek and slapped a hand to her chest. At the end of the hallway, a gray-haired woman with a deep scowl stood with her hands on her hips and a massive dog at her side. The black Newfoundland let out a thunderous bark and launched into a gallop toward Elena. She barely had time to stretch out her palms to ward off the coming attack before the dog jumped and planted his paws on her shoulders. Elena collided with the railing to the staircase as she stumbled under his weight. With another loud *woof*, the dog dragged his long tongue up the side of her face.

"I *said*, who the hell are you and what are you doing in Vlad's house?" the old woman demanded.

"Can you please call off your dog?" Elena begged. She loved dogs. All dogs. In fact, she preferred dogs to most humans. But this one could fit her whole head in his mouth, and she wasn't sure if the licking meant *I love you* or *I'm going to eat you.*

"It's not *my* dog," the woman said.

"Well, whose is it?" Elena asked. Had Vlad gotten a dog and not told her about it? She thought his rejection in the hospital stung, but not telling her that he'd adopted a pet would be an outright *fuck you.*

"I'm not answering any of your questions until I know who you are," the old woman argued. "Are you some kind of stalker? One of those lunatic groupies who chase after famous athletes or whatever? How did you even get in here?" She spoke over her shoulder. "Call the police, Linda."

Elena snapped out of her stunned state. "I don't think so," she said, gently pushing the dog away. He dropped all four paws to the floor and wagged his bushy tail. Elena gave him a tentative pat on the head and sidestepped him to face the intruder at the end of the hallway. "*I* will be calling the police."

The old woman snorted. "For what? We have a right to be here."

"Really? So do I."

"Bullshit. Who are you?"

Elena crossed her arms. "*I* am his wife."

Just then, two more women raced into the hallway to stand next to the gray-haired one. They wore matching expressions of *OMG*.

"*Elena?*" the old woman croaked.

"Holy crap," said the one in the middle. Was that Linda? Elena realized upon closer inspection that she looked like a younger and less-intimidating version of the older one. The third woman, a trim fifty-something in yoga pants and bright lipstick, squeak-gasped and covered her mouth with her free hand.

"I can't believe it," the older one hissed. "You have some nerve, showing up here like this. Does he even know you're here?"

Elena stiffened in indignation. "Yes, he knows I'm here. I spent the night at the hospital with him."

"That's a lie," the old woman said.

"Ma!" The younger one glared. "Stop."

"What?" the old one snapped. "You expect me to be nice to her after everything she has put him through?" She turned an accusing finger at Elena. "You have no idea what he's been like the past few months."

Wow. This woman really, really hated her. What had Vlad told them?

Probably the truth.

Elena swallowed her own reproach. The dog, as if sensing her discomfort, scooted closer to her and leaned against her legs. Elena had to brace her hand against the railing of the staircase to keep from falling again.

"Ignore my mother," the nicer one said. She walked forward and extended her hand. "I'm Linda. It's nice to finally meet you."

Elena stared at the woman's long fingers skeptically before slowly accepting the handshake.

"That is my mother, Claud," Linda said, gesturing reluctantly to the cranky one. Then she nodded to the one in yoga pants. "And this is Andrea."

"We're Vlad's neighbors," Andrea said. "When we heard about what happened, we decided to come by and help get the house ready for him. We were cleaning out his fridge."

Elena tucked her hands under her arms. "That's very kind of you, but I can take care of everything."

Claud made an ugly, nasally noise.

Linda looked at the ceiling as if praying for peace and said, "Ma, please."

The dog, whose owner had yet to be determined, woofed and leaned harder into Elena's legs.

"We're the Loners," Andrea said.

"The what?" Elena said.

"That's what we call ourselves because our husbands are all dead."

Elena cleared her throat. "How . . . unfortunate."

"Technically," Andrea clarified, "I got divorced before my ex-husband died."

"My condolences."

Andrea shrugged. "We started coming over here almost every day to have coffee with Vlad when he's home, and now he's a member of our little club. We swap recipes, gossip about the neighbors, stuff like that."

"I see." Actually, Elena didn't see. At all. Every word out of their mouths wove a thicker and thicker cobweb in her brain. The beginnings of a headache throbbed a warning behind her temples. Elena pressed her fingers into one as she tried to make sense of the situation. "I don't understand. Why exactly is Vlad in your club?"

"Because he's alone, too, thanks to you," Claud sneered.

"Ma," Linda hissed. "Stop."

Elena squared her shoulders. "I am sure he will appreciate that you stopped by to help, but I have to get ready for the team to drop off some equipment for him—"

"And then you'll be leaving, right?" Claud said.

"Ma!" Linda said. "Vlad wouldn't like this."

"Because he's too tender for his own good." Claud lowered her voice. "And what will Michelle think?"

Elena blinked as the name of another woman rocketed through her. "Michelle?"

"Another member of our club," Andrea said quickly. Too quickly. "Except her husband isn't dead. They're divorced because he cheated on her, so we just wish he was dead."

Elena rubbed both temples.

Claud pointed that accusatory finger again. "Why did you come back here? Afraid his injury means he won't be able to play anymore and you'll be cut off from his money?"

The oxygen evaporated Elena's lungs in a whoosh. Claud's words hit a target deep inside Elena's worst insecurities and shame.

"Let's go," Linda said, tugging her mother's elbow. Then to Elena, she said, "I'm sorry. She's very protective of him."

"So am I."

"If that were true, you'd leave," Claud said.

Once again, the woman's words hit their mark. And once again, it was because Elena knew she was right. But Elena had just enough self-respect left to not want to give Claud the satisfaction of knowing how much the old woman had hurt her. Or to tell her that Elena would, in fact, be leaving soon because Vlad didn't want her here anymore than Claud apparently did.

Elena steeled her spine. "You can think whatever you want about me, but I am here for one reason only. To help Vlad. Whether you believe me or not is out of my control. Now, if you'll please excuse me, I have a lot to do to get ready for my husband to come home."

"Of course," Linda said calmly. "Please tell Vlad we're thinking of him."

"I will." Elena reached down and scratched the dog's ears.

"His food is in the kitchen pantry, by the way," Linda said, gesturing to the dog.

"This *is* Vlad's dog?" She asked the question before realizing it simply proved Claud's point that she was a shitty wife.

"No," Andrea said. "He belongs to the people across the street, but he sort of adopted Vlad too. He'll bark at the door to leave eventually."

More cobwebs. "Someone else's dog comes here to hang out?"

Linda shrugged. "There's a cat that comes around too. Vlad had a pet door installed in the garage to let her come and go as she pleases."

Of course he did. Because he was Vlad.

Linda grabbed her mother's arm and started to tug her toward the front door. "Let us know if we can do anything to help," she said.

"Thank you."

Andrea paused next to Elena. "It's really nice to meet you," she said with a giggle. "You're as pretty as he always said you were."

Cheeks blazing, Elena crossed her arms across her chest and watched the three women leave. When they were gone, she looked down at Neighbor Dog—that would have to be his name for now—and patted his head. He woofed and wagged his tail. At least *he* didn't have any preconceived notions about her.

Sighing, Elena picked up her backpack and grabbed the handle of her suitcase. Neighbor Dog followed slowly behind her as she lugged both up the stairs and down the long hallway on the second floor. Her room was the last on the right, directly across from Vlad's. Her door was closed, and when she opened it, the silence inside was like an accusation. Everything was the same. Exactly as she'd left it. And though nothing was really hers—not the paisley bedspread or the white dresser or the matching lamps on either side of the bed— she remembered them. Like a child who goes to visit an aunt after several years and ends up sleeping in the same room as the last visit. Everything was familiar but strange.

Elena set her things on the floor by the bed. Someone had cleaned in here recently. The carpet bore the stripes of a recent vacuuming, and there wasn't a speck of dust to be seen on the TV, the desk, the dresser. Even the attached bathroom was spotless. A peek under the sink revealed all her products were still there, waiting for her return. Shampoo and conditioner and shaving cream and honeysuckle-scented bodywash. She'd left them here when she went to school, and Vlad had stored them for her eventual return. She lifted the bodywash, flipped open the lid, and inhaled the scent. She closed the lid and put it away before it brought back too many memories.

She returned to the bed and gave in to the weakness in her knees, much like she had the first night she spent here. It was the nicest bed she'd ever seen. Plush and full, with enough pillows to accidentally smother someone. Or, as she discovered, to smother the sounds of crying. She did a lot of it that night. And then, hours later as she lay awake in the dark, eyes puffy and head throbbing, she vowed she'd never cry again. And she hadn't until six months ago when she'd stood in front of him, looking sexier than any man had a right to in his tuxedo, and told him she was leaving him.

Even now, months later, she couldn't forget the way he'd looked at her at the wedding. So full of hope and joy. Until he wasn't. She'd broken him. The man who had saved her. The man who had been her childhood best friend.

Neighbor Dog leaped onto the bed and flopped down with his head in her lap. She buried her fingers in his thick black fur. He sighed contentedly and closed his eyes. Vlad had always wanted a pet, but his travel schedule made it impossible because he couldn't leave them alone. Something else she'd stolen from him.

The sudden blare of her phone made her jump a full inch off the mattress. It was a Nashville number she didn't recognize. "Hello?"

"Mrs. Konnikova? This is Tess Bowden. I'm one of the trainers from the Vipers. We're going to be there in a few minutes with the home rehabilitation equipment. Are you ready for us?"

"Yes, I'll watch for you."

"Great," the woman said. "We're about ten minutes away."

Elena left her room with Neighbor Dog at her heels and found herself staring at the open door to Vlad's bedroom. She could count on one hand the number of times she'd been in there. Which was as sad a commentary on the reality of their marriage as anything. At first, she'd avoided going in there because it was awkward. But then because it was too painful. Every time she stepped foot in his private space, the ring on her finger would grow heavy with the weight of his disappointment.

Now, temptation mingled with curiosity, propelling her feet forward until she stood at the threshold. A glance around the space told her very little had changed since she'd last been here. The same king-size bed sat in the middle of the room covered by the same plain, navy blue comforter. Matching tables sat like bookends on either side with twin lamps. She had no right to snoop around his things, but voyeuristic need overrode her sense of propriety. A few feet inside the room, the door to the master bathroom stood open on the left. She paused to look inside. The products and toiletries lined along the sink were like intimate insights into his daily rituals. A towel was folded haphazardly and draped across the sink. Heat filled her chest cavity as her mind pictured him there, wrapped in a towel as he dragged a razor down the hard angle of his jaw. Such a simple task. Such a manly task. One that wives around the world watched their husbands do every single day, but not Elena. She'd never witnessed her husband engage in that particular act of grooming.

Elena tore her eyes away, swallowed hard, and approached the bed. Only one side was disturbed or appeared like it was regularly slept on, and the relief that flooded through her at that thought was as swift as it was humiliating. A quick scan of the room revealed no evidence that a woman—a *Michelle*—regularly stayed there. Elena returned to the bathroom and studied the products on the sink again. All men's things. No lotions or nail files or ponytail holders or boxes of tampons.

But when she walked back out, the glint of gold caught her eye. She approached his dresser. And there, on top, discarded like yesterday's mail, was his wedding ring.

"You're my best friend, Elena. I want to take care of you. Come to America. You can start over and make a new life."

"I don't understand. What are you saying?"

Vlad dug a pair of rings from the pocket of his jeans. One, a simple, manly gold band. The other, a circle of diamonds that twinkled in the light of the streetlamps above. Life moved in slow motion as he lowered to one knee.

"I'm asking you to marry me."

She was so stunned that she couldn't speak, and he took her silence as rejection. His cheeks blazed red as he stood. "I'm sorry. It's stupid. Forget I said that. Or, maybe just think about it. I—"

She whispered her answer. "Yes."

Her brain had revisited that moment so many times. Wondered how things might have been different if she'd said no. If she'd had the presence of mind to recognize her own vulnerable desperation and his eager generosity for what they really were—a toxic combination that was doomed to combust. Elena had long since accepted that she'd made the only decision she could at the time, but she had also wished a million times since then that she could go back and do things differently, to stop herself before she made selfish choices that would inevitably hurt him. She wouldn't do that to him again. Maybe Claud was right. Maybe the best thing she could do for Vlad was to leave as soon as possible.

Elena looked down at her own ring, still wrapped snugly around the finger where he'd placed it all those years ago. She tugged it off and, after a moment of hesitation, laid it next to his.

A knock at the door signaled the arrival of the team staff. She walked out, Neighbor Dog closely behind, and pulled the door shut.

"The Western conference finals will end tomorrow with either the Nashville Vipers or the Vancouver Canucks heading to the Stanley Cup, but the Vipers will face a battle without their best defenseman, Vladislav Konnikov, who is recovering in a Nashville hospital from surgery for a broken tibia suffered in Friday night's game. Team sources say it is uncertain when he will return to the team. The Vipers have moved Adam Lansberg into the rotation to replace Konnikov—"

Vlad zapped off the TV, casting his room in darkness but for the lights from the parking lot outside. The shadows matched his mood. All day, he had prayed for privacy amid the constant stream of team staff, nurses, and other medical personnel. But now that he had silence, he longed once again for distraction because the instant his mind was disengaged, it replayed the sound of Elena's suitcase wheels growing fainter down the hallway.

He'd told Elena that his mother would get her hopes up if she knew Elena was here. Which was true. His mother would say it was a sign that she was right all along, that Elena had just needed time to get over what happened with her father so she could love Vlad fully. Mama would read something into the fact that Elena had dropped everything and hopped on a plane in the middle of the night to stand next to his bed, run her fingers over his hair, and assure him everything was going to be okay.

But that wasn't why Vlad sent Elena away. It wasn't only his mother's hopes he worried about. It was his own. *He* would think it was a sign that she'd hopped on a plane in the middle of the night. At least with his mother, he could blame her eternal optimism on being a natural romantic. She was a literature professor at Omsk State University, a specialist in the great Russian poet Alexander Pushkin. Whenever he had doubts, Mama was ready with a Pushkin quote to encourage him to hang on a little longer, to believe in the future of his marriage.

But seeing Elena had made at least one thing clear. He couldn't avoid his parents any longer. He'd never gone this long without calling home. He couldn't even be sure when he last did. April, maybe? It had simply become too painful to keep lying to them, especially Mama, so he cut them off as much as his friends. Telling her the truth—that he and Elena were getting a divorce—was going to be torture. But it was time.

Vlad pressed his mother's name in his contacts list, put the phone to his ear, and braced for impact.

"Finally."

Vlad winced. It was a feat of linguistic majesty the way his mother could convey an entire spectrum of human emotions with a single, curt word. "I'm sorry, Mama. It's been busy here and—"

"Too busy to tell your parents that you're okay? The only person we've heard from is Josh."

"I know—"

"And do you know how we found out that you were hurt? A journalist called us, Vlad. For comment. We didn't even know!"

"Let me talk to him," his father said in the background. Then, a moment later, his father's voice boomed clearly. "If you weren't already injured, I'd break your other leg."

"Papa, I'm sorry. I haven't had a chance to call until now."

"You haven't called *in months*."

"Let me talk to him again." His mother returned to the phone, this time with a slightly softer tone. "How are you? Are you in any pain?"

"Not right now. I can't really feel anything." In his leg, at least. His chest was caving in on itself.

"Josh said you'll start rehab in about a week?"

"Yes, I hope so."

His mother paused, and he could hear her brain working. "You are going to need someone to help out."

"The team will provide someone—"

"Don't be ridiculous. Elena will do it. She's almost done with school."

And there it was. Elena had found her way into the conversation like he knew she would. "Mama—"

"Have you called her yet? She must be so worried."

Vlad dropped his head to the pillows and closed his eyes. "Mama, listen to me—"

"Please tell me you've called her. How are you ever going to have a normal marriage with her if you always hold her at arm's length?"

His eyes flew open. "What are you talking about?"

Mama made a dismissive noise.

Vlad pressed his hand into the bed to sit higher. "*She* is the one who moved to Chicago. You told me to let her go."

"Yes, but I never told you to make her believe she would never be welcomed back."

Vlad wanted to pound the heel of his hand against his head to make sure his ears were working correctly. Was Mama blaming *him* for the state of his marriage? She had never spoken to him like this. Never. "All I have ever done is give her the space you said she needed."

"You're right. It is all you've ever done. So call her now, Vlad. Tell her you need her *now*. Before it is too late."

Vlad had to clear his throat twice to form his next words. "It— it is already too late."

"Not if you call her."

"Mama, you're not listening to me."

His mom's silence was as loud and bone-shattering as a defensive hit against the boards. He could imagine her standing straight in the kitchen, her hand fluttering to her ever-present strand of pearls. They'd been a gift from his father on their tenth anniversary, and Vlad had never seen her without them.

His mouth was suddenly dry. "Mama, Elena and I—"

"No."

"We're getting a divorce."

"Why, Vlad?" she asked in a voice that finished him off.

He closed his eyes against the assault of guilt. "You know why."

"No, I don't. You two are meant to be together. You always have been—"

"She's coming back to Russia," he blurted out, cutting her off.

"What?" His mother breathed. "What do you mean?"

"She wants to come back and become a reporter like her father."

"No. That can't be true. She married you so she could get out of Russia."

Yeah, and that was the only reason, which was the problem. "I guess she changed her mind."

"And I suppose you've done nothing to try to stop her."

There it was again. The insinuation that this was all his fault. He swallowed against the burn of irritation. "Of course I tried."

"Really? Because it seems to me you just did your normal shut-down-and-withdraw routine."

"What does that mean? What is my shut-down-and-withdraw routine?"

"You're like a skittish, hibernating bear when you are scared, Vlad. You shut people out and go into hiding. Like an absolute bear."

He resisted the urge to growl like one. "She's leaving me."

"Leaving you. Is that how you see it?"

"How the hell else am I supposed to see it?"

"If you opened your eyes, maybe you'd see that you left her a long time ago."

"I—I can't believe you're saying this. You are the one who has told me for years to keep hanging on, to give her time, to—"

"Have you ever told her you love her?"

It was his turn to go silent.

"I assume that means no," she said.

"I told her that when she was done with school, I wanted a real marriage with her."

"That's not the same thing as telling her you love her."

"There's no point. Not when there is only love on one side."
Oh shit. He slapped a hand over his eyes and held back a groan. But
it was too late. His mother pounced like a panther.

"Oh, Vlad. You *do* love her."

"That's not what I said."

"But it's what you meant."

What was the point in denying it? "Mama, it doesn't matter."

"It would matter if you simply told her."

He opened his eyes and turned his head to stare out the window.
"What makes you think it would change anything?"

"Vlad, love changes everything."

"Only in books." And he was done with those. Done with the
fairy tales. The Alexander Pushkin romanticism. The unrealistic
expectations. He'd even once thought he could write his own book,
but not anymore. He hadn't looked at his manuscript in months.
He was done with all of it.

"I hope you don't really believe that," Mama said, her tone
heavier with disappointment than he'd ever heard.

"Tell Papa I said goodbye."

"Vlad—"

He hung up.

CHAPTER FOUR

Elena awoke the next morning to the sound of a mournful meow.

After blinking in confusion for a second, she sat up and kicked off the blankets. She found a cat draped across the floor in front of Vlad's bedroom, poking its paws through the tiny space between the closed door and the carpet.

"Sorry, kitty. He's not home."

The cat rolled over when Elena spoke.

"Come on," she said. "I will feed you."

The longhaired calico followed her all the way downstairs and into the kitchen. She must have known where Vlad kept the food and treats, because she began to meow at the pantry door. Elena picked her up and checked the collar for a name tag. There wasn't one.

"Guess we'll have to settle for Neighbor Cat for now," she said, setting her down.

Neighbor Cat didn't seem to care what she was called once Elena poured a small bowl of food.

According to the clock on the microwave, it was nearly nine—much later than Elena normally slept. She decided to blame it on the fact that it had taken hours to fall asleep last night and not on the fact that the bed was more comfortable than she remembered. It was unbelievably soft, like sleeping on top of a giant down pillow. She hadn't been in the right state of mind during the few months she had lived with Vlad to appreciate it then, but now? Now it would be hell going back to the concrete block that was her futon. But it was well past time to figure out how and when she was going back. She hadn't booked a plane ticket yet and didn't even know if she could get a flight out today. If she couldn't, she'd stay in a hotel by the airport. Vlad clearly didn't want her at the house when he came home, and she wasn't going to take advantage of his generosity by asking if she could. She didn't even feel comfortable raiding his fridge for breakfast or making tea. This was his house, his space. She was a visitor and always had been.

Elena sat down in one of the tall leather chairs that lined the long island in the center of the kitchen. She'd left her laptop on the counter before bed last night and now booted it up to search online for a flight. When the travel website prompted her to select a return date, she checked the button for one-way and sucked in a shuddering breath as it hit her that this was the last time she would ever be here. When she left this morning, she would never be coming back. And though she'd known for months that she would eventually face these lasts—last time in the house, last time seeing Vlad—the reality of it soured her stomach. There were things she still hadn't said to him, things she wished he knew and understood. But maybe that was just as selfish as her decision to marry him. He obviously was ready to move on. She had no right to burden him further with her excuses.

She chose a flight for late that night from Nashville to O'Hare. Then, because she didn't trust herself not to start crying, she busied herself with getting ready to go. She showered quickly and, after dressing, left her wet towel in the laundry room on the second floor. She repacked her few belongings quickly and then walked back into his bedroom to get some clothes for him to drop off at the hospital on the way to the airport. Searching through his drawers felt like an invasion of his privacy, so she simply grabbed the first things she saw—a sweatshirt, a pair of shorts, and some boxer briefs. Next, she grabbed a toothbrush and some toothpaste from the bathroom. In his closet, she found an empty drawstring backpack to put them in.

The orderly line of clothes hanging on one side of the walk-in closet made her pause for a moment. The neatness of it all, the tidiness, brought a pang of homesickness she had no right to feel. This wasn't her home. But the sight of his suit coats, some still in the plastic bags from the dry cleaner, felt intimate. She ran her fingers down the sleeve of one, a dark navy that probably looked amazing against his olive-toned skin. She'd seen pictures of him walking into arenas before games, dressed in one of these suits with dark sunglasses shading his expression from the cameras. Sometimes, she'd watch his games and marvel, *That's my husband*, but he never really was.

And now it was time to say goodbye.

Neighbor Cat was asleep at the bottom of the stairs. Elena crouched and gave her a scratch. "Take care of him, okay?"

Her heart wanted to linger, to look around a little longer. Her brain told her to go. She drove one of his cars—a spacious SUV— and would leave it at the hospital so someone could drive him home in it. She'd just call an Uber to take her to the airport from there.

The security guard didn't question her this time, but she felt like a zoo animal on display when she exited the elevator on the fourth floor, dragging her suitcase behind her. A small circle of people wearing tracksuits bearing the team's logo stood next to the nurses' station, consulting with an official-looking man in a sport coat and a tie. They turned as one and stared at her with unmasked curiosity. Madison was among them, so Elena waved like they were old pals.

"Tell him I'll be in in a few minutes to go over the rehab plan," Madison said.

Elena nodded but didn't stop. Their eyes followed her every step down the hallway toward his room and when she paused at his closed door. Did she need to knock? With the eyes of the staff burning a hole in her back, she quickly rapped her knuckles on the door and opened it before he could respond. She braced herself for whatever he might say, but she found him staring listlessly at the TV on the wall, the remote in his non-IV hand.

He turned it off when he saw her. "Hi," he said, pressing his hand to the mattress to straighten against his pillows, gingerly, though, so as to not disturb his injured leg in the harness.

He was slightly more covered today. The hospital gown now hid his chest, but tufts of dark hair still poked through the top. And rather than detracting from the muscular appeal of his body, the thin, diamond-printed gown accentuated it. His biceps looked like they'd rip the fabric if he flexed. Vlad wasn't the flexing kind of guy, though. His body was a machine with one purpose—hockey. And he was as oblivious to his stunning physique as he was to the way his smile could make a person want to lean into him to absorb some of his warmth. He'd never understood how handsome he was, how attractive women found him. Elena had always felt lucky to know that his sexiest quality was his kindness.

Elena left her suitcase by the door and averted her eyes from his exposed skin as she walked to the side of his bed. "I wanted to bring you some things before I left," she said in Russian. "Clothes and a toothbrush."

"Thank you."

She set the bag on the table next to his bed. "The keys to your car are in there too. I hope you don't mind that I drove it here. I just thought someone could drive you home in it."

He thanked her again, studying her face in a way that heated her blood and scrambled her brain.

She bit her lip. "Did you sleep okay last night?"

The purplish smudges beneath his eyes said he hadn't, but Vlad nodded. "Yes. You?"

"Good."

"You found everything you needed in the house?"

"Yes." Elena shoved her hands in her back pockets, desperate for something to cover the awkwardness. It didn't used to be like this between them—useless small talk bracketed by heavy silences. But the man who'd once been her best friend was now like a stranger. Still, awkward was a lot better than the subtle aggression he'd shown toward her yesterday. "I met your friends."

"Which friends?"

"The Loners." She toed the floor with her sneaker. "They were at your house when I got there yesterday. I don't think the old one likes me very much."

Vlad dragged a beleaguered hand over his hair and spoke on a sigh. "What did Claud say?"

"I don't remember exactly, but it was something like, 'You're a heartless bitch who should be hit by a train.'"

Vlad's eyebrows pulled together as his expression darkened. "She said that?"

"Maybe not those exact words, but that was clearly the

meaning." She shrugged and adopted what she hoped was a self-deprecating smile. "Hey, if I were dead, then you'd be a real member of their club, at least."

Her attempt at humor missed its mark. "Elena, don't ever say anything like that again."

She squirmed again under his examination. She self-consciously scratched a nonexistent itch on her face as she thought of something to say.

"You're not wearing your ring."

She shoved her hand back into her pocket.

"You had it on yesterday." His voice had dropped an octave.

"I saw yours on your dresser. I figured since you weren't wearing yours . . ." She shrugged. "I left mine next to it."

"I only take mine off for games, Elena. I've been wearing it."

"Oh." Her heart hammered a confusing beat. Why was he telling her that?

A brisk knock on the door interrupted them. Madison poked her head in. "Can I come in?"

"Yes, of course," Elena said, switching back to English. She turned away from Vlad, hands still in her back pockets, as Madison walked in. Madison greeted Vlad, checked his incision, and then introduced the two other trainers with her—a pair of eager-looking grad assistants who seemed like they couldn't wait to start torturing him with squat thrusts.

Done with the introductions, Madison smiled and said, "So, I bet you're ready to get out of here."

"Very much," Vlad answered.

"Since you're here, Elena, does that mean you're staying, or . . . ?"

The empty, sour feeling returned to her stomach. "No, I am going back to Chicago."

"You can stay." Vlad said it in Russian, and at first, Elena wasn't sure she'd heard him correctly. But when she looked down at him, his expression confirmed it. A pink tinge rose above the dark outline of scruff on his cheeks, giving him a boyish, sheepish look. "If—if you still want to."

"But you said—"

"I was a jerk yesterday."

Heart pounding, she glanced at Madison, who was quietly conversing with the two other trainers. Even though none of them could understand her conversation with Vlad, Elena appreciated the attempt at privacy. She stepped closer to his bed. "I don't understand. You—you want me to stay?"

His response was a single nod.

A warm bloom in her chest began to melt the cold loneliness that had been slowly turning her heart to ice. "I bought a plane ticket for tonight. I don't know if I can cancel it."

"Just don't get on the plane."

"But the money . . . I always cost you so much money."

His expression became wounded. "I don't care about the money, Elena. If you want to go, then go. But I'm asking you to stay. Do you want to or not?"

Just like that day so many years ago when he'd crouched before her with two shiny rings, she hesitated before answering. And just like then, a smile spread across her face, and when she finally found her voice, it was a whisper. "Yes."

His features relaxed, as if he'd been holding his breath in anticipation of her response. He nodded and swallowed hard. "Okay."

He looked at Madison and switched back to English. "Elena is staying."

"Great," Madison said, grinning in an oddly victorious way, as if she'd known all along this would happen or, at least, had hoped for it. "Shall we go over the rehab plan together?"

Before either of them could answer, Madison whipped out a single sheet of paper from the folder she carried. "This is just a basic outline. It will change as needed, but this is what we're looking at for the next few months." Madison handed Vlad the paper. Elena inched closer to his bed to read over his shoulder.

The plan was broken down week by week, but that was almost the only thing Elena understood. Simple instructions like ice and elevation were complicated by clinical terms and acronyms. *Six weeks in a brace with full extension. Ice to reduce pain and inflammation. Gait training with crutches, NWB.*

She looked up. "What does NWB mean?"

Madison and Vlad answered at the same time. "Non-weight bearing."

"The next few days, you need to take it easy," Madison said. "You can obviously get up to use the bathroom, to bathe, and to stretch, but for the most part, you need to stay off your feet and keep the leg elevated above your heart."

Patella mobility drills. Multi-plane open kinetic chain straight leg raising. Week two, begin proprioception drill emphasizing neuromuscular control.

"Is he supposed to know what any of this means?" Elena asked, not even trying to hide the rising alarm in her voice.

"That's what we're for." Madison smiled.

Vlad absently scratched his jaw, the scrape of his fingertips against his thick whiskers drawing Elena's attention. Transfixed, she studied the pop of a vein atop his hand that wound all the way up his forearm. As if feeling the weight of her stare, Vlad suddenly looked up. Their eyes collided, and she felt a kick in her chest. The reality of the close quarters they were about to share became its own presence in the air between them.

Elena tore her eyes away to find Madison watching them with a curious, amused glint in her eye.

Elena's cheeks grew hot. "What about nutrition? Will you put him on a special diet to help him heal, or can I make him anything he wants?"

"Lots of fruits, vegetables, and protein," Madison said. "And, of course, gluten-free."

"Why gluten-free?"

"I was diagnosed with a gluten allergy late last year," Vlad answered quietly in Russian.

"You never told me that."

"I planned to, but . . ."

But she broke his heart instead.

Madison cleared her throat. "Well, we're going to leave you alone now so you can get ready to go home. We'll be in touch tomorrow, but call tonight if you need us, okay?" She spoke with the quick cadence of someone anxious to leave. She all but pushed the two grad students toward the door.

"I have no idea how to cook gluten-free," Elena said, nibbling her lip. "I'll have to do some research on how to adapt recipes."

"I don't need anything fancy."

"But I want to make all your favorites from home."

Vlad shifted against his pillows to sit up straighter. "You're sure you don't mind doing this?"

"I'm sure." She swallowed and hugged her chest. "But can I ask you something?"

He nodded tentatively, as if he feared the question.

"Why did you change your mind?"

He gave a one-shouldered shrug. "You were right. It will be nice to not have a stranger in my house."

It was an ironic answer, since she felt like a stranger around him. But maybe this time together was exactly what they needed to correct that, so that when the time finally came for her to leave, they would part, at last, as friends again. It was the best she could hope for, and more than she deserved, but she wasn't going to waste this opportunity to start making things right between them.

CHAPTER FIVE

Several hours later, Elena kept a steady beat of nervous chatter all the way home, but Vlad was too shell-shocked to respond with much more than single-word answers.

The hospital had sent him home with a pair of crutches, some painkillers, and a stern warning to take it easy for the next few days. They gave him nothing, however, to deal with the reality of his rash decision to let Elena stay. What the hell had he been thinking?

He *hadn't* been thinking. That was the problem. He'd simply been reacting. The crushed look on her face when she told Madison she was going back to Chicago had awakened a side of him he'd long thought dead. It was the same side that had convinced him to propose to her. The side that believed his mother when she assured him that Elena would eventually find her way back to him. The side that once read every romance novel he could get his hands on to learn how to make it happen.

Vlad must have made a noise, because Elena quickly glanced over at him. "What's wrong? Does it hurt? Do I need to pull over?"

"No. I'm fine." Which was the biggest lie he'd ever told. He was anything *but* fine. The car was too small with her in it, and he was too keenly aware of how desperately he needed a bath. Something he was not going to be able to do alone.

"Are you hungry?" she asked.

"Not right now."

"I could make dinner when we get home, or we could order something. Do you know if you're supposed to take your pill with food?"

"I'm not sure."

"I'll find out. I did a bunch of cleaning yesterday so the house would be ready for you. I mean, it was already really clean. I just made your bed and removed all the rugs in the bathrooms and stuff so you don't trip on them. I'll make a grocery list tonight."

The comments continued at a rapid-fire pace, too fast for him to respond. But it was clear that she didn't actually intend for him to contribute to the conversation. This was her way of dealing with the tension in the car. While he stared out the window and grunted, she gave voice to every thought in her head.

She barely took a breath until she pulled into his driveway. "Do you want me to park in the garage so you can go in that way?"

"The front is probably easier."

She turned the car off and jumped out. Vlad opened his door, but she barked at him to stay put. His crutches were in the back seat, so he waited for her to get them before attempting to get out. Using one crutch for leverage, he swung his braced leg out and then rose slowly on his good leg.

Elena handed him the other crutch, hovering and biting her lip as he wedged it beneath his armpit.

"Careful," Elena said, holding her arms out, presumably in

case he toppled over. Which was pointless. If he fell, he'd take them both down.

"I'll shut your door," Elena said.

Vlad crutched forward a couple of times to give her room. The door slammed behind him, and then Elena raced around, and her frenetic questions started again. "Do you need help? I'll open the front door. Can you get up the porch steps?"

"I'm fine, Elena. But yes, it would be helpful if you opened the front door."

She took off like a speed skater and bounded up the few steps to his porch. She used her key to unlock and push open the door before turning and racing back to him.

"So, do I—do you need help?"

"I can do it."

"Right. Okay. I just, I don't know what to do."

Vlad paused in his slow approach to the porch. "Look at me."

Her wide eyes blinked up at him. Something shifted in his chest, and he wished the painkillers could numb his heart. "I'll tell you if I need something, okay? You don't have to hover."

"Okay." She backed up a step. "Sorry."

"Don't be sorry. I appreciate the help."

Her minuscule nod did more damage to his chest cavity. This woman was going to kill him slowly with her presence alone. Was that her goal? Was that why she was doing this? To finish off what remained of his pathetic carcass?

"Could you maybe bring in my bag?"

"Yes," she said, nodding with far more enthusiasm this time. "Yes, I can do that."

He crutch-hopped up the steps as she retrieved his duffel bag, and by the time he made it inside, she was already behind him, hovering once again.

"Okay, so do you want to go straight upstairs or maybe sit on the couch for a little while?"

He inched toward the staircase. "My bed is better. More room to elevate my leg."

"Right. Of course. That was stupid."

He hopped up the first step, and she followed closely behind. He was breathing hard and sweating by the time he reached the top.

"Now what?" Elena said behind him.

"Now I ice it for a little while."

"I will get some after we get you settled in bed."

Just hearing the word *bed* out of her mouth made him want to groan. Except for the hospital room, which really didn't count, they hadn't been in a bedroom together for any significant time in years. And even then, they'd shared the space for mere moments. And not for what husbands and wives usually shared a bedroom for. This was going to be torture.

The minute he sat on the mattress, Elena moved in between his splayed legs to take his crutches. "I'll lean them here," she said, oblivious to the effect she was having on him by just standing. "That way you can reach them."

"Thanks," he grunted.

He reached behind him for a pillow to put under his leg. Elena raced forward. "Let me do it."

She bent over him, and he must have made another one of those tortured noises, because she leaped back suddenly. "Oh my God, did I hurt you?"

"Nope. Just trying to get comfortable." His voice scraped like rusty skates on pond ice.

"Lean back so we can move your leg," she said.

He obeyed, mostly to get as far away from her skin as possible, because his hands were developing a mind of their own. He lifted his leg then as she plumped the pillow for him to rest it on. "Is that good?" She looked over at him.

He gulped. "Thank you."

"Okay. I'll go get the ice."

She raced from the room, and Vlad clunked his head against the headboard. He wasn't going to survive this. Five minutes at home with her, and his mind was already occupied with thoughts of things that would definitely not help him heal.

In his leg or his heart.

She returned a moment later, panting as if she'd bounded up the stairs two at a time. She carried a plastic bag full of ice cubes and a thin kitchen towel. "Do we just put the ice on the brace, or on the skin?"

"On the skin," he said, sitting up. "I can open the brace—"

She waved his hands away. "I can do it. I need to learn how."

"Icing my leg probably won't be one of the things I need help with." He tried to inject some levity to his tone but failed. It came out stressed.

She straightened and apologized. Again. "You're right. I'm being annoying, aren't I?"

"No." Vlad took the ice and set it beside his hip. "Elena, listen."

She gulped and crossed her arms across her chest in that same protective pose that she'd adopted yesterday at the hospital, as if she were afraid of what he was about to say. He couldn't blame her. He'd been an asshole yesterday.

"You don't have to do every little thing for me."

"Okay. Right. I'm sorry."

"And you don't have to apologize all the time."

"Right." She laughed with a nervous little puff of air.

"And you have to promise to tell me if this becomes too much work."

"I will. But it won't." Beaming confidently again, she nodded in the general direction of the door. "I'm going to bring the rest of your stuff in from the car. Do you need anything else for the next few minutes?"

"No, I'm—I'm fine."

He didn't exhale until he heard her open the front door. He'd either made the biggest mistake of his life or . . . there wasn't an *or.* He'd just made the biggest mistake of his life.

The ice was quickly numbing his hip, so he leaned forward to open up his brace and rest the baggie on top of the incision. The movement was just enough to remind him that he'd gone way too long without a shower, and there was no way he was going to ask her to help him with that. He was putting his foot down—the good one—on that.

His phone was on the nightstand, and though he dreaded making this call, it had to be done. Colton answered on the first ring. "Holy fuck, dude. The guys and I are going nuts. You send us one text, and that's it?"

"I am sorry, but—"

"We've had to get all our information from ESPN, for fuck's sake. I was just on the phone with Mack. We were about to storm the damn hospital."

"I am not there anymore."

"Where the hell are you?"

"Home."

"Who took you home? Someone from the team? Jesus, man. We would've done that."

"It was not someone from the team."

"Why the hell do you keep cutting us out like this?"

"Colton, please—"

"You can't just ghost us like this anymore, man. We're your family, and we know you need us, so why are you—"

"Because Elena is here!"

Silence. The deafening kind.

Colton made a dramatic play of clearing his throat. "I— What did you say?"

Vlad puffed out his cheeks and let the air seep out. "Elena is here. She came to help. She is the one who drove me home."

"Like, she's here for the day, or . . . ?"

"She is going to stay for a while and take care of me."

This time, in the silence that followed, Vlad could almost hear the gears turning in Colton's brain and his lips curling into a grin that meant he was already reading way too much into it. "Well, well, well."

"It is only temporary."

"If you say so."

"I do. But I still need your help with something."

Downstairs, the front door opened and closed again. He didn't have much time before she came back upstairs.

"Anything, man," Colton said. "Just name it."

"Can you give me a bath?"

Colton laughed and then sobered. "I'm sorry, but it sounded like you said you need help taking a bath."

Vlad groaned and leaned back against his pillows. "That is what I said, yes."

"But I thought your wife was there."

She was, and from the sound of it, she was in the kitchen now. "I cannot ask Elena to do it."

"Why not?"

"You know why!"

"Because of the divorce? I hardly think she's going to mind, given the circumstances."

And for the second time that night, Vlad blurted out something he wished he could take back. "Because she has never seen me naked!"

Silence again. Longer this time. And far more ominous. "Okay, first of all, neither the fuck have I. But more importantly, why exactly has your wife never seen you naked?"

"Please, Colton. I cannot explain over the phone." Elena's footsteps padded softly on the stairs. "Just . . . please. Can you come over in the morning?"

Colton made several noises under his breath that sounded like very dirty words. He finally returned to the phone. "I'll be there. But believe me, I'm not coming alone."

He hung up before Vlad could protest but also just in time, because Elena chose that moment to walk back in. She had a bottle of water, a plate of cut-up fruit, and the information Madison had given them.

"I know you said you aren't hungry, but I think you should eat something. I was reading the information about the painkillers they gave us, and it says the pills can make you nauseous if you take them on an empty stomach." She stopped short. "I—I'm sorry. Are you on the phone?"

Vlad lowered his cell to his lap. "I was talking to Colton."

"I can come back."

"No, it's fine. He hung up."

"Everything okay?"

"The guys are coming over in the morning."

"Oh," she said, blinking rapidly. "Okay. That's good. I'm sure they want to see you."

"They're going to help me take a bath," he blurted.

Her cheeks turned a soft pink of understanding.

"I didn't want to impose on you," he said.

She set down the plate of fruit on his nightstand. "No, of course. I understand."

"I just thought it might be embarrassing since, you know . . ."

The pink became the color of a Detroit Red Wings jersey, and he cursed himself. There was no need to be specific, as if she didn't know as well as he that the most intimacy they'd ever shared was a single kiss on their wedding day.

Her movements were stiff as she backed away from the bed. "That is very considerate of you. It would probably be embarrassing for both of us. And I need to get groceries tomorrow anyway, so maybe I'll do that while they're here."

"Good idea."

She backed up farther. "You should eat and then try to get some sleep. I know you didn't get much last night. I'm going to unpack my stuff, and then we can turn the game on."

He cleared his throat. "That's not necessary."

"You really do need to get some sleep."

"No, I mean, the game. I'm not going to watch it." He looked away from her and from the inevitable questions in her eyes. If she voiced them, he wouldn't be able to answer. Not coherently. Not in a way she could possibly understand. But he just couldn't do it. He couldn't watch his team play without him.

"Vlad—"

"No game."

A moment passed before she nodded. "Okay. No game. I'll check on you in a little while."

She retreated, her footsteps leaving tiny indentations in his carpet. Though she was just across the hallway, she felt a million miles away suddenly. Which was ridiculous. She'd been a million miles away from him for forever, it seemed, and absolutely nothing about that had changed just because she was here. He strained to listen to the sounds of her in her room, just like he'd done every night during the four months she'd lived with him after she came to America. Every slide of a drawer, every creak of her mattress, every splash of water in her bathroom. They were nails on the chalkboard of his psyche.

That smile she'd given him earlier had filled up his room with light, and now it was dark again. The fact that her smile was already a source of emotional vitamin D for him was all he needed to know about why this was a bad idea. Soon, she'd be gone for good, and it would be like the sun burning out completely. He'd endured that particular kind of winter before. He wouldn't survive it again.

If he was going to get through this, he would need a distraction, more than just the daily job of rehabbing his body. Something he could disappear into to avoid the reality of his situation. For the first time in months, Vlad opened the drawer to his nightstand and withdrew the pages of his manuscript.

He traced his thumb across the title, *Promise Me.*

His story with Elena was on its last chapter. If he couldn't have his own happy ever after, maybe he could try again to write one.

Promise Me

March 1945

Ninth Air Force Base
Erlangen, Germany

"It's almost over, isn't it?"

Tony Donovan sucked on his last Lucky Strike and then snuffed out the glowing butt with the toe of his size 10 boots. It melted a speck of frozen grass before extinguishing in a final puff of smoke.

Almost over. They'd been saying the same damn thing since D-Day. *We've got 'em on the run, boys. Germany's beat. Just a few more days. Nothing left of Jerry but young boys and old men.*

Usually, the declarations were uttered with enthusiasm. But his jeep driver, Private Rogers, spoke the words with the disappointed whine of a kid who was afraid of missing the fireworks on the Fourth. Tony understood on one level. The kid was eighteen years old—a jittery, impatient type who got in line to enlist the minute he met the legal age requirement. But instead of storming the beachhead of his hero-fevered dreams, he found himself saddled with the inglorious task of driving around a weary war correspondent who'd seen more combat than half the soldiers in the army.

But that's where Tony's empathy ended. Private Rogers had no idea what he'd been spared. The sounds and smells and images of war would forever haunt Tony's sleep. The horror of what man could do to man. He'd seen enough to know that no one should ever have to see it. But Tony would still give anything to trade his pen for a rifle.

But since a pen was the only weapon he was allowed, he had vowed at the beginning of the war to wield it until the end. And now he was about to set out on what could be one of his most dangerous assignments yet. With Allied forces pushing through Nazi Germany from the west and the Russian Army clearing a swath from the east, rumors were spreading of prisoner of war camps being evacuated by the SS all across Germany and Poland. The prisoners—most of them American and British airmen—were being force-marched through the bitter conditions to places unknown. Reports had been trickling in of prisoners dropping dead of exhaustion and starvation. He needed to get on the move, but his goddamned photographer was late.

Not just any photographer, though.

Anna Goreva.

There wasn't a GI in the European campaign who hadn't heard of her. Beautiful and brave, she'd once distracted her own jeep driver so much by simply smiling at him that he crashed into a ditch. Some people dismissed the story as gossip, but Tony knew it was true. He'd been in the back seat.

When his boss told him that she'd be accompanying him on this assignment, Tony had argued to no avail.

"You need a photographer who speaks Russian and has been

on the front before," George Burrows, his editor, had told him. "You've got one. Now go. She'll meet you in Erlangen."

Tony shoved his hands in his coat pockets and stamped his feet to stave off the now-familiar sting of cold. He should have fought harder. He should have been more up-front about the reasons for his concerns. Like the cold air, the memory of their parting a year ago stung like a slap in the face.

A gust of wind knocked her bag from her hands. It opened at her feet, and she lunged for several pieces of paper that fluttered out. One landed on the toe of his boot. He grabbed it before she could and turned it over. The gentle face of an American airman stared up at him. Anna swiped the photo from him and shoved it back in her bag.

"Who is he?"

"Nobody."

"I doubt you would carry around the photo of nobody in your bag."

Her body language gave her away. He was more than a friend. Someone important. Tony had to unclench his teeth. "Is he one of your lovers?"

"That is none of your business."

"Isn't it?" Jealousy raged inside him, hot and irrational. He had no right to feel any claim on her. They'd shared nothing more than a single passionate kiss, and that had been the result of a near-miss with a German mortar. "I'm your boss, Anna. The last thing I need is some khaki-whacky Jane at my side who wants to wage her own personal charm offensive across Europe—"

"How dare you!" She planted her hands on his chest and shoved. He stumbled more out of surprise than from her strength. "How dare you judge me when you know good and well that

you're perfectly fit for service. I'm doing everything I can for the war. What about you?"

"Tony."

The sound of his name from that unforgettable smoky voice brought him around and into a collision with brown doe eyes and red bow lips that he hoped he'd never see again. "You're late."

"I had to stop at the hair salon first in my charm offensive across Europe." Sarcasm dripped like hot tar from her voice as she threw his own words back at him.

She extended a gloved hand to Private Rogers. "Anna Goreva."

The poor kid turned red and stammered like he'd just met a Hollywood starlet. Christ.

"Go get the jeep and come back for us," Tony barked.

As the private sauntered off, Anna eyed him coolly. "I see your personality hasn't improved since the last time I worked with you."

He inched closer to her, as close as he dared. "Let's get one thing clear, Anna. I didn't want you on this assignment, so if you hope to stay on it, you do what exactly what I say."

"No."

"*No?*"

"I'm here because *you* need *me*. I speak Russian. You don't." She cocked a hip and raised an eyebrow. "This time, we're doing things my way."

CHAPTER SIX

Three things in life terrified Vlad.

A flare-up without a bathroom in sight.

Running over an animal with his car.

And *this*. Waking up to find his friends circling his bed, their arms crossed and eyes narrowed in matching expressions of *resistance is futile*.

He was about to get book clubbed.

Vlad scooted high on the mattress against the headboard and prepared for the onslaught. At the last second, he grabbed a pillow to hug. "Where is Elena?"

"She left a note on the counter that she went out to get groceries," Noah said.

"Which is good," Malcolm added, "because it would be best if she weren't around to hear what we have to say to you."

Vlad gulped.

"You have no idea how pissed we are at you," Mack said. "And since we've never been pissed at you, even that pisses us off."

"I'm sorry—"

Malcolm cut him off with a point as a single, intimidating eyebrow arched over his eye. "First, we bathe you, because, *damn.* And then you tell us *everything.*"

Vlad nodded. There was no point in doing anything else.

Malcolm looked at Colton and Del and then nodded with his chin. "Help him into the bathroom. I'll get the water started."

Colton and Del each took a side and helped Vlad out of bed. Colton whiffed and grimaced as they helped him to the bathroom. "Jesus, man. You really stink."

Vlad scowled. "I am a hockey player, and I have not showered for two days."

"Damn," Del said, pretending to gag. "And I thought baseball players stank."

Gavin hovered closely behind. "I've actually heard that baseball clubhouses are way smellier than any other professional sport."

Malcolm snorted. "Who the fuck told you that?"

Gavin shrugged. "A reporter told me that once."

"There is no way that is true," Vlad said, voice straining as he eased sideways to squeeze through the bathroom door. "Hockey gear? It smells like rancid bear."

Malcolm turned on the water in the tub, so Gavin had to raise his voice to be heard. "Yeah, b-but baseball players are out in the hot sun for hours."

Colton eased Vlad down on the edge of the tub. Yan picked up the conversation and looked at Malcolm. "What about football players?"

He shrugged. "We can peel the fucking paint from the walls."

"Boys, trust me, you're all equally rank," Colton said. "Can we just get Vlad hosed off, please?"

"You don't have to wash me," Vlad grumbled. "Just help me in and out."

"No way, dude," Gavin smiled. "I want to wash your hair." He made a scrunchy gesture with his fingers. "All that thick, glossy luxuriousness."

"Fuck off," Vlad growled.

"Okay, stank ass," Colton said. "We gotta stand you up and strip you naked."

Vlad grabbed Colton's outstretched hand and stood on one leg. Balancing, he lifted his T-shirt and tossed it. Someone wolf-whistled, and Vlad growled again.

"Now the pants," Colton said. "Just whip 'em down and get it over with."

After some awkward maneuvering, he managed to pull down his shorts one-handed just enough for him to sit back down on the tub. Gavin stepped forward and pulled them off his legs, and then Vlad spun around on the edge of the tub. He lowered the foot of his good leg into the water. Once again holding on to his friends, he stood so he could inch forward into the tub. But before he could move, Yan whistled. "Damn, man. You could bounce a quarter off that ass."

Vlad looked over his shoulder. "Why would you throw a quarter at my ass?"

"It's a phrase, nut sack," Colton said. "Means you have a nice ass."

"Of course I do. I am a hockey player. I have hockey butt." He crouched with their help so he could sit in the water.

"What's hockey butt?" Gavin asked.

"From skating," Vlad grunted, easing farther into the water.

"We get big thighs and butts compared to the rest of our bodies. Makes it very hard to buy pants."

Del nodded. "I've actually heard that before."

"Whatever," Colton said. "Can we talk about the body hair? You gotta do something about that."

Vlad glowered at him. "What is wrong with my hair?"

"It's not supposed to be everywhere."

Vlad gestured at his body. "This is how I am made. I am big, and I have a lot of hair."

Colton shrugged. "I'm just saying a wax treatment on your chest every now and then wouldn't be a bad idea."

Malcolm smacked his head. "Knock it off, Colton. Body-shaming is unacceptable."

"I'm not body-shaming. I'm saying the dude has a hairy chest."

"Yeah, that is body-shaming. A man can't help how much hair he's born with any more than a woman can control whether she has a thigh gap. All bodies are beautiful."

Vlad squeezed his eyes shut and thanked God that Elena wasn't around to overhear any of this.

"Okay, we got your magnificent ass in the tub," Malcolm said. "Do your thing, Gavin."

"I can wash my own hair," Vlad grumbled.

Mack pointed at him. "Shut up and let us take care of you."

Gavin crouched on his knees next to the tub. "Someone hand me the shampoo."

Vlad heard the creak of the glass shower door, and then Del handed Gavin a blue bottle of men's shampoo and conditioner combo.

"Dude, that cheap shit will dry out your hair," Mack said as

Gavin squeezed a large dollop onto Vlad's head. "You should be using a regular conditioner at least once a week."

"I don't use a conditioner," Gavin said, digging his fingers into Vlad's hair like he was kneading dough. Vlad closed his eyes because it actually kind of felt good.

"And your hair is dry," Mack pointed out to Gavin. "It would look better if you took care of it."

"Not all of us are blessed with hair like you and Vlad," Gavin said.

"And Noah," Vlad added. "Noah has good hair."

"Thanks, man," Noah said. "Means a lot."

"So does Malcolm. Very thick and soft."

"I use expensive products," Malcolm said. "Mack's right, dude. You should be trading up from that store-bought stuff. You gotta buy from a salon. Hair like yours is a thing of beauty. You should protect it."

"Tilt your head back so I can rinse," Gavin ordered, reaching for the handheld showerhead attached to the faucet. Malcolm turned on the water for him, and a moment later, warm water washed over Vlad's head.

"There," Gavin said, standing. "We'll turn around so you can wash yourself, and then we'll help you out."

Vlad grabbed the bar of soap and started to bathe as the guys looked away. Nearly all of them were professional athletes, too, and knew the rules. No staring during the washing part.

"I'm done," Vlad said, breaking the silence. "Can you help me out?"

Noah reached in to drain the tub as Vlad used his good leg to scoot himself onto the edge of the tub again. Colton took one arm and Malcolm the other to help him stand. Gavin was waiting with a towel, which he wrapped around Vlad's waist.

It started to fall, so Colton tugged it tighter and tied it. "There you go, little butt," he said, patting an ass cheek.

Vlad glared over his shoulder.

Colton shrugged. "That's what my grandma used to say when she gave me baths as a kid. She'd dry me off and say, *There you go, little butt.*"

Del shook his head. "We have spent a lot of time discussing the Russian's ass tonight."

"It's worth talking about," Yan said.

Malcolm gestured toward the bedroom with his chin. "Let's get him back to bed."

They hobbled out of the bathroom, Malcolm and Colton on either side of him, while the others trailed behind. After getting him settled back into bed, the wet towel still wrapped around his waist and his leg elevated on a pillow, Vlad braced himself.

"There," Colton said. "You don't stink anymore. Now you get to tell us why the hell your wife has never seen you naked."

Vlad paused. Took a breath. Looked away as he searched for words they would understand.

After a moment, he looked up again. "Elena and I . . . we are in a marriage of convenience."

They reacted like he knew they would. A moment of stunned silence followed by a slow exchange of glances and then . . .

"Holy fucking shit." Mack dragged his hand over his perfect hair.

"Are you serious, dude?" That was from Colton.

Del and Gavin adopted matching poses—mouths agape, hands hanging loosely at their sides, and eyes full of *what the fuck.* Malcolm tugged at his long beard, and Noah made a noise like someone had just insulted his LEGO collection.

Yan shook his head. "I don't understand. What does that mean?"

"What do you think it means? You have read the manuals. We've read a hundred marriage-of-convenience books."

"Yeah, in *historicals*," Mack said. "Are you saying she married you for your money?"

Vlad swore under his breath. "No." He clunked his head against the headboard, suddenly weary and wishing he could just close his eyes and sleep for a week. Maybe fatigue was a defense mechanism. The body's way of protecting you against the emotional onslaught of finally telling the truth. "It wasn't about money," he said, rolling his head to look at them. "She needed a way out of Russia. I offered to marry her so she could come to America."

The guys processed the information in exhales and long glances between them.

Malcolm sat down on the edge of the mattress. "But . . . isn't that illegal? I thought green card marriages were against the law."

"It's not a green card marriage," Vlad snapped, defensiveness rising along with the hair on the back of his neck. "That's when someone marries a stranger to avoid being deported. Elena was my best friend. We've known each other since we were children. Marriages have been built on far less before, so it was a real marriage. It just . . . it was not real in every way. Not in the way I always hoped." His face flamed in humiliation.

"Just so we're clear," Colton said.

Vlad groaned. He knew what was coming, and so he answered before Colton could even finish the question. "No. We've never had sex."

"You've been married for six years!" Colton choked.

"And she has lived in Chicago for most of that time," Vlad ground out.

"Okay, but even from afar, the topic never came up?"

Mack coughed. "Bad choice of words, dude."

Vlad glared. Mack had the decency to look chagrined. "Sorry."

Malcolm stroked his beard. "Maybe you should start at the beginning."

The beginning? Vlad wasn't even sure what that was. Did he go all the way back and explain how their fathers had been friends at university? That after Elena's mother died, she and her father moved from Moscow to Omsk and lived just a few blocks away from his family? Or did their story start when he was sixteen and he realized that his feelings for her had changed from friendship to something else? And that when she accepted his proposal, he felt like he'd just won the lottery. He was marrying the most beautiful woman in all of Russia.

And it was all a lie.

"Her father was a journalist," Vlad finally said. "He wasn't home very much, and since her mother died when she was nine, Elena spent as much time at my house as she did at her own. Maybe more. She became very close to my family." He took a breath to continue. "Her father made many enemies uncovering corruption in industry and government. A couple of months before we were married, he was working on a story, and he went missing."

The gravity of the statement sucked all the air from the room. "Jesus," Malcolm breathed. "What happened to him?"

"We still do not know. But after her father disappeared, Elena was all alone and frightened. She had my family, of course. She is like a daughter to my parents. But she has no other family. No siblings or grandparents. She needed a fresh start."

The guys exchanged silent looks, starting to fill in the plot holes on their own.

"I had just finished my first season here in America. I went home to Omsk to see if I could help or just to see how she was doing. My mother . . . she knew I always had feelings for Elena. She suggested that I—that I propose to her. If we were married, she could get a visa to come live in America with me as my spouse. So she could start over in America."

"And she said yes?" Del asked.

"Yes." Elena took one step forward and threw her arms around his waist.

The air vacated his lungs in one exhale, and Vlad quickly returned her embrace. "It's going to be okay now, Lenochka," he whispered, using her nickname. "It's going to be okay."

"We got married right away. Very small ceremony. Just my family. I thought she would come back here with me immediately, but there was delay in getting her visa approved. Probably because of her father, but that was never explained. I had to get back to America for the start of the summer training camp, so I had to come back without her at first. She finally came over a month later."

The next part was difficult. "But when she finally got here, she . . . things weren't easy. She cried a lot. Locked herself in her room. Wouldn't talk to me or open up to me. It was like we were strangers. When she said she wanted to go to college in Chicago, how could I say no? I thought it would be good for her. She was obviously miserable here with me, and her visa does not allow her to get a job. I thought she just needed space. I thought that if I was patient, she would eventually come back to me and we could officially start our lives together. I was wrong. She told me at your wedding that she wants to return to Russia and be a journalist like her father."

"I don't understand," Mack said, shaking his head. "In all that time, you guys never talked about the future? About what this marriage would eventually be?"

"There are a lot of misunderstandings between Elena and me."

"Horseshit," Mack snapped. "Misunderstandings can be fixed with a simple conversation. You've had plenty of time for that. So something tells me that's not really what's going on here."

"People only let misunderstandings linger when they're afraid to talk about them," Malcolm said, nodding in that annoying *we've got you figured out* way of his. "Or when they're too afraid to hear the truth."

"Even if that were true at one time, it's too late," Vlad said.

The guys exchanged long looks. He knew those looks. He'd been in on those looks before. The guys were starting to read something into all of this, and that meant they were going to try to make him read something into all of this, and that would be a mistake because there was nothing to read here. And even if there were, he'd already skipped to the end of the book, and it was not a happy ending. Something he would need to remind himself repeatedly over the next several weeks.

A tear dripped down his cheek. "I know what you are thinking, my friends, but this isn't a situation the book club can fix. There is no manual for this one."

"That's why you've been avoiding us," Noah said. "Isn't it?"

Vlad looked at his lap. "It was too humiliating. I couldn't tell you the truth."

"But that's what we do in book club, man," Malcolm said. "And I know you didn't mean to deceive us maliciously, but I feel a little betrayed right now."

Yan pouted. "After everything we've been through, the way

we've all spilled our guts over the years, and you never once told us what was going on in your own marriage?"

"I'm sorry," Vlad said. "I did not want to burden you. Not with everything you've all been dealing with." That, at least, was true. The things these men had endured over the past few years—from Gavin's marriage troubles, to Mack and Liv's struggle to get together, to Noah and Alexis's fight to turn friendship into love—had always made his own issues seem small.

"How can you say that?" Mack crouched next to the bed and met him eye to eye. "We're a family, Vlad."

"We're brothers," Malcolm said, clapping a hand on Mack's shoulder. "We are always here for you."

"I'd b-be divorced right now if not for you," Gavin said, his lifelong stutter emerging with his emotion. "D-do you really think I wouldn't drop everything to do the same for you?"

Vlad's eyes blurred with tears. He might have screwed up so many other things in life, but finding these guys, joining them in their effort to become better men, was the best decision he'd ever made. "I'm sorry," Vlad said, voice tight. "I should have told you. But it would not have made a difference."

"I don't believe that," Del said.

Vlad shook his head. "It is too late."

"It's never too late," Mack said. "Haven't you learned that yet?"

"Russian," Yan said reverently, "think about it. You are living a real-life romance novel."

Vlad frowned. "No, I'm not. A real-life romance novel would have a happy ending. My story will not."

"You don't know that," Noah said. "Trust me. When you guys brought me in, I thought it was a hopeless fantasy to think Alexis and I could ever get together. But you made it happen for us."

Vlad scoffed and looked away. "It's not the same."

Noah crouched beside Mack on the floor next to the bed. "Why not?"

"Because you and Alexis loved each other. You wanted the same things."

Mack softened his voice. "Are you sure that you and Elena don't?"

"I'm sure."

"Then why is she here now?" Yan asked.

"Because she feels obligated. She said she wants to *pay me back* for everything I've done for her. Like our marriage was just a business deal." He wiped his eyes with the heels of his hands, but another tear quickly dripped down Vlad's cheek. Then another. And suddenly it all came out. Vlad covered his face with his hands and released all the pent-up emotion he'd been holding in for months. Without words, his friends gathered around him in a silent, supportive huddle, waiting him out as he got his shit together. Usually, he was the one giving the hugs, letting someone cry it out on his shoulder. He hadn't been prepared for it to be his turn. But it felt good. He'd missed them so much.

Malcolm finally pulled back and patted his leg. "You gotta find a way to move on, man. You owe it to yourself to find some kind of equilibrium. Because you can't go on like this. We won't let you."

Mack stood. "And if there's truly no hope, then you're going to need some way to distract yourself while she's here."

Vlad glanced at his nightstand, where the pages of his manuscript were stacked in a neat pile. He'd forgotten to put them back in the drawer last night, but at least he'd turned the pages over to hide the words. Unfortunately, these guys missed nothing.

"What are you looking at?" Colton asked, eyebrow raised.

"Nothing." Vlad tore his gaze back to the group. Insecurity made his heart pound. He'd never told a single soul about his book.

"You're obviously looking at something," Mack said. "What is it?"

"*Nothing.*"

Del crossed his arms. "You just admitted that you've been lying to us for years. You going to keep doing it?"

Dammit. Vlad banged the back of his head against the bed several times. What did it matter? He was already humiliated. Why not make it complete? He sucked in a breath and spoke on the exhale. "I'm writing a book."

"You're doing what now?" Colton said.

Vlad groaned. "I'm writing a romance novel."

For the second time that morning, confused silence descended on the room. His dread deepened as the guys had another conversation with their eyes.

"That's it," Mack finally said, grinning.

"Totally," Colton laughed. "I'm so fucking in."

Vlad fisted his fingers into the blanket. "Oh shit. What are you talking about?"

"Same, dude," Del said, doing the man-clasp with Colton. "This is going to be awesome."

Vlad hugged the pillow again for support. "What are we doing?"

Colton planted his hands on his hips. "We're going to help you finish your book, little butt."

Vlad coughed. Tiny explosions inside his brain made dots dance across his vision and the blood roar in his ears. If he shook his head any harder, he was going to end up with a concussion. Nope. No way. They were absolutely not going to help him write a book.

His protests were pointless, though.

"Don't even bother saying no," Colton said, waggling his eyebrows. "I'm already thinking about the sex scenes."

Noah scoffed. "We're not letting you anywhere near the sex scenes. I've worked on your computer security. I've seen the links you click on. You're twisted as fuck."

"Hey," Colton said, pointing. "Don't yuck someone else's yum."

Vlad gulped. "How can you help me write a book? You've never written one."

"But we've read a million," Del said. "We know what readers want and expect. That's gotta help, right?"

"My friends, please—"

"Look, man," Malcolm said. "We've missed you. You've been avoiding us and keeping a lot of secrets from us. It's time to let us in."

Vlad gulped. "If I do this—"

The guys whooped in unison. Vlad held up his hand and glared. "*If*, I said. If I do this, it is *only* about my book."

Colton shrugged innocently. "Of course. What else would it be about?"

"I mean it. If any of you think you are going to use this to try to save my marriage, I will put a stop to it."

They all raised their right hands as if swearing an oath.

"Just about the book," Yan said. "Promise."

For the first time ever, Vlad wasn't sure if he trusted his friends.

CHAPTER SEVEN

When Elena got home two hours later, she eased the car into the garage but didn't immediately get out. The guys were still there, so there was no avoiding them this time, and she needed a few minutes to gather her strength.

The first and only time she'd met Vlad's friends, it was through a sheen of tears as she fled Mack and Liv's wedding. She doubted they would welcome her warmly today. But this wasn't about her. It was about Vlad. So, if she had to endure another round of skepticism and hostility from another set of his friends, so be it. Elena gulped down two deep breaths of oxygen and slid out of the car.

The door from the garage led to a back room, which opened into the kitchen. She walked in to find six men circling the island. There were seven of them in all—two Black men, a Latinx man, and four white guys—and together they looked like a photo from a sexy calendar shoot. They were whispering like conspirators, but when she cleared her throat, they jumped apart, looking guilty.

She lifted her chin. "Good morning. Thank you for being here. I'm Elena."

A heavy pause followed her words, but then the guys all began to introduce themselves at once. She could barely keep their names straight as they went around the room. Malcolm. Mack. Colton. Del. Gavin. Yan. Noah. She recognized most of them even though she'd only seen them from afar at Mack's wedding.

"How is Vlad?" she asked.

"Sleeping like a baby," Colton said. "He took a pain pill and fell asleep in mid-sentence."

"And his bath? You made sure he didn't get his incision wet, right?"

"Yep," Mack answered.

"And he didn't put any weight on his leg?"

"All good," Del said, darting his gaze around the room to communicate *something* with his friends.

"Did he eat something before taking his pill?"

Noah nodded. "He had some tea, and I brought him some gluten-free muffins." He pointed to a bakery bag on the counter with a logo for a shop called ToeBeans Café. "My fiancée owns it. There are some more, if you're hungry."

He had probably only offered it to be polite, but she hadn't even expected that, so it took her a moment to respond. "Thank you," she finally said.

"So, can we help you carry in the groceries?" Yan asked.

"That is not necessary but thank you."

"Nah, we got this," Mack said, gesturing with his head toward the garage. They all followed him, and a task that would have taken her ten trips back and forth was done in two. She unpacked the bags as they brought them in.

"Wow," Colton said, surveying what she'd bought. "So, like, did you just raid the gluten-free aisle at the grocery store?"

Elena adopted a sheepish look. "I want to make him his favorite meals, but I wasn't sure what to get to adapt my recipes, so I sort of got a little of everything."

The guys all exchanged more of those none-too-subtle looks that made her squirm.

"So," Mack said, shoving his hands into his back pockets. The pose was far too casual to actually be casual. "Vlad told us you're almost done with school."

Her hands stilled against a box of gluten-free crackers. "Um, yes. That's right. I'm getting my master's degree."

"Congratulations," Noah said.

"And you're planning to go back to Russia," Colton said. His tone was flat, careful. Probing without being accusatory.

"Yes," she said. "To be a journalist."

"We need good journalists, now more than ever," Noah said.

"Yes, I agree." She carried the crackers and two boxes of gluten-free cookies to the walk-in pantry. The silence outside the small space became unbearable, like a heavy humidity had descended on the kitchen. She didn't need to walk out to know they were likely having another one of those eyes-only conversations about her.

"Vlad told us about your father," Malcolm said when she re-emerged. "We're very sorry about what happened. We had no idea."

Guilt forced her gaze downward. "He has kept a lot of secrets for me. To protect me."

"It's great you could be here now to take care of him," Del said. "How long do you plan to stay?"

"Until he doesn't need me anymore."

They did it again. Looked at one another meaningfully, as if they could read one another's thoughts. It was quickly becoming annoying.

"Well," Mack said, standing tall. "We'll get out of your hair now."

"Thank you again for coming," she said.

"Some of us will be back tomorrow to hose him off again," Colton said. Del smacked him upside the head as they walked out. The rest of the guys bid her goodbye and filed from the kitchen. Only Malcolm remained behind.

He shoved his hands in his front pockets. "Vlad is one of the best men I've ever known."

Her heart hammered. "Me too."

"He's been here for every single one of us during some of the hardest times in our lives. We will be there for him too."

"I'm glad. He's lucky to have friends like you."

"To be honest, I'm not sure we deserve him."

To her horror, tears turned her vision watery. She quickly looked away. "I know exactly what you mean."

He studied her a moment longer and then said he'd see her tomorrow. As soon as she heard him leave, she gripped the kitchen counter and leaned against it. They hated her for what she'd done to him. Sure, they'd been polite, but it was obvious that they held her in no greater esteem than the Loners. She wished it didn't matter, and really, it shouldn't matter. She was leaving. And though she was relieved Vlad had such a strong group of friends, being surrounded by them filled her with loneliness. She was his wife, but those men were his family.

She quickly finished putting the groceries away and then went upstairs to check on Vlad. Just as they said, he was sound asleep. A blanket covered most of his lower half, but once again, his broad chest was open to her thirsty stare. It lifted and lowered in a steady rhythm with every deep breath. Her fingers itched with a sudden, insane urge to touch him. To feel that coarse chest hair beneath her soft palms. To curl up next to him and press her cheek to the place where his heart beat strong and sure.

A heat rash rose up her neck as she backed out of the room, clicked the door shut, and leaned against it. She had to get over this, this . . . lust. There was too much to do to stand around ogling him. She'd bought enough food to make several of his favorite meals this week. For her, nothing was as distracting or as comforting as cooking. So she headed back to the kitchen and got to work.

She wanted to make his favorite soup for lunch—solyanka, a thick, briny broth with sausage, pickles, and dill—and then beef stroganoff for dinner. She also wanted to get started on the pelmeni for tomorrow's dinner. The Russian dumplings were another of his favorite. His mother used to fill them with potatoes, mushrooms, and onions, but all the gluten-free recipes she'd found recommended letting the dough sit overnight. The dumplings were a lot of work, but she'd cook all night if necessary to make them perfect for Vlad. The distraction would be welcome, too. Anything to keep her mind off the delicious man he'd clearly become.

How could she still be so affected by him? Clearly, her libido had not caught up to reality. Maybe she was just sex starved, but if that were the case, she would have the same reaction to every good-looking man she encountered or any man who showed interest in her. But she didn't. Only Vlad had ever made her stomach flutter, and she'd never forget the first time it happened. That first whiff of womanly awareness, of gut-tugging breathlessness that forever changed him in her mind from boy to man, from friend to . . . something else. She was sixteen, and he was eighteen, and like a million times before, he whipped his shirt off in front of her to jump into the pool. But unlike the million times before, she *saw* him. Really saw him. Gone was the lanky boy from childhood, and in his place was someone who made her heart jump around.

Her heart was still jumping. Maybe it always would. Maybe that was her personal cross to bear. Her penance.

Elena shook off the memory and threw herself into the cooking. An hour later, the soup was simmering and the dough was done for the dumplings when she heard a dog bark out front.

Elena peered around the corner from the kitchen. Neighbor Dog had his nose pressed to the window to the right of the door. His tail wagged when he saw Elena, and he let out another enthusiastic woof. Elena walked to the door. "Um, go home, doggie."

"You can let him in."

Elena whipped around to find Vlad leaning heavily on his crutches at the top of the stairs.

"What are you doing up?" she asked, rushing up the stairs two at a time. "You should've called for me."

"I smell solyanka," he said, voice thick with the remnants of sleep. He'd put on a shirt and some basketball shorts. One side of his hair stood on end as if he'd fallen asleep on it while it was still wet.

"It's almost done. I'll bring you some. Go back to bed."

"I want to come downstairs."

Elena hovered behind him as he crutched down step by step. The dog woofed again when he spotted Vlad.

"Let him in," Vlad said, nodding to the door.

Elena opened the door, and Neighbor Dog bounded inside. "Your leg!" she warned.

Vlad simply snapped his fingers, and the dog sat in obedience.

"Good boy," Vlad said. He looked up at Elena. "Do you need any help in the kitchen?"

"I'm supposed to be helping *you*. Let's go to the couch."

Neighbor Dog kept pace at his heels as Vlad made his way down the hallway before turning left into the living room. The spacious room was sparsely furnished but cozy. A long gray sectional couch faced a large fireplace, which was flanked by two plush chairs and wide windows overlooking the backyard. A leather ottoman doubled as a coffee table in the center, and above the mantel hung a large flat-screened TV.

"Sit," Elena ordered. "I'll push the ottoman closer for your leg. Do you need ice?"

"Not right now," Vlad grunted, scooting backward until his knees touched the couch. Then, holding his crutches for balance, he lowered slowly to sit. Elena quickly shoved the ottoman until he could rest his leg on it. He sank back against the couch cushions and rubbed his eyes. Neighbor Dog rested his head on Vlad's good knee in search of a scratch.

Vlad obliged. "How long was I asleep?"

"About two hours."

"I don't remember when my friends left."

"They said you sort of passed out."

He scratched his hand down his thickly whiskered jaw. "I feel drunk."

"And you were going to come down the stairs like that?" One corner of his mouth quirked up in an apologetic smile, and her heart jumped. "I'll go get you some soup."

She raced back to the kitchen before he could see what he was doing to her. Then she dished up a bowl of the simmering broth, poured a tall glass of milk, and carried them both to the living room, where she set them on the small table next to the couch. "I should get you a tray or something."

"I don't need one," Vlad said, reaching for the bowl. "I pretty much eat all my meals like this when I'm home."

"That's not very Russian of you."

He shrugged with one shoulder. "It's too quiet to eat at the table alone."

The image that conjured was so full of loneliness that Elena felt a swell of something inconvenient in her chest. Vlad ate alone with someone else's dog at his feet.

Vlad swallowed a large spoonful, and a moan escaped from his lips. "Holy shit, Lenochka."

This time, her heart completely stopped. *Lenochka* was the affectionate nickname that he and his parents used to call her when they were young. It was a common diminutive for Elena in Russia, but her own father had never even called her that. It had been years since she'd heard it.

"It's good?" she asked, her voice strangely tinny.

"Better than good. I'm going to eat the entire pot."

That was exactly the response she'd been hoping for, and she couldn't hide her satisfied smile as she sat down on the opposite end of the couch. "Well, save room for dinner. I'm making beef stroganoff tonight, and tomorrow I am going to make pelmeni."

"You are going to spoil me." He shook his head, but as far as protests went, it was a weak effort. "Pelmeni is a lot of work. You don't have to do that."

She shrugged. "I want to. You're going to need to eat well if you're going to heal, and I like cooking."

"I know you do." He swallowed another heaping spoonful and then looked at her. "Did you already eat?"

"Not yet."

"Go get some and eat with me." He then added in a rush, "If you want."

"I— Yes. Okay. I'll be right back."

She served herself a smaller portion and returned to her spot on the couch. After tucking her legs beneath her, she dug in. The flavors exploded on her tongue. Spicy and sweet and sour. She could have made this for herself in Chicago, but the memories it conjured were too powerful. Like now. "This was the first thing your mom taught me to make."

He looked over quickly. "It was?"

"Whenever she made it, I would eat so much that she finally offered to show me how to make it for myself." She smiled into her bowl. "I started cooking it for my dad almost once a week after that. I think he got sick of it, but he didn't want to hurt my feelings, so he ate it."

Vlad tensed next to her. "He should've been making it for *you*."

"I would've starved. He could barely fry an egg."

"He should have learned like a normal father."

She stirred her soup. "My father was never going to be that."

"He could have if he'd tried."

The stern gruffness of Vlad's tone plucked a familiar chord of resentment, and the disharmony that hummed between them was an old song. Vlad had never hid his anger at her father for how often he was gone when she was a child, because Vlad had never understood the importance of her father's job. Which was one of the reasons she didn't want Vlad to know she was trying to finish her father's story. He would never, could never, comprehend why it was so important to her.

The scrape of spoons against bowls was the only sound in the suddenly and uncomfortably quiet room.

"Let's watch TV," she suggested.

Vlad picked up the remote from where it rested between them and hit the power button. It was tuned to a local sports channel, which was showing a preview of that night's game of the Nashville Legends, the team that Gavin, Yan, and Del played for.

"Do you ever go to their games?" Elena asked, grateful for the chance to change the subject to something safer.

"Once my season ends, yes," Vlad answered. "I went to a few games last summer with the rest of the guys."

"Do they ever come to yours?"

"Of course. We are very supportive of one another."

He probably hadn't meant it as a dig against her, because Vlad never said anything intentionally harsh, but it stung all the same. As if reading Elena's mind, the sportscasters suddenly changed direction and began to talk about Vlad's team.

"For the first time in franchise history, the Nashville Vipers have won the Western Conference finals and earned a spot in the Stanley Cup championship. The Vipers defeated the Vancouver Canucks last night four to three in game seven of the conference series."

Elena reached for the remote.

"It's okay," Vlad said, covering her hand with his. The unexpected touch strummed an entirely different tune inside her, and she discreetly slid her hand from beneath his before she gave herself away. Vlad didn't seem to notice. His eyes were locked on the TV.

"The Vipers will face the New York Rangers in game one of the Stanley Cup at seven o'clock Saturday night in New York. It's a bittersweet victory for the Vipers and their fans without their top defenseman, Vlad Konnikov."

Elena looked over at Vlad. He sat eerily still but for the up-and-down bobble of his Adam's apple beneath the scruff of whiskers darkening his neck.

"Team sources tell us he is now recovering at home from surgery to repair his broken tibia—"

The chime of the doorbell sent Elena nearly out of her seat. Soup sloshed onto her hand. With a quiet curse, she set the bowl on the table next to her side of the couch and stood. "I'll get it."

She braced herself in case it was the Loners again, but when she glanced out the windows on either side of the front door, just one person stood on the other side.

A very beautiful woman.

Elena opened the door slowly, and the woman smiled brightly. Elena forgot for a moment that she was expected to smile back. She was Russian. Smiling at strangers was an American trait that still did not come naturally to her. "Can I help you?" she asked belatedly.

The woman's smile faltered. "Oh, I'm sorry. Are you Elena?"

"Yes."

"It's so great to meet you finally," the woman said. "I'm Michelle. I'm a neighbor of Vlad's. The Loners told me you were back."

Oh, God. This sophisticated woman was the mysterious Michelle? She wore a stylish outfit of white jeans and a sleeveless black blouse, and her hair was pulled back in a sleek ponytail—the kind Elena could never pull off with her naturally wavy hair.

"Yes. I am back," Elena finally said. Then, when she realized the woman was waiting expectantly to be invited in, Elena moved away from the door. "Do you want to come in?"

"I don't want to disturb you. I just wanted to drop this pie off for Vlad. I meant to come by earlier, but I thought I should wait until he got settled."

Elena accepted the pie from Michelle's outstretched hands. "Is it gluten-free?" she blurted.

Michelle blinked. "Y-yes. I know he can't eat gluten."

"He's in the living room eating lunch," Elena said, trying to edge out the flatness of her voice with her long-forgotten smile.

Michelle nodded politely and gestured with her hand. "I'll follow you."

The woman's fancy sandals clicked on the floor, and Elena suddenly felt as frumpy as she knew she looked in her shorts, oversize Medill sweatshirt, and house slippers. Elena was tempted to tell Michelle to take her shoes off, but apparently Vlad was not as strict about maintaining that particular Russian tradition at home as she was. None of the Loners or his friends had removed their shoes either.

Elena walked into the living room first. Vlad looked over his shoulder. "Who was it?" Before she could answer, Michelle strode in behind her. Vlad did a double take.

"Michelle," Vlad said, clearing his throat. "Hi."

Unease pooled in Elena's stomach. Why did Michelle make him nervous? "She brought you a pie."

Vlad glanced at it and then back at Michelle, who was rounding the couch to stand in front of him. "Thank you," Vlad said. "That was very nice of you."

Michelle clasped her hands in front of her. "I'm so sorry about your injury. The girls and I were watching the game when it happened. They're so worried about you."

"The girls?" Elena asked.

Michelle smiled at her. Did this woman ever not smile? "My kids," Michelle explained. "They love watching Vlad play hockey. He got us tickets earlier this year for one of their home games, and the girls *still* talk about it."

Vlad cleared his throat again. "It was good of you to come." He seemed to remember the bowl in his hand. "Would you like to eat? Elena made one of my favorite soups."

Not for her. The thought arose with surprising ferocity along with an urge to storm into the kitchen and deposit Michelle's pie in the trash.

"No, thank you," Michelle said quickly. "It smells wonderful, but the girls will be back from their dad's soon, so I should probably get home. I just wanted to stop by and see how you're doing."

"I'm good, good," Vlad stammered. "The surgery went well."

"Are you in any pain?"

"No. Not yet. Maybe when the morphine shot begins to wear off, though."

Every nervous utterance was a tiny needle in Elena's nerves. Which was ridiculous. What did it matter that a pretty, kind woman had brought Vlad a homemade pie? Michelle met Elena's gaze, and there was that smile again. Too genuine for Elena to trust it. She really was her father's daughter.

"Do you have everything you need? Can I do anything to help?" Michelle asked.

The correct response was probably something like, *That's very kind*, but all Elena could manage was, "We are fine for now."

"Well, if that changes, I am just a couple of blocks away." Michelle shrugged with a deep breath. "I'll get out of your hair now. Please do call me if you need anything."

"I will walk you out," Elena said.

"No need. I know the way. You have your hands full already."

Politeness dictated that Elena walk her to the door anyway. Jealousy sent her instead straight to the kitchen. Elena set the pie on the counter next to the bowl with dough for the pelmeni. Her enthusiasm for making them had selfishly waned.

"Elena."

With a startled gasp, she spun around. Vlad stood just inside the kitchen, leaning on his crutches. She'd been so lost in her own thoughts that she hadn't heard him approach.

She smoothed the front of her sweatshirt. "Michelle seems really nice."

"She's a friend from the neighborhood." He spoke too carefully, as if he could see right through her.

"It was nice of her to make this for you." Elena gestured toward the pie. "Do you want a piece? Go back and sit down. I'll bring it to you."

Vlad stared with an unblinking expression before giving her a brief nod of acknowledgment. His crutches pounded out a soft thud-scuff rhythm as he returned to the living room. As soon as he was gone, Elena leaned against the counter and sucked in a deep breath. She needed to get her shit together, to use an American phrase she'd grown especially fond of. Lusting over him? Shuddering over the touch of his hand? Flushing with jealousy over a woman sharing her pie? She had no right to feel any of it. She was here to help him heal, nothing more, because there could be nothing more. And if she was going to survive the time with him, she needed to remind herself as often as necessary that this was temporary. Once Vlad was healed, only one thing was in her future.

Elena dug her phone from her pocket. Before she could talk herself out of it, she hammered out a text.

You said to call if I ever needed anything. Can we talk?

CHAPTER EIGHT

Elena awoke early the next morning because she wanted to make syrniki for breakfast. The Russian pancakes were another one of Vlad's favorites and one more of many dishes she learned to make in his mother's kitchen.

She showered and twisted her wet hair atop her head before throwing on the only thing left that was clean—a pair of jogging shorts and a plain white T-shirt. Before heading downstairs, she peeked in at Vlad. He was asleep under only the sheet. Neighbor Cat was curled against his side.

"Hussy," Elena whispered.

The cat blinked and stretched out her paws before burrowing closer into Vlad's chest.

Elena had just set out all the ingredients for breakfast when someone rang the doorbell. She apparently wasn't the only person who'd gotten up early. Colton and Noah stood on the other side of the front door, both of them grinning.

"Vlad is still asleep," she said, letting them in. "But I was just about to start breakfast."

Colton rubbed his hands together. "I was hoping you'd say that. What're you making?"

"Syrniki. They're like pancakes with cheese in the batter."

"Cheese pancakes?" Colton said. "I'm going to eat the shit out of those."

Noah handed over a pastry bag that matched the one from yesterday. "A present from Alexis, my fiancée."

Elena peeked inside to find a variety of pastries. "Wow, please tell Alexis I said thank you."

"You got any coffee going?" Colton asked, holding his fist to a yawn.

"Um, no."

"I'll do it," Colton said.

Another car pulled into the driveway. Elena peeked through the window.

"That'll be Mack and Malcolm," Noah said, following Colton toward the kitchen.

Elena opened the door again, and sure enough, Mack and Malcolm strolled up the sidewalk. "You guys are here to bathe my husband too?"

"It's the highlight of our day," Mack said. "Bro's got an ass that won't quit."

"Um—" Elena shut the door.

"Ignore him," Malcolm said. Then he bent and kissed Elena's cheek. She had no response other than stunned disbelief as he followed Mack to the kitchen. Yesterday, Elena had been convinced Vlad's friends hated her, and now a kiss on the cheek and pastry gifts? Elena wanted to pound the heel of her hand against her head, because once again she felt like cobwebs were growing in her mind. Like she'd been dropped into the second act of a play.

She returned to the kitchen to find Colton filling the coffee maker with water. Mack sat on the floor with Neighbor Cat in his lap. He looked up. "I didn't know you guys had a cat."

"We don't. Er, I mean, Vlad doesn't. It's not his cat."

Mack's hands paused in the act of petting the cat's fur. "Whose cat is it?"

"I don't know. Animals just show up here a lot."

Noah snorted. "Of course they do."

Elena began to work on the pancake dough—syrniki was not made with the kind of liquid batter Americans were used to—but another knock at the door brought a quick interruption. She looked at the guys. Mack shrugged. "We're all here. Gavin, Del, and Yan have an early game today, so they aren't coming."

Elena gulped. That could only mean one thing. She returned to the front door slowly, as if she'd filled her house slippers with pebbles. This time, the face on the other side of the door greeted her with what Elena assumed was a permanent scowl. Elena fought the urge to cross herself as she opened the door. "Good morn—"

Claud pushed her way inside. "Where is he?"

"It is lovely to see you, too, Claud. Vlad is still asleep."

"Go wake him up," Claud demanded.

Linda let out a long, weary sigh. "I'm sorry about her. Truly. She's grumpy in the morning."

Elena lifted an eyebrow. "Just in the morning?"

Andrea walked in last with a dish in her hands. "I made a quiche."

"Do you know what a quiche is?" Claud asked.

"Yes, I know what a quiche is. I grew up in Russia, not on the moon." She returned her attention to Andrea. "Thank you. I am just about to make breakfast, but I'm sure Vlad will enjoy this, as well."

"Whose cars are in the driveway?" Claud asked as they all returned to the kitchen. She stopped short at the sight of Colton, Malcolm, and Noah gathered around the island. Mack was still on the floor with the cat.

"I know you," Claud said, pointing at Colton. "You're that country singer Vlad hangs out with. Cat Whaler or whatever."

Mack and Noah laughed into their coffee mugs. Colton tipped the brim of his nonexistent hat and winked. "Cat Whaler, at your service."

"I hated your last song. It was vulgar."

"I do aim to please, ma'am."

"Ma!" Linda said, rushing forward. "Be nice."

"Don't mind her," Elena said to Colton. "She's just mad that someone turned her hair into snakes."

Malcolm and Mack exchanged grins.

"Coffee?" Elena asked to no one in particular.

"Thank you," Linda said. "We can get it ourselves."

"Well, *I* am Andrea Sampson," Andrea said, setting the quiche on the counter. She held out her hand to Colton. "And I'm a huge fan of yours."

Colton picked up her hand and brushed his lips across her knuckles. "It's a pleasure, darlin'."

"Don't encourage her," Claud scoffed. "She got hit on last night at Silver Sneakers. Now she thinks she's Brigitte fucking Bardot."

"Who is Brigitte Bardot?" Noah asked.

Claud hissed through her teeth as she accepted a cup of coffee from Linda. Then she plunked down on a stool at the island and muttered something about goddamned millennials.

Elena returned to the pancake dough and began to roll it into individual cakes. "What is Silver Sneakers?"

"Aerobics for people whose joints crack in the morning," Linda said.

"Hey, I took that class by accident once," Colton said. "It kicked my ass."

"How did you take it by accident?" Malcolm asked.

"I had the times wrong. I thought I was going into Six-Pack Abs. I was super confused when all these old ladies walked in. I was too embarrassed to walk out."

"Old ladies?" Claud scoffed.

"It's a compliment," Colton said. "They ran circles around me. I've had a thing for older women ever since then, to be honest." He winked again at Andrea, who preened and smiled.

Elena carried the dough cakes to the stove and heated a skillet with oil. Claud snorted. "What're you making?"

"Syrniki," Elena said. "Russian cheese pancakes. Do you know what pancakes are?"

Claud muttered under her breath, and Elena could've sworn something crawled up the back of her neck.

Elena set each cake in the skillet and put on the cover. They needed about five to seven minutes on each side to get puffy. As they cooked, she walked to the fridge and pulled out sour cream and blueberries for toppings. Probably only she and Vlad would use those. In the pantry, she found powdered sugar and syrup for everyone else.

"So, Elena," Noah said in a tone that conveyed some kind of preplanned speech. "The guys and I were talking, and we'd like to help out as much as possible. Maybe put together a meal schedule or help out with his rehab appointments—"

Claud snorted. "Why are you talking to her about it? She's leaving again in a few days."

Elena lifted the cover of the skillet and flipped the pancakes. "I'm not, actually. I'm staying for as long as he needs me."

Claud sputtered like a rusty tractor. "You can't stay."

"Why not?" Elena replaced the lid. About five more minutes, and they'd be done.

"Because . . . because. You can't. He needs to move on with his life, and he can't do that with you here."

Elena turned quickly so no one could see the reaction on her face.

"Ma!" Linda snapped.

"Well, now, that was downright harsh," Colton said in a deceptively dulcet tone.

Elena busied herself with gathering plates from the cupboard. She heard Mack rise from the floor.

"Seems to me it should be up to Vlad to decide whether he wants Elena here or not," Mack said, "and he's agreed to it."

"Do you even know how to cook, girl?" Claud grumbled.

Elena shot Claud an *are you serious?* look over her shoulder.

"Anyone can make pancakes," Claud said dismissively.

"I've been cooking since my mother died when I was nine," Elena said, setting the plates on the island so everyone could get their own. "Vlad's mother taught me how to make all of his favorites. I don't suppose you know to make pirozhki? Or maybe kholodets or Pozharsky cutlets?"

As she spoke, the guys did that talk-with-their-eyes thing again.

Elena returned to the stove and turned off the burner. Then she piled the finished syrniki on a platter. "You are all welcome to eat with us," she said, setting it next to the stack of plates. "I'm going to go wake up Vlad."

Neighbor Cat followed her upstairs. Vlad's bedroom door was still partway open from when she'd checked on him after she woke up. She tiptoed inside and found him in the same position as this morning, which was the same position as when she'd checked on him last night. Flat on his back, leg propped up on the pillow, his head turned slightly to the left.

"Vlad," she whispered, creeping up next to the bed. His breathing didn't even change. "Vlad." She said it louder, bending closer to him. He turned his face the other way with a deep breath. Dammit. Elena pressed her hand to his shoulder and gave it a small shake. "Vlad."

His eyes flew open. "What? What's wrong?"

Elena jumped back. "I'm sorry. Did I hurt you?"

He dragged a hand across his face. "No. I'm fine. What time is it?" He focused on her face then and rose up on his elbows. "What's wrong?"

"Your friends are here."

He narrowed his eyes. "Did they say something inappropriate?"

"What? No. But I think there's going to be a food fight with the Loners."

"They are *all* here?"

"Yes, and I swear Claud just put a hex on me."

The corner of Vlad's mouth curled up in a tired smile as he reached a hand up to rub his whiskers, which had grown overnight officially into a beard—the wild, unkempt kind—but the ruggedness was offset by the tired softness of his eyes. Neighbor Cat leaped onto the bed, rubbed against him, and began to purr. Elena couldn't blame her. If she had a chance to curl up next to Vlad, she'd probably purr too.

Vlad absently scratched the cat's ears.

"Does this one have a name?" Elena asked.

"Angel. She lives across the street."

"She was in your bed this morning."

A powerful yawn split his mouth wide, and he stretched his arms high over his head as he sat. "She is a good girl," he said. "One of my favorites."

As if Vlad had ever met an animal he didn't like.

He swung his legs off the bed and nodded self-consciously to the bathroom. "I need to, um . . ."

Oh, right. Bathroom stuff. All over the world, other married couples were perfectly unembarrassed about nature's calling, but Elena's cheeks blazed like she'd just stuck her head in a pizza oven. She handed him his crutches and hovered nearby as he slid one under each armpit.

"I'll just wait out here?"

He avoided her gaze. "Sure."

She turned away as he shuffled to the bathroom. He used the foot of his crutch to shut the door behind him. Moments later, the toilet flushed and then water splashed in the sink. It lasted for a minute, and she realized he was brushing his teeth.

She turned around when the door opened again. He came out looking rough and vulnerable at the same time. An insane, over-whelming urge to hug him nearly propelled her forward from her safe spot by the bedroom door. Instead, she backed up so he could pass by. She followed him to the stairs, and then he let her pretend to help by giving him an arm to hold as he went down on one leg. Not because he really needed the help, but probably because she'd yelled at him yesterday for coming down the stairs alone.

When he entered the kitchen, the guys all stood and greeted

him with hugs and *how are ya?* and *you look like shit*. Which was not true. He looked the opposite of shit.

The Loners repeated the greetings with much nicer sentiments. Even Claud lost her scowl.

Andrea and Linda rose from their seats and practically ran to him. They each hugged him, and Elena met his eyes over Linda's shoulder. He smiled tiredly at her, and Elena was momentarily distracted by the warm familiarity of it.

"Breakfast is done," she said, heading back toward the stove. "Do you want some tea?"

"I'm good for now. Don't rush around." He crutched to a seat at the island. Mack and Noah got him settled and moved another stool closer so he could elevate his leg. Elena quickstepped to the freezer and removed one of the baggies of ice she'd filled last night. She grabbed a towel and returned to his side as he ripped open the Velcro straps.

"How is it this morning?" She leaned over him to study the incision. It was still reddish with green and purple bruising forming around it. She looked up. "Is it supposed to do that?"

"Bruising is normal." He reached for the ice and smiled when she handed it over.

"You're sure? Maybe we should take a picture of it and send it to Madison."

"If it gets worse by tonight, we can do that," he said calmly.

"Maybe we should have iced it again last night."

"It's fine, Elena. Don't worry."

The silence in the kitchen suddenly became obvious. Elena looked up to find everyone watching with bemused expressions. Everyone but Claud, who looked murderous.

"What?" Elena asked.

"Nothing," Colton said quickly. Too quickly. He met Malcolm's eyes, and they both looked away. Those damn silent conversations were becoming really annoying.

"You were speaking Russian," Noah finally said.

"Oh yes. We tend to do that." They slipped in and out of it so naturally with each other that she hardly noticed. "Sorry. We will try to stick to English when you are around."

"I think it's cute," Andrea said.

Claud muttered something under her breath, and Elena's eye started to twitch. She turned to Vlad and switched back to Russian. "Did you hear that? By midnight, I'm going to break out in pulsing boils."

Vlad pressed his fist to his mouth to smother a laugh.

Elena pointed to the platter of pancakes. "Who is hungry?"

Colton rubbed his hands together. "Hot damn, I am."

"Everyone fix a plate," she said. "I hope there is enough. I can make another batch if we need it. We also have the quiche that Andrea brought—"

The feel of Vlad's hand on her back brought an abrupt end to her nervous speech. She looked down at him, and his warm gaze melted her insides. "It's enough, Lenochka. Get your food and eat."

She nodded because it was the safest thing she could think of in response, the only thing that wouldn't reveal that the feel of his fingers on her spine had left her breathless. She quickly fixed his plate and set it in front of him with a fork.

"This looks delicious," he murmured in Russian. "You didn't have to do this."

"I wasn't sure if they'd still be good with the gluten-free flour."

"They look perfect."

"Sour cream or syrup?"

He lifted a single eyebrow. Right. She knew the answer to that. She handed him the sour cream and waited for him to plop a large dollop on top of his pancakes. The room grew quiet again, and she looked up to find everyone eyeing them with disgust.

"Did he just put sour cream on his pancakes?" Colton asked, fork paused halfway to his mouth.

"Russians put sour cream on everything," Vlad said, adding a handful of blueberries on top. "This is how we eat syrniki."

"It's how we eat everything," Elena said.

Colton shoveled a huge bite into his mouth. "These are amazing."

Elena filled her own plate and sat down next to Vlad. "They'd be better with tvorog, but I couldn't find any at the store."

"What's tvorog?" Mack asked over a mouthful.

"It's a kind of Russian cheese. You can't have real syrniki without it, so I had to use ricotta cheese instead."

"They don't sell it in stores?" Andrea asked.

"Not usually, at least not in America," Elena answered. "Some international markets will have it, but that's pretty rare. It has to be served fresh or it will spoil quickly."

"I might know a place that would have it," Colton said.

Vlad coughed, and Elena watched as he locked eyes with Colton and engaged in one of those silent conversations of his own. A moment passed in which Colton seemed to have been scolded, because he finally shrugged and looked away.

Andrea suddenly sighed dramatically. "Anyway," she said, "I need advice."

Claud rolled her eyes. "Here we go."

"What? I need to talk about this. And that's what we do in our morning coffee hours. We talk about things."

"I'm listening, darlin'," Colton said.

Andrea gave him a coy smile but then she sighed again. "I don't know what to do about Jeffrey. He really wants to, you know, take things further. I just don't know if I'm ready for that yet."

Claud snorted. "You mean you don't know if you're ready for him to know the truth about your boobs."

Mack coughed into his coffee, and Colton grinned. "I'm suddenly extremely interested in this conversation."

Andrea crossed her arms, probably to show off the very boobs they were discussing. "For the last time, there is absolutely nothing wrong with breast enhancement."

"Oh, I heartily agree," Colton said.

Elena snuck a glance at Vlad. He seemed as unfazed as he was unsurprised by their conversation. Apparently, Andrea's boobs were a regular topic of conversation during morning coffee hours.

"I just, I'm still so gun-shy from Neil," she said. She looked at the Elena and the guys. "That's my ex-husband."

"Ah," Elena said.

"I mean, I care about Jeffrey. I do," Andrea continued. "But what if he's just another Neil? We were so perfect together for so many years, and then . . . it just fizzled."

"Before or after he died?" Elena asked.

Vlad snorted and then coughed to again cover up his laugh.

"See, that's your problem right there," Claud said, pointing at Andrea. "You're still waiting on your knight in shining armor who will make you all giddy and sparkly for the rest of your life. What you should be looking for is someone you're still willing to have sex with after they make you look at pictures of their colonoscopy."

Malcolm spit out his coffee.

"That's what's wrong with so many young people today," Claud continued. "You think marriage is this grand romantic adventure that's never going to end. That's not what it is. It is a partnership. A legal agreement that makes it so damn annoying to get out of that you stick by each other even when you want to beat him with a giant zucchini—"

Elena opened her mouth, but Linda waved her off. "Don't ask."

"—because it's just too much of a pain in the ass to break up."

Noah pounded his chest to clear the last of his choking fit. "Well, I'm excited to get married."

"You shouldn't be excited to get married. You should be *ready* to get married. There's a huge difference. Most people are excited for a wedding but never think about what happens after that or what marriage really means." Claud leaned forward. "You know what my mother told me on my wedding day?"

"Double, double toil and trouble?" Elena said.

Vlad grunted another laugh.

"She said, 'Claudia, I know you are so happy right now that it's hard to imagine things will ever be bad. But there will come a day when you'll be sitting across from him as he is eating his breakfast, and all you will think is *why?* And then you'll get over it, and things will go back to normal.' That is marriage. Security and stability with the occasional *what the hell was I thinking?*"

Elena turned a pointed gaze at Vlad and whispered, "'Thus heaven's gift to us is this . . .'"

His chuckle came out a surprised puff of air before he finished the couplet. "'That habit takes the place of bliss.'"

"Your mama was right. There is a Pushkin quote for everything."

"Who is Pushkin?" Colton asked.

Vlad shook his head and wiped his mouth. "We are with heathens, Elena."

Elena sighed dramatically and plunked her elbow on the counter. "Now you've done it."

Vlad leaned back in his chair, still shaking his head. "Alexander Pushkin is only Russia's most famous and important poet in all of history."

Elena adopted a theater whisper. "His mama is a literature professor at the university in Omsk and teaches a course on Pushkin."

"Who is Pushkin?" Vlad muttered again. "He is to Russia what Shakespeare is to Britain."

"Between the two of us, we've probably memorized every one of his poems. His mama used to make us sit for hours and analyze every word, every translation." Elena adopted a matronly tone of voice. "*'Literature is life, and Pushkin is its beating heart.'*"

Vlad grinned, a wide, toothy thing that showed off the tiny gap between his two front incisors. "You sounded exactly like her."

"Damn, boys," Mack said. "Been a long time since we've seen the Russian smile like that, huh?"

"Indeed," Malcolm said, nodding with an almost Zen-like quality. "Indeed."

The guys did that talking-with-their-eyes thing again.

"Well," Linda suddenly said. "We've invaded your space long enough this morning. We should get going."

Claud scowled. "I'm not ready."

Linda grabbed her mother's arm. "Yes, you are."

"Breakfast was incredible," Andrea said. "Can we help clean up?"

"No," Elena said, waving her hand at the mess. "I'll take care of it."

"Before you go," Colton said. "We have an idea that perhaps you ladies would like to help us with?"

Vlad's eyebrows tugged together, as if he didn't quite trust whatever was going to come out of his friend's mouth.

"Since Vlad can't be with his team during the Stanley Cup championship—"

Elena snuck at a glance at Vlad to gauge his reaction. He had none. He'd gone impossibly still.

"—I was thinking that we should throw him a party here on Saturday to watch the first of the Nashville games with him."

Vlad's throat went taut with a hard swallow. Apparently, this was news to him. His fingers crumpled his napkin into a tight ball. Elena wasn't even sure he knew he'd done it.

"A party with Colton Wheeler?" Andrea gushed. "Count me in."

Colton winked. "Be sure to bring Jeffrey."

Andrea winked back. "Who?"

"We were thinking that everyone can bring food to share," Mack said. "I know Liv and Alexis are both hoping Elena will make some authentic Russian dishes."

Elena didn't respond to Mack's suggestion. She was too absorbed in watching Vlad's reaction. She couldn't tell if he was mad or . . . *Oh, Vlad.* His bottom lip swelled beyond the outline of his beard and trembled. He cleared his throat and reached for his crutches. "Excuse me for a minute."

Silence followed his retreat from the kitchen. The crutch-hop of his gait grew softer and softer as he headed down the hallway.

"That man is too pure for this world," Andrea said.

"We'll clean up," Noah said to Elena, but his eyes were following his friend. "Go make sure he's okay with this."

Elena found him leaning on his crutches and staring out the French doors in the dining room. Neighbor Cat wound around his good leg, purring up at him. At Elena's appearance next to him,

Vlad dipped his face to swipe one-handed at the wetness on his cheeks.

"You have incredible friends," she said quietly.

"I know."

"It felt like a real Russian meal in there for a minute."

"Loud and chaotic?"

"Exactly." She tilted her head. "Are you okay with the party?"

He bit his lip.

"Hey." Elena stepped closer and pressed her hand to the center of his chest. He looked down in surprise and . . . something else she would think about later. Something that made it difficult to form her next words. "You don't have to do it. I'm sure they would understand."

"No, I—I want to do it. I need to."

"Good. I think it will be fun. I'll make a ton of food, and we can all wear your jersey."

His bottom lip wobbled again, and it was like seeing her old friend after a long absence. Her gentle giant. Her hug in human form. The man she had never deserved and never would. This time, when the urge to hug him flared, she didn't fight it. She wrapped her arms around his waist and pressed her cheek to his chest. Within her embrace, his breath caught and his muscles stiffened.

"It's been a long time since you hugged me." His voice was thick and gravelly.

"You looked like you needed it."

He lowered his forehead to the crown of her hair and inhaled deeply. "I did."

A moment later, the sound of someone clearing his throat extra loud brought them apart. Elena jumped back and found Vlad looking down at her, face unreadable.

"Thank you," he said.

"For what?"

"Being here."

Colton appeared around the corner. "Okay, little butt. Let's go. Time for your bath."

Elena watched him follow his friends upstairs, Neighbor Cat tagging along. As soon as he was out of earshot, she let out the heavy breath she'd been holding. He wasn't the only one who'd needed that hug, but he at least was able to walk away from it without feeling the Earth tilt beneath his feet. She was suddenly tipsy, spinning in her own head.

She couldn't do that again. Not if she wanted to leave here with any piece of her heart intact.

Promise Me

The house was abandoned, as they all were. Empty, broken shells from the time before, when children huddled around dining tables and fireplaces with no idea of the hell that was to come.

Anna had spent countless nights in houses like this. Places that once radiated warmth and light were now nothing but cold, dark stay-over shelters for the weary. At least this one had an actual bed. It had long since been raided for its blankets and pillows, but Anna wouldn't complain. The mattress was soft, and it wasn't the ground. She'd take it, even if she knew she wouldn't actually sleep. She rarely did anymore. How could anyone sleep in a world like this?

Two years. That's how long she'd been in Europe. Her bosses at the *Seattle Times* wouldn't even entertain her request to send her overseas as a correspondent after Pearl Harbor. *You're lucky to have a job at all, sweetheart.* So when United Press Associations put out a call for Russian-speaking journalists, she applied using only her first initial. She wasn't the only woman covering the war, but there were few enough of them that most men had no idea how to treat her. Only Tony had treated her like a real journalist.

At first.

His accusations, which were no different than a million others that had been hurled her way, hurt more than she could ever admit to him. Being paired with him now was only fitting. A soulless assignment alongside a man with no heart.

Heavy footsteps outside her door made her breath catch in her throat. Not out of fear, but from tension. Two weeks on the road, and she and Tony had yet to reach a truce. She heard him breathe—a deep intake followed by a defeated exhale.

Anna called out quietly, "I know you're out there, Tony. What do you want?"

The door slowly creaked open. She could barely make out his tall frame in the darkness. "Did I wake you?" he asked gruffly.

"No." She sighed and sat up. "I sleep about as much as you do."

He folded his arms across his broad chest. "You need to rest, Anna. We're leaving early."

It was the kind of everyday gallantry that men like him expressed without thinking, but it always made Anna feel weak. Like she needed to be protected. A woman like her couldn't afford to be treated that way. Everyone in this war had made assumptions about her from the minute she landed in Europe, all of them wrong and all of them based on old notions of what a woman should or should not be, do, say. She was pretty, so they assumed she was a lightweight. She was flirtatious, so they accused her of sleeping around. She was brave, so they called her risky. "*You're* not asleep," she countered. "Do men need less rest than women?"

Tony's sigh was long and weary. "Not everything I say is a

knock against you, Anna. I'm just trying to make sure you're ready for what we're likely to find tomorrow."

A hasty burial ditch. That's what the villagers had told them. Remains of American and British POWs who'd tried to run but were caught and executed. "I'm well aware of it."

He hesitated, and she felt more than saw his gaze upon her. His voice, when he finally spoke again, was low and raspy. "I'm 4F."

A hot flush rose up her cheeks as shame turned her blood to sludge. The designation—4F—meant he'd been denied entry into the military on medical grounds.

"A heart murmur," he said. "I tried to enlist three times after Pearl Harbor. The last time, I got caught using a fake name. I was almost arrested, so that's why . . ."

Anna stood up. "Tony—"

He pulled away from the doorframe. His boots scuffed against the floor as he turned to leave. Anna acted without thinking. She crossed the room. "Wait. I'm sorry."

"For what?" he asked over his shoulder.

"You know what. What I said to you back then was rude and ignorant and inconsiderate. I know as well as anyone that being a war correspondent is every bit as important to the effort as being a soldier on the field of battle, and I also know what it's like to have people make the wrong assumption about you."

Tony turned around and shoved his hands in the pockets of his coat. "I overreacted. Let's just forget it."

Frustration bubbled as he walked away from her toward the other bedroom. "Jack Armstrong," she blurted.

Tony turned around in the cramped hallway. "What?"

"That's his name, the man in the photo."

Tony approached her slowly. "He's a pilot?"

"Was."

Her quiet answer brought a curse under his breath. "I'm sorry, Anna."

She tried to shrug, but it was a weak effort. "That's war, right?"

"What happened?"

"I don't know. Technically, he's missing in action. They said his B-24 went down over Frankfurt."

"He could have been taken prisoner," he offered quietly.

"I know." She raised her chin. "I know more than anyone what we might find tomorrow, but I need you to know that's not why I'm here, Tony. I am every bit the professional that you are. I am here to document this war in all its ugliness, just the same as you. When you questioned my motives before, it hurt. Especially coming from you."

They stood just inches apart now. "Especially from me?"

"I've stopped caring what most people think of me, but I care what you think."

His eyes held hers, and she felt it—that quiver in her belly that she thought she'd never feel again, the low tug of awareness and need that only Jack had ever evoked inside her. Until she met Tony.

"You're the bravest person I've ever known." His voice was as taut and tense as she felt. "My admiration for you exceeds all others."

Her lips quirked up in a sad smile. "Spoken like a true newsman."

"I don't possess poetry in my verbal arsenal."

"I don't need poetry. I just need honesty."

Longing ebbed and flowed between them. Not like the one time he'd kissed her. That was a passion borne of extraordinary circumstances, a spontaneous expression of joy at having survived.

This was different. This was the tension of wanting someone, needing someone.

Tony's rough hand scraped along the curve of her jaw. Like a cold, lost kitten seeking heat and comfort, she leaned her cheek into his touch. "Anna . . ." Her name was torn from his lips on an agonized breath.

But whatever he'd been thinking about doing, he thought better of it, because he suddenly backed away.

"Go to sleep."

CHAPTER NINE

"What the fuck, man? Why didn't he kiss her?"

Wednesday afternoon, Vlad realized he'd made a horrible mistake. He and the guys were gathered at Colton's palatial estate outside Nashville to work on his book, and it was clear they were taking it very, very seriously. Colton had set up a classroom-size whiteboard in the middle of his living room, and Yan arrived with a backpack full of how-to-write books.

"I've been studying," Yan said, turning his backpack upside down to let his entire library fall out. "This shit is great. They have all these books to teach you how to write a novel. Have you read any of these?"

In his mind, Vlad rose from the couch and sucker punched Yan. In reality, he simply smiled like every writer who has had to deal with tips of nonwriters. "Yes, I have many of those books."

That wasn't the only thing bothering him, though. Elena had been distant ever since she hugged him yesterday. He'd been so surprised that all he could do at first was stand rigidly in place, breath locked in his lungs. But then he'd found his voice, and she leaned into him, and it took all his willpower not to drop his crutches and wrap both of his arms clear around her. Instead, he'd turned his face into her hair and inhaled deeply.

And it had been weird since then. She'd thrown herself into party planning, almost as if she was using it as an excuse to avoid long stretches of time with him. Part of him realized it was maybe for the best that they spend as little time together as possible. The other part of him already missed her and wanted to sniff her hair again.

He'd been looking forward to this little book-plotting session with the guys for that very reason. Until now.

"It's not the right time for him to kiss her," Vlad finally said, answering Colton's question.

"Uh, it's always the right time for kissing," Colton snorted.

Mack nodded. "It's true, man. Nothing beats the first-kiss scene."

Yan clutched his hands to his chest. "Especially if it's one of those passionate, almost angry kinds of kisses, like they just can't control themselves kinds of kisses."

Mack nodded. "Fuck yeah. I love a good spontaneous angry kiss in a book." He made a little growl noise and shuddered. "Gets me all worked up."

Del sighed. "I'm sorry, but nothing beats the soft, tender forehead kiss. It's like, the real feelings are coming out then. Gets you right here, every time." He pressed his hand to his breastbone.

"Okay, but what about the almost-kiss," Gavin said. "I love an almost-kiss."

Noah got a dreamy look on his face. "The staring-at-the-lips thing? Damn. Sexy as hell. Tony should have at least stared at her lips or something."

"He needs to, like, *notice* her," Yan said.

Mack cupped his own face. "The curve of her jaw."

"Or the way her hair always slips free and falls across her forehead," Gavin said.

Del sighed. "I mean, is it even a romance novel if she doesn't chew on her bottom lip when she's concentrating?"

Mack shook his head. "Damn, I love that shit."

Malcolm nodded with wisdom. "It's one of the best parts of romance novels. The celebration of all those small, important moments of awareness, of noticing someone for the first time, of feeling alive when they're near you. Of wondering when they became so important to you. It's romantic as fuck, man."

Vlad realized they expected him to say something. "They can't just kiss for the sake of kissing," Vlad argued. "And nothing ruins a first-kiss scene like when you can tell that the author just put it there for the sake of having a kissing scene. It has to feel natural."

"But they obviously want to kiss," Del pointed out.

"Yes, but they can't give in to the longing yet."

"Why not?" Mack asked.

"It would not be true to the characters."

Colton stuck out his bottom lip. "Are you saying this is going to be a slow burn? I wanted to help write the sex scenes."

"It has to be a slow burn," Vlad said. "They have too much history to move too quickly."

"Too much history, huh?" Noah said. "Interesting."

Vlad narrowed his eyes. What did that mean?

"Look," Malcolm said. "All we want to know is what's going to happen next. You really left us hanging here."

"But . . . you liked it?"

"It's brilliant, Russian," Noah said. He leaned over and riffled Vlad's hair. "We're so proud of you."

"It's true," Mack said, lowering to the sit on the floor. He kicked his legs out straight and leaned back on his hands. "You've got us hooked, man. Give us some more to read."

The momentary surge of confidence he'd felt at their praise deflated like a pin in a balloon. He slumped and picked at the edges of the Velcro keeping his bone in place. "If I knew that, I would've written it."

"You don't have any more written?" Yan asked in a pouty way.

Vlad shrugged with one shoulder.

"How long have you been stuck?" Malcolm asked.

"Couple of years," Vlad mumbled.

"Couple of years?" Yan's jaw dropped to nearly to his chest.

"You've been staring at it for *two years*?" Colton asked.

"If you'd ever tried to write a book, you'd understand," Vlad grumbled. "It's not easy. I feel like I've been writing and rewriting the same few chapters over and over again but can't figure out how to move forward in the story."

"According to all these books," Yan said, gesturing at his super-helpful pile of resource guides, "if you are stuck, it's not because you can't figure out what should happen next. It's because you probably got something wrong in what you've already written. So we just need to fix that."

"Wow," Vlad deadpanned. "Is that all?"

"Obviously, they need to have sex," Colton said.

Everyone ignored him.

"I agree in theory with Yan," Del said, ripping open the bag of gluten-free crackers that Elena had sent along for snack time. "Maybe you can't figure out how to move forward because you haven't dug enough into your characters' backstories."

Mack and Malcolm looked at each other and spoke in unison. "Backstory is everything."

Vlad tried not to growl in frustration. He knew backstory was everything. It was one of the central rules of book club. Whatever happened to a character before the first page of the book determined who they were *on* the first page of the book, and that dictated how they navigated every page afterward. "I already know their backstory," Vlad grumbled.

"Then why are you struggling?" Malcolm countered.

"I don't know."

Del popped a cracker in his mouth and then immediately let it fall out. "That tastes like cardboard. Is this the kind of shit you have to eat all the time?"

"What? No. There are a lot of good gluten-free snacks."

Del shoved the bag away. "This isn't one of them."

"Focus, boys," Colton said.

"Let's start with Tony," Malcolm said, leaning forward with his elbows on his knees. "Why didn't he tell Anna that he was 4F when she first accused him of not doing enough for the war effort?"

"Because he was offended."

"Sure, but why?" Malcolm asked.

"Because it was a rude assumption to make."

"True," Mack said, "but that doesn't explain why he didn't just set her straight, tell her that her assumption was wrong."

Malcolm jumped in. "Maybe he wasn't offended. Maybe he was scared. In all the books we've read, characters fear something at the start of the book, and that fear drives their behavior. Which isn't all that unlike people in real life, right?"

Gavin nodded like a man who'd seen some shit. "Fear forces us to do stupid things, brother. Make bad decisions, often against our own best interests and against wh-what we really w-want in life." The reappearance of his stammer told him how much he spoke from experience. Gavin and his wife had been through hell before book club helped them repair their marriage.

"Fear has led every single one of us down very bad paths in our relationships," Malcolm said.

Mack took over again. "So what is Tony afraid of?"

Vlad blinked. Little pinpricks of creative electricity were coming alive in his body. "Not being good enough."

Del nodded. "And why does Anna target that fear when she comes into his life?"

The creative electricity illuminated a light bulb. "Because she is everything he wants but thinks he doesn't deserve."

Malcolm pointed at the white board. "Write that down, Colton." He returned his attention to Vlad. "And why would that be?"

Vlad stared at the notebook on his lap. His pen was poised and ready for brilliance.

"Dig deep," Malcolm said.

Light bulb. Vlad started writing notes. "Being 4F has made him ashamed that he can't fight like his brothers. Anna . . . she is so brave and talented and—and fearless. He thinks he will not measure up for someone like her. And when she drops the photo, he realizes she is in love with a brave pilot, which just makes him feel worse."

"Can you go deeper with that?" Del prompted. "Why does her being in love with a pilot directly target his fear?"

"Because the pilot was able to fight, but Tony couldn't," Vlad repeated. Shit. Another answer appeared, and he bent over his paper. "He's afraid that his whole life will be like that. He'll always be the guy who didn't fight. The man who wasn't quite a man."

"A man who failed when it mattered most?" Yan prompted.

"Yes," Vlad breathed. He blinked as the story began to slowly take shape in his mind. "He wasn't there when it mattered."

"And Anna is a reminder of that," Malcolm said. "So, of course he's going to react badly when she calls him out for not being in uniform. It directly targeted his—"

"Sense of self," Vlad said.

Yan whistled. "Damn. That's some deep shit. We're getting somewhere now, boys."

Colton reached for the bag of crackers. "Hey, speaking of going deep, when *will* there be some sex in this book?"

Vlad shifted uncomfortably. The fear of his own backstory being discovered had suddenly pulled up a chair and started telling *that's what she said* jokes. He'd promised to stop keeping things from the guys, but some secrets did not need to be revealed. "I don't know," he finally said.

"How about a kiss?" Noah asked. "Will *that* at least be in the next chapter?"

"I don't know," Vlad repeated, more forcefully now. "They are both too vulnerable."

"Fair enough," Malcolm said. "Just remember that fear of vulnerability—physical or emotional—is usually a fear of something else."

The ToeBeans Café.

Wasn't that the name of the café that Noah's fiancée owned?

The one with the gluten-free muffins that Vlad liked? Elena was running some errands for the party while Vlad was at Colton's for some kind of playdate, and when she saw the sign for the café, she turned around and parked across the street.

The café was located in an artsy section of Nashville, where cute shops and restaurants lined the sidewalks. In front of the building, an outdoor dining space held four tables with umbrellas, and most of them were taken when Elena walked up. The line inside was nearly to the door, which jingled when she opened it. The blast of air-conditioning was a welcome relief from the humidity outside. Her Medill sweatshirt was way too heavy for June in Tennessee. She really needed to get some new clothes soon.

Elena took her spot at the end of the line and practiced what she might say when or if she actually met Alexis at the counter. This sort of thing did not come naturally to her. As a journalist, she could fake it. As a person, not so much.

She didn't have to practice long, though, because someone suddenly gasped. "Elena?"

Elena turned to the left. A woman she recognized from Mack's wedding was quickly approaching. She wore an apron with the café's logo on it and had her curly hair piled high on her head in a messy bun. A colorful, bohemian scarf was tied around it, the long ends flowing down her back.

"Alexis?" Elena asked tentatively.

The woman beamed with a wide smile. "Oh my gosh, it is you!" Before Elena could say more than a quick hello, Alexis threw her arms around Elena's neck in a tight, quick embrace.

"I can't believe you recognized me," Elena admitted. After all, they hadn't actually been introduced at the wedding.

"A face like yours is hard to forget," Alexis said, pulling back.

Was it a good thing that she had a face that wasn't easy to forget? Alexis seemed too nice for it to mean something bad.

"I'm so glad you're here," Alexis said. "What brings you by?"

"I was out getting some things for the party this weekend—"

Alexis let out a little squeal and gripped Elena's elbows. "We are all so excited about the party."

"—and I drove past the restaurant and recognized the sign. I thought I would come in and say thank you for the pastries you gave us and maybe pick up some more."

"Oh my gosh, you are *so* welcome." Alexis tugged on her elbow. "Come on. Friends don't wait in line."

Elena followed, the word *friend* an unfamiliar wiggly thing burrowing in her chest. She didn't have friends. Vlad had been her only true friend, and well . . . things were different now between them. Even if it had felt for a moment like old times during breakfast yesterday, her reaction to the simple act of hugging him afterward had been a quick reminder of how much the old days had changed.

Alexis led her to a table by the window. "Have a seat. Can I bring you something to drink?"

"Oh no. You're so busy. I don't want to take up your time."

"My staff has it under control. Do you like lattes? Tea? Something stronger?"

"I'll take whatever your favorite is."

Alexis grinned. "Honey soy latte, coming right up."

She returned a few minutes later with her drink, a bakery bag bursting at the seams, and a plate of various pastries. Alexis sat down after setting it all on the table. "On the house," she said, grinning still.

"Oh, I cannot let you do that," Elena protested.

"Already done. I put some cookies in the bag for Vlad to taste along with some more muffins."

"Vlad will be so happy. Thank you."

"He's my official taste tester for gluten-free products."

Elena sipped her latte. The sweet flavor was light and airy on her tongue. "This is very good. Thank you."

"My pleasure." Alexis leaned forward then with a sympathetic wince. "How is Vlad?"

Elena was getting used to this question but still stumbled over her answer. "Good. I mean, he's upset about missing the Stanley Cup, of course. But he's not in any pain."

"The party will be good for him," Alexis said. "Noah and the guys have been so worried about him for the past few months."

That was the second time someone had mentioned Vlad being in a bad way in recent months. She thought Claud was just being mean when she mentioned it, but Alexis didn't seem like the type to say things out of spite.

"What do you mean?" Elena asked, bracing for the answer.

Alexis's eyes pinched at the corners. "He sort of dropped off the face of the Earth after the wedding. After . . . well, you know."

Elena swallowed against a sudden bitterness. Alexis immediately reached over and rested her hand on Elena's arm. "I'm sorry. I didn't mean to upset you."

"It's okay. What do you mean that he dropped off the face of the Earth?"

"He really withdrew from the guys. Stopped hanging out. Stopped answering calls and texts. Eventually, only Colton could ever get ahold of him."

Elena thought she was the only one he'd stopped communicating with. And at least that would make sense. "Why would he do that? He is so close to the guys."

"I don't know," Alexis said, squeezing Elena's arm. "I just know that Noah and the guys are really happy to see him smiling again."

Elena sipped her latte and hoped the warm drink would loosen the constriction in her chest.

"Anyway," Alexis said in that tone of voice people used when eager to change the subject. "I cannot tell you how excited Liv and I are to taste some of your authentic Russian cuisine on Saturday. Noah is begging me to figure out how to make the pancakes you served yesterday."

"I can give you my recipe," Elena smiled. "Oh, actually. You might be able to help me."

"How's that?"

"I'm looking for an international market or maybe a specialty shop that might sell tvorog. It's—"

"Russian farmer's cheese," Alexis said. "I've had it before."

"I know I could try to make it myself, but it's one thing I have never mastered. Do you know of anyplace around here?"

Alexis bit her lip. "Well, maybe."

"Really? Where? I've tried everywhere I can think of."

Alexis looked around as if making sure no one could hear them. Then she leaned forward. "I don't know if I should tell you or not."

"Um, why?"

"Vlad might not like it."

"I don't understand."

Alexis looked around again. Her voice became a conspiratorial whisper. "Ask him about the Cheese Man."

* * *

Vlad was grumpy.

The book club meeting left him eager to write but also annoyed for reasons he couldn't pinpoint. And even *that* made him grumpy. Colton drove him home and helped him inside. They both stopped short in the entryway. Something smelled amazing.

Tangy and rich, Vlad knew immediately what it was. Stewed cabbage. Another favorite. With one inhale, he was home. He smelled cold fingers wrapped around a bowl of hot soup. Aching muscles and a clean T-shirt. Howling wind and a crackling fire. His mother's hug and his father's laughter. Elena sitting at a table helping him with his math homework after practice.

"Whatever she's making, I'm eating some," Colton said, taking off down the hallway.

Vlad bristled. He didn't want Colton to stay. He wanted a moment alone with his wife before heading upstairs to write. And that thought made him grumpier. He couldn't think about Elena like that, as *his wife*. But when he entered the kitchen, he stopped short again at the scene that greeted him. Elena stood at the island with her hair coiled on top of her head, which was bent to study a piece of paper, a pen poised in her hand. Sometimes, her fresh-faced beauty caught him so off guard that he forgot to breathe. Like now.

A sudden memory hit him hard.

"Elena, are you staying for dinner?"

His mother stirred the sautéing bacon and onions. Elena looked up from the counter, where she'd been finishing an essay for her literature class. "No, thank you. My dad promised he'd be home tonight."

Vlad met his mama's eyes over Elena's head. Her father's promises were as reliable as a Soviet-era nuclear reactor.

Mama kept her tone even. "Why don't you take some home, just in case?"

Elena returned the empty bowl the next day. Her father had broken his promise. Again.

Vlad cleared his throat. Elena looked up. Her eyes flashed with a welcoming warmth for a moment before withdrawing into cool distance again. It seemed forced, as if she'd reminded herself to do it.

"Hey," she said. "I made stewed cabbage."

"I know. It smells incredible."

"It should be done by now. Are you hungry?"

"Starving."

"Yo," Colton whistled. "You guys are doing the Russian thing again."

Elena switched to English as she looked at Colton. "Are you hungry?"

"Hell yes."

"How come you never eat at home?" Vlad grumbled, crutching to a seat at the island.

"Because I don't have an Elena."

Neither did Vlad. Not for long, at least. And suddenly grumpy became downright cross.

"Will you fix a plate for Vlad?" Elena asked Colton. "I'm trying to finish this grocery list for the party."

"Didn't you buy out the entire store last time?" Colton joked from the stove. He raised the plate to his face. "Goddamn, this smells good."

He carried it to Vlad and set it down. "You need a bib, little butt?"

Vlad muttered a Russian curse word. Elena looked up sharply. "Vlad, be nice."

After Colton filled his own plate and sat down, Elena capped her pen and faced them with her hands on her hips.

"Vlad."

He looked up from his plate. "What?"

"I really, really need some tvorog."

"Um, okay. Maybe we can find a store."

"Vlad."

He gulped. "What?"

"Tell me about the Cheese Man."

Vlad went cold, and he dropped his fork. "Where did you hear that name?"

"What is it? Is it a store?"

Vlad shook his head. "No. It's nothing. Forget you ever heard that name."

"What name? Cheese Man?"

Colton set down his fork. "Come on, man. What's the harm?"

"You know the harm, Colton! It is a dark path. I cannot drag her down it. I will not."

"I'm sorry," Elena said, looking back and forth between them. "What dark path?"

Vlad and Colton locked gazes again for a moment before turning to look at her. "The path to the best cheese you'll ever eat in your life," Colton breathed.

"No. To an addiction you will never break," Vlad warned. "The price is too high."

Elena waved her hands in front of her chest. "Wait. I don't understand. What are we talking about? Who exactly is the Cheese Man?"

"No one really knows," Colton said. "He appeared last year.

People started whispering about him. Have you tried the Cheese Man yet? Have you heard about the Cheese Man? We have a lot of connections, you know, and so I started asking around, and someone finally hooked us up."

Elena crossed her arms. "Does he have store, or something?"

"God, no," Colton said. "He basically runs a speakeasy. Like, like a speak cheesy."

Laughter barked from her chest. Elena pressed a hand to her mouth to smother the sound, but it was no use. She sucked in a breath and bent over as if she hadn't laughed in a year. The sound was so pure, so beautiful, that Vlad got lost in it for a moment. But only a moment, because the reality was ugly. "Cheese Man is no laughing matter, Elena. Once you start, you can't stop. He will own you for life."

Elena wiped her eyes and stood up. "Sorry. I just . . . this is absurd."

"To get in, you have to show this," Colton said, digging his membership coin from his wallet.

"This is a joke, yes?"

Vlad glowered at Colton. "Put that away. And no, Cheese Man is not a joke, Elena."

"But will he have tvorog?"

"He has everything," Colton said. "And if he doesn't have it, he'll know how to get it."

Elena nodded. "Great. When can we go?"

"No," Vlad said, shaking his head. "Absolutely not."

"Tomorrow?" Colton said.

Elena nodded. "Tomorrow."

Vlad swore in Russian again.

Colton grinned. "Prepare to be amazed."

CHAPTER TEN

Elena was not amazed.

This couldn't actually be the place. The building where Vlad had directed her the next afternoon looked like the aftermath of a rabies outbreak. *This* was the cheese shop?

"Elena." Vlad's hand shot across the center console and grabbed hers. "There's still time to back out."

"I really need that cheese, Vlad."

He closed his eyes. "God forgive me."

He let go of her hand and opened his door. Elena ran around and helped him with his crutches. "Stay behind me," he ordered her.

"You can't be serious," she said.

"Just do what I say, Elena. Please."

She slid behind him and immediately felt invisible. His massive shoulders dwarfed hers, hiding her from whatever bogeyman he feared as they approached the decrepit black door.

Vlad knocked three times in quick succession and then twice more.

A moment passed, and someone from inside knocked once. Vlad knocked two more times.

"There's a secret knock?" Elena whispered.

"Be quiet," Vlad hissed. "And don't laugh. He doesn't like it when you laugh."

"Sorry." Elena cleared her throat.

A single window in the center had something covering it. The scrape of wood against it made her stand on tiptoe to peer over Vlad's shoulder. A pair of eyes looked out through the previously blocked window. "Coin," a dark voice said.

Elena slapped a hand over her mouth to cover the bark of laughter that threatened to ruin it all. Vlad held up the Swiss cheese coin like the one Colton had shown her. There was a sound of locks turning, and the door opened. A burst of cold air from inside rushed out.

Vlad crutched forward slowly, and Elena stayed as hidden as possible behind him. But when Vlad crossed the threshold, the mysterious man began to close the door. Elena shoved her foot in the door as Vlad whipped his head around.

"Wait—"

The man's hand shot out and gripped her shoulder, holding her back. "Who is this?"

Vlad swiveled on his crutches, an ominous look turning his face into an intimidating mask, and Elena got the first glimpse of what he must look like to opposing players on the ice. She'd be lying if she said it didn't sort of do things for her.

"Do not touch her," Vlad warned.

Whether it was the tone or the expression, it worked. The man dropped his hand but shook his head. "You know the rules. No nonmembers."

"It's my wife," Vlad said in that same menacing tone.

The man narrowed his eyes. "Where has she been? Why hasn't she been here before?"

"She's been away at school," Vlad said. He balanced a crutch against his side so he could extend his hand to her. "Elena, come here."

She skirted around the man and skidded toward Vlad. He pulled her against his side. "She knew nothing about this until now," he said. "I've never told her about this place."

Elena glanced around the tiny, dark space. It had probably once been the welcoming entryway to a small shop or pub but had long ago decayed into the kind of moldy, cramped staging area she always imagined for illegal organ-harvesting operations. Which wasn't that far-fetched. Her father had uncovered just such an operation several years before his disappearance.

Behind them, a short hallway ended with a slight ramp, where a thick black tarp of some kind hung low to the ground and blocked her view of whatever was beyond.

"He's not going to like this," the man said.

Now that Elena's eyes had adjusted to the darkness, she could actually see him. He wore a red bandanna around his forehead, and a tight hairnet covered what appeared to be the smallest man bun ever attempted. The smudges on his black-rimmed glasses told her he spent too much time in the dark.

"Well, bring him out here," Vlad said. "Let's ask him directly."

"No. I can't do that. Only coin holders get to see him."

Vlad shifted to pull Elena closer to him, but at the same time, the movement caused his crutch to dislodge from under his arm. It fell to the floor, and inside the small space, it was as loud as a gunshot and had nearly the same effect.

Man-bun Man jumped half a foot and whipped a short-handled prong knife from his pocket. The kind used for soft and medium-hard cheeses and, in this case, maybe their throats.

Vlad lunged forward on one leg, grabbed the man's wrist, and simultaneously shoved him against the wall. "That's a fancy cheese utensil you've got there," Vlad said in a deceptive drawl. "I'd hate to have to break it."

Elena muttered a Russian curse word and stepped forward. "Stop this! You're going to hurt yourself."

Vlad didn't turn around. "Elena, stay back."

She shoved his crutches at him. "For God's sake, I just need some tvorog."

The scuff of the tarp brought a collective gasp from all three of them. At once, they turned their heads in time to see a tall, dark figure emerge from behind the curtain. He wore a long apron and carried a towel on which he slowly wiped his hands.

"A woman who knows her cheese. Color me aroused."

His voice was smooth, warm, like a melted raclette, soft and creamy and hot. Elena felt herself sink into it like a crust of bread in a fondue pot. She turned toward it and began to walk.

"Elena, no." Vlad's fingers skimmed her elbow, but it was no use. She was under a spell.

The man descended the ramp. When he finally stepped into the dim light, he spoke to the dude with the bandanna. "It's okay, Byron. Let them in."

To Elena, he extended his hand. "I am Roman. You are?"

"Elena," she breathed.

"A beautiful name for a beautiful woman." He raised her knuckles to his lips. "It is a pleasure."

"That's my wife," Vlad said behind them.

Roman lifted a perfectly formed brow. "A gorgeous woman who is also a turophile? You are a lucky man, my friend." He cupped Elena's elbow. "Please, let me show you to my fromagerie."

The click-scruff of Vlad's crutches behind them had an aggressive cadence to it as he followed. Roman lifted the black plastic curtain. When she walked through, bright lights automatically turned on, momentarily blinding her. But after blinking a couple of times, she slapped her hand to her chest. This was a cheese paradise.

Elena wrapped her arms around her torso and shivered.

"My apologies, love," Roman said, brushing a fingertip down the goose bumps that had erupted along her triceps. "We must keep it cool in here. Your husband should have warned you to bring your coat."

Vlad made an ugly noise.

"As you can see," Roman said, bending seductively close to her ear, "we have everything you could want."

"Tvorog?"

He turned and pointed with a long, slender finger. She followed with her eyes and . . . there it was. "You have it," she whispered, her feet moving of their own accord toward her quarry. Her mouth watered.

"Ah yes," Roman said, following closely. "Authentic farmer cheese. I use the original recipe of my great-grandmother."

Elena looked over sharply. "You are Russian?"

"On my father's side. My great-grandparents came over in 1911."

"Do you speak any Russian?"

He winked and made a dirty proposition in their native language that made her cheeks flame.

Vlad squinted in suspicion. "You have never spoken Russian to me."

"I only know enough to get me in trouble." He laughed in Vlad's direction.

"I don't understand," Elena said, shaking her head. "This is amazing. Why don't you open a store to the public?"

The air seemed to escape the room. She glanced at Vlad, who was frozen in place, a slice of Havarti halfway to his mouth.

Roman chuckled quietly, but his laughter held a sinister undertone. "Big Cheese would never let it happen."

"Big Cheese?"

"Corporate dairy farms. They lobby the government to pack the FDA with their friends who set regulations that make it impossible for a small cheesemaker to succeed. They set standards that strip away the joy, the artistry. They have sold their souls"—he pounded his fist into his other hand—"to factory-made cheese. And then they destroy the environment with their mass-production farms that milk their cows too often."

Elena blinked. "How often do they milk their cows?"

"Three times a day, Elena. Three times!"

"And how many times should they be milking them?"

"Two times, max."

"I see."

"Do you know how hard it is to get a real Brie in this country, Elena? American pasteurization laws make it impossible. What you buy in the stores is a watered-down version with none of the texture and seduction of the real thing."

Elena didn't know what those words meant in regards to cheese, but he was on a roll, so she didn't want to interrupt him.

"That is why I must operate in the dark," he said. "In the underground."

"So you're like a resistance fighter against a cheese conspiracy?"

"At the highest levels of government and dairy."

"And you can make authentic cheeses that others cannot?"

"Yes. And anything I do not make, my network of underground fromagers can provide."

"Cool. I'm in." She fist-bumped him. "Because we are having a party on Saturday, and I'm going to need a lot."

"A party, huh?"

"Yes. You should come."

"It is a party for friends only," Vlad growled.

"Then I am doubly honored to be invited." He lifted Elena's hands to his lips and kissed her knuckles. Elena might have swooned a little. "I'll be sure to bring something extra special."

"That's the last time we're going there."

Vlad eased his leg into the car and slammed his door shut. Elena started the car, a dreamy look on her face that made him want to punch the dashboard and add broken fingers to his list of problems.

"All that cheese," Elena breathed, pulling onto the road. "It was like a dream."

"It is a nightmare, and I cannot believe you invited him to the party."

"It seemed rude not to."

"I don't want him anywhere near our party." Vlad glared out the window at the passing buildings as she drove. He suddenly hated those buildings and for no particular reason other than they happened to be in his line of vision at the time of his bad mood.

"I'm going to make cottage cheese bars," she said in that same wispy voice. "And vareniki."

"That's too much work."

"And a kurnik."

His stomach growled that the mention of another one of his favorites. It had been years since he'd had the traditional layered chicken pie.

"Oh, and dressed herring."

She moaned it in a way that snapped every last nerve. "We don't need all that. Make some tea cakes and call it good."

"I just want your friends to get the full Russian culinary experience."

"They eat pizza and wings. They won't know the difference."

"Colton seems to like my cooking."

Vlad cracked a knuckle. Colton needed to start eating at home. He didn't like this feeling, whatever it was. His skin felt too tight over his bones, and something burned in his chest.

She finally glanced over. "Why are you so grumpy?"

"I'm not grumpy."

"You're acting grumpy."

"Have you decided where you're going to live in Russia?" he asked, because why the hell not? He was already grumpy.

"What?" she asked. She did a double take, tearing her eyes briefly from the road. "Where did that come from?"

"It's something we should probably talk about, don't you think?"

"*Now?*"

"Why not?" He twisted in his seat to look at her and then instantly regretted it because all he could see was the gentle curve of her jaw. "What about your car? Are we going to ship it?"

Her hands tightened on the steering wheel. "I—I don't know. I haven't thought that far. I'll probably leave it with you."

"You can't leave it here. What will you drive in Russia?"

"I will buy a new one."

"That's ridiculous. Why would you do that when you already have a car?"

"Because I'll be making my own money. I'm not going to keep relying on you, Vlad."

It annoyed him when she said stuff like that. A reminder that all of this had been nothing but a transaction to her. He rubbed the center of his chest again.

"There's no use fighting about this stuff now," she said. "I don't even have a job yet."

"You should apply to the paper in Omsk. You could live with my parents."

She rolled her eyes. "Oh yes. I'm sure they would love to have their son's ex-wife move in."

"You are like a daughter to them, whether we are married or not."

"Well, the last time I looked, the paper in Omsk doesn't have any openings."

"But I'm sure they would make an exception for you—"

"Vlad, stop," she snapped, once again peeling her gaze from the road. "You don't understand how journalism works. Could you just send your résumé to any hockey team and ask to play for them? No."

"Why are you being so stubborn?" Vlad asked, eyebrows tugging together.

"Why are *you* being so stubborn?"

"Because I'm just trying to protect you, Elena."

She turned onto his street. "I don't need your protection. Maybe you haven't noticed, but I'm not the same scared little girl you married."

"I have noticed," he said as she pulled into the drive. "And I'm proud of you. If I haven't said that before, I'm sorry."

"There's a lot we don't say to each other." She eased the car into the garage and killed the engine. Irritation was evident in her movements when she threw open her door and slid out. He waited for her to come around to his side before opening his door. She handed him his crutches like always and stepped back so he could get out. But in the cramped space between the car and the wall of the garage, she could only move so far. She was blocked between his open door on one side and his body on the other.

The mundane suddenly became meaningful, and he began to notice all those small moments of awareness about which Malcolm had waxed so poetically. The fresh-aired scent of her hair. The light spray of freckles across her nose and cheeks. The way her lush bottom lip curled out farther than the top, giving her a perpetual look of someone who'd just been kissed. The way he suddenly felt like he was seventeen again, sitting next to her along the banks of the Om River, his body hyperaware of hers in a way he'd never experienced before. The way the air moved against his skin whenever she flipped her hair off her shoulder. The way his fingers itched to catch a soft tendril and tickle it across his palm. The way her collarbone formed a straight, sensual line above the swell of her breasts beneath her shirt. The urgent, overwhelming, burning need to kiss her.

Her eyes strayed to his mouth and lingered there. Every breath became a labor of willpower under her scrutiny. *Kiss me.* The words were there on the tip of his tongue. Why couldn't he say them? Why couldn't he move, take that first step? Now, like then, he couldn't do it. "Elena," he rasped.

She blinked, and that cool detachment returned. She stepped

back with a forced smile. "Thank you for taking me today. You should go inside and rest your leg."

"My leg," he said, disappointment weighing his voice down. "It's why I'm here, right?"

Right. And as soon as he was healed, she'd be leaving. How many times was his brain going to have to remind his heart of that fact?

CHAPTER ELEVEN

"Wakey, wakey, hands off snakey."

Vlad thought he'd imagined every kind of possible hell. Now he knew he'd missed one—waking up to find Colton leaning over him.

"Time to wake up, little butt," he said. "You're going to be late for your appointment."

Vlad rose up on his elbows. "What time is it?"

"Almost nine. You're supposed to be at the arena in a half hour. I let you sleep too long."

He had his one-week post-op appointment today. He didn't recall any plans for Colton to take him. "Where is Elena?"

Colton shrugged and crossed the room to Vlad's dresser. "I figured you'd know. She texted me this morning and asked if I'd take you because she had something to do."

Vlad sat up in alarm. "She didn't say where she was going?"

Colton opened the top drawer. "Maybe she had some more errands to run for the party. She didn't tell you?"

No. She didn't. Vlad checked his cell phone to see if he'd missed any texts from her. But nope. Nothing.

Colton pulled out a T-shirt and a pair of shorts. "Did you guys get in a fight or something?"

Vlad swung his legs off the bed and reached for his crutches. "No."

"Then why didn't she tell you she was leaving?"

"I don't know," Vlad lied. He knew exactly why. Because after whatever that was in the garage yesterday, she'd withdrawn back into her shell. After serving him dinner, she disappeared into her bedroom like every other night this week.

Vlad got dressed, brushed his teeth, and thought briefly about shaving. But at this stage of beard growth, it would take more time than he had. Colton helped Vlad down the stairs and into the front seat of his car before tossing the crutches into the back seat.

"Thank you for doing this," Vlad said.

"Did you get any more writing done?" Colton asked as he pulled out of the driveway.

Vlad grunted.

Colton turned at the corner. "Is that a yes or a no?"

"Yes."

"And?"

Vlad scowled at his reflection in the window. "And what?"

Colton waggled his eyebrows. "Did they kiss yet or not?"

"No."

Colton tsked. "Don't cheat your readers, man. It's a romance. Give us the romance."

"I know it's a romance, but it has to make sense. And kissing right now would not be in character for them."

"Or maybe you just don't want it to be in character for them."

Vlad twisted in his seat. "Why would I not want it to be in character for them? I like kissing. I love kissing. But the timing is still wrong."

"Why?"

"Because Elena doesn't want him to! She has made that absolutely clear."

Colton tore his eyes from the road. "You mean Anna."

"What?"

"You said Elena."

Heat erupted from his cheeks. "No, I didn't."

Colton sucked on his teeth. "Yeah, you kind of did."

"Obviously, I meant Anna."

"Obviously."

Vlad felt a vein pop in his forehead. "Fuck off."

Colton started whistling to the radio.

They arrived at the arena twenty minutes late, but it was still more than enough time for word to spread that Colton Wheeler was in the house. Vlad left him signing autographs and posing for selfies in the hallway outside the medical facility.

Madison told him to wait for her in one of the consultation rooms. While he waited, he glanced at his cell phone for the hundredth time. Still no message from Elena. Of course, he could text her, but what would he say? *Where did you go?* That would sound whiny. *Why didn't you tell me you were leaving?* That would sound needy.

Why didn't you kiss me yesterday? That would be downright pathetic.

Madison walked in then, knocking as she opened the door. "Ready for me?"

Vlad leaned on his hip and shoved his phone in his pocket. "Ready."

The two grad students walked in behind Madison as she approached the bed. "We're going to take a look at the incision before sending you in for the X-ray, so why don't you lie back?"

Vlad reclined as Madison opened up the brace. "How's the pain?"

"Fine. I haven't had much."

The other two trainers moved in next to Madison. "We're going to take you through some range of motions, okay?"

Vlad tensed as one of the trainers slid a hand beneath his knee and gripped his ankle with the other. "Just relax," Madison murmured.

Relax. Sure. His entire body was a lit fuse. His career was on the line. His wife was nowhere to be found. And his nerves hummed with frustration of the sexual kind. He forced himself to let out a long breath and loosen his muscles. One of the trainers lifted and bent his leg, heel toward his glutes.

"Good," Madison said quietly.

For the next ten minutes, they manipulated his leg to gauge strength and flexibility. Every new position made him hold his breath, but there was no pain, and Madison seemed pleased with his progress.

"Okay," she said finally. "You can sit up."

Vlad crunched his abs to haul himself up. "Now what?"

"We're going to have you put some weight on it."

The trainers helped him off the table. He balanced on one foot and waited for Madison's instructions.

"We just want you to stand, nothing else. Okay? When you're ready, lower your foot to the floor."

He held loosely onto the trainers' arms as he extended his leg and touched the floor for the first time since the injury. He winced in anticipation of pain, of weakness. But when the sole of his shoe touched the ground, he felt neither. The trainers let go of him, and he damn near pumped his fist in victory.

He was standing.

On his own.

"Good," Madison murmured. "How does it feel?"

"Fine. It is good."

Madison smiled. "You're doing great. Let's get an X-ray to make sure the bone is healing well, and I think we'll be ready to move you into the next phase of rehab."

Madison handed him his crutches, and he followed her out of the room and down a hallway to the on-site X-ray room. They draped him in protective gear and once again had him lie down on a long table. The technician took several pictures from different angles, and then Madison told him to wait for her back in the consultation room as she reviewed the images.

He checked his cell phone as he waited.

Still nothing from Elena.

When the door opened again, Madison walked in with a confident smile. "Everything looks great."

A half hour later, he crutched back out into the hallway with an updated rehab plan, a new brace, and still no message from Elena. He found Colton in the hallway, this time leaning suggestively toward a young woman in a trainer uniform who clasped an autographed towel to her chest.

"I'm done," Vlad announced.

The young woman stammered and turned red as she jumped away from Colton like she'd just been caught making out with him. Colton turned around and grinned. "Hey, little butt. Do I still have to give you your baths or what?"

The woman excused herself and scurried away.

"Sweet girl," Colton said.

"Leave her alone. She is probably still in college. And no, you don't have to bathe me anymore. I can get the incision wet now."

Colton gave a last look as the girl walked away. "So does that mean you're healed, or what?"

Vlad crutched down the hallway. "No. But I get to start putting some weight on it next week and daily rehab."

"Guess that means Elena doesn't have to stick around much longer, huh?"

Vlad punched the button for the elevator. "What the hell does that mean?"

Colton shrugged innocently. "You're going to be up and around on your own soon. No reason for her to stay."

"I'm not going to be up and around on my own soon. I still have to use crutches for several weeks."

"Yeah, but you won't be quite as helpless."

The elevator arrived, and they walked in together. Vlad punched another button. "What is your point, Colton?"

"Nothing. Just that she might not feel like there's any reason to stay much longer."

Vlad imagined throwing Colton against the boards. Instead, he rubbed the center of his chest. The feeling he didn't like was back.

"You wanna grab some breakfast?" Colton asked. "I can call the guys, see who can meet us."

The Six Strings Diner was their regular gathering spot, a local-favorite restaurant in downtown Nashville where he and his other highly recognizable pals could eat in peace. More than one painful secret had been shared over plates of enormous American breakfasts.

"Come on," Colton cajoled. "I'm hungry, and we need to talk about all the sex your characters aren't having."

"Fine," Vlad grumbled. At least it would give him something to do besides sitting at home and waiting for his wife. Colton texted the guys and asked who was available. Mack said he could be there in fifteen, Malcolm in ten, and Noah responded he was on his way. No one else could make it.

"You could just call her, you know," Colton said as he pulled down the parking ramp.

"If she wanted me to know where she was, she would've told me."

"You're kind of stubborn, you know that?"

"Shut up."

Colton obeyed, miraculously. Noah and Malcolm were already at the diner when they arrived and had grabbed their normal table. Colton earned a few surprised gasps and excited points, but for the most part, other customers left them alone. That was one of the reasons the guys ate there. It was a local place with few tourists to interrupt them.

"Good news," Colton said, dropping into a chair. "Our boy here got clearance to wash his own magnificent ass from now on."

"I've been washing my own ass," Vlad said, picking up the menu. He had the whole thing memorized, though, so it was really just for hiding behind.

"He's also really grumpy," Colton said. "Elena left his morning without telling him where she was going."

Mack walked in then and joined them at the table. "How'd your appointment go?"

"I am healing on schedule."

"Well, that's some news worth celebrating," Mack said. "But does that mean we don't get to bathe your stupendous ass anymore?"

"For the last time, I can wash my own ass!"

The waitress appeared right at that moment. She blinked but said nothing. The Six Strings staff was used to bizarre outbursts from their table. The guys all ordered their usual, and the waitress said she'd be back with their coffee and tea.

"Make any progress on the book?" Malcolm asked.

Colton snorted. "I already asked, and they still haven't kissed."

Noah groaned. "*Come on.* Do I have to smoosh their faces together?"

Vlad shook his head. "No. They are still not ready."

"Or maybe Tony is just a wuss." Colton shrugged.

Malcolm tsked. "That's a gendered insult that you need to erase from your vocabulary, Colton."

"What? No, it's not. I use that word all the time."

"It is a merging of *wimp* and *pussy* and is used to describe weak men with an implication of effeminacy. You can trace its roots to both misogyny and homophobia." The guys all stared in reverent silence. Sometimes, Malcolm morphed into a professor, and they all learned something that made them better men. "Our society has allowed men to get away with a lack of emotional intelligence by equating the expression of a full range of human emotion with femininity."

"My apologies," Colton said. "What I'm trying to say is that Tony is a big, fat scaredy cat."

The waitress returned with their drinks. When she left, Vlad growled. "He is not afraid. He is realistic."

"Maybe it's the author who's afraid, then." Malcolm said it with a raised eyebrow, a challenge against Vlad's authorly manhood if he'd ever seen one.

"I am not afraid of my own book."

Colton snorted. "Hell, you're too scared to even let Tony admit to *himself* how he really feels about Anna."

"He loves her!" He wanted to grab the words and shove them back in, because now that they were spoken, the guys would stop at nothing to make him do something about it. To make *Tony* do something about it, that is.

"Um, duh," Noah said. "Anyone who can read sees that. The question is why you're not letting him tell her."

"You do not understand."

"Obviously, because the way we see it, things are pretty simple," Mack said. "Tony loves her. Anna obviously loves him—"

Vlad stiffened. "That is not obvious. She pulls away time and again. She gives him little tiny crumbs, just enough to make him want her, to make him have hope, and then she runs away every time. She is going to leave the minute she gets a clue about where Jack might be, and Tony knows that."

"But she's with Tony *now*," Noah said calmly.

"Only because it's her job." He scowled.

"Bullshit," Mack said. "He was a complete and utter asshole to her at first. She could have packed her things and hightailed it out of there. She even had plenty of reasons to do so. But she chose to stay with Tony. He just won't see it."

"No. That is not true."

"She's asking him to give her a reason to stay with him," Noah said.

Vlad frowned. "Which is not the same thing as telling him she cares for him."

"But it's a goddamned start," Mack said. "Why are you being so obtuse?"

"Because he can't believe she could really want him!"

The silence that followed his outburst was humble and solemn. Probably because this time, the admission was like ripping open his chest and letting his heart fall right out onto the table while he bled out in a slow, agonizing death.

"Jesus, man," Mack breathed. "Why would Tony think that?"

"He has his reasons."

"Does Anna know the reasons?"

He shook his head. No. Anna didn't know, because Tony couldn't stand to think about what would happen if his reasons simply pushed her further away.

"You know, all that baggage that characters carry from their backstory," Mack said. "Eventually, that fear becomes less of a motivation and more of a stubborn hindrance. Characters have to change during a book to earn their happy ever after."

"I know that," Vlad grumbled. He paused again when the waitress showed up with their breakfasts. Vlad scowled at his egg-white omelet.

"But Tony isn't changing," Malcolm said when the waitress walked away. "He's clinging to his page-one fear. You have to give him some kind of midpoint plot twist to open up a new path."

"And then he has to take it," Mack said.

"He cannot risk it yet."

"Risk what?" Malcolm asked. "His heart?"

Vlad nodded, poking his eggs with his fork.

"Jesus, dude, have you learned nothing from the manuals?" Mack snorted. "A man's heart is the only thing truly worth risking."

"But also the most dangerous," Vlad fired back.

"Look," Mack said. "You have two choices. Tony needs to tell her how he feels, or he needs to accept that she's going to slip through his fingers, and you will have written the shittiest romance novel *ever*."

Vlad stuck out his bottom lip. What he thought earlier, that he'd welcome their help, he was wrong about that. This sucked.

Malcolm steepled his hands beneath his chin. "Midpoints are a chance for characters to start rewriting their own stories. Let Tony start to rewrite his."

CHAPTER TWELVE

Elena returned home—correction, returned to Vlad's house—just before noon with more party supplies. It was probably cowardly to ask Colton to take Vlad to his appointment, but she needed some space to think.

Last night, she'd finally gotten a response to her text asking for a favor. Call me when you can.

She had convinced herself to wait until tomorrow to call him back, but when she returned home—correction, returned to Vlad's house—and realized he was still gone, she knew there was no reason to put it off any longer.

Neighbor Cat was waiting at the door when she walked in, so Elena let her in. The cat followed her upstairs and into her bedroom. Elena shut the door to her room and, hands shaking, dialed the number for a man she hadn't spoken to in years. It was nearly eleven o'clock in Moscow, and she knew he'd still be awake. Journalists like him always were.

The phone rang in her ear twice before an impatient voice answered in Russian. "Elena?"

Relief at the sound of his voice was as potent as a stiff cocktail. She sank to the bed. "It's me. I'm sorry to call so late, but with the time difference—"

"I was so happy to get your text. God, it is good to hear your voice."

"You too."

"How is America?"

Elena let Neighbor Cat crawl into her lap. "Good. Good. I mean, for now."

"For now? What does that mean?"

She should've known Yevgeny would pick up on that. He was a journalist. He missed nothing. "You said to call you if I ever needed anything."

"Yes, of course. And I meant it."

"I hope so. Because . . ." She sucked in a fortifying breath. "Because I need a job."

Her words were met with nothing but the sound of a newsroom in action somewhere in the distance. Editors shouted. Televisions blared. Reporters joked and cursed. He was still at work. Because of course he was.

"Yevgeny—"

He interrupted her again. "So it's true, then. There were rumors, but I refused to believe them."

The sweat on her brow chilled as icy fear wormed through her veins. "Rumors? What rumors?"

"That you wanted to come back."

The fear turned her voice to a rasp. "Where did you hear that?'

"This is Russia, Elena. Very little is secret. And you think I haven't kept tabs on my own goddaughter?"

She should have been warmed by the reminder of their lifelong connection, but she was instead plunged deeper into a cold bath of determination. "Then as your goddaughter, I am asking for a favor. I want to be a journalist like my father. I'm ready."

The creak of a desk chair told her he'd either stood up or leaned back. Either way, she could picture him. He'd look just like her father used to. Sleeves rolled up over his forearms. Tie loosened or tossed aside altogether and the top button undone on his standard button-down shirt. All journalists around the world wore the same bland uniform.

"Elena," he said, voice tight as if he were reining in the worst of his thoughts. "I'm sure your father would be very proud that you want to follow in his footsteps."

"He wouldn't be," she snapped. "We both know it. He told me a thousand times that the last thing he wanted was for me to be a journalist."

"So why are we even having this conversation?"

"Because I have to do this. It's in my blood." *And because I owe it to him.*

"There's a reason he didn't want this life for you. Even before he—before what happened . . . he knew this was no life for you. It's dangerous. You know that better than anyone. You've spent nearly six years in America. It might be a hard adjustment to come back here after living and studying in a place that has freedom of the press enshrined in its DNA."

She stiffened. "It's not perfect here either. The press is vilified on a daily basis. People walk around with T-shirts threatening to hang reporters. Journalists get spit on at political rallies. They are called fake news and enemies of the people."

"But do they mysteriously disappear from train stations there?"

His words packed a punch, one that knocked the air from her lungs.

"I'm sorry," he said. "I should not have said that."

"I'm not naive, Zhenya," she said, using his nickname. "I know the dangers better than anyone. I'm not afraid."

Yevgeny paused again, and this time she could hear the silent pity all the way across the time zones. "What about Vlad?"

"We're getting a divorce."

He cursed under his breath, and again, she could picture him. He'd be just like her father. Rubbing a hand over his hair and staring at the ceiling as if praying for patience and wisdom but coming up short. "I'm sorry to hear that," he finally said. "Truly."

"I don't need you to feel sorry for me. Just give me a chance. Treat me like any other entry-level reporter. Give me the shittiest assignments. Teach me. Please."

"I need to think about this."

"I'll interview with anyone you need me to talk to. I don't expect you to just hand me a job."

"Before I do anything, I need to ask you something, and I expect the truth."

"O-okay."

"Why are you really coming back?"

She gulped. "What do you mean?"

"You could be a journalist in America."

"No. My visa does not allow me to work here."

"There are always ways around that. If you apply at a U.S.

newspaper and get hired, they can arrange for you to get the necessary classification. Foreign journalists are hired by U.S. newspapers and broadcast networks all the time."

"Yes, but—"

"Are you coming back here to try to find out what happened to your father?"

"No. Of course not," she lied.

"Because if you are—"

"I'm not."

"Because if you are," he repeated, "I will not hire you. Do you understand? If I hire you, and I find out that you're digging into what happened to your father, I'll have no choice but to let you go."

Her heart thudded against her rib cage so hard that she was certain he could hear it. "I understand. Of course."

"Good. Then I will get back to you in a few days."

Elena couldn't keep the relief from her voice. "Thank you, Yevgeny."

"Don't make me regret this."

"I won't."

Elena dropped the phone on her bed and fell onto her back. The entire conversation had lasted less than fifteen minutes, but a lifetime had passed since the minute she'd dialed his number. Until now, it had been an abstract concept, but now it seemed real.

Soon she would go back to Russia, and Vlad would finally be free to move on.

The thought should have made her happy. Instead, she wanted to curl onto her side and bury her face into a pillow and sob like she did all those years ago. Back then, it was because she knew coming here was a mistake. Now, it was because the thought of leaving felt like one.

Elena pressed her hands into her temples and rubbed at the beginning throbs of a headache. Neighbor Cat purred and curled up into a ball next to Elena's hip. The idea of joining her in a long nap was almost too tempting to ignore, but the hum of a car in the driveway brought her upright with a sigh.

She listened as the car doors opened and closed, followed a few seconds later by the front door. That should have been followed by Colton's sarcastic tenor asking for food, but the door opened and closed again. For once, Colton hadn't stuck around. Which meant the buffer she'd become dependent on was not going to be there when she walked downstairs.

Elena forced herself to get out of bed. Neighbor Cat meowed in protest but followed. She stopped at the top of the stairs to find Vlad standing at the bottom. "Hi."

He looked up at her. "I was just coming upstairs to find you."

Neighbor Cat made a dash down the stairs toward her boyfriend. Elena suppressed her jealousy. "How was your appointment?"

"Good. I can start putting weight on my leg twice a day."

"That's great."

"I can also start bathing myself again." He said that part with a half smile. It lifted his bearded cheek into a round ball.

Elena descended the stairs. "I'm sure your friends will appreciate that part."

Vlad inched backward to make room for her when she hit the bottom step. "Where did you go this morning?" he asked.

"I had some errands to run."

"For the party?"

"Yes." She shoved her hands in her back pockets. "Are you hungry?"

"No. I met the guys for a late breakfast."

"Okay. Well, I need to get started on some of the food for tomorrow, so . . ." She waited for him to move back so she could pass, but he didn't. Neighbor Cat wound in and out of their legs. "I think your girlfriend missed you."

He blinked, confused. "What?"

"The cat."

"Oh." He looked down. "Yes."

"You should sit. I'll bring you some ice."

"I'm tired of sitting. I need to do something."

"Then keep me company in the kitchen while I make the vareniki."

He lifted one sexy eyebrow. "You making them with mushrooms, onions, and potatoes?"

She scooted away from him. "Like I'd make them any other way."

"Let me help," he said, following her into the kitchen. "I don't have to just sit here."

"Careful what you wish for, or I'll make you peel the potatoes."

"If that's what you need, I'll do it."

She pointed to a chair by the island. "Sit and get that leg up."

While he got settled, she pulled out all the ingredients for the vareniki. They were every bit as time intensive as pelmeni dumplings, but the recipes were slightly different. Like everything else, Vlad's mom had taught her how to make them, but they were often a family affair. Vlad and his parents—and often, Elena—would circle the table and work together to shape and fill the dumplings. Those hours were some of her favorite memories, full of laughter and teasing and affection. But they were also tinged with a bitter aftertaste, because it was during those hours around the family table that Elena began to realize how different her own family was. Her father's job never allowed him to be home in time for dinner at a normal hour. There were no traditions, no recipes to pass down.

Elena slid the bag of potatoes and a paring knife across the island to Vlad and then handed him a large bowl for the finished potatoes. "How many should I peel?" he asked.

"The whole bag, if you can. I want to make a lot."

Elena stood on the other side of the island and began to dice the mushrooms and onions. Occasionally, she glanced up to watch him work but had to look away each time. His fingers—long and thick— appeared graceful as they swept the knife back and forth across each potato. It was all too easy to imagine his fingers sweeping across her, and that was a train of thought that would end with her cutting herself.

They worked in silence for a while, each concentrating on their own tasks and lost in their own thoughts. When they were done, he leaned back. "Now what?"

"Want to roll out the dough while I cook?"

"Anything but that." He groaned when he said it, but then he grinned again and, holy God, he winked at her. Elena forgot her own name for a moment. When she opened the fridge to pull out the dough she'd prepared last night, she was tempted to lean her head all the way in to cool herself down.

"I might need a quick tutorial on this part," Vlad said, watching her as she carried the dough to where he sat.

"You don't remember how?"

"Only vaguely. Mama usually did this part."

Elena grabbed the gluten-free flour, the rolling pin, and a wooden cutting board. After dusting the board with flour, she put the ball of dough in the center. "Start with small strokes," she said, leaning across him to show him how. "Just keep doing it until the dough starts to flatten out." She stood back and looked at him. "Got it?"

He chuckled, and their faces were so close that she felt his breath on her face. "What's so funny?" she asked, voice stretched tight.

"You have . . ." He lifted his hand to her face, and one of those long, graceful fingers brushed her cheekbone. "Flour. You have flour on your face."

"Oh." She wiped her cheek with the back of her hand.

His smile grew. "You just made it worse."

Flustered—not by the flour, but by him—she backed away. "Okay, I'm going to get started on the filling."

They worked for several hours, shaping, filling, and boiling the dumplings. Long stretches of conversation were bookmarked by content silence. When they were finally done, Elena stretched her arms over her head and winced at the catch in her neck.

"You okay?" he asked.

"Just stiff." She rolled her head back and forth against tight muscles.

"Go sit on the floor in the living room."

Elena blinked and slowly lowered her arms. "What? Why?"

"Just do it," he chided gently. "I'll be right there."

Elena washed her hands and dried them as Vlad disappeared into the downstairs bathroom. Then she did what he told her to. She went into the living room and lowered herself to the floor in front of the couch. Vlad joined her a moment later and wedged behind her.

"What are we doing?" she asked.

"You are going to sit there. I am going to rub your neck."

"You are?" Her voice came out as flittery as butterfly wings. Excitable and frantic.

"Let me take care of you for a change."

Behind her, he widened his thighs to create a cocoon around her. "Scoot back," he said gruffly.

Her pulse pounded in her ears as she did so.

"Where does it hurt?" His voice was a warm, soothing baritone.

Elena pressed her fingers into the spot on her neck where the cords and tendons were stretched tight. Moments later, his fingers brushed hers aside and began a magical slide across her skin. Elena melted. Instant goo. A low moan escaped from her throat as he spread his fingers wide and wove them up into her hair. Slowly, he massaged her scalp in wider and wider circles, her hair tangling around his fingers. When he slid them down again, he brushed over the source of her pain—a knot in her neck. He paused. "Is that where it hurts?"

"Yes," she whispered.

Vlad pressed his thumb into the knot and rubbed a small circle around it. Elena tilted her head to give him greater access because it felt so good and she was so rarely touched. "You're going to put me in a trance."

"I would settle for putting you to sleep."

"I don't know how to take that."

He chuckled, and the warm vibration of it set her heart jumping. "I just mean that I know you don't sleep much. You need to relax."

"How do you know I don't sleep?"

"I can hear you at night when you get up and walk around." He pressed the pad of his thumb into the knot again, and she sighed. "You're working too hard, Lenochka."

"There's no such thing."

"That sounds like something your father would say."

"It is. He said it often." His fingers stalled against her neck, so she plowed forward before he could say anything to match the tension in his hands. "He did the best he knew how to do, Vlad. He never expected to have to raise me alone."

Vlad spread his hands down to her shoulders and squeezed the tight muscles there. "People have to make hard choices all the time for the ones they love. He was no different than anyone else."

She snorted. "Yes, he was. How many kids are taught a secret code word to know if their father is in trouble?"

Vlad's voice sounded like it had been dragged across gravel. "What are you talking about?"

She picked at the cuff of her shorts. "If he texted me that word, then I knew something was wrong. And we had this whole plan about what I was supposed to do. I had to take his hard drive from the computer, burn his journals in the woodstove. We had a motel room that we would meet at. He changed the location every few months."

His hands paused again. "When did this start?"

She shrugged with one shoulder. "I don't remember. When I was twelve, maybe."

"What was the code word?"

"Sparrow." At his questioning silence, she explained. "From the proverb. *A word is not a sparrow.*"

Vlad finished the old Soviet-area saying. "Once it flies out, you can't catch it."

"He only used it once. That night."

His hands rested against her shoulders, protective and warm, drugging her with their soothing weight. And so she kept talking. About something she swore she never would. "I got home from work around eleven o'clock. He was gone, of course, but that wasn't strange. He was almost always gone somewhere. I'd been . . . We'd been fighting a lot. I wanted to move out and go to college and be normal for a change, but he wouldn't let me. He said I was still too young, and he was working on something too dangerous. But he'd been saying that my whole life, and nothing had ever happened. So, I started rebelling and sneaking out when he was gone. Going out and . . ." She sucked in a breath and let it out, sparing him the *and* part. The part where she sought temporary comfort in the arms of a string of bad decisions.

"Anyway, when I realized he was gone that night, I went out and left my cell phone at home as if that was some way to get back at him. I got home at four in the morning, and I realized he had texted me while I was gone. It was just that word. *Sparrow.*"

Vlad let out a long breath and rubbed the pads of his thumbs up and down the tense strains of her neck.

"I just stared at it, like I couldn't understand the word. I almost called him to ask if he was serious. But then I just snapped into action. I went through all the steps. Dug out his hard drive. Burned his journals. Grabbed my bag and went to the motel." She picked at her cuticles. "I waited and waited and waited. But he never showed up. I waited for him in that hotel room for three days, too scared to even go to the vending machine. I nearly starved."

Vlad's fingers stalled again. "Christ, Elena. Why didn't you ever tell me that?"

The same reason she hid all her notes in the bottom drawer of her dresser upstairs. Why she kept it a secret that she was trying to finish her father's story. And why she knew she had to leave him when every part of her longed to stay right there in the warm cradle of his body. To protect him.

With a forced yawn, she sat forward. "I need to clean the kitchen."

His hands cupped her shoulders and tugged her back again. His voice was as gruff as his hands were gentle. "Your father never should have put you in that position. It was selfish. You deserved better, Lenochka."

"Better than what?"

"Better than him."

"But I had you."

Vlad's breathing grew heavy with the weight of his pause.

Hers rushed out in a single gush when his lips lowered to the top of her head. "You still do," he murmured.

Elena rose to her feet and slowly turned in the opening of his legs. He gazed up at her, his eyes smoldering with the same *something* from when she'd hugged him earlier that week. It lit a fire low in her belly that burned long into another sleepless night.

CHAPTER THIRTEEN

Elena set her alarm for extra early the next morning so she could tackle the rest of the cooking for the party. She showered and dressed quickly. When she walked out of her room, she discovered the door to Vlad's bedroom open. A quick peek inside revealed an empty bed.

She found him in the kitchen, back to her as he filled a mug with one hand, the other holding on to a single crutch. The other was propped against the island. Neighbor Cat was happily scarfing down her treat by the pantry.

Elena cleared her throat to announce herself. Vlad looked over his shoulder. "Hey," he said, a tired lilt to his voice and a shy smile on his lips.

"Good morning."

"I made you some tea." He nodded with his chin toward another mug on the island.

"Thank you." She slid the mug closer to her. "You should have waited for me, though."

"Why?" He turned around, putting the bulk of his weight on

his crutch. She winced in anticipation as he lowered his broken leg all the way to the floor.

She let out a breath. "That's why."

"I'm supposed to start putting weight on it, remember?"

Yeah. But that didn't make her any less worried. He leaned back against the counter and raised his mug to his lips. Over the rim, he met her gaze and smiled with his eyes alone. Her heart jumpy-jumped clear into her throat. Mornings were an intimate routine they had yet to settle into, and this was why. Because it was moments like this, like last night, that would be hardest for her to give up and forget. Even with ten feet of distance between them, it felt suddenly too close, the kitchen too small. His hands dwarfed the mug, and as he raised it to his lips again, the short sleeves of his T-shirt protested against the bulge of his bicep. If she pressed her nose into the space where his pulse pounded in his neck, she knew he would smell like warm skin and sleepy man.

"How can I help today?" he asked, interrupting her ogling.

She shook her head. "Just relax and take care of your leg."

"I can't relax if I know you're working yourself to the bone in the kitchen."

"I'll try to rein myself in for your benefit."

"Thank you." He smiled over his mug again.

He really needed to stop doing that, or she was going to suffer cardiac arrest. She stood with purpose. "Do you want breakfast?"

"I ate a muffin."

"Okay, well, I sort of need to get started, so . . ."

He laughed. Not one of those big, boisterous laughs that invited people to join in, but one of those quiet, *just between us* kinds of laughs. "I get the feeling you are trying to kick me out of the kitchen."

"More like gently nudge."

"I'm going." He downed the rest of his tea. "I'm actually looking forward to bathing today since I can do it by myself again."

She bit her lip. "You're sure you don't need help?"

That sexy eyebrow did its thing as he gazed across the island at her. "Are you offering?"

"I'm telling you to be careful." Her voice was stern but the bright heat of her cheeks likely gave her away. She was rather unused to his flirting but enjoying it all the same.

"I'll get out of your way now." Using both crutches, he slowly rounded the island, stopping briefly at her side. "But if you *were* offering—".

"Go." She pointed.

His laughter followed him down the hallway. Elena returned to her seat and lightly banged her forehead on the counter. Neighbor Cat meowed at her feet.

"What are you waiting for?" Elena asked the animal. "He's about to get naked upstairs. Now's your chance."

A few minutes later, the water turned on overhead, which brought to mind an image of him naked. She really needed to get busy, because—a loud thud split the thought.

No. Oh shit. Elena ran down the hallway and up the stairs. "Vlad?"

His bedroom door was open, so she ran inside. The bathroom door was halfway shut. Oh, God, if he fell . . .

"Vlad!" She threw open the bathroom door.

And skidded to a stop.

Vlad was on the floor, one hand raised to ward her off. "I'm okay. I slipped. But I'm fine. I didn't hurt my leg."

Elena planted her hands on her hips. "I told you it was too dangerous."

Vlad winced and lowered his hand.

And that's when she realized.

He was nude.

As in naked.

As in, oh, sweet Jesus, the man was cut from stone.

Elena sucked in a gasp and spun around. "I'm sorry. I—I should have knocked. But I heard the thud and I was worried." Her breath came in tiny pants. "What—what can I do to help?"

"Nothing. I've got this."

"If you think I'm going to let you get off the floor alone, you are deranged."

"I don't want to put you in an awkward position."

"If you don't want me to see you naked, I can close my eyes and hand you a towel to put around you or something. I promise not to look."

He made a frustrated noise.

She repeated it. "Vlad, we're adults. This is ridiculous."

"Fine," he rasped. "Let's just get this over with."

Elena fortified herself with a deep breath and turned around. She locked eyes with the wall. "How do we do this?"

"Just let me hold your arm while I get into the water."

Okay. She could do that. She waited with arms outstretched as he hauled himself from the floor and onto the edge of the tub. His bare legs brushed against hers as he reached for her hand for balance. Unbidden, her mind conjured an image of what she was purposely not looking at, and she had to close her eyes to chase it away.

"That bad, huh?" His voice had gone from annoyed to grumpy again.

"Huh?"

"You look like you'd rather die than catch a glimpse."

"You didn't want me to look."

"That's not what I said." He muttered it under his breath.

"So you want me to look?"

"I want you to stop acting like you'll turn to stone if you do."

"Make up your mind, Vlad. Do you want me to look or not?"

"I want you to open your damn eyes before *you* fall down."

She obeyed and found herself staring intently at a popping vein along his temple. "I told you this was a bad idea," he said.

"Just get in the tub."

"I need your hand again."

"Right. Okay." She needed to get her shit together. She was acting like a teenage girl with her first crush. Which he was, of course. Her first crush. Her forever crush.

He held on tightly as he turned around and lowered his good leg into the water. Then he let go of her hand so he could instead grip both sides of the tub. With ease, he lowered his body fully, relying on the strength of his thick, massive thighs to take all the weight off his lower leg.

"You're looking."

Flames burst from her cheeks. Elena turned around so abruptly that she stumbled. "No, I'm not."

"I cannot help that I have a hairy chest."

That's what he thought she was staring at? His chest hair? And anyway, why would it be bad to stare at the thick blanket of dark hair that covered his sculpted pecs and dipped enticingly toward his defined abs?

She squeaked out a response. "There's nothing wrong with your hairy chest."

"Colton says I should wax."

"Colton is a stupid American."

He looked up with an apologetic grimace. "I'm sorry you have to do this."

"Shut up and let me wash your hair."

His grimace lifted into something resembling a smile. "You're bossy."

"And you're stubborn."

"I could have just called Colton."

"So he can insult your chest hair again? I don't think so."

His smile became a chuckle as he relaxed. Elena squeezed a dollop of shampoo into her hands, rubbed them together, and then slowly massaged the liquid into his wet hair. Suds formed between her fingers, turning his thick, dark locks into foamy spikes. She spread her fingers wide to slowly scrub along his temples and then down behind his ears. The smooth outline of his head took shape in her imagination, and the need for exploration overtook all common sense. Her fingers dipped lower to the cords of his neck, where tiny, wispy hairs were already growing back from his last haircut. Such a simple thing. Washing someone's hair. But there was nothing simple about the layers of complex emotion competing inside her as he turned himself over to her. Touching him like this was at once intimate and innocent. Seductive and sweet. Dangerous and natural.

He sucked in a breath, and she immediately paused. "Am I hurting you?" Her voice sounded like sandpaper over glass.

"No," came his gruff response. "I would let you do this all day."

She suddenly wanted to. She splayed her fingers again and scraped them up into his hair, massaging his scalp inch by inch like he'd done for her last night. His head moved with her, toward her touch. And when he tilted his head all the way back, she saw that his eyes were closed.

Her own eyes betrayed her, and they drifted downward to the

place she swore she wouldn't look, along a dark trail of hair down the center of his abs that pointed farther south to a thicker patch.

What would it be like with him? It had been so long since she'd allowed herself to imagine it, but now her body insisted on painting every vivid pornographic picture in her mind. To feel those powerful hips move against hers. To press her fleshy breasts against that coarse, dark hair, that hard, granite chest.

His breathing changed, and her eyes snapped back to find his now open, watching her with an unreadable expression.

She should have been embarrassed, but she couldn't summon any emotion beyond the tightly coiled sexual kind. Her hands stalled against his scalp. "You have a beautiful body, Vlad."

His throat moved with a deep swallow. But when he didn't respond, the embarrassment finally pushed through. She forced a lightness to her voice that she didn't feel. "Like you need me to tell you that."

"I do," he rasped.

The lightness evaporated. "Why?"

"What husband doesn't want to know his wife finds him attractive?"

"I've always found you attractive, Vlad. You just never invited me to look before."

"I'm inviting you now."

Reality collided with fantasy. What the hell was she doing? She pulled her hands away and stood. Oxygen was in short supply, and so was sanity. "Can you rinse without me?"

"Elena—"

"I'll wait outside in case you need me again."

Coward. She cursed herself as she fled to hide in the bedroom, too afraid to hear or see his reaction. But maybe also because she was too afraid of herself and the feelings coursing through her, the desire that lingered still.

It was just physical. A natural reaction. That's all it was. What woman wouldn't feel a surge of lust with her hands on a man like that? What woman wouldn't begin to imagine all nature of naughty things when presented with a specimen like him?

Except she wasn't just any woman, and he wasn't just any man. And the body wasn't a nameless or faceless specimen. It was Vlad. Her lifelong friend. Her husband. The one she was, in fact, divorcing. And she'd just all but admitted to him that she wanted him.

Desire became humiliation. Years of hiding it, poof. Gone. Exposure was a thief, stealing the protective veil she hid behind until she felt like the one who'd been stripped naked.

"Maybe this is a mistake."

Elena plastered herself against the wall outside Vlad's bedroom. She hadn't meant to eavesdrop, but Vlad had one of those voices. The deep baritone kind that carried even when he was trying to be quiet. He and his father had disappeared after his father's toast, and she went to look for him because she had gone long enough without her husband by her side.

Husband. *She couldn't get used to the word. That morning, she'd nearly called the whole thing off. Vlad didn't need a burden like her, no matter how she felt about him. But the minute she saw him in his suit, waiting for her at the city office with that warm smile and those tender eyes, all her fears evaporated. Maybe she was always meant to marry this man, her best friend. And he'd kissed her with such tenderness after their vows that a hundred forgotten dreams were restored. She wasn't sure what would happen tonight, their wedding night. But hope and desire had quickly made her drunk with possibilities.*

Until now.

"Maybe I should have just told her the truth," Vlad said.

Elena's stomach clenched. What truth?

"Yes," his father scoffed. "I'm sure she will just open right up when you tell her you only proposed because your mother suggested it."

Her skin, so hot a moment ago, was now ice-cold. It was a lie. All of it. He was marrying her out of obligation. Nothing more. She tiptoed away, hid in the bathroom, and cried for ten solid minutes. When she was done, she vowed he would never know the truth of how foolish she was. He would never know she'd been stupid enough to believe he wanted her as much as she wanted him.

In the bathroom, the sound of splashing water was followed by the draining of the tub. The squeak of wet hands on the tub. The quiet thud of a foot on the floor, the swish of a towel.

She crept closer to the door, steeled herself, spoke into the small opening. "Do you need help?"

"I think I got it." His voice betrayed nothing.

"The floor might be slippery."

"It's fine. I'll be right out."

She wanted to run away, lock herself in her own bedroom and hide. But she couldn't. Not until she knew he'd made it safely out of the bathroom. So she waited, wincing, as the sounds of his crutches approached the door. She pulled it open for him and put enough distance between them to avoid any chance of touching him again. He'd wrapped a dry towel around his waist again, but rivulets of water dripped down his back from his hair.

"I—I'll get some clothes for you."

"I can dress myself."

"Fine. I'll, um, I'll be downstairs."

"Dammit, Elena. Stop."

She hovered in the doorway and stared at the closed door to her room, caught between two worlds. Across the hallway, all her notes, all her work, her future. Behind her, all her desires, all her longings, her past. But he didn't feel like her past anymore. He felt real. He felt present.

"What just happened?" he asked, managing to sound both wounded and confused.

"Nothing."

"It wasn't nothing."

"Then it's something we need to forget."

"*Why?*"

She turned around and found him in the same spot as before. Rooted and stuck. "I had a job interview yesterday."

His face drained of color. "What are you talking about?"

"The *Moscow Independent*."

He washed a hand down his face.

"I mean, it wasn't really an interview, but I called Yevgeny, and he said he would get back to me in a few days. I have no reason to think he won't offer me a job."

All the warmth and softness evaporated from his eyes. They became as hard as his jawline, his expression as dark as his beard. "Congratulations."

"This was always the plan, Vlad."

"Not always." He turned around on his crutches. "You can go now. I don't need your help anymore."

CHAPTER FOURTEEN

By six o'clock, the food was done, the house was full, and Elena wished she could be anywhere else.

They hadn't spoken again all day, and Vlad had barely even looked at her. For everyone else, he offered smiles and hugs. But whenever their eyes crossed paths, his face turned to stone. Shortly before the game was supposed to start, the guys got him settled on the couch and then huddled around him in the way they always did. From her spot on the opposite side of the room, she felt the weight of their stares. She looked up to find Mack, Malcolm, and Noah watching her and whispering. They quickly looked away, making it obvious that she'd just busted them talking about her.

Vlad had probably told them about her job interview and now they hated her too. She gave them her back and pretended it didn't matter. She sensed someone else staring, but this time it was Alexis, who studied her with a slight tilt to her head and a questioning look in her eyes.

"I'm sorry, did you say something?" Elena asked.

"I asked if there was anything I could do to help?"

"Oh. No, thank you." Elena shook her head to clear the fog. She gestured toward the table covered in food. "Please just enjoy yourself."

Alexis looked back and forth between Elena and Vlad before quietly excusing herself.

"Heads up, girlfriend." Colton's sudden voice over her shoulder was a fierce whisper. "Your friends are here."

Great. Just when she thought the night couldn't get any worse, the Loners marched in single file. Elena slapped a hand over her right eye as it began to twitch.

"What's wrong?" Colton asked.

"Hex."

Colton tugged her hand away. "Courage, woman. Don't let them intimidate you."

"I'm not intimidated," Elena hissed.

But then Michelle walked in, and her voice died. Michelle once again carried a pie plate, but this time she'd added a bottle of wine and a dose of understated sophistication that made Elena wish she'd put a little more thought into her own appearance. Compared to Michelle's sharp blue shorts and sparkly Vipers T-shirt, Elena felt downright frumpy in her jeans and V-neck jersey.

Michelle set her pie down among the other food on the dining table and then made a beeline for Elena, smiling brightly. "I brought you a gift," she said, handing over the wine.

"For me?" Elena blinked.

"For the hostess," Michelle said warmly.

Elena accepted the bottle, unsure of what to say. "I— Thank you. That is very kind."

"It's my favorite. It's from a winery in Michigan."

Claud barreled in like the bull she was. "Where's Vlad?"

Elena pointed to the living room. At the sound of his name, Vlad turned and looked over the back of the couch. He lifted his drink in greeting. The movement tugged his shirt across his chest, and Elena's mouth went dry. She tore her eyes away.

Michelle picked up a plate. "This looks amazing. Did you make all this yourself?"

"I did. I've been cooking for days."

"Wait until you taste everything," Colton said. "Elena is a genius."

"Anyone can follow a recipe."

"Ma!" Linda shoved a plate at her mother. "Be nice."

Andrea gushed. "If any of this is half as good as the pancakes you made, I'm going to walk out of here a satisfied woman." She preened for Colton's sake as she dropped a dumpling onto her plate.

Colton took the bait with a wink and a lean. "Darlin', I guarantee you'll walk out of here satisfied if you stick with me tonight."

Michelle caught Elena's gaze, and they shared an eye roll and a hidden smile that made Elena think they'd be friends in different circumstances. But circumstances were not different, and the fleeting sense of belonging left a hollow space inside her.

Alexis leaned over the table and gasped. "Are those blini?"

"They are," Elena said, surprised.

Alexis made a lustful noise and plopped two of the cheese-filled crepe-style pastries on her plate. "Oh my God, I haven't had these in so long."

"Where have you had them before?"

"Culinary school," Alexis said. She took a bite and moaned in a way that brought Noah swiveling around. "We didn't do a lot of Russian foods, but a few. These are my favorite. I cannot believe you made these. I'm going to eat them all."

The praise mattered more than it should. Elena lifted her shoulder. "I like to cook."

"Well, that's convenient," said Liv, Mack's wife, as she elbowed past Alexis. "Because Vlad likes to eat."

Elena forced a smile on her face and tried to participate in the conversation as if nothing was amiss. "I think I'm driving him crazy, to be honest. I fuss too much."

"All men liked to be fussed over," Andrea said. "Makes them feel loved. Of course, some sexy lingerie never hurt anyone either."

"Except your husband," Claud snorted.

"Ma!"

Elena met Michelle's smile with one of her own. A real one this time. The unfamiliar sense of camaraderie grew.

"So you and Vlad grew up in the same town?" That was from Malcolm's wife, Tracy.

"Yes," Elena nodded, sneak-glancing at Vlad again. "We grew up in Omsk. It's in the southern part of Siberia."

"I'm afraid I don't know much about Russian geography," Andrea admitted, selecting a cookie. "How far is Omsk from Moscow?"

"Very far. Almost three thousand kilometers. I was born in Moscow, actually, but we moved to Omsk after my mother died."

Alexis made a sympathetic noise and rested her hand briefly on Elena's arm. "I'm so sorry. How old were you?"

"Nine."

The pity on their faces stiffened her spine. She could read their minds from the look in their eyes. Poor little Elena, who had to marry her best friend to get out of Russia like an unloved orphan.

Who had to learn to cook as a child because her father was off saving the world.

She lifted her chin. "And to answer your question, Claud, yes, I am leaving soon. I had an interview yesterday with a newspaper in Moscow."

It was like a record scratching in the room. Even the TV blaring from the surround-sound speakers seemed to quiet as every eye in the room widened.

One of the guys did a shitty job of whispering to Vlad, "Is that true?"

"Yes," Vlad answered, and she didn't have to see his face to know he was forcing the word through a clenched jaw. "It is true."

So apparently, he hadn't told his friends yet. And they were not happy about it, judging by the way they crowded around him and began to gesture like a pack of hyenas on a kill.

"Wow," Andrea said, stammering to cover the tension. "Congratulations on the interview."

"Yes," Michelle said. "Congratulations. That sounds like a great opportunity."

Claud huffed. "When will you be gone?"

Linda shoved a cookie in her mother's mouth.

"I don't know yet. It was just a preliminary interview, but I—" Elena paused and cleared her throat. "I will be going back to Chicago first anyway. Probably soon." The words left a sour taste on her tongue.

"Are you sure?" Alexis said. "We've only just started to get to know you."

"It's for the best," Elena said, forcing her chin higher.

"Just promise me you won't leave until we have a chance to get together again," Michelle said. "Please, Elena. Promise me."

She put just enough sincerity into her voice that Elena could almost let herself believe she was part of the club. Or that these women wanted her to be.

But she knew better. These were Vlad's people. Vlad's family. She didn't belong here.

The doorbell rang, and the entire room let out a relieved breath.

"I will get that," Michelle said, setting down her plate and glass.

A few moments later, she returned with a dazed, glassy-eyed expression followed by a man in a tight pair of jeans and a leather jacket.

Every woman swayed on her feet.

Cheese Man.

Vlad tipped back his glass and demolished an ice cube with his molars.

He and the guys were huddled like a sad rec-league team watching the opposing players warm up and wondering where the hell they found the new, young sniper. In the dining room, Cheese Man stood center stage like a celebrity chef at a food show. The women surrounded him, seduced by his every word as he explained the virtues of the slow dairy movement.

"Do you know what happens when a cow is milked too many times a day? Their stress levels increase, like an overworked mother who just needs a little tender loving care."

In the center of the table, he'd set up a Girolle wheel and a fresh hunk of Swiss. With every crank of the handle, he shaved off a feather-thin layer of cheese and a year from Vlad's nerves.

"Stress affects the quality of the milk, and that affects the quality of the cheese. They must be treated with tenderness." He turned the crank and added a little twist to his hips. "Worship the miracle of their bodies. They must be caressed and nurtured. And you can taste the difference."

He lifted a slice of cheese and leaned toward Elena, who opened her mouth like a goddamned baby bird and let Cheese Man place it on her tongue. She sighed and closed her eyes.

"You taste the difference, don't you?" he murmured, trailing a finger down her jaw.

"Mmmm," she moaned.

Vlad tossed another ice cube in his mouth and broke it in half. "Who the hell does he think he is?"

Colton shrugged. "A super-hot man who knows how to make cheese sound like an orgasm."

"He's hitting on every woman here. Why aren't any of you mad about it?"

Mack shrugged. "I don't care if Liv wants to taste his cheddar. She's coming home to my salami."

The guys all groaned in disgust.

"That was beneath you, dude," Noah said, his tone betraying his own anxiety about Alexis's rapt attention to the way Cheese Man gripped his Gouda.

Elena giggled at something Cheese Man said. Vlad felt the blow of it all the way across the room like he'd just been Kronwalled onto his ass. "I'm going to break his balls."

"This is a side of the Russian I've never seen before," Mack mused, downing the last swallow of a beer.

"What side is that?" Vlad crushed another ice cube.

"Jealous."

"I am not jealous."

"You sure seem jealous."

"I am annoyed. This is my party and my house, and no one is even watching the game because . . . look at him!"

They all turned in time to see Cheese Man hand a Brie-smeared cracker to Michelle. She plucked it from his fingers with her lips. A swoon went up from the women.

Vlad tipped his glass back again but found it empty. He cursed under his breath.

"This is interesting," Malcolm said, stroking his beard. "I am always intrigued by what it is that finally pushes each man over his limit, what it takes to bring out that inner caveman we're always trying to suppress. It is a process to overcome a lifetime of toxic masculinity and to—" His voice cut off as Cheese Man picked up Tracy's hand and kissed it. "I will break his balls."

Vlad pointed with his empty glass. "Ha, see? It is not so easy to ignore when it is *your* woman he is hitting on."

The guys all lifted a collective eyebrow. Vlad realized his mistake. "Not that, I mean . . . Elena is not my woman. We are getting a—a . . . you know."

Mack tilted his head. "Are you trying to say divorce?"

"You know what I'm trying to say!"

"I do. What I find interesting is that you can't bring yourself to say it."

"Shut up."

Mack faced him head-on, blocking his view of the women. "Why won't you just admit it, man?"

Vlad gripped his empty glass tighter. "I have nothing to admit."

Noah snorted. "How about the fact that you don't want a divorce?"

Vlad hissed at him to keep his voice down. But a quick peek at the dining room told him no one had heard. The women were still too transfixed by how Cheese Man turned his crank.

Mack laid a hand on his shoulder. "It's okay, man. You don't have to keep up this lie. Not with us."

"I've made my peace with the status of my marriage," he finally said.

"The expression on your face right now is not one of peace, man."

"Then consider it one of acceptance."

"It's one of defeat, nut sack." Mack snorted.

"You heard her. She had a job interview in Moscow. She's leaving."

"Don't you want to fight for her?" Noah asked.

"I'm done fighting for her."

Another squeal went up from the dining room. Cheese Man was now waxing poetic about the aphrodisiac qualities of Parmesan.

"I hate him so much," Vlad seethed.

"Kick him out. It's your party."

Cheese Man trailed his fingers up Elena's arm before feeding her a slice of Parm.

Then the room became painted in a red filter as Cheese Men lowered his head.

And kissed his fucking wife.

CHAPTER FIFTEEN

And just like that, the party was over.

One minute, Elena was wincing in anticipation of a kiss on the cheek. The next, Vlad was standing on both his legs and bellowing for everyone to get the fuck out.

The guys all gathered their wives with *we'll talk about it later* urgency and hurried them outside, followed quickly by the Loners, who were already whispering like gossiping hens.

Face flaming, Elena walked Cheese Man to the door. "I'm so sorry. I don't know what got into him. He's not usually like this."

Cheese Man lifted her knuckles to his lips. "I have a pretty good idea."

"No, you don't. We're getting a divorce."

Cheese Man studied her with a small smirk. "Are you sure about that?"

Elena shut the door, clenched her fists, and stormed back to the living room. She found Vlad huffing and puffing, his hand wrapped around a half-empty glass of something that was probably bad for his stomach.

"I. Cannot. Believe you." Elena grabbed the remote from where it had landed on the floor when Vlad leaped to his feet. She zapped off the game. "What the hell were you thinking, jumping up like that? You could have hurt yourself again. And do you have any idea how humiliating that was?"

"I have some idea, yes." He took a long drink and hissed at the burn. He downed the rest of the liquor and dropped the empty glass to the floor.

"You need to stop drinking. That can't be good for your stomach."

Vlad pointed. "Stop taking care of me. And you want to know what is humiliating? Watching another man kiss my wife right in front of me."

Indignation burned like a bite into a scalding pelmeni hot from the oil. "You have no right to be jealous, Vlad."

His voice dropped an octave. "He kissed you."

"He kissed *my cheek*."

"Only because you turned your face at the last minute. If you hadn't, he would have shoved his tongue down your throat."

"Which is a lot more than you ever did to me!"

"Maybe because you've never wanted me to!"

Elena advanced on him in angry steps, drew back her fist, and socked him in the chest. He hopped back on one foot, blinking in surprise. Since he was obviously clueless, she did it again. Her fist landed in the valley between his pecs with a dull thud.

"Elena—"

"Of course I want you to kiss me. I've always wanted you to kiss me. I wanted you to kiss me when you proposed. I wanted you

to kiss me on our wedding day. I wanted you to kiss me *last night*."
Whack. Another punch. "And I want you to kiss me *right now*."

Elena grabbed the front of his shirt, yanked him down, and
smashed her mouth to his.

For the first time since they said *I do* at the altar, she kissed
him, but this time, there was nothing chaste about it. There was no
pretense this time, no confusion. No one to convince but each
other. She softened her lips against his, pressing gently in an un-
spoken plea to let her in. With a whimper, she nudged his mouth.
Once. Twice. Until finally she felt him give in. Vlad parted his lips
a fraction of an inch, and she slanted her mouth to go deeper.

At the touch of her tongue against his, Vlad came to life. With
a groan, he palmed the back of her head with one hand and pressed
the other against her back, pulling her tightly against him. Together,
they stumbled until she collided with the wall, never breaking
contact, never letting their mouths lift. Her arms wound around his
neck as she rose on tiptoe. He devoured her. Consumed her.

Years of wanting, wondering, longing collided with a reality
that exceeded all fantasy. His hands cradled her. His arms held her.
His mouth made love to her. There was a sweetness to his passion,
a tenderness in his brute strength. He kissed with an innocence
that spoke of purity but a gentle proficiency that suggested experience, and she did not want to think about that.

He manipulated the angle of her mouth to feast on what remained of her senses as she pressed into him, the front of her pelvis
brushing against the bulge of his arousal. He made a noise that was
part human, part animal. With a gasp, she wrenched her mouth
away to gulp in oxygen, tilting her head back, eyes closed. Vlad
trailed his lips down her jaw, her chin, her throat. Her fingers dug

into his scalp as he tasted the delicate skin, breathed in her scent, nuzzled the tender pulse point that raced ever faster with every flick of his tongue.

"Vlad . . ."

He answered her whispered plea with a slow slide of his hand down her side, pausing as if to memorize every inch, every dip and curve. Then his fingers fumbled with the hem of her shirt, and her breath became lodged in her lungs as his fingers met her skin and began a journey back up her body.

His fingertips brushed the underswell of her breast for a fraction of a second before his palm covered the lacy fabric standing between his exploration and the taut nub of her nipple.

She gasped his name, arched into his touch.

He groaned and jerked away from her. Vlad planted his hands on the wall on either side of her body and dropped his head between his shoulders. Defeated. Deflated.

"Vlad?"

He finally backed up, limping. "I can't do this, Elena."

Elena tugged down on her shirt. "Do what?"

"Whatever this is. For years, you've wanted nothing to do with me. You tell me you want to go back to Russia, to leave me, but then you come here and suddenly you're hugging me and looking at me naked and telling me I'm beautiful and kissing me. Do you know what I've had to do to move on from you?" He smacked the center of his chest. "What I've had to do to move on from you *in here*? And now here you are, and I have no idea what is going on with us."

"I—"

He grabbed her shoulders. "What the hell is going on with us?"

"I don't know," she whispered.

He let her go. "I need you to figure it out. Because I'm not a machine. You either want me or you don't. Just please, God, make up your mind."

Elena peeled her body from the wall. "And what about you? When are you ever going to make up your mind?"

"What are you talking about?"

"You can't ignore someone for almost six years and then show up out of the blue to say you want a real marriage now."

"Ignore you?" He slapped one hand into the other palm. "I *married* you. I vowed before my family, before our church, to marry you and protect you, and that meant something to me."

"No, it didn't."

"Wh-what?"

Her hands balled into fists. "I heard you!"

"Heard me when?"

"With your father. The night of the wedding. I heard you. I know the truth, Vlad. I've always known the truth. You proposed out of a sense of obligation, not love or passion. You proposed because your mother told you it was the right thing to do."

In her mind, she was a cartoon character with her legs spinning in the air as she tried to grab the words back. But it was too late.

He winced. Deeply, until lines formed around his eyes. "No. That's not . . . Elena, you misunderstood."

"Did I? You didn't even kiss me after you proposed."

"You didn't kiss me either!"

"Because I had no idea if you wanted me to." Her voice came out a whimper, and she hated it, the weakness of it.

"I can't believe this," Vlad breathed. "Why . . . why didn't you *say something?*"

"Because it hurt too much."

"And that's why . . . why *everything*?" He threw his arm out with the word.

"I was twenty years old. I was scared and confused and—"

"Six years, Elena!" He cut her off, smacking his hand into the wall. "Six years of our lives!"

"I know," she whispered, because that was all she could muster in the face of his rage.

"Why didn't you just talk to me?" His voice was a sonnet of agony.

"Because I didn't know how! I was humiliated and—"

"Bullshit. We were friends, Elena. We used to talk about everything."

"Yeah, and then we got married."

Vlad stacked his hands on his head and looked at the floor.

Weariness stole all her fight. She sank back against the wall. "The girl you proposed to, she wasn't the one you knew when you were younger. That girl was gone. She disappeared along with her father. And in her place was a terrified and lonely person who had no idea what she was supposed to do next, and then you came along like a white knight. When you proposed, it was like you'd thrown me a life preserver. I clung to it. To *you*. But when I overheard that conversation with your father, it was like finding out the life preserver was actually an anchor. It just dragged me further under. Once again, I was nothing but a burden. And I was so mad. So humiliated."

He looked up, his eyes dark with regret.

"And everything you did after that let me believe I *was* just a burden. You filled my bank account and paid my tuition and bought me a car. But you never once told me that it was because you cared about me. You let me go to Chicago without ever once telling me that you didn't want me to go. Or, God forbid, that you loved me."

His face scrunched up in pain.

"I would have been a wife to you if you'd asked me to, Vlad. But you never asked me to. Not until six months ago. And by then it was too late."

She whispered the words, but their truth was as loud as a shout. They stared at each other, chests rising and falling in a unified battle with oxygen and anger. And hovering above it all was the potent realization that perhaps things could have been different if they'd just been honest with each other back then.

Except no.

Things could not have been different because *they* had not been different. They were stuck with a present defined by a past that could never be changed.

Vlad sucked in a shaky breath and turned his face away from her, but not before she saw a tear drip down his cheek.

"Vlad—" She reached out to him.

"Don't." He shook his head and let out a noise that was half agony, half anger. "I swore I'd never ask you this, but I've had about four of those drinks tonight, and even that hasn't been enough to erase the memory of you staring at me in the bathtub, and now I get to add on top of that the image of another man kissing you. So fuck it."

Elena steeled herself, but nothing could have prepared her for what came next.

Staring straight ahead, he swallowed hard and rasped, "Have you been with anyone since we've been married?"

"What . . ." she breathed, too hurt and shocked to say anything else.

"Don't make me repeat it."

Her indignation returned. "How dare you? That's what you want to say to me right now? That's your only burning question? To ask if I slept with anyone in Chicago?"

His hand shot out and braced against the wall so he could lean against it. His voice was a tortured plea. "Just tell me. *Please.*"

"No!" Elena threw up her hands. "No, I have not been with anyone since we've been married."

He turned into the wall and dropped his forehead against it. "Thank God."

"But can you honestly say the same?"

He lifted his head. His red, glassy eyes were suddenly alert and wounded. "Are you serious?"

"You get to ask me, but I don't get to ask you? You're a man. A very sexy man, and a professional athlete. I'd have to be the world's most naive fool to think you'd go all this time without . . . that."

He opened and closed his mouth. Rubbed his hand over his jaw. A puff of sad air escaped his lips. "You have no idea what you're talking about. Jesus, Elena, you have no idea how faithful I've been to you."

"What the hell does that mean?"

Vlad limped back to the couch. He rounded to the front and sank onto the cushions. He stared with empty eyes at the dark TV screen. When he spoke again, his voice was flat and lifeless. "I've never been with *anyone*, Elena. Ever."

Elena shook her head as he tried to piece together the meaning behind those words. What . . . what did he mean? He couldn't mean. Did he? "Vlad," she whispered. "What—"

"Yep," he said with another one of those humorless laughs. "That's right. Your husband is a virgin. A virgin who *waited for you.*"

Elena pressed her fist to her mouth. The *tick-tick-tick* of a grandfather clock in the corner chronicled the seconds, but nothing could measure the chasm between them. "Vlad, I—"

"I don't need your pity."

"I don't pity you. I'm angry with you. Furious, actually."

He turned around on the couch, his expression a twisted combination of surprise and confusion.

"I never asked you to wait for me, Vlad. You did that all on your own, so don't put that one on me. But I'm sorry, anyway. I'm sorry for messing up your life in so, so many ways."

She spun on her heel and stormed to the stairs. She had to leave. Now. She ran to her room and shut the door. Barely a minute had passed before she heard him on the other side of it, but by then she'd pulled out her suitcase and started throwing her meager belongings into it.

"Elena, what are you doing?" He tried to turn the knob but she'd locked it. "Please let me in."

She threw her toiletries into her suitcase and zipped it shut. Vlad tried again. "Elena, open the door. Please."

The only thing left was her notes. She shoved them in her backpack and hauled it onto her shoulder. When she pulled open the door, he nearly stumbled into her. But then he saw her things—the suitcase, the backpack—and he sank backward on his crutches.

"What are you doing?"

"I have to go."

His head shook back and forth. "No. No you don't."

"We both know it's for the best."

He dropped one of his crutches and shoved his arm across the doorframe to block her path. "It's not. Please, Elena."

"Don't make this any harder than it already is."

He suddenly palmed the back of her head and pressed his brow to hers. "I don't want you to go," he choked.

"You will," she whispered, unable to find the strength to pull away from him. "Eventually, you will. Marrying me was a mistake. I'm trying to fix it. You have to let me."

He lifted his head from hers. Tears streamed down his cheeks and turned his eyes red.

"I was wrong to come here. I thought I was doing something good for you, something to repay your kindness and your friendship, but I was wrong. You don't need me here. You never did. You have your amazing friends, and your team, and even the neighborhood pets. And obviously you have Michelle. I'm just making things worse."

Elena dragged herself through the doorway and past him into the hallway.

He didn't try to stop her as she fled into the night.

CHAPTER SIXTEEN

Elena awoke just after dawn in a strange, cold room with a pounding headache and a hole in her chest. She'd barely slept, and even when she did, she'd clenched her jaw to the point of pain amid a movie reel of angsty dreams.

After leaving Vlad's last night, she'd chosen the first generic chain hotel that came up in her search results, and as soon as she checked in, she booked the first available flight to Chicago she could find. She snagged a last-row middle seat leaving at nine o'clock tomorrow morning. She'd have to text Vlad the location of his car in the airport parking lot before she left. Maybe one of the guys would help him get it back.

She rose gingerly, feeling like a bruise. Everything hurt. Two Tylenol and a hot shower eased some of the physical pain, but there was no medicine for the other kind of hurt.

For the first time in a long, long time, she felt the full weight of her loneliness. She had no schoolwork to distract her, and the thought of poring through her stack of dead-end clues in her investigation had all the appeal of a Pap smear. But the idea of staring at the lonely white ceiling all day in a bland white room was only slightly less tempting.

She wondered if he was awake yet. Did he even go to bed last night or just go back downstairs and pass out on the couch?

A twinge of alarm made her breath catch in her lungs. What if he fell? Elena grabbed for her phone and called up the number she'd programmed in for Colton. He'd likely ask questions, but she had to contact him. She hammered out a quick text.

Will you check on Vlad? I'm not there anymore. Want to make sure he is okay this morning.

It was several minutes before Colton responded.

COLTON: What do you mean, not there anymore?

ELENA: I'm going back to Chicago.

COLTON: Oh.

That was it. *Oh.*

ELENA: Will you check on him?

COLTON: Yes

Another one-word answer. They were back to hating her. It shouldn't matter, but it did.

Before she could talk herself out of it, she got dressed and went out to the car. And even though she didn't make a conscious decision about where she was going, it also seemed inevitable when she pulled along the curb in front of the house two blocks away from Vlad's.

She ambled along the sidewalk, indecision turning her feet to cement blocks. They weren't friends. They barely knew each other, and as an added bonus, Michelle was probably going to start dating her husband the minute Elena boarded her plane.

Yet she still walked up to her front door and knocked. A few moments later, Michelle opened the door wearing a surprised expression and a typical Sunday-morning suburban mom outfit. Leggings. T-shirt. Messy bun. Her disheveled appearance was actually a relief. Even Michelle could do sloppy.

Her expression quickly softened. "Oh my gosh, Elena, hi."

"I'm sorry for just showing up like this," Elena stammered. "I didn't really think this through, but you made me promise to come see you, and I just . . . Can I come in?"

Michelle blinked rapidly but then backed up. "Of course. Please."

Elena crossed the threshold into Michelle's house. Her house was nowhere near as big or grand as Vlad's, but it was nice. To the right of the entry was a wide staircase leading upstairs, and to the left was a formal dining room that looked like it doubled mostly as a place for the kids to do their homework and Michelle to fold laundry. Straight ahead was a long hallway that led to a kitchen.

"I'm sorry about what happened at the party," Elena said.

Michelle swung the door shut and laughed softly. "Don't be."

"Vlad should not have done that."

"Truly, there is no need to apologize."

They hovered awkwardly in the entryway. Elena looked around, biting her lip. Michelle finally gestured toward the kitchen. "I just made some coffee. Would you like some?"

"Oh, I—I don't want to impose."

"Not an imposition at all."

"Then yes," Elena breathed. "Coffee would be very nice."

Elena's stomach churned as she walked down the hallway. The walls were lined with framed professional photos of Michelle and her girls. This was a happy family. This is what Vlad wanted. What he deserved. What she had denied him with her immaturity and selfishness.

The kitchen was clean but cluttered. A small stack of dirty dishes filled one side of the sink, and someone had forgotten to put away the bread and peanut butter after making a sandwich.

"Excuse the mess," Michelle said as she pulled another mug from a cupboard. "I didn't have a lot of time before the party to clean up last night, and I slept in this morning."

"It's not messy. It just looks like a family lives here."

Michelle smiled as she filled Elena's mug. "We tend to live a lot messier than most. My girls are pretty active."

"How old are they?"

Michelle handed the coffee to Elena. "Seven and ten. Cream or sugar?"

"Sure. If you have them."

Michelle laughed again. "Are you kidding? Only a psycho drinks it black."

Elena's shoulders lost some of their coiled tension. Michelle was a lot more relatable than Elena realized.

"Shall we sit?" Michelle gestured toward the living room just beyond the kitchen. The house was a wide, open-concept style, which was probably good for a mom. She could cook dinner and still see the kids.

Elena followed Michelle to a long sectional couch and sat down on the end opposite her. Various toys were strewn across the floor, and a suspicious cat stared from behind the leg of a decorative table.

"What is your cat's name?"

"Dolphin."

At Elena's questioning glance, Michelle laughed. "The girls named him. They thought it was hilarious."

"Vlad loves cats."

Michelle tilted her head. "Yes, he has told me that before."

Elena looked around the room again. As much as it pained her to admit it, Vlad would fit in so nicely here. Michelle's house was soft and homey. Cozy and welcoming. Mismatched pillows decorated the couch, big fluffy things that would be perfect for a nap on a football Sunday and for cuddling on cold winter nights.

"Do your kids like Vlad?"

Michelle's coffee mug stalled halfway to her mouth. "Um, yes, of course. I mean, they don't know him very well, but—"

"Vlad is very good with children. He will make an excellent father someday."

"I'm sure he will be . . . someday."

"You can tell a lot about a man by how he treats animals. And Vlad is so gentle with animals."

"I suppose that is true."

"Are your girls asleep?"

"No. They are with their father this weekend."

"What—what happened with your husband?" Elena shook her head and winced. "I'm sorry. Forget I asked that. We barely know each other. Sometimes I forget that not everyone is an interview subject."

Michelle let out a quiet laugh. "It's okay. Really. I don't mind talking about it anymore. And frankly, I don't have a lot of female friends my age, so it's kind of nice to talk to someone, I guess."

More tension eased from her shoulders. "I don't have a lot of friends either."

Of *any* age. She wondered if Michelle noticed the omission. Except for Vlad, Elena had never had any real friends. Her father's job made it too risky for her to venture outside the tiny circle he trusted when she was growing up. While other kids her age were out having fun, playing sports, and dating, she was at home or at Vlad's.

"My ex-husband," Michelle said, inhaling. She let it out slowly. "He's a lawyer and worked, *works*, long hours. I have a degree in library science, but I was working part-time because of the kids and his hours. I came home one day not feeling well, and he was here. And he was not alone."

"He was cheating on you?"

"In our bed."

Elena swore in Russian.

Michelle tipped her mug in Elena's direction. "I have no idea what that means, but ditto."

"It means he is a pig."

"Yes. Very much." She shrugged. "Anyway, I discovered during the divorce that the woman I found him in bed with was not the first. He'd been cheating me on since our first year of marriage. I got the house, went back to work full-time at the Nashville Public Library, and the girls and I are making a new life."

"You are very strong."

"I have to be for my girls."

"You are alone in Nashville?"

Michelle's face turned compassionate, as if Elena had revealed some kind of hidden subtext in her question. "No. Not at all. I mean, my family lives two hours away, so they can't help much on a day-to-day basis. But we get by. We have amazing friends."

"So does Vlad. He has built a very good life here. I'm—" Elena bit her lip. "I'm glad you're part of that."

Elena sipped her coffee to cover the tremble of her bottom lip.

"Elena," Michelle said gently. Her tone suggested a lot of practice dealing with stubborn children. "I think I know why you're here."

"You do?"

Michelle nodded and set her mug on the coffee table. "So, I think I should just be straight with you."

"It's okay," Elena said, jumping in before Michelle could continue. "I know . . . I know about you and Vlad."

"Yeah, see, that's what I think I should be straight about. There is no me and Vlad."

"Maybe not now, but it's obvious there is something between you two—"

"Elena, there is *nothing* between Vlad and me. I like him very much. He is one of the sweetest men I've ever known, and maybe there is a part of me that might be tempted to pursue something with him, because who wouldn't? But there's just one massive problem."

"What?"

"You."

Elena looked over. "No. You have my blessing." The words cut like broken glass, but she had to say them. "You are smart and sweet and . . . you are actually what he wants and deserves. I won't get in your way."

Michelle pressed her hand to the cushion between them. "You misunderstand. It's not that I'm worried about you being in the way."

"Then what are you worried about?"

"The inconvenient fact that he is and will always be in love with you."

If Michelle had said those words twenty-four hours ago, Elena would have insisted they weren't true. Now, she didn't know what to believe. Not after all the things he said to her last night. But there was something she knew with certainty still. "It's too late."

"No, it's not."

"I'm leaving tomorrow."

That set Michelle back. Her mouth opened and closed before she let out a disappointed sigh. "Why, Elena?" Her voice was at once sorrowful and recriminatory.

"Because some things became very clear last night. I'm hurting him by being here. It's better for him if I go back to Chicago now."

"But do you *want* to go?"

Elena sloshed hot coffee on her hand.

"Is that a *no*?"

Elena sucked on the burned portion of her thumb and realized she was too exhausted to do anything but tell the truth. "No, I don't want to go."

"Thank God," Michelle breathed. "I was afraid I was going to have to beat you with a giant zucchini."

"It's barely been more than a week! How can I already be this confused? How can I already be reconsidering everything that I've been working toward? What does that mean?"

Michelle shrugged. "That you're human. That love is complicated."

Elena set her mug on the coffee table and stood, too agitated to remain seated. She began to pace. "I feel like I've been walking around my whole life with smudged glasses and have finally cleaned them or something. But instead of seeing things better, I'm just bumping into walls I never knew were there."

"Starting over is never easy."

"I'm not starting over." Her words came out like a petulant child insisting she wasn't tired.

"Look, I know a little about what you're going through. It's hard to redefine yourself after so long of seeing yourself as one way. I was his wife. That's who I was. I never stopped to ask myself if I was happy in that role. If I even recognized myself in that role. I think that's why I ignored all the warning signs for so long. It's not that I loved him so deeply that I couldn't imagine not being with him. It was that I had lost touch with myself so deeply that I couldn't imagine who I was without him. Redefining yourself is scary."

Elena understood that on such a deep level that she felt tears prick the back of her eyes.

"When my ex-husband moved out, I spent about three weeks in this fog, you know? And then one day, I got out of the shower, all wet and naked. And I realized . . . *I'm clean.* I was really, really clean. I'd washed away all that disappointment and broken promises. I didn't get dressed for an hour. I just walked around my house bare naked. I've never felt so free."

"But—" Elena returned on the couch and faced Michelle. She shook her head at the last second and took a drink of her coffee.

"But what? You can ask me anything."

"When you were first together . . . you loved him, right?"

"I did. I really did."

"So, what went wrong?"

"*He* went wrong. I'm not saying I was a perfect wife or that I didn't contribute to the problems in our marriage. But in the end, he just couldn't stop chasing something that I could never give him."

Something sour sprouted in Elena's stomach and began a slow crawl up her throat. "What was he chasing?"

"I don't think he ever really thought he was good enough. It makes me sad to think about it now, because he was so talented and smart. He had so much to offer, but somewhere inside him, something was broken. Something told him he always had to be better, make more money, chase the next big thing, the next big win. He forgot to appreciate what he had. And for so long, I let him run and chase those things. I thought I was happy to run along beside him. Until I realized I wasn't beside him. We weren't in the race together. He was running ahead, leaving me behind, and there was nothing I could do or say to make him slow down. It took me a long time to realize it wasn't my job to convince him *I* was the prize worth fighting for."

Elena felt every word like a thousand tiny pinpricks.

Michelle must have seen something in her face, because she rested a reassuring hand on Elena's arm. "Elena, you and Vlad are not my ex-husband and me."

"But I've been chasing something, too, and leaving him behind."

"But I'm willing to bet that it's not because you don't love him."

It's because I do. Elena looked at her lap. "He deserves better than me."

"He has a house full of romance novels that suggests he would disagree with that statement."

Elena lifted her head. "Romance novels? What are you talking about?"

"The book club he has with his friends," Michelle said. Her eyes widened. "Wait. You don't know about that?"

Elena blinked.

"I just assumed you knew," Michelle said apologetically.

"Vlad and his friends read romance novels? Like, as a joke?"

"Far from it," Michelle said. "They're super serious about it. They read them because they think it will make them better husbands and lovers and people. He seriously has never told you?"

"There's a lot we've never told each other."

"Elena, he joined the club for *you*."

"F-for me?"

"He wanted to figure out how to make you happy and come back to him."

Out of nowhere, tears sprang into her eyes. Elena leaped to her feet and turned away from Michelle, blinking rapidly to fight them off. It was no use. Twin tears leaked down her cheeks.

"Oh shit," Michelle said, rising. She instantly wrapped her arms around Elena from behind. "Don't cry. I didn't mean to upset you."

"When did he join the book club?"

"A few years ago, I think."

A few *years*? "He never told me. Why didn't he tell me?"

"Maybe it's time to get to the bottom of that and a lot of other things," Michelle said soothingly, tightening her embrace. "Everything is going to be okay."

The words were simple but so, so ironic. Vlad had hugged her almost the exact same way when she saw him after her father disappeared, and he'd said the exact same words. *It's going to be okay.*

Michelle gave Elena a moment to collect herself before patting her shoulder. "Can you wait in here for a second?"

Elena's eyes tracked Michelle's rise. "Where are you going?"

"To call in reinforcements."

Elena's eye began to twitch. "Wh-what kind of reinforcements?"

Michelle smiled. "I promise, everyone is on your side."

"No. Claud hates me. She put a hex on me."

"She will come around as soon as I fill her in."

Elena rose to her feet to follow Michelle from the living room. Michelle pulled her cell phone from a multi-device charging station in the kitchen.

"Michelle, please," Elena said. "I know what you're trying to do, and I . . . I am so touched. But Vlad doesn't want me to stay. He thinks he does, but he doesn't."

Michelle burst out laughing as if Elena had just told the funniest joke she'd ever heard. She put the phone to her ear. A moment later, she said, "Can you come over? She's here."

Elena gulped as Michelle met her eyes.

"I'm not entirely sure," Michelle said, "but she just told me I have her blessing to date her husband."

Another moment passed, and Michelle ended the call. A glint in her eye preceded a giggly little clap. "I'm so glad you came here this morning. We have so much work to do."

"But it doesn't matter. I'm leaving."

"Are you really, though?"

"I—I have a plane ticket."

"Doesn't mean you have to use it."

The front door burst open, bringing with it a gust of the west wind and a creepy-crawly feeling along the back of her neck.

"Where is she?" Claud stormed in with a general's determination. She was trailed by Linda and Andrea, good little foot soldiers.

"In here," Michelle said calmly. Elena fought the urge to stand behind her for protection.

"For God's sake, girl," Claud said, huffing and out of breath. "It's about damn time one of you got your head out of your ass."

CHAPTER SEVENTEEN

Vlad smelled bacon.

That was impossible, though. Elena was gone. She'd taken her things and driven away in his car last night. And even though he had known it would happen eventually, had always known she would one day leave, it gutted him. Just like he knew it would.

Vlad threw an arm over his eyes and prayed for sleep to drag him back under. His stomach warned of a punishing day of retribution for last night's whiskey binge. The bizarre bacon smell wasn't helping.

A quiet noise on the floor drew his gaze to the right.

He blinked. Rose up on his elbows. Blinked again.

A chicken was in his room.

A chicken in a diaper.

Vlad sat up fully and pressed the heels of his hands into his eyes. But when he looked again, the chicken was still there. She walked slowly near his dresser, beak pecking at something she'd found on the floor.

Dear God, he'd broken his brain last night. He was officially seeing things.

"Oh, good. You're awake."

Vlad nearly jumped out of his skin. Mack stood at his bedroom door holding a tray of food. "Brought you a friend," he said, nodding at the chicken as he walked in. He set the tray on the nightstand. Curls of steam rose from a mug of tea and a plate of scrambled eggs, bacon, and cut-up fruit.

"Is that Hazel?" Vlad could barely speak over the sandpaper of his throat.

"Yep. These are her eggs you're about to eat too."

Hazel was Vlad's favorite chicken. Probably not everyone in the world had a favorite chicken, but Vlad did. She was from a farm outside the city where Mack's wife had once lived and worked, and when Vlad was there one time, he and Hazel had bonded because a mean rooster named Randy had been attacking her.

Vlad held out his arms. Mack bent, scooped up the hen, and deposited her on Vlad's lap. Hazel cooed and settled down with her legs tucked beneath her. Vlad ran his hands over her soft feathers until the hen's eyes closed. She was a good chicken. Vlad bit his lip to keep it from trembling and cleared his throat. "What time is it?"

"Almost noon."

Elena was probably already on a plane back to Chicago by now. Or maybe she was driving his car. Either way, she was far, far away.

"Malcolm, Del, Noah, and Colton will be up in a few minutes," Mack said, reaching for the chicken. "You need to eat."

"I am not sure I can." Vlad pressed a hand to his stomach.

"Give it a try. You need to soak up the damage from last night."

Vlad pulled the tray to his lap, studied the food, and opted to start with the tea. "Elena is going back to Chicago," he said.

Mack set Hazel on the floor. "We know."

"How do you know?"

"She texted Colton to ask him to check on you."

She was still watching out for him. Even after everything they'd said to each other last night. His stomach clenched, and not because of his gastrointestinal sensitivity. This was pure mental anguish.

The rest of the guys came in a few moments later. Vlad braced himself for the cross-check. The yelling about what an idiot he was for what happened at the party and for letting Elena leave.

"Just say it," he grumbled.

"Say what?" Malcolm asked, leaning casually against the bed-frame.

"Tell me I'm an idiot who screwed up the best thing that ever happened to me and I'm an idiot for letting her go."

Colton shrugged. "I mean, yeah, that sort of sums it up well."

Mack dragged his hands over his hair. "What happened last night after we left?"

"It doesn't matter. She's going back to—"

"Russia. Yeah, so we've heard." Mack shook his head. "But we also watched you lose your fucking mind over another guy even thinking about kissing her last night after you insisted you were *at peace* with the divorce, so maybe it's time to cut the shit and just be straight with us."

Vlad poked at his eggs. He wished he could hug Hazel again.

"You don't want a divorce," Malcolm said. "And neither does she."

"That's not true. She's leaving."

"Because you're letting her."

"No," he said, choking on that damn emotion he knew he couldn't hold back much longer. "Because I told her the truth, and it was too much for her."

Mack groaned. "The truth about what? You keep talking in circles."

Vlad shook his head. He knew how these guys worked. Once you started talking, it was all over. They wouldn't let you stop until you had spilled your guts and were a weeping mess on the floor. The good thing about his friends is that they would be there to pick you back up again with some tissue for your snotty nose and a shoulder for your heavy head. The bad thing was, emotions were flying at him like a speeding puck across the ice. At least with the puck, he could visualize the scene and make the kind of split-second decision that had made him one of the best defensemen in the NHL. But right now, he was useless. The puck was going to hit him square in the face.

He scanned his friends, all waiting patiently, except for Colton, who had sunk to the floor to play with Hazel. Mack sat down on the narrow edge of mattress next to his hip. "Listen, man. We've all had to share our secrets before. You know how this works."

Yeah. He'd just never been on this end of it before.

"You can do it, man," Del encouraged.

Noah nodded. "Just tell us—"

"I'm a virgin!" He held his breath as his blurted confession settled on the group.

He expected an explosion.

He got silence.

"No shit?" That was from Noah. "Huh."

He looked around the room, incredulous. "That's it? That's your only response?"

Malcolm shrugged. "So you're a virgin. Big deal."

"It *is* a big deal. I am an almost thirty-year-old professional athlete who has never had sex, even with his wife of six years. I'm a living, breathing—"

"*Human being*," Mack said.

Vlad muttered obscenities in Russian. "You are missing the point. I told her I am a virgin, that I've waited my entire life for her, and she ran off saying she has ruined my life and she could never repay me and that it was a mistake to come here, and then she left me. *Again*."

"Something tells me there was a little more to it than that," Del mused.

Vlad's cheeks grew hot and he looked at his lap. "She might have kissed me."

"Wait, what?" Mack squawked.

Vlad lifted a single shoulder. "She kissed me."

"Holy shit," Colton breathed with a grin.

Malcolm lifted an eyebrow. "And then what?"

"I pulled away."

And then came the explosion.

Mack swore and tugged at his hair. Malcolm pointed at Vlad, sputtering nonsense. Colton and Noah both stood at the same time and accidentally clunked their foreheads together. Del muttered, "I give up," and started to leave.

Hazel squawked like she'd laid an egg.

"Why the hell did you stop her?" Mack seethed.

Del turned around and returned to the side of the bed. "I'm not leaving until I hear this. Not because I think it's worth hearing, but because I want to file it away the next time we think we've met the dumbest fucker on the planet, and I can say, 'Oh, no, remember the fucking Russian?'"

"I was confused, okay?" Vlad protested in his own defense. "One minute, she wants to go back to Russia. The next she is kissing me and looking at me naked and—"

"Uh—" Colton held up his hand. "What is the naked part?"

Noah smacked his arm. "He's on a roll. Don't interrupt him."

Vlad sighed and ran a hand down his jaw to cover the sudden tremble of his lip. "I couldn't do it. Not if she was just going to leave me. I couldn't survive that. So I stopped her and told her to make up her mind, and that led to an argument, and I told her I was a virgin, and she left."

Mack met Malcolm's gaze, and together they shook their heads. Mack looked at the ceiling. "Jesus, you are so obtuse when you want to be."

"What am I being obtuse about? I gave her a chance to tell me what she wants, and she left."

Del leaned over and smacked Vlad upside the head. Vlad leaned away and rubbed at the spot that now stung from Del's hand. "What was that for?"

"For being an obstinate ball sack." Del bent forward and glared menacingly. "You didn't give her a chance. You made her feel like shit. She took a huge risk in kissing you, and what did you do? You blamed her for your own choice to remain celibate."

Vlad's stomach lurched. "I didn't blame her." But he had. She'd even called him out on it. *I didn't ask you to wait for me. Don't put that on me.*

"And as an added bonus, you cemented in her mind her greatest fear, that she has fucked up your life, that you're better off without her," Del said. "No wonder she left."

Vlad could barely hear anything over the roar of his own rapid heartbeat. "I'm going to be sick."

Mack backed up. "For real? Like, you're going to puke? Or just, like, you're going to be figuratively sick?"

Vlad wasn't sure.

Colton pretended to study his fingernails. "Hey, guys? Do you think now might be the right time to put him out of his misery?"

Noah crossed his arms. "Yeah, we've probably tortured him long enough."

Vlad glowered. "What are you talking about?"

Colton shrugged. "She hasn't left."

Vlad's heart stopped. "What?"

Colton grinned. "I happen to have it on good authority that Elena is currently just a few blocks away at Michelle's house."

A small blood vessel burst in Vlad's brain as an overload of conflicting feelings fried his nerve endings. She was still here. *She was still here.*

Mack grinned. "Ooh, look at that. Plot twist."

"You knew this all along?" Vlad growled.

Del shrugged. "We like Elena. We weren't going to tell you until we were sure you deserved to know."

"I am going to break your balls."

Mack crossed his hands over his heart. "Is that any way to talk to the friends who are going to help you get your wife back?"

Vlad's hands shook as he moved the tray to the nightstand. "I—I do not know what to do."

Mack picked up Hazel and plopped her back on Vlad's lap. "Well, I might not be a writer, but I would think your next chapter ought to include you making sure she knows you want her to stay."

Colton laughed and ruffled Vlad's hair. "Drink your poop tea, little butt. Because you just got your midpoint moment, and you have to decide if you're willing to start rewriting your own story."

CHAPTER EIGHTEEN

Michelle's bedroom was broken into three parts—the bedroom part, a sitting area, and a closet the size of a Starbucks.

They told Elena to wait while they disappeared into the coffee shop.

"What are you doing?" she said after five minutes. She had to raise her voice to be heard.

Michelle came out loaded with a pile of clothes so high that Elena could barely see her face. Michelle dumped the pile unceremoniously on the other chair in the room. She leaned a hand against the wall to pant. "Lucky for you, I have way too many clothes."

"Lucky for me?" Elena asked. "What is going on?"

"Don't take this the wrong way, but I am going to burn that sweatshirt," Michelle said.

"This is my school," Elena said, looking down at the word *MEDILL* emblazoned across her boobs.

"You've worn it every day that you've been here."

"I didn't have a lot of time to pack." Of course, even if she had more time, most of her wardrobe looked exactly like what she'd been wearing. Leggings. Sweatshirts. Ripped jeans.

"Well, you also don't have any time to go shopping, so you're going to shop in my closet."

"Shop for what?" She was afraid of the answer, especially when Michelle laughed.

"What else? For seduction."

Linda and Andrea came out then, also loaded down with clothes. They dumped them next to the stack that Michelle had unloaded. Only Claud came out empty-handed. Apparently, she'd been the manager.

"Seduction?" Elena squeaked. "No. No, no, no, no. I can't do seduction. We're getting ahead of ourselves. I haven't even talked to Vlad. He might just throw me out."

Michelle held up a black dress with a deep V-neck. "Not if you're wearing this, he won't."

Elena looked down at herself and made eye contact with the mounds of her generous breasts. "No way. I'll look like a pool floatie."

Four sets of hands grabbed her at various joints and forced her into the bathroom. Michelle handed over the dress. "Try it on."

Five excruciating minutes later, Elena walked back out. Michelle and the Loners adopted the same expression—openmouthed and wide-eyed.

"I told you this was a mistake," Elena said, turning back around.

Once again, everyone grabbed her, but this time they dragged her to the full-length mirror by the closet door.

"Look at yourself," Michelle said. "You look ah-may-zing. I would never look this good in that dress."

"I look like the women who used to hang out at the ice rink after the men's senior competitions."

"Well, I don't know what that means, but if those women looked like *this*"—Andrea emphasized the word with a wave that gestured vaguely to Elena's body—"then they were some hot women."

Michelle laughed. "Vlad is going to faint."

Heat that would rival Mount Vesuvius blazed across her cheeks. "This dress is way too obvious."

Claud snorted. "Men don't do subtleties, honey. You have to hit them over the head with things, and even then, you have to give them an explanation why."

"Yeah," Andrea said, pulling the V-neck even lower. "So, make sure you show these off."

"Oh yeah," Michelle said, nodding. "Those are the goods. Show 'em off."

"I can't do this." Elena crinkled her nose. "I—I don't even know how to seduce someone. I can't just show him my boobs."

Claud snorted again. "It's like you've never met a man in your entire life."

"I've met Vlad. He won't even touch me without permission."

"Even a gentleman can lose his mind over a pair of fleshy boobs."

Elena laughed. "Why are you all helping me?"

"Because we want Vlad to be happy."

"But what changed your mind about me?"

Claud came to stand in front of her. "Because you came to Michelle's to offer your blessing even though it clearly broke your heart. Only a person who truly cares about a man would do something that selfless."

"I am not selfless. I . . . I hurt him."

Michelle gave her a sympathetic look. "You gotta give yourself a break. Nothing about your marriage has been normal. Neither one of you has made wise decisions. He is as much to blame for things as you are."

Elena returned to the mirror and tried to see herself, see *things*, in a new way. She smoothed her hands down the fitted curves, tried to imagine his reaction, tried to imagine him taking it off her. A tug low in her gut made her sweat. "You're absolutely sure about this dress?"

Michelle nodded. "Yes, and now we need shoes."

"High ones," Andrea said.

Claud smirked. "Fuck-me pumps."

Dear God.

An hour later, Elena had enough borrowed clothes for a month of outfits, but her Medill sweatshirt was mysteriously missing. She changed into a pair of white jeans Michelle loaned her—she had to roll up the legs because Michelle had a good three inches on her—and a sleeveless black T-shirt that was slightly too tight in the chest, because Elena had a couple of inches on Michelle in that area. She returned to the kitchen, where the Loners waited for her with fresh coffee.

"Look at you," Michelle said, shaking her head. "Look what you've been hiding beneath that sweatshirt."

"Speaking of which, I can't find it."

Michelle whistled and looked away.

"Time to make a plan," Claud said.

"A plan for what?"

Claud eyed her like a teenager trying to explain TikTok to her. "For getting your man back."

Elena looked at the floor. "I never really had him."

"Yes, you did. He's always been yours. You're just two very stubborn people."

There was a knock at the front door. Michelle got a quizzical look on her face. "I have no idea who that could be. It's too early for the girls to be back."

She excused herself, and Elena held her breath as momentary panic imagined Michelle opening the door to find Vlad there to ask her out finally. She hid in the kitchen and ignored the quiet murmur of voices.

The door closed, and a moment later, Michelle reappeared. Her grin was as wide as her face, and she carried an envelope the size of a greeting card. She held it out to Elena. "This just arrived for you."

"For me? From who?" Elena took the card from Michelle's fingers just as Michelle answered her question.

"Seeing how it's written in Russian, I have a pretty good idea."

Елена

Her name was scribbled on the front of the envelope in Vlad's unmistakable script.

Elena's hand fluttered to her lips. "But he doesn't know I'm here."

"Well, he actually probably does by now," Andrea said. "I sort of told Colton." She did a little giggle and dance then. "I can't believe I have Colton Wheeler's cell number."

"Well, are you going to open it or not?" Claud demanded.

"Maybe she wants some privacy," Linda suggested.

The pounding of her pulse in her ears drowned out their voices as Elena slid a finger beneath the seal of the envelope. It flipped open with a simple tug, and her fingers shook as she pulled out a card with a spray of Russian sage on the front. She'd carried a bundle of it at their wedding.

Inside, in his masculine scrawl, was a poem she knew well.

"Well?" Claud demanded.

Elena could only whisper. "'I still recall the wondrous moment when you appeared before my sight . . .'"

"What the hell does that mean?" Claud asked.

Elena looked up from the paper to find her unexpectedly new friends watching her closely and waiting for an explanation. "It's a poem."

"Awww." Andrea clutched her hands to her chest. "He wrote you a poem?"

"He didn't write it," Elena said. But it wouldn't have meant more even if he had. She looked down at the words again, but this time they swam through a watery lens.

"Does it mean something important?" Michelle asked quietly.

Yes, it meant something. It meant everything. It was a Pushkin poem about a man who fell in love with a woman but lost her, only to find her again years later.

It was a poem about second chances, about forgiveness and starting over.

It was, Vlad seemed to be saying, a poem about them.

At the bottom, Vlad had written a note. *It was a wondrous moment when I woke up in the hospital and saw you there. I don't want you to go. Will you have dinner with me tonight?*

"So?" Claud prodded impatiently. "That's it? Just a poem?"

"No," Elena said, looking up again. "He wants me to have dinner with him tonight."

Michelle squealed and did a little dance before pointing at Elena with an *I told you so* expression.

"What did I say? That man would die for you."

"I don't want him to die for me. I want him to be happy."

"And he will be if you get over your stubborn self, put the past behind you, and give your marriage a chance at a real future."

"But what if I can't make him happy? What if—"

She swallowed the rest of the question, but it remained a loud voice in her head. What if she was too broken after all this time? What if it was too late to overcome all the mistakes, the misunderstandings? What if her past was just another anchor destined to drag their future into a dark well of water?

"No more *what ifs*," Claud ordered. "It's time to decide, once and for all. Happiness is the harder choice, but you're strong enough to risk it. I wouldn't be standing here if I didn't believe that."

"I still have things to tell him," Elena whispered, her voice weakening along with her resistance.

"And you'll have plenty of time for that later," Michelle said. "But for now, you just have to take the first step."

The first step toward a new future. Was it really that simple?

Elena swallowed and sucked in a breath. "Okay," she said with a fortifying nod. "What's the plan?"

CHAPTER NINETEEN

She said yes.

An hour after he'd sent her the poem, Elena sent a note back saying she would be home at five, and the guys immediately sprang to action. They shaved him. Fixed his hair. Dressed him up in his best suit. Noah asked Alexis to make a special dinner, and then the two of them arranged the patio table outside the same way he'd arranged it her first night in America.

With a half hour to spare, Vlad took to pacing with his crutches as the guys tried to calm him down.

"Take deep breaths," Malcolm said.

"I can't. I'm too nervous."

"About what?"

He stopped and glared.

Malcolm held up his hands. "There is no reason to be nervous about that right now. This is your first chapter of a new story together. Sex might not even happen tonight."

"But what if it does?" Oh, God. He was going to puke.

"If it does, congratulations," Mack quipped.

"But what if she doesn't . . ." He couldn't even finish the sentence. He could even say the word *orgasm.*

Malcolm stood in front of him. "You know what? There's actually a really good chance she won't just from intercourse itself."

Vlad groaned.

"But that could be true whether it's your first time or your fiftieth. No matter what, just remember to take care of her first."

Vlad closed his eyes. And then wrenched them open. "Oh shit. What about condoms? I don't—I don't even know if she's on birth control."

Mack patted his chest. "Taken care of, my dude. We bought you some and put them in the drawer next to your bed."

Vlad wished the ground would open up and swallow him. "This is so embarrassing. I can't believe I have to talk to you guys about this."

Mack scoffed. "Are you kidding? This is what we're here for, man. Think about how much healthier all men in this world would be if we could be this open with one another all the time."

Malcolm nodded and crossed his arms. "Virginity is nothing to be ashamed of. It's just one more artificial measurement of how we define manhood. We raise men in our society to treat sex like a contest, a race to be won, instead of the joyful expression of love that it can be. And that's not to say that casual sex is wrong, or that a person's reasons for wanting to have sex are ever a reason for judgment. Sex for pleasure's sake is perfectly healthy and normal. But so is waiting. We tell women they're sluts for not waiting long enough and men that they're losers for waiting too long. It's a twisted message that hurts everyone. But look at you, nervous and embarrassed, when you actually have a chance to experience something amazing."

Malcolm gripped the back of Vlad's neck and squeezed. "You are going to get to fully experience your first time with a woman you love at an age when you can actually appreciate it."

"You're just saying that to make me feel better," Vlad said.

"No," Mack said. "I don't even remember my first time. I remember the girl, but not the act itself. I was in a rush to shed my virginity, and that was all that mattered to me. I'm ashamed of it now. But you? You waited, man. You put yourself in cold fucking storage for years to wait for the woman you loved. You really are a romance hero."

"But my leg . . ."

"Means you can have fun and get creative," Malcolm said.

"The important thing is to just be honest with her about everything," Mack said. "Tell her you're nervous and why. Tell her you're afraid she won't orgasm. Tell her you're concerned that you might have to experiment to find the right position. Tell her all of it. Intimacy is an act of communication. Hold nothing back."

"But remember," Malcolm said. "The most important thing tonight is to *talk*. Tell her what you should have said last night."

Colton ran into the room. "She's on her way," he said. "Everything is ready."

Oh, God. Vlad had never been this nervous. Not even when he proposed to her.

"Okay, we're going to take off now," Malcolm said. "Just be honest with her, man."

Vlad listened to them leave. The sound of their cars' departure, however, was quickly followed by another car pulling in.

She was here.

Vlad scraped his hand down his jaw and swore. He was already growing a shadow. He crutched to the front door and pulled it open just as she slid from the front seat of the car. She wore a black dress and high heels that made his heart pound and his eyes bug out and his chest break open with the surge of floaty champagne bubbles.

She stopped halfway up the sidewalk. "Hi," she whispered.

He tried to calm his breathing, but his voice shook anyway. "Welcome home."

And then all his careful plans collapsed, because she burst into tears. Shit. SHIT.

She quickly closed the distance between them, walked into the house, and threw her arms around his neck. She buried her face against his clean-shaven jaw and clung to him. "I'm sorry," she whispered. "I'm sorry."

Vlad cupped the sides of her cheeks and tugged her back. "For what?"

"For everything. For leaving. For crying. For six years. For everything."

"Don't do that," he murmured. "Not yet. Just be here with me."

"Okay." She nodded, sniffled, and backed up. "This was not what I was going to do when I saw you."

A bubble of laughter found its way north as he wiped a tear from her cheek. "What were you going to do?"

She sucked in a breath and stood tall. Then, in a clear but shaky voice, she said, "'Bound for your distant home, you were leaving alien lands. In an hour as sad as I've known, I wept over your hands.'"

The champagne bubbles rose all the way to his eyes and began to pop and fizz until a sheen of water formed across his vision. She was reciting the first stanza of another Pushkin poem, "Bound for Your Distant Home."

"Elena," he whispered.

In a breathy, smoky voice, she continued the story, a tortured tale of two lovers exiled from each other, surviving only on a futile fantasy of seeing each other again and sharing a long-awaited kiss. To Vlad, the poem had always felt despairing, forlorn and full of loss. But now, hearing it from Elena's voice as she stood in his doorway, finally home and gazing at him with tears and the promise of something more in her eyes, the words became symphonic, the message hopeful. In her voice, there was nothing futile about having faith in a fantasy of finding each other once more.

A whimper stole from Vlad's chest, and he tugged her close again. As he buried his face against her shoulder, her hands threaded into his hair. She held him like that, cradled him, as she whispered the remaining lines of poetry until she reached a fevered verse about a sweet kiss at last.

He couldn't take it anymore. Vlad lifted his head and repeated the words with her. Then her hands came around to cup his cheeks, and she kissed him.

Oh, how she kissed him. Slid her hand around the back of his neck, drew his mouth the rest of the way to hers, and breathed in the little sigh he made when he slanted and slid into her. She moaned low in her throat, and he was gone. Just like that. Gone. He dug his fingers into her back and poured all the longing and sweetness and fireworks he felt into his kiss. Their pose was awkward because of his crutches, but it didn't matter. Their mouths mingled and merged in a sensual conversation that was six years in the making.

He reached behind her and swung the door shut. Then he wrenched his mouth away to suck in a breath. If he could, he'd carry her upstairs right then, but Malcolm's reminder was fresh in his mind. They needed to talk. "There's something I want to show you," he said.

It took a giant's dose of willpower to remove his lips from her body, to set her apart from him, to grab hold of his crutches instead. She followed closely to the patio outside. The guys had set it up exactly as he instructed. Candles flickered on the table. Their plates were set for dinner, which was warming in the oven, and on her plate was a wrapped present he should have given her a long time ago.

When she saw it all, her hand fluttered to her mouth. "It's just like . . ."

"Your first night here. I wanted to try it again, since I screwed it up so badly the first time."

"No, you didn't. It was me."

He nodded toward her seat. "Open your present."

Elena's heels clicked quietly on the concrete patio as she walked to the table. She picked up the gift, the paper now dusty and faded. As she peeled away the tape, the paper fell away and revealed a picture frame.

She bit her lip. "Where did you get this?" She slowly sat down in her chair, staring at the photo.

He made his way to his own seat next to her and sat down. He set the crutches on the ground and stretched his leg out under the table. "My mom took it."

The picture was from their wedding just after his father had offered a toast. The moment was seared in his memory. He and Elena stood next to each other, and halfway through his father's speech, Elena had looped her arm through his and leaned into him. Surprised by the affection, he'd looked down to find her smiling up at him. For one split second, it all felt real. And somehow, his mother had captured it in a snapshot.

"Do you remember what I said to you when you walked down the aisle?"

"That I looked beautiful."

He lifted a corner of his lips. "After that."

"You said everything was going to be okay."

"I *promised* you." His voice wobbled. "I haven't kept that promise."

"Yes, you have. You've taken care of me. You've made so many sacrifices for me."

"But that's not the same thing. You were right, what you said last night. I shouldn't have just let you go to Chicago without telling you how much I wanted you to stay. I thought that if I let you go, that if I gave you the space you needed to heal and to find yourself after what happened with your father, that you would find your way back to me. But you never did. You just slipped further away, and it's my fault. Because I never made it clear that I wanted you to come back."

When she looked up, the candlelight caught the glint of the tears shimmering in her eyes.

"I waited way too long to tell you what I really wanted out of our marriage. That's my fault. So, I'm telling you now. I didn't propose to you *only* because my mom suggested it. She simply gave me the courage to do what I always wanted to do." He started to shake on the inside. "Maybe we were too young to be married. Too young to know how to say the things we needed to say. To understand the problems we created by not saying them. But we're not too young now."

Her chest rose and fell in deep, shaky breaths as she absorbed his words, let their meaning settle into her mind.

"I don't want you to go, Elena." His voice was thick, and his eyes stung again. "When I said that last night, what I meant was, I don't want you to *go*. I never wanted you to go." He wiped away the tear that slipped down his cheek. "I will learn to be okay with whatever you decide, but if you think there's a chance that you could want to start over—"

"Shut up." She laughed thickly.

"Wh-what?"

She stood and gazed down at him. "Shut up and kiss me."

Vlad rose on wobbly legs, using the table for leverage. With a gentle tug, he pulled her flush against his body. She rose on tiptoe and placed a soft kiss upon his lips that took his breath away. Not with its passion, but with its promise.

"Do you want to eat dinner?" he murmured.

She shook her head.

"What do you want?"

She caressed his cheek. "I want my husband."

His entire body trembled. "Are you sure? Because if you're not ready, Elena, we can wait."

"Don't you think we've waited long enough?"

Yes. Yes, they had. He crushed his mouth to hers, devoured her in a single slant. Her hands slipped inside his jacket and explored his chest, his back, his stomach. Oh, God. This was really going to happen. Between them, the urgency of so many years of pent-up desire swelled and nestled against her stomach. She gasped and pressed against him until he saw stars. He'd never wanted to be naked so badly in his entire life, but at the same time, he was grateful for the boundary of clothing. He didn't want to go too fast. Every second of this was precious, and he wanted to stretch each one out as long as possible.

He pulled back and rasped against her lips. "Meet me in bed."

CHAPTER TWENTY

As her footsteps padded quickly up the stairs, Vlad blew out the candles and then went into the kitchen to turn off the oven. Every part of him shook. He needed to get it under control. Otherwise, he was going to explode the instant he was inside her. He groaned at just the thought. He wanted this to last. He wanted to savor every second, every taste of her skin, every sound of her breath. He wanted to make it good for her.

Vlad went into the downstairs bathroom and splashed water on his face. Shit. SHIT. He was almost desperate enough to text the guys for advice.

Hell, he *was* desperate enough to text the guys. He dug his phone from his pocket and typed CODE RED to the group text.

The replies came in immediately.

MACK: Oh, fuck. What happened?

COLTON: Shit. Did you fuck up already?

VLAD: She's waiting for me in bed.

COLTON: Holy. Fucking. Shit. ALREADY?

NOAH: Damn. You're a legend.

MACK: Liv says to put the food in the fridge if you didn't eat it. She worked hard on that meal.

MALCOLM: Why aren't you in bed with her?

VLAD: Because I'm freaking out.

MALCOLM: Where are you?

VLAD: In the bathroom.

MACK: NOOOOO

COLTON: JFC, dude. Light a match.

NOAH: She can't hear you, can she?

DEL: Seriously. Nothing kills the mood like a fart.

MACK: Maybe he should try to squeeze one out just in case, you guys.

COLTON: No fucking way, Mack. That could go very badly. I've made that mistake before. I was at a girl's apartment and thought it was a fart but it wasn't and that got awkward.

VLAD: I have medicine now!

MALCOLM: Ignore them, Vlad. You've got this. You love this woman. Just remember that.

VLAD: But what if she's disappointed?

COLTON: You're asking the wrong guy.

MACK: Shut the fuck up, Colton. Vlad needs our help.

MALCOLM: She won't be disappointed. Just show her how you feel and remember what you've learned in the manuals.

COLTON: And if you think you have to fart—

Vlad closed out his text messages and stood.

He stared in the mirror. Ran a hand down his face. A face he'd looked at a million times but now seemed different. Because he was seeing it through her eyes all of a sudden. She'd called him beautiful. And she wanted him.

And he was hiding in the goddamned bathroom.

He threw open the door and crutched as fast as he could up the stairs. When he entered his bedroom, she shot to her feet from where she'd been waiting on the edge of the bed. "I was afraid you'd changed your mind."

"Never."

He advanced toward her in quick, long strides on his crutches before tossing them to the floor. Standing on both feet, he hauled her against him and lowered his mouth to hers. The frantic kissing began again. With thick, clumsy fingers, he found the zipper at the back of her dress and tugged it down. As the dress pooled at their feet, every careful plan to go slowly, to cherish every second, evaporated in a haze of need. Patience was a virtue he no longer possessed, replaced by a hunger he couldn't control. And his one fleeting coherent thought was to at least recognize her own ravenous response. She clung to him, and he clung to her.

Beneath his hands, the skin of her back was hot and smooth, soft where he was rough. When he slid his hands up her spine, he brushed the clasp of her bra. Panting, he whispered, "Can I?"

"Yes," was her breathless answer.

Like a bumbling teen, he fumbled with the hook until it finally gave way, and he had just enough functioning brain power left to laugh at the absurdity of fact that he'd just unclasped his first bra. But that, too, evaporated the instant she stepped back from him and the straps of her bra fell down her shoulders. The curves of her breasts kept the lace in place, the cups molded around each soft mound of flesh. As he watched, she shimmied once, and the lace dislodged. The bra fell to the floor, leaving her bare to his gaze. And only then did time finally screech to a halt. How long had he imagined this moment? Dreamed of it? So many years of longing, but now that she finally stood before him, he froze with indecision. His hands twitched with a need to feel that soft flesh beneath his palms, to thumb her taut nipples. Did he . . . could he just reach out and touch her?

"Vlad," she whispered. As she spoke, she placed her hands atop his, which had somehow come to rest uselessly at her hips.

He tightened his fingers. "I'm so nervous."

"So am I."

"You are?"

"This is as important to me as it is to you."

"I don't want you to be disappointed."

"How could I be?"

"Because I'm not going to last long. Once I'm inside you, I—" He chuffed out a laugh and pressed his forehead to hers.

"I don't care how long you last. I want you."

"Lie down." The words came out an order, gruff and urgent, because just as he feared, he was about to lose control. And he nearly did as she sat down on the mattress and reclined. His fingers trembled as he shed his jacket and worked at the buttons of his shirt. When the sleeves got stuck on his wrists, he swore a blue streak and ripped them from his body. Before him, Elena shimmied out of her panties and reached for him.

Oh, God. God. It took three tries to undo his pants, and even then, all he could manage was to shove them down over his hips before he crawled one-legged onto the mattress and covered her body with his. His erection found a soft nest between her thighs, and every cell in his body exploded. With a groan, he buried his face against her neck.

Beneath him, Elena wiggled her legs around his waist.

Wait. Shit. He lifted his head. "Condoms. In the drawer."

"I'm on birth control."

Thank God. Elena reached between them, encircled his erection with her fingers, and guided him toward her entrance. If he had a single functioning brain cell, he'd try to imprint the memory of this. The first time making love to his wife. But his body had become a machine with a single mission. To be inside her. To consummate their marriage. To claim her.

"Please," she begged.

Without fanfare, without foreplay, he entered her in a hard thrust. A sound emerged from his throat that was barely human. She gasped and arched into him, driving him farther inside her body. She was tight and warm and wet, and . . . Oh, God. Vlad sought her mouth with his. Anything to distract from the fission reaction erupting inside him. She moved beneath him and lifted her legs.

"Vlad," she moaned, fingers digging into his back.

Bracing his good knee against the mattress, he moved inside her. Somehow, his body knew how, but what it didn't instinctively know, he'd learned from the manuals. He slowly withdrew to the tip and then back into the embrace of her body. She cradled him with her arms, her body, her heat. Together their bodies found a rhythm, a pace as natural as if they'd done this a hundred times before. As if this was what they'd been meant for all along.

And beneath him, she made noises that drove him mad, but tenderness was there too. And gratitude. The guys were right. This was a gift. A sacrament. A promise all its own.

"Elena," he gasped. His body was its own master. Seeking pleasure, giving pleasure, finding pleasure like he'd never felt before. He could never write this. How could he ever capture in the written word what this felt like? "This— I'm sorry. Oh, God, I'm sorry. I can't stop."

She clung to him tighter and urged him on. "Don't stop. I just want to be with you."

Not yet. Not yet. He chanted it in his mind, but it was no use. Atoms collided. Stars exploded. He choked out her name and shuddered as wave after wave released inside her. He collapsed in a heap of weak knees and stunned muscles. She sought his kiss with a shuddered breath, and still nestled inside her, he feasted on her mouth languidly. Atop the blanket, he found one of her hands and laced their fingers together. Tenderness swelled in his chest, and the urgency of desire faded into a sweeter ache to simply hold her, breathe her in, finally stretch out the seconds.

"I waited so long for you," he whispered. A tear dripped from his eye to her cheek as he pulled back to gaze at her. "There's never been anyone else for me, Elena, because I never wanted anyone else."

A muted sob tore from her throat. "I'm sorry I hurt you."

He silenced her with his lips. He didn't want any more regrets between them. Not tonight.

Vlad gingerly rolled to the side, careful not to wrench his leg. She leaned over him, placed a soft kiss in the center of his abs, and told him she'd be right back. He lifted his head so he could watch her naked body walk across the room. When the bathroom door closed, he sat up and undid his brace so he could finally remove his pants. Then he returned to bed and reclined against the headboard. When the bathroom door opened, his entire heart walked out with a shy smile.

"Come here," he said, holding out his arm. "I need to hold you."

She crawled across him and then stretched out along his side. With her hand pressed to her chest, she traced a lazy circle atop his heart.

"How do you feel?" he asked.

"Happy. How do you feel?"

"Pushkin himself could not find the words."

She sighed and pressed her cheek to his chest. "You are absurdly romantic."

"Elena, I don't know how to tell if you . . . Did you . . ."

She kissed his chest. "No, but it doesn't matter."

"It matters to me. I want you to feel everything I do."

"I do. And it was perfect."

"Next time, I will take care of you first."

She rose up on her elbow and grinned down at him. "There's going to be a next time?"

He scowled playfully. "There's going to be a next time in about twenty minutes. Sooner, if I can recover quicker."

She laughed and lowered her brow to his. "We have to be careful with your leg."

"I don't care about my leg. You healed my heart."

She lifted her head, lips trembling. "There you go again. Being absurdly romantic."

"Not romantic. Just happy." A tear rolled down her cheek. He brushed it away with his thumb.

Then he held her against him, heart to heart, stroking away her pain and scars, until finally, at long last, husband and wife fell asleep together for the first time.

CHAPTER TWENTY-ONE

Elena couldn't remember the last time she'd slept so well. No bad dreams. No jaw-clenching headaches. No middle-of-the-night anxieties. Just a deep, cleansing sleep. Waking up was even better, because she opened her eyes to find a pair of soft brown pools of molasses staring down at her.

"Hi," she whispered.

He dropped a gentle kiss on her lips. "Good morning."

"How long have you been awake?"

"About ten minutes." He brushed a curl from her face.

"Have you been watching me sleep?" Her cheeks heated at the thought. She was not a cute sleeper. She drooled and made weird noises sometimes.

"I have," he said smoothly. "I've waited a really long time to wake up next to you. I wanted to remember it."

He kissed her again, this time with a little more intent. "I wish we could stay in bed all day."

"What time do you have to be at the arena?" He was supposed to start longer rehab sessions today with the on-site trainers.

"Ten."

"What time is it now?"

He nuzzled her neck. "A little before nine."

"I missed my plane again," she whispered.

"Money well wasted." He hauled her across his lap. As he crunched to a sitting position, his arms came around her, and he kissed her deeply. And before long, he was hard and insistent between her legs. But when Elena reached between them to guide him inside her, he shook his head. "You first."

Vlad leaned back on one hand and slid his other hand between her legs. She gasped and tipped her head back as he began to stroke and circle. "Rub on me," he coaxed.

Her eyes flew open. She didn't know what he meant. He flexed his hips, and his hard length slid back and forth through her wetness. "Like that," he rasped. All the while, he continued to stroke her with his fingers.

Elena gripped his shoulder to hold on. The sensations he generated were too much and not enough. When he crunched up again, bringing her sex against the coarse hair of his hard stomach, she lost all sense of time. She rocked against him.

"You're so pretty, Elena," he whispered. "I can't stop looking at you."

She gazed down at him. Between their bodies, he covered her breast with his hand and flicked his thumb across her nipple before bending and sucking it into his mouth.

"Vlad," she cried, throwing her head back.

"That's it, my love. Let me take care of you."

His thumb once again found the pulsing nub of her sex, and

she seized up in an explosion of color and sound. Wave after wave of pleasure rocketed through her from the tip of her head to the ends of her toes. She trembled and shook and called his name over and over again.

He held her tightly as he thrust up inside her, and the sensations began again. She moved atop him, riding him faster and faster until their groans merged and mingled, until she crested again and felt him shudder, her name wrenched from his mouth.

"Oh, God," she moaned, dropping her forehead to his shoulder. "I can't believe we waited this long. All this time, this is what we've been missing."

Panting, he fell back against the bed. "I don't think I would have been very good at it when I was younger."

She gazed down at him, his eyes closed and his brow sweaty. "Why are you good at it now?"

The corner of his mouth curled up in a cheeky smile. "I watch a lot of dirty movies."

She laughed. "Liar. I know your little secret."

He peeled open one eye. "What secret?"

Elena crawled off his lap and settled next to him. Both eyes open now, he watched her carefully. "What secret?" he asked again.

"Tell me about your book club."

Vlad blinked and then coughed. "Who—who told you about that?"

"Are you mad?"

"No. I just . . . I wanted to tell you myself."

"Did you really join the club because of me?" she prodded.

He opened and closed his mouth before finally answering. "Yes. At first. I was desperate to find a way to make you want me the way I wanted you."

She closed her eyes. "Vlad, I'm sorry—"

"Hey." He stroked her arm. "Look at me."

She opened her eyes reluctantly.

"You remember that old coach I had, the one you hated?"

"Yeah?" What he could possibly have to do with this conversation, though, Elena had no idea.

"You remember how my parents pulled me off his team when I was sixteen?"

"Yeah."

"We told everyone it was because the schedule was getting in the way of school, but that wasn't the truth." His Adam's apple bobbed in his throat with a hard swallow. "He was pretty abusive to me."

"Abusive how?" Her brows pulled together in a single, angry line.

"I didn't exactly meet the ideal of a manly Russian hockey player."

Elena sat up fully. "What are you talking about? You were one of the best players on the team!"

"I was soft."

"I don't even want to know what that means." She crossed her arms under her breasts.

"I'm emotional, Elena."

"Yeah, so?"

"I cry. A lot."

She threw her hands out. "So?"

"I never had a girlfriend. Never disrespected girls the way the other guys did. I read poetry, for God's sake. Plus, my best friend was a girl. Coach picked on me for it. He used to call me some pretty vicious names. Ugly names. I'm sure you can imagine."

Her heart thudded with rage. It didn't take a genius to figure it out. Russian men embraced some toxic ideas about masculinity.

"My parents overheard him once, and they defended me. He said I was lucky just to be there. That every team needed a duster. If I tried to stick around, that's all I'd be because I was . . . I was too much of a pussy for higher play."

She pried her clenched jaw apart. "I am going to find that man and remove his balls with a spoon."

"How very Russian of you." He brushed her hair off her forehead. "The point is, I didn't realize how much his words had become part of how I defined myself until I found the book club. I thought I was reading romance to fix our marriage, but I ended up realizing I need to fix myself too. To accept myself."

"You learned all that from romance novels?"

"Not just the novels, but my relationship with the guys. I've never been so accepted, so valued. I realized there are a lot of men like me. Men who aren't afraid to be vulnerable. And these books, they show you what it's like to be truly respected. I didn't just see how I wanted to be treated in a relationship. I saw how I wanted to treat myself. How I deserved to be treated. How I deserved to be loved."

Her heart sank. "And that you deserved better than me?"

"No." He sat up and cupped her face. "That's what I'm trying to say. When I joined the book club, I thought you left me because you didn't believe I was good enough for you."

Her heart cracked. "Vlad—"

He pressed his fingertip to her lips. "But I realized that I was the one who believed that. I'm still working on it. Even right now, there's a part of me that is scared this is just a dream, that you're not really here, that you couldn't possibly feel about me the way I've always felt about you."

A tear dripped down his cheek. Elena wiped it away before

pressing her brow to his. "How could you ever not know that you deserved to be loved?"

"How could you ever think that you were just a burden?"

She laughed thickly. "It's sort of a miracle we've made it this far, isn't it?"

"Maybe this is just how our story was supposed to be written."

She kissed him and wiped her cheeks. "So what do we do now?"

Vlad tugged her back down to his chest and wrapped his arms around her. "We get up, take a bath together"—she mmm'd against his skin—"and we take it day by day for a while."

"I like the sound of that," she said, burrowing closer to his warmth.

He hugged her tighter. "It's going to be okay now, Lenochka. Everything is going to be okay."

A little less than an hour later, Elena pulled into the employee and player parking lot of the arena.

"Can I walk in with you?" she asked.

Vlad grinned. "I'd love that."

The entire building vibrated with an indescribable energy. The next game in the Stanley Cup was tomorrow night, and it was in Nashville again. A small piece of her heart broke for Vlad that he was missing out on what was essentially the pinnacle of any player's career, but he displayed none of the sadness that he had a week ago. They approached a T at the end of the hallway, and she followed Vlad when he turned left. A short distance later, two automatic doors blocked their way. Vlad swiped his player credentials on the keypad to their right, and the doors swung open with a whoosh and a rush of air.

Her steps faltered just inside the doors of what was basically a small-town hospital. A bright center room featured what looked like rehab equipment, and along the perimeter were separate rooms for X-rays, MRI machines, trainers' offices, and— "Is that an operating room?"

"Sometimes we have to get stitched up before going back out on the ice," Vlad said. He stopped and hopped around to face her. "Should I just text you when I'm done?"

"Sure."

"What are you going to do while I'm here?"

"I think I'll go to Alexis's café and get you some more gluten-free cookies."

"She will be happy to see you."

They stared at each other awkwardly. Elena bit her lip. "Um . . ."

He smiled. "Come here."

She rose on tiptoe as he dipped his face toward hers. And there, in full view of the entire training staff, he kissed her. "See you in a little while," he said.

Elena wondered as she walked back out to the car if it was normal at her age to still feel the kind of teeth-tingling giddiness of a teenage girl. Whether normal or not, she felt it. And soon, the entire team staff was going to likely know about it. Not just that Vlad's wife had been there, and not just that he'd kissed her, but that she walked out grinning and sighing like the front row of a Harry Styles concert.

When she walked into ToeBeans a few minutes later, Alexis once again spotted her immediately and greeted her with the same enthusiasm as the first time.

"Elena!" Alexis raced over and hugged her. All of Vlad's friends were huggers. She was trying to get used to it. Alexis pulled back. "I'm so glad you're here. Is Vlad with you?"

"No, I just dropped him off at the arena for rehab." Elena's face grew warm. She hadn't seen Alexis since the disaster at the party. "I'm sorry about what happened the other night."

Alexis shook her head and waved a dismissive hand. "No need to apologize. We all rather enjoyed seeing Vlad lose it over you."

Elena blinked rapidly for a moment. "You did?"

"That man wears his entire heart on his sleeve, and it's all yours." Alexis shrugged with giddiness. "We're so happy that you two are trying to work it out."

At whatever expression must have crossed Elena's face, Alexis winced. "I'm sorry. That was rather personal. I'm not trying to pry."

"No, don't apologize. It's just all very . . . *new*. I don't really know what to say."

"I understand," Alexis said. "When Noah and I finally got together after being just friends for a long time, I was so scared to jinx it. It's scary when a relationship changes from one thing to another."

For some reason, Elena felt herself opening up to Alexis. "There are things I need to figure out."

"Of course."

"I still want to be a journalist."

"And you should try to find a way to make it happen."

"I just have a lot of questions about the requirements of my visa and . . . sorry. I don't know why I'm dumping this on you."

"Because I asked, and because we are becoming friends, I hope."

"I hope so too."

"I don't know if this helps or not, but a good friend of mine is an immigration attorney. She specializes in asylum cases, but maybe you could talk to her."

"Yes, I—I would love that. Thank you."

"Her office is just up the street, actually. You probably passed it. Her name is Gretchen Winthrop. I'd be happy to let her know you might be calling."

Elena filed the name away in her memory as she nodded. "That would be incredible. Thank you." She laughed self-consciously again. "You've all been so nice to me when you didn't have to be."

"Are most people not nice?"

"In my world, yes."

"Well," Alexis said, laying a gentle hand on Elena's arm. "You're in a different world now. And we care about one another in this one."

Once again, before she could formulate a response, Alexis plunged forward into the next subject. "Anyway, I have been seriously dreaming about your blinis from the party. They were so good."

She tugged Elena toward a table.

"I will make you some more, if you'd like."

Alexis beamed. "*That* would be awesome."

Elena hung out at the café for a half hour, and then she walked up and down the street to visit some shops to kill time. Finally, Vlad texted her that he was done. He was waiting for her just outside the parking lot when she pulled up. She helped him get in, and as soon as she returned to the driver's side, he leaned across the console, wrapped a hand around the back of her head, and kissed her.

"How fast can you drive?" he rasped.

She drove very, very fast.

CHAPTER TWENTY-TWO

"Something smells good."

The next morning, Elena looked up as she pulled a tray of biscuits from the oven. She'd woken up early to make some breakfast before Vlad had to leave for rehab. Colton was going to take him, because they apparently had a book club meeting afterward, but she wanted to feed him first.

When Vlad crutched into the kitchen bringing all his morning sexiness, though, she wished she'd stayed in bed and woken him up another way.

"Good morning," she greeted. He reached around her to grab a biscuit.

She batted him away. "They're too hot. They'll lose their shape."

"But I'm hungry. We didn't eat much last night, remember?"

He stood behind her, lips on her shoulder, hands on her hips. "Can I help?"

She pointed to a stool on the other side of the island, a very safe distance away. "No. Sit. You need to take it easy on your leg today."

"You're as bad as the trainers." He winked as he said it, though.

He grabbed a bag of ice from the freezer and sat on one of the stools to balance it on his knee.

"You okay?"

She looked up at his tone. "Why wouldn't I be?"

His cheeks pinked. "I got a little aggressive when I woke you up in the night."

Wonderfully so. And more than once. Last night had been incredibly eye-opening about how much her tenderhearted husband had learned from the pages of romance novels.

Elena bit her lip. "I liked it."

"Yeah?" That lazy smile returned, and so did her libido. He removed the ice from his leg, stood up, and crutched around to stand behind her again. His lips nibbled her earlobe.

She laughed throatily but tipped her head to the side to give him access to that tender spot where her pulse betrayed her dirty mind. When his hands snuck up the front of her shirt, she turned into a hussy. "How much time do we have?"

"More than enough."

Elena spun in his arms and peeled her shirt from her torso. Vlad didn't need any more encouragement. He wove his fingers in her hair, tilted her head back, and commandeered her mouth. All the while, his other hand caressed her until she whimpered.

She was halfway to *oh, God* when the back door opened.

"Not a single word."

A half hour later, Vlad slid into Colton's front seat and slammed the door shut.

Colton threw his hands up. "Why the hell didn't you check your texts? I told you I was going to be early."

"Because I was *busy*. And I'd still be doing it if you hadn't walked into my house without knocking."

"I did knock. No one answered. Why was the door unlocked?"

Because he'd been too torqued up yesterday to remember to lock it. Christ. Vlad had managed to cover Elena's body with his own before Colton could see anything, but he'd seen enough. And heard enough.

"But, I mean, it seems like things are going well—"

"Not. One. Word."

Colton did a bad job of not laughing as he started the car.

"You are going to apologize to her in an appropriate way that doesn't further traumatize her. You violated her privacy. You violated *my* privacy. And you abused the boundaries of friendship. Are we clear?"

"Yes, but—"

"Are. We. Clear?"

Colton sulked silently for a moment. "I don't like it when the Russian is mad at me," he said.

"I don't like being mad at you either."

They shared a tense glance, and then Colton grinned. "Things are good, though, right?"

Vlad groaned and banged his head against the seat. But then he stopped and felt his own mouth curl into a matching grin. "Yes, it is good."

"Look at you, Fabio." Colton peeled one hand from the steering wheel and punched Vlad's arm.

The drive to the arena took longer than normal because the city had detoured traffic an entire block around the arena. Vlad had Colton pull up to one of the police officers at the barricades.

He was about to introduce himself when the cop said, "Holy shit. You're Vlad Konnikov."

The officer reached through the open window with an open palm. Vlad accepted the bro-shake.

"How's the leg? Damn, I can't believe you're not playing."

"I'm here for rehab. I'll be back out there next season."

The officer pounded the door and waved them through. Colton laughed. "I never knew what that felt like until now."

"What *what* felt like?"

"Being totally ignored next to someone famous."

"He's obviously more of a hockey fan than country music."

"Blasphemy." Colton pulled onto the parking ramp and found an open player's spot close to the door. He helped Vlad get out and walked slowly to keep pace with Vlad's slow crutch.

"What are you going to do while I'm here?" Vlad asked.

"I'll find another college girl to thrill with my presence."

Vlad glowered. Colton laughed. "I'm kidding. I have a book to read."

He left Colton sitting in one of the massage chairs and met the trainers in the rehab room. An hour later, he was pretty sure they were actively trying to kill him.

Vlad grunted through pain as Madison hovered nearby and ordered him to do one more rep. Vlad growled in her direction and she rolled her eyes. "You don't scare me, Vlad. I used to work for the Red Wings."

He let out an *argh* and pushed through the last rep. Then he collapsed on his back on the floor in a heap of whimpers. Being injured sucked. Of course, most of his weakness this morning was from lack of sleep, and he wouldn't trade that for anything.

Madison handed him a bottle of water, and as he sat up to gulp it down, a shadow appeared next to him. He looked up to find his coach, Sawyer Mason. It was the first time Vlad had seen him since the injury.

"Just thought I'd come check on our boy," Coach said, holding out a hand to help Vlad to his feet. Or, rather, foot. Madison was waiting with his crutches.

"I am good. Things feel good."

"Madison and Doc have been keeping me posted."

Most people, including Elena, figured a coach would be more closely involved when a player got hurt, but a head coach was like the CEO of a corporation. He was in charge of everything and relied on his lower-level staff to deal with the daily operations. So, Vlad was touched that Coach had taken the time today of all days to come see him.

"I hope you're coming tonight," Coach said.

"To the game?"

"No, to my daughter's ballet recital," Coach snarked. "Yes, the game. It will be good for the team to see you there. Bring your wife. Use the owner's suite."

Vlad's heart pounded. "The owner's suite?"

"There's plenty of room, and Rudolph would much rather have you to talk to than his asshole family." Miles Rudolph was the team's owner.

Coach didn't give Vlad time to refuse. "I'll tell them you're coming tonight. Don't let us down." Then, with a hearty pat on the shoulder, he left.

Vlad found Colton facedown on a massage table getting a shoulder rubdown from the same trainer as the other day.

He cleared his throat. "I'm done."

The trainer jumped back, face red. Again. Colton thanked her and sat up before she raced off. Vlad waited by the door, and when Colton approached, Vlad smacked him upside the head. "She is too young for you."

"She offered to help with the kink in my neck."

"I bet."

"The guys are already at the diner," Colton said.

Malcolm, Mack, and Noah were at their regular table when Colton and Vlad arrived. Del, Gavin, and Yan were on the road with the team and wouldn't be joining them.

"Well, well, well," Mack crooned. "Would you look at that, boys? Someone's got a smile on his face this morning."

At Mack's teasing, Vlad quickly lifted the enormous menu to hide his red cheeks.

Mack tipped it back down. "You're not getting off that easy. Spill it. How are things going?"

Colton clapped his hands. "Oh, let me tell, please?"

Vlad scowled at him, but it quickly became another goofy smile. The entire table broke into laughter.

"Seriously?" Mack gaped.

Vlad's cheeks got hot. "Things are going well."

"Oh, they're better than *well*," Colton snorted. "When I walked in this morning—"

Vlad pointed. "No."

Mack lifted his eyebrows. "What happened?"

"Let's just say I walked into the kitchen at the wrong time."

"Hey," Vlad snapped. "That is my wife you are talking about."

"The kitchen?" Mack snorted. "Damn. You're not wasting any time."

Vlad sheepishly shrugged, and his cheeks heated.

The guys clasped their hands in front of their hearts and let out a collective *awwww*. The entire restaurant swiveled to stare and then quickly looked away. Most of them were regulars, too, and were used to the weird shit that came from the Bro table.

Vlad hid his blush behind the menu again, but the guys laughed and yanked it away. "Why are you embarrassed?" Malcolm asked. "This is wonderful, man. Wonderful."

Mack leaned back in his chair. "Now *this* is a version of the Russian I like."

"What version is that?" Vlad asked, grinning because he felt fucking fantastic all of a sudden.

"The *I got my girl back* version," Noah said, leaning forward to offer him a hearty handshake.

"Careful, though," Mack said. "Don't get too far ahead of yourself. Remember to take this slowly. You two are in that awesome early stage of your relationship, but you have a lot to unpack."

Noah smacked Mack upside the head. "Way to be a downer, douchebag. Let the Russian enjoy the moment."

"I'm just telling him to go slow. I went too fast with Liv at first, and it damn near blew up in my face."

Vlad closed his menu, suddenly eager to change the subject. "Let's talk about my book."

Colton shook his head. "If Tony and Anna haven't done the humping yet, I'm not interested."

Elena pulled into a parking spot in front of an office building with a sign announcing the law offices of Gretchen Winthrop, the immigration attorney Alexis had recommended. Elena fed some quarters into the parking meter and locked the car. A bell over the door jingled when she walked into the unassuming square of worn cubicles and stained carpets in the street-level corner of a building a few blocks from Alexis's café.

The waiting room was a small square with two rows of beige chairs and the odor of mold. A receptionist sat behind a raised counter to the right of the entry. "Can I help you?"

Elena approached the counter. "I am Elena Konnikova. I'm here to see Gretchen Winthrop."

The woman smiled. "Do you have an appointment?"

"Yes. I called this morning."

"Have a seat, and I'll let her know you're here."

The walls of the waiting room were lined with framed newspaper articles about immigration cases and signs listing KNOW YOUR RIGHTS and WHAT TO DO IF ICE SHOWS UP.

"Elena?" She stood as the receptionist returned. "You can head on back."

The office was small enough that she needed no other directions than that. Gretchen's was the only office with its own door, which now stood open. Elena knocked and Gretchen waved her in.

"It's nice to meet you," she said, gesturing toward the chair facing her desk for Elena to sit. "Alexis gave me a heads-up that you'd be calling. What can I do for you?"

"I'm just exploring some options right now, and I have some questions."

"Hopefully, I will have some answers, but I should warn you that I don't specialize in your type of immigration."

"I know," Elena said, setting her purse at her feet. "I'm not just here about me."

Gretchen leaned back in her own chair. "Okay."

"I wonder if you ever work with victims of sex trafficking."

Gretchen lifted an eyebrow. "Seriously?"

"Yes, I am serious."

Gretchen smiled. "That was sarcasm. Nearly half of my clients are victims of some kind of human trafficking. Why?"

"What options do they have? Immigration wise, I mean."

"Some are given refugee status in the U.S. if they were brought here illegally and against their will. It varies widely."

"What about Russian or Ukrainian girls? Have you ever helped them?"

"Some. Why?"

Elena crossed her legs. "My visa does not allow me to work here."

Gretchen squinted at the sudden change of subject. "That's correct. Your status allowed you to attend college, but you cannot hold a job under your visa."

"Do you know why I had to leave Russia?"

Gretchen covered her ears. "If you're about to confess something about the nature of your marriage, I strongly advise you to stop now."

"What I mean is, are you aware of what happened to my father?"

"No."

"He went missing while working on a story about sex trafficking of girls. I believe the story is why he was—" She stumbled on the words. "Why he disappeared."

"I'm afraid I'm not following."

"If I stay here, is there *any* way I can work as a journalist without violating the terms of my visa?"

"Well, I assume you and Vlad will petition for green cards at some point. Most professional athletes do."

"But that could take years, yes?"

Gretchen shifted in her chair. "Look, Elena. I hope this doesn't come across as rude, but this is not exactly a bad problem to have. You're married to a very wealthy man who is all but guaranteed permanent residency. What is the rush?"

"Because I want to work. I want to do something that matters. I have something important I've been working on."

"I understand. I didn't mean to insult you. I just—" Gretchen cut herself off with a sigh. She stood, walked to one of several file cabinets lining the wall of her office, and opened the top drawer of the first. "See this?" She turned around. "This is just the As. These are people I am currently representing or have represented, hard-working people who want the chance to stay and work in the United States just like you. The difference is"—she slid the drawer shut — "they have *no* options. They are driven by desperation."

She returned to her chair.

"The American immigration system is designed specifically to cater to people like you. Rich, white people from equally rich, white countries. You are in very little risk of being deported. Your husband was able to cut to the front of a very, very long line simply because he can play hockey. Americans love immigrants like you."

"You don't seem to like my husband and me very much."

"What I dislike is the system that gives you the ability to explore your options to best suit your needs, when the majority of immigrants to our country have almost no options."

"Even for refugees?"

Gretchen snorted in an ugly way. "The word is almost meaningless." She tilted her head and studied Elena. "There are ways to make a difference here without violating your visa, Elena. That is what you're trying to figure out, correct?"

Elena nodded. She just had been too skittish to say it out loud. It still felt so sudden. The thought of leaving now, well, she couldn't stand to think about it. But how could she turn her back on everything she'd worked for? How could she turn her back on the women like Marta? How could she turn her back on her father?

"There are plenty of nonprofits who need volunteers, and someone with your skills would be incredibly valuable. Your language skills alone would be vital. I know it wouldn't be the same as earning money for your work, but you could still accomplish some of the things that are important to you."

Gretchen glanced at her watch. "I'm afraid I have to cut this short. I have another meeting in ten minutes. But I can assure you, if you are looking for ways to use your journalism skills to help clients like mine, the need is endless."

Elena thanked Gretchen for her time. She didn't get any real answers, but she got enough for her brain to start turning.

She'd just gotten back into her car when her phone rang. Assuming it was Vlad, she answered immediately.

"Elena, it's Yev."

Her free hand white-knuckled the steering wheel. "Yev. Hello."

He chuckled. "You sound nervous."

"Yes, to be honest." At least that wasn't a lie.

"Well, no need. I'm very pleased to be making this call."

"Oh . . ." She sounded breathless, like a little girl.

"Is everything okay? Did I catch you at a bad time?"

Yep. Totally bad time. Because her entire life and what she thought she knew and wanted had changed in the past week. "Of course not," she breathed. "This is perfect."

"Good," Yev said. "Because I would like to officially offer you a job."

A sensation she hadn't been prepared for greeted his words. *Disappointment.* "Thank you. That is . . . wow."

"We understand that it is a big move from America, so we don't expect you immediately. But do you think you can start in a month?"

A sour taste stung the back of her tongue. "A month?"

"If you need more time, we can make that work."

"Um, no, that's not it."

"You're sure you're okay?"

Elena winced but then reminded herself this was a man she'd known all her life. "Yev, I am so grateful for the job offer, but I actually think I will have to decline."

There was a pause and then a creak of his chair. "Well, this is unexpected. May I ask why?"

"I might not be quite ready to leave America yet." He made a noncommittal noise, so she rushed forward. "I will always be so grateful that you were willing to take a chance on me."

"Well, it was the least I could do for your father. But can I be honest? I'm kind of relieved."

She laughed. "You are?"

"Now I don't have to worry about you." Another creak of his chair, and she pictured him standing. "What are your plans, then?"

"I don't know yet. I haven't made any plans. I met with an immigration attorney, though, and she at least gave me some things to think about."

"Good for you."

"Yev, thank you so much for understanding."

"Of course. You're like family, Elena. You know that."

"I do. And it means a lot."

"You'll let me know if you need anything else?"

Elena held her breath. "There actually is one thing."

"Name it."

"I sort of lied to you before."

He paused. Then, "I'm listening."

"When you asked if I was looking into my father's disappearance—"

"Oh shit, Elena. What have you been doing?"

"I've been trying to finish his story. I've been doing my own investigation, as much as I could from here."

Silence, then, "And did you find anything interesting?"

"A lot of false leads and dead ends."

"Well, that's not surprising."

"There's one thing I wonder if maybe you'll look into for me."

His sigh could have powered a steamboat. "Elena, you know how dangerous this is."

"I know. And I'm sorry if I'm putting you on the spot."

"What is it you want me to look at?"

"Nikolei 1122."

Silence again. Then, "Where did you hear that?"

Her heart hammered at his tone. "Does it mean something?"

"Not immediately, no. But it could be part of a classification for a police report. The name of the officer and the date, but it could mean anything. Where did you hear that?"

"I have a source inside one of Strazh's clubs."

He let out a string of curse words that had her pulling the phone away from her ear. "Yevgeny—"

"This is madness, Elena. Please tell me you're lying."

"I need to know what happened to him. Don't *you* want to know?"

He swore under his breath. "Does Vlad know what you're working on?"

Cold seeped down her spine. "Not yet."

Seconds ticked by when all she could hear were the sounds of the newsroom in the background and his angry breathing into the phone. "Fine," he finally said. "I'll see what I can find out."

"Thank you—"

"But if I can't find anything, you have to promise me that you'll drop this and move on with your life."

"I promise," she breathed.

Yevgeny hung up without saying goodbye. Elena tossed her phone onto the passenger seat and rested her forehead against the steering wheel. She waited for the panic to set in. She'd just turned down the job she'd always wanted. A job that would have given her everything she thought she needed, everything she'd been working toward. A chance to honor her father's legacy. Access to the information and people who could help her figure out what really happened to him. A chance to save women like Marta.

But she didn't have to go back to Russia to do those things. She had options she'd never considered before because she'd never *let* herself consider them before. She'd never allowed herself to believe that she could have any kind of future in America because she'd never believed she could have any kind of future with Vlad.

She eased the car back onto the road and pointed it toward home. When the phone rang again, she knew this time it was Vlad.

"Hey," he said when she answered.

She considered telling him immediately about her call with Yevgeny but decided to wait. There was too much to tell him. And she *would* tell him. Just not yet. "How'd it go today?"

"Good. My coach came to see me."

"Finally."

"He, um . . ." Vlad cleared his throat. "Would you be willing to go to the game with me tonight?"

"Like a real hockey wife?"

"Like *my* wife."

She bit her lip to stave off emotion. "I would love that," she finally answered.

He let out a relieved breath, as if he had actually thought she'd say no. "What time will you be home?" he asked.

"In about a half hour."

"Good. Meet me in our bed."

CHAPTER TWENTY-THREE

The team sent a car for them just before seven that night so they wouldn't have to navigate the downtown traffic.

"I'm nervous," Elena said.

Vlad slung his arm around her in the back seat and kissed her hair. She smelled like orange blossoms and looked amazing in her too-big hockey jersey with his name across the back. "It will be fun."

"What if people ask me questions about where I've been or—"

"They won't. And if for some reason they do, I'll be there to deal with them."

Vlad was nervous, too, but for a different reason. It had already been released to the media that he was planning to attend the game, and the team's media staff wanted him to do a live on-air interview after the first period. All of which meant there was zero chance that an image of him with Elena wouldn't find its way into Russian media. But he still hadn't told his parents that Elena was even here with him, much less that they were *together*.

Vlad dug his phone from the pocket of his jeans. "We need to make a phone call."

She looked up at him. "Who?" She immediately made an *o* with her mouth.

"I don't want them to find out from a picture in the press."

"I don't either."

Vlad hit the button for his mother's contact. It would be almost six in the morning in Omsk, so she'd be awake by now. He held his breath as he waited for her to answer.

"You *do* remember my phone number," she said in lieu of hello.

He cut her off before she could lecture him again or, God forbid, get his father involved. "Mama, before you get going, there's someone I want you to talk to."

Elena gave him an *are you kidding?* look as he handed her the phone. But she took it and pressed it to her ear. "Hi, Mama."

Vlad could hear his mother's voice. *"Elena?!"*

Vlad pressed a fist to his mouth to smother a laugh, and Elena pounded her fist into his chest.

"Yes, I'm here," Elena said before pausing. "Well, right now we're on our way to the game." Another pause. "Since the day after the surgery." Elena winced and handed the phone back to him. "She wants to talk to you."

"Vladislav Konnikov, you have so much explaining to do. You lied to me. How long has she been there? When is she leaving? Have you even tried to talk to her?"

"Mama, slow down."

"No, I will not slow down. What is going on?"

"I swear I will explain more later. I just wanted to call so you weren't caught off guard if you see a picture of us together tonight at the game."

"What do you mean *together*?" His mother's voice held the upward lilt of hope.

Vlad met Elena's gaze as he spoke. "I—I took your advice, Mama."

"What do you mean?" she asked again, this time breathlessly.

Vlad traced Elena's lower lip with his thumb. "I think maybe I'll keep some of those details between Elena and me."

She laughed in a weepy way. "Of course. Of course. Oh, I can't wait to tell your father. But what does this mean? Is she staying in Nashville?"

Vlad held Elena's gaze. They hadn't talked about their plans, and he didn't want to answer for her.

Vlad gripped Elena's chin between his thumb and finger and tugged her mouth upward. It turned out that keeping a kiss silent made it all the more potent. It took every bit of willpower he possessed to pull back from her and remember he had his mother on the phone. "I promise I'll tell you more later, but we're almost to the arena now."

"I'm so happy, Vlad. So happy."

"So am I, Mama."

He ended the call. "I have something for you," he murmured against Elena's lips.

She leaned back and gave him a coy smile. "In the car?"

He barked out a laugh and set her back from him. Then he lifted a hip so he could dig into his front pocket. When he pulled out their rings, a small gasp escaped her lips.

"I thought maybe—" He gulped, nervous again. "Since we're going to be in public, I thought maybe we could wear them so people won't ask too many questions."

"Yes," she whispered. Her fingers trembled as she held out her hand and he slid her ring back on. After she repeated the gesture with his, he hauled her onto his lap. He leaned in to kiss her, but she held back. "I heard what Mama asked. If I'm staying in Nashville."

He held his breath.

"Yevgeny offered me the job today. I turned him down." Elena lowered her head to his shoulder. "I have never felt at home anywhere. Not in a long time anyway. Even before my father disappeared, I felt alone. Never safe. Never settled. The only time I feel at home, have ever felt at home, is with you."

Vlad cupped the back of her head and tilted her face toward his. "What are you saying?"

"I want a real marriage too."

The moment called for passion, but the thick swell of emotion in his throat rendered him useless. He pressed his forehead to hers and sucked in a shaky breath. They stayed that way, silently holding each other, until the car slowed and pulled into the traffic around the arena.

The arena was just one block away from the main strip of honky-tonks and music venues that Nashville was famous for, and the driver had to stop several times to let a wall of people and partiers cross the road before advancing toward the same barricade that Colton had driven up to this morning. With a flash of credentials, the police officer let the car through. Elena plastered her face to the window. "There are so many people," she breathed.

And for the first time in his career, Vlad was one of them. Just another spectator relegated to the stands while his team played without him. It stung, but not as badly as it did before. He was healing on pace, and he had Elena, finally, by his side.

The driver dropped them off by the players' entrance. One of the trainers was waiting to meet them with a medical cart to drive them to the service elevator and up to the top floor where the suites were located. That way he wouldn't have to crutch the entire length of the arena.

"Are you going to go see your teammates first?" Elena asked.

"They're warming up already," Vlad answered, waiting for her to get into the golf cart first. "And it's bad luck. I don't want to mess with their concentration."

"You mess with my concentration, and it doesn't end up badly."

He winked at her.

The team owner was already in the suite with members of his family when they walked in. Miles Rudolph waved and walked over to greet them.

"Vlad, so good to see you upright." Rudolph patted him on the shoulder.

"Thank you for letting us use the suite tonight." Vlad moved his crutches aside so he could settle his hand on Elena's back. "This is my wife, Elena."

Rudolph shook her hand. "Finally, I meet the mysterious Elena." He backed up and waved for them to come in. "Please, come in. Get settled. If you need anything at all, let one of the waiters know."

Elena's eyes widened as they walked into the luxurious suite. A full bar was along the right wall, where a bartender filled drinks for the dozen or so guests who were already there. A mouthwatering buffet was set up along the opposite wall, but Vlad had eaten before they left the house because he could never guarantee at events like this that even food labeled gluten-free hadn't been cross-contaminated.

Vlad bent toward Elena's ear. "You want something to drink?"

"I can get it," she said. "You should sit."

"I sit all day."

She lifted an eyebrow at him, and that fiery little expression got him hot and bothered again. God, this was going to be a long night.

"What do you want?" she asked.

"Just water. Thanks." He dropped a kiss on her lips, drawing a surprised look from more than one person in the room. He understood now why she worried about people asking questions. This was the first time most people had ever seen her, and they were not shy about hiding their curiosity.

Vlad crutched slowly toward the set of VIP seats just beyond the glass wall overlooking the ice. He balanced his crutches along the railing. Below, his team skated and warmed up without him. Loud music pulsated from the speakers, and the jumbotron that hung from the ceiling played videos and commercials to distract fans before the game. He'd dreamed his entire life of being here. The Stanley Cup. Thousands of fans screaming and cheering. And he wasn't down there.

"Hey." Elena jolted him out of his brief pity party. She carried a glass of wine for herself and a bottle of water for him. He twisted off the top and downed half the bottle in a long gulp.

"People are looking at you," she said.

He followed her gaze to the stands below, and yes, several fans were turned around in their seats with excited grins. Vlad lifted his hand in a polite wave, and the fans acted as if they'd just been blessed by the ghost of Gordie Howe.

"You should sign autographs for the kids," Elena said.

"I didn't bring a Sharpie."

"I'm on it," Elena said. She set her wine in the cup holder of one of the seats before jogging back up the steps. A moment later, she returned with a marker and a member of the team's PR staff. She started giving orders, and the staffer had no choice but to obey. "Let's invite some of the families with young children to come up here to meet Vlad." She pointed at one family with four children who'd been staring since the minute Vlad appeared. "Just one family at a time."

The staffer nodded and opened the gate that separated the VIP seating from the rest of the stands. They watched as the young man quietly tapped the father on the shoulder, spoke and pointed behind them, and then as the family all gasped at the same time.

A moment later, they all jogged up the stairs to the railing. "Oh my gosh, this is so exciting," said the woman whom he assumed was the mother.

"Would your kids like an autograph?" Elena asked.

After signing his name to two souvenir pucks, a T-shirt, and a game program, he offered to take a picture with the family. Elena stepped away to get out of the photo, but Vlad tugged her back in.

And that's how it went for the next twenty minutes. The PR guy brought up families with children for signatures and selfies, and it was exactly the distraction Vlad needed from the fact that he wasn't down on the ice with his team. Somehow, Elena had known what he needed. Just like she'd known his favorite meals would heal his soul and that he had needed a hug when the guys suggested a party to watch the game.

Elena looped her arm through his and leaned into him. "You okay?"

"I wouldn't be without you."

"There you go again. So romantic."

"Elena?"

She looked up at him. "Hmm?"

"I need to tell you something."

Her lips parted. "What is it?"

"I love you."

She sucked in her bottom lip as her eyes shone with a wet sheen. Around them, the noise of the crowd and the music faded. It was just them, suspended in a collision of past and present.

After a torturously long moment, Elena raised her hand to cup his jaw. "I love you too."

Vlad wiped away the tear that dipped down her cheek, and then he lowered his mouth to hers. He kissed her lightly, lingering just long enough to let her know he meant it and couldn't wait to start the rest of their lives.

Promise Me

"Down. Get down."

Tony grabbed Anna and dragged her back into the ditch. They flattened against the Earth as the rumble of trucks grew louder, closer. Tony covered her with his body as he peeked above the side.

"What do you see?"

He nearly fainted in relief. He rolled onto his back. "Americans. They're Americans."

Tony lifted both hands in the air and slowly stood. A nervous private could still shoot his nuts off if he made too many fast moves. He approached the road, and one of the trucks slowed with a grind of the gears.

"Press," Tony panted. "American."

The driver tipped his cap. "What the fuck are you doing out here?"

Anna scrambled up the side of the ditch. The driver winced. "Sorry, ma'am."

"We need a ride back," she said. "Can you take us?"

"We can get you as far as Minsk, but after that, I don't know."

Anna and Tony jogged to the back of the truck. A young GI held out his hand to help Anna aboard, and Tony shot him a warning dagger with his eyes when the kid admired her too closely.

Then he accepted the outstretched hand of one of the GIs. They sank against the hard benches. Anna closed her eyes and dropped her head back, panting.

"Where you coming from?" Tony asked.

"Barth," the captain answered. "POW camp."

"We're investigating the marches," Tony said. "You find any evidence of them?"

The captain spit on the wooden floor. "Fucking bastards. Some got away. But most that ran were shot. We picked up a couple of stragglers from the sixty-third and left them at the aide station."

Anna's eyes flew open. "The sixty-third?"

"Yeah," the captain said. "Why?"

Anna shot to her feet. Tony grabbed her arm. "I know what you're thinking, but you can't."

She pulled her arm away. "They were in the same camp as members of the 579th," she breathed. Jack's squadron. "I have to talk to them."

She stumbled as the truck lurched. "You can't just jump off, Anna," he said, but she was already threading her way toward the flap of the truck.

She looked back at him. "I have to."

In his two years as a war correspondent, Tony had seen and experienced every kind of horror. But he'd never, not once, panicked the way he was panicking now. He watched her jump off the truck and hesitated a mere second before he took off after her. He landed awkwardly on his leg. "It's too dangerous, Anna. These roads are still crawling with the enemy. I'll be shot if we're captured, but you—" A tortured noise cut off his words.

She kept walking. "I have to go. I have to do this. They might know where Jack is. Don't you understand?"

"I can't let you."

"It is not your decision."

"Anna." He grabbed her arm and whipped her around, tugging her close to his body. "Don't do this to me. *Please.*"

His eyes held hers before dipping to stare longingly at her lips. He lowered his mouth to hers in an almost punishing kiss. She clung to the front of his shirt and let him plunder her mouth, his thumbs digging into her jaw and his fingers pressed against the side of her head. He pulled back just enough to steal her gaze.

She stared at the long road ahead before turning back to him. "Tony," she whispered. "I have to go."

Anna backed away from him with shaky, stumbling steps. She walked away, taking with her the sun and the moon and the tides and the gravity that had become his life force.

"Anna," he pleaded.

"Please, Tony. Don't make this harder."

"Anna, I love you."

Her footsteps faltered.

"I love you, and you don't have to do this. Stay with me. *Stay with me.*"

Suddenly, she was in his arms. "I love you too. I'll stay with you. I'll stay."

CHAPTER TWENTY-FOUR

"Look, I know things are all hot and happy in your house these days, but you can't end the book this way."

Vlad popped a gluten-free cracker in his mouth as he looked up from his notes the next afternoon at Colton's. While he and the Bros plotted out the rest of the book, Elena was meeting the Loners at Alexis's café to talk about cats and Russian tea cakes or something. Then they would join the guys to watch the next Stanley Cup game.

Vlad had been feeling pretty good about life and the book so far, until now. "Why not?"

Mack twisted off the top of a beer. "Because there's no conflict. She just up and decides that she's going to stay with Tony because he asks her to? It's not very satisfying."

"They end up together. How is that not satisfying?"

"Because they haven't really earned their happy ever after," Malcolm said.

Mack pointed with his beer. "Thank you. Yes. You ever get to the end of a book where they end up together without having to overcome any significant obstacles? It sucks. You feel cheated."

Malcolm reached for the bag of crackers, tossed one in his mouth, and immediately spit it out. "This tastes like an Amazon box."

Vlad bristled. "They have faced a ton of obstacles. They've been nearly shot, and they were chased by the SS, and—"

Del shook his head. "Those are external problems, man. *External* obstacles. You have to make them face their internal fears before they can truly have a happy ending." He reached for the crackers. "Let me try one."

"It's your taste buds," Malcolm warned.

Del took a bite and spit it out. "I'd rather shit my pants."

"No, you wouldn't," Vlad snapped. "It is not funny when it is your pants you are shitting."

"It's not like I'd shit someone else's pants."

Noah kicked his feet up on a leather ottoman in front of his chair. "I know I'm the newest member of the group and all and I still don't know much, but I concur with everyone else. I want to see Tony and Anna have to dig deep one last time."

"Not every book has to have some big, dramatic *all is lost* moment," Vlad pouted.

Gavin piped in. "But every book needs a last push to the end that forces a character to have a final epiphany that helps themselves see clearly for the first time."

Vlad crossed his arms and scowled. "So you're saying she shouldn't stay with Tony? She should leave him and go find Jack?"

"She *has* to go look for Jack," Malcolm said. "Otherwise,

has she really chosen Tony? How will he know that she really chose him?"

"Why the hell does that matter?" And why the hell was he taking it so personally?

"It matters because Jack is the one thing still standing in their way emotionally," Malcolm said. "He's everything Tony fears he lacks as a man, and he's the past that Anna can't forget. Until they deal with those issues, it's a cheap way to end the book."

"Did you read the scene?" Vlad argued. "He just told her he loves her. You guys have been riding my magnificent ass to get Tony to advance the relationship. It's the one thing he has feared more than anything else. How is that not digging deep?"

"You said that telling her how he felt about her was his greatest fear," Malcolm said. "But is that really it? Is that what truly scares him?"

"*Yes.*"

"What if she'd left anyway?"

Vlad scowled as he pondered Malcolm's question. "What do you mean?"

"What is the worst possible thing that could happen to him at this point?"

"For her to not feel the same way."

"No," Colton said, suddenly somber in a way Vlad rarely saw his friend. "For her to love him, too, but to leave him anyway."

Silence descended over the room. The reverent, *damn, that's some deep shit* kind of silence.

"Vlad, does Tony believe that Anna would ever choose him over Jack?" Malcolm asked.

"No," he breathed.

"Which means she *has* to go look for Jack," Mack said. "Otherwise, has she really chosen Tony? How will he know that she really wants him?"

"He has to let her go," Noah said.

Vlad shook his head. No. That was too mean. He couldn't do that to Tony.

"More importantly," Malcolm said, "he has to find the faith that their love is strong enough for her to come back to him."

Vlad tossed his notebook. "If you guys know my characters so damn well, then you write it."

Colton tsked and opened a beer. "Sorry, dude. Only you can write the end to your own story."

"I don't think this looks right."

Michelle pulled her tray from one of the large ovens inside the ToeBeans Café kitchen and set it on the cooling counter with a skeptical eye.

Elena peeked over Michelle's shoulder at the golden-brown pastry cups. "They're perfect."

Elena was teaching them how to make korzinochki, a sweet little sour-cream tartlet that had been one of her father's favorites and would be perfect for the watch party later.

"I don't think *that* looks right," Andrea said, pointing at Alexis's cat, Beefcake.

Since ToeBeans was a cat café—Alexis hosted cat adoption events on the weekends—Beefcake came to work with her every day to sit in a window box and intimidate customers. He looked like the bad end of a failed science experiment.

"I should get a cat like that," Claud said, watching from a stool next to the stainless-steel counter inside the kitchen. She declared that morning that she'd be happy to eat the cakes but wanted no part of making them. "I need something to sit in a window box and bare its privates and hiss at men."

"Isn't that basically what you do every day?" Elena asked.

Michelle smothered a laugh and turned around, shoulders shaking. Elena looked at Claud, who had a small smile on her face.

"Okay, these can cool while we make the filling," Elena said.

Alexis gathered all the ingredients—heavy cream, sour cream, and powdered sugar—and measured them into her professional-size mixer. Once the white concoction was the right consistency, they spooned dollops onto the pastries.

"You're pretty damn good at this, you know," Alexis said a few minutes later, adding sliced strawberries to each pastry. "Can I lure you to work for me?"

Elena smiled at the praise. "If I *could* work in America with my visa, I would be a journalist. But I appreciate the offer."

"So, what *are* you going to do now that you've decided to stay?" That was Andrea. "Can you do any kind of journalism?"

"Only on a volunteer basis maybe. I met with Gretchen Winthrop, and she said she has some ideas for me on how I can help. I think I'd love to tell the stories of refugees and asylum seekers who are stuck in the immigration system."

"You'd do it for free?" Linda said.

Elena nodded. "The stories matter more than me getting paid for now."

Claud snorted. "No one is that pure."

Michelle and Elena looked at each other and spoke in unison. "Vlad is."

Alexis smiled and hugged herself. "I can't help but notice your ring."

Elena blushed.

Andrea sighed. "I miss being in love."

"What happened to Jeffrey?" Elena asked.

"It fizzled."

Elena bit her lip. "But, like, he's alive?"

Andrea sighed. "Alive. Just boring."

"This means you're definitely staying, right?" Michelle said, redirecting the conversation to Elena.

"I am. I have some loose ends I need to tie up, but yes. Vlad and I are staying together."

No one asked her what she meant by loose ends, and she was relieved. She still hadn't even told Vlad about the loose ends yet.

Alexis hugged her and squeezed. "I am so glad. You two belong together."

"Should we head over to Colton's?"

Andrea did a little dance. "I cannot believe I'm going to Colton Wheeler's house."

Alexis and Elena carefully boxed up the pastries in pretty pink boxes emblazoned with the logo for ToeBeans and then loaded them into Alexis's car behind the café. Elena was parked up the block in the public lot. Michelle had driven the Loners in her own car and had already headed out.

As Alexis and Elena walked back into the café, Elena's phone buzzed in her pocket. She pulled it out and checked the number on the screen.

Her skin turned to ice.

Vlad curled his phone into his hand as Elena's number went straight to voice mail again.

"She did not say who was on the phone?" he asked.

Alexis hugged herself and shook her head. She'd arrived at Colton's fifteen minutes ago and told him Elena had gotten a strange text and quickly left. Now, she wasn't answering his call.

"It shook her up," Alexis said. "She tried to act like it didn't, but I know it did. I hope I'm not being too nosy." Noah rubbed Alexis's back.

"No. Thank you for telling me." Vlad dialed Elena's number again.

Again, it went straight to voice mail. Something was wrong.

"I'm sure it's nothing to worry about, dude," Mack said. Everyone was gathered in the kitchen, smiling at him with varying degrees of reassurance and concern.

"Can you give me a ride home?" Vlad asked. "I just want to check on her."

Colton nodded, already digging keys from his pocket. He looked at Mack. "You guys hang out here. We'll be back in a few minutes."

Mack nodded. "Keep us posted."

Colton drove faster than normal for him, which was saying a lot, because he tackled every road in his life like the cops were on his tail. The SUV was in the driveway when they got there. It was pulled up in front of the door, crooked, as if she'd raced home so quickly that she couldn't be bothered with the garage.

Colton followed him inside. Vlad called her name from the entryway. When she didn't respond, Colton said he'd check the backyard while Vlad went upstairs. He called her name again. At the top of the stairs, he heard her voice, muffled and frantic, coming from the guest room. The door was closed.

"Elena?"

He knocked on the door and nearly fell backward when she pulled it open. She immediately returned to pacing, phone pressed to her ear.

"I don't understand," she was saying. "Why are you telling me this if you won't give me the report yourself?"

"Who is it, Elena?"

She gave him a fierce headshake. His eyes took in the rest of the scene. Papers were strewn across the bed—folders and scraps of notes and printouts from websites. He crutched closer. There was no rhyme or reason to the chaos. He picked up a folder, flipped it open, and skimmed the top page. None of it made sense. There were notes in her handwriting of what looked like an interview, but about what, he couldn't decipher.

"Elena—"

She held up her hand to silence him again. Then into the phone, she said, "Just wait. You can't drop this on me and then refuse to help. Why the hell did you even call me?" She paused again, and her eyes bugged out. "You know I can't do that!"

Whoever was on the other line ended the call. Elena folded her phone into her hand and began to shake.

"Elena, what the hell is going on? What is all this? Who was that?"

Elena sank onto the mattress. Her pupils were dilated like someone high on Adderall or adrenaline. Her hands shook. Her knees bounced. And when she finally looked up at him, her gaze scared the shit out of him.

Colton's voice called up the stairs then. "Hey, I'm coming up. Is everything okay up here?"

Vlad swiveled on his crutches and hobbled back to the hallway just as Colton appeared at the top of the stairs. "I found her."

"Everything okay?"

He had no idea. "I will be down soon."

Colton looked unconvinced but turned around and headed back down the stairs. Vlad returned to the guest room to now find Elena standing and frantically sorting through the mess on the bed. Frustrated with his inability to move, Vlad tossed his crutches and tested the weight on his foot. He hobbled to her. "Elena, you have to talk to me. What is all this?"

"I have to go back."

"Go back where? Chicago?"

Her hands stalled. "No."

His stomach plummeted. *"Russia?"*

"Just for a few days," she whispered, voice shaking. "Maybe a week."

"Why?"

She turned to face him, a mixture of regret and entreaty tightening her features. "I should have told you about this. I was going to, but there hasn't been time, and—"

"Told me about *what*?" Jesus, it was like they were having two different conversations. He asked her what color the sky was, and she gave him the recipe for borscht.

"This," she said, gesturing toward the mess on the bed. "What I've been working on."

Vlad gripped her shoulders. "Look at me," he said, trying to calm his voice. "Just start at the beginning."

Elena sucked in a breath and let it out. "Okay. But you have to promise not to freak out."

"I'll do my best."

"I've been trying to finish my father's story."

He freaked out. His knees grew weak, so he sank to the edge of the bed and tried to keep up as words spilled from her mouth, but they were gibberish, meaningless. Or maybe it was just his brain refusing to listen, to process.

"Elena." He coughed to clear the sand from his throat. "I don't understand. How long have you been working on this?"

"A while."

"How long?"

"Since I've been in Chicago."

He freaked out a second time. "Are you kidding me?"

"It took me a long time to start to piece everything together, but I've finally started to make progress, Vlad. Real progress."

He stood, carefully, the ginger movement incongruous to the steel in his voice. "This is too dangerous. You have to stop."

"No. I've been careful. I use untraceable email addresses and burner phones. I—"

"Burner phones?" His eyes nearly fell out of their sockets. "Do you hear yourself?"

"Yes. I sound like a journalist. That's what I am."

He raked his hands over his hair.

"Look," she said, picking up something from the bed. "Look at this."

He was doing his best to keep an open mind, but the further he stretched it, the more terrifying possibilities poured in. "What am I looking at?"

"A report from the witness who said they saw my father get on the train that night. But the witness lied. He was nowhere near the train station that night."

"How do you know?"

She hesitated. "My source."

"The person on the phone just now?"

"Yes." She put the paper back and resumed gathering everything into an organized stack.

"Who is he?"

"I can't tell you."

"Jesus, Elena. This isn't a game." He regretted the words and his tone this time, so he tried again. "How does this source know the truth?"

"Because he has seen the original witness report, the one he gave before it was changed. I need that report, Vlad."

"And you have to go to Russia to get it."

"He has a copy. But it's too risky to email or fax. I have to get it in person."

He swore under his breath. "And what then? What happens after you get that report?"

"And then . . ." She shook her head, grabbed the entire stack of notes, and shoved them in her backpack. "And then I don't know."

She started to walk away, so he gripped her arms to stop her. "Why didn't you tell me any of this, Elena?"

She unartfully dodged his question. "I'll only be gone a few days. Maybe, maybe a week. I can get a flight to New York in a few hours and then to Russia from there tomorrow night."

"No." He shook his head, his jaw a wedge of granite. "You can't go."

She looked at him with beseeching eyes. "I need to follow this lead."

"What lead?" he exploded. "Your father is dead, and nothing is going to change that."

"I know that," she yelled, yanking free of his hands. "But I have to know what happened to him, Vlad. I'm trying to find out *what happened to him*."

"No, you're not! You're trying to justify in your mind why his job was always more important than you!"

Her face fell as the color drained from her skin. "His job was important. Journalism is important."

"Is that how you justify the fact that you hid in a hotel room for three days with almost nothing to eat? Why my mother had to buy you your first tampons? Why he never, ever remembered your birthday?"

She wrapped her arms around her torso and looked as small and defeated as she did the day that he snapped at her in the hospital. He wished he could take it away—the pain of what he said—but he couldn't. She had to face it, because the guys were right. It was just like in fiction. This was her internal conflict, and until she truly faced it, they would always end up right back here.

Vlad bent to grab his crutches. He was tired and sore and all out of fight. He slid them under his armpits and leaned heavily.

"What are you doing?" she breathed.

Irony turned his voice to vinegar. "What I always do with you. I'm letting a captive bird go winging."

"Vlad . . ." Her voice was a hoarse, wrenching rasp that would've made any Russian romanticist proud, as if it had floated up from the depths of some hidden well of feelings where she'd been hiding them. He recognized the sound because he had one of those wells too. The difference was, he wasn't afraid of the dark water below. She was still searching for a life preserver.

Vlad closed the distance between them and cradled her head

against his chest. "I love you, Elena. I don't want you to go, but I'm not going to stop you, and I'm not going to make you choose. But I'm done trying to convince you to choose me."

Elena straightened and pulled away from him. "Why can't you just support me on this? Why can't you accept that this is who I am?"

"Because you're chasing something you'll never be able to catch. And I can't compete with a ghost."

"I'm not asking you to compete with my father."

"He's not the ghost I'm talking about. Decide what you want, Elena. Once and for all."

The trek down the stairs was the longest of his life. Colton was crouched on the bottom step, waiting for him. He stood up when he heard Vlad's descent.

"Let's go," Vlad said.

"Um, where's Elena?"

Vlad crutched around him to the door. "She's not coming."

"Is she okay?"

Vlad didn't answer. He threw open the door and crutched outside. Colton followed slowly. "Dude, talk to me. What the fuck is going on?"

Vlad spoke purely out of pain. "I need to make a stop."

"Thought we were never coming back here," Colton said, car idling in the seedy, weedy parking lot.

"You can wait in the car." Vlad got out with his crutches. He banged on the door with his fist, and when the window slid open, he held up his coin. A moment of palpable surprise from the eyes staring out at him made him scowl. "Let me in."

Colton appeared beside him as the door squeaked open. Byron

ushered them inside, a leery look on his scraggly face. "He's not going to like this. He said you're banned."

"I don't give a shit what he said."

Byron made a quick decision about the difference in their two sizes and told them to go inside. Colton was blessedly silent as he followed Vlad up the ramp and through the heavy curtain. When they walked inside, Roman didn't even look up from where he arranged a delicate array of cheese curls. "Didn't think you'd have the balls to show up here again."

"I need a hit."

Roman snorted.

"Ädelost," Vlad said, pointing at the blue-veiny Swiss cheese. He scanned the day's selection and landed on a semihard from Denmark. "Samsø. And . . . Époisses."

Colton and Roman both reeled back. The creamy French cheese was known for its pungency. Only the most hard-core of cheese connoisseurs could stand its aroma.

"Dude, no," Colton said.

"That is strong cheese, my friend," Roman said.

"The stronger the better." Vlad pulled his wallet from his back pocket.

"A man only drowns himself in cheese like that when he's looking for a fight," Roman said.

Colton lifted an eyebrow. "Or when he's just been in one."

Vlad lifted his chin to the end of the table. "Throw some of that Edammer in there too." Because why the fuck not? He was going to drown his sorrows in the decadent nutty flavor alongside some chilled peaches until he passed out. And then maybe he could wake up and realize it had all been a dream, and she was not going back to Russia.

Roman tossed him the bag, and Vlad dropped two hundred dollars on the table.

"Tell your wife I said hello."

Vlad growled, and Colton dragged him away. "What the hell is going on?" he asked, helping Vlad into the car. He threw the crutches in the back and jogged around to the driver's side. "I mean it, Vlad. You either tell me what's going on or—"

Vlad ripped open the bag. The pungent, offensive odor of the Époisses immediately filled the cab of Colton's truck. Colton gagged and opened a window. "Christ. That smells like athlete's foot."

Vlad tore off a hunk of the Samsø, set it on his tongue, and rolled it around in his mouth. "It's an acquired taste."

"Caviar is an acquired taste. *That* is the end stages of gangrene." Colton gagged again as he pulled out of the parking lot. "Start talking."

"She's going back to Russia to find her father."

"Elena?"

"Yes, of course Elena."

"What the fuck? Why now?"

Vlad relayed the key details of what Elena had told him.

"And you're not going to stop her?"

"What's the point? She was always going to leave me."

"If you still think that after all this time, then you haven't learned a goddamn thing. Have you been paying attention at all?"

Colton made a call on his hands-free calling device.

Mack answered immediately. "What's the story? Is everything okay?"

"No," Colton said, glaring pointedly at Vlad. "Assemble the bros. We have a magnificent ass to kick."

The minute they pulled back into the driveway at Colton's, Claud and Michelle met them on the front porch.

"What did you do?" Claud demanded.

"Vlad, what is going on?" Michelle, at least, used a nice tone of voice.

"I like that girl," Claud said, following Vlad inside. "If you hurt her, you will answer to me."

The guys dragged him to the basement. The yelling commenced as soon as Vlad explained himself.

"So . . . you gave her an ultimatum?" Malcolm looked ready to tackle him.

"No! I told her specifically that I was not going to make her choose."

"Which is an ultimatum to a woman who thinks she doesn't *have* a choice," Mack argued.

Vlad felt a kick inside his chest.

"Oh, is that a light bulb going off?" Mack snorted.

Malcolm sat down next to him and settled a hand on Vlad's knee. "You're the heart and soul of this friendship. But sometimes the most tender people can be the most stubborn, because they have the most to lose when things go wrong."

"*She* is the stubborn one."

The guys all exchanged a *get a load of this douchebag* look. "Vlad, why do you think she never told you about any of this before?"

The question was from Noah, who had mostly refrained from yelling until now.

"Your lack of answer tells me you know what it is," Noah said.

"She said she knew I would freak out."

"And you did, didn't you?" Malcolm prodded.

"I told her I love her. I told her—"

"That your love comes with strings attached when she needs you most." Noah's tone of voice managed to shame Vlad as much as the words themselves.

Malcolm was there again, this time with an arm around his shoulders. "There's a big difference between letting someone go because you have faith that they'll come back to you and letting someone go because deep down you're convinced they won't. One is an act of love, the other an act of fear."

I let a captive bird go winging . . .

He'd spent six years clinging to his mother's interpretation of the poem, that Elena was a frightened bird who needed to fly free for a while before returning to the nest. But didn't that mean their marriage was, and had always been, a cage from which Elena had to be set free? Didn't that trap him in the role of the beast holding her against her will until he chose to open the door to the cage?

All his time in book club, all the lessons he thought he'd learned, and he never learned the most important. He wasn't the cage. He wasn't the captivity to which she had to eventually return.

He was the air beneath her wings. She needed him to fly with her.

"I need to go home," he rasped.

Colton dug his keys out again. "Yes, you do. You have a lot of groveling to do."

Colton drove as fast as he could, but it was too late.

Elena was already gone.

CHAPTER TWENTY-FIVE

The hotel by the freeway had only gotten more depressing since she'd last checked in. She couldn't get a flight out until the morning, but the thought of staying in the house was too painful, so she ended up back here.

In all her lonely years, this was the loneliest she'd ever felt. She was in a hotel by herself, headed back to a place that was no longer home. But the only home she did have left was suddenly cold and empty. Vlad had taken its light and warmth and walked out the door with it, leaving behind nothing but ugly accusations.

You're trying to justify in your mind why his job was always more important than you.

It wasn't true. It wasn't.

You're chasing a ghost.

No.

Is that how you justify the fact that you hid in a hotel room for three days with almost nothing to eat? Why my mother had to buy you your first tampons? Why he never, ever remembered your birthday?

Elena didn't realize she was crying until she felt the dampness on her pillow when she rolled onto her side.

What happens after you get that report?

A bone-deep fatigue settled into her limbs, because the answer to *that* question was a dark horizon. A cliff she couldn't see over. Clue after clue after clue. None of them led anywhere definitive. How long was she going to do this? How long was she going to ignore the beauty of her present for the ugliness of her past?

Vlad was right. She was chasing a ghost. *She* was the ghost. The little girl she once was before she realized how different her life was from others. Before she figured out that no matter what she did, her father was never going to come home on time. Never going to help with her homework, make sure she had a good lunch or clean clothes. He was never going to take her ice skating or to the movies. He was never going to remember her birthday. She'd spent years trying to figure out why she mattered so little to the one person who was supposed to love her above all else.

Tears soaked her pillow now as sobs racked her body. What was she doing? Why was she leaving the man who *did* love her above all else? Who always had, even when she'd rejected him, even when it was clear that she didn't deserve him.

She didn't want this. She didn't want to spend her life blindly chasing something in her past until she was unable to see what was right in front of her.

Elena shot out of bed, wiping madly at her face. What was she doing here? There was only one place she wanted to be, one place she belonged. Home. And home was with Vlad. She shoved her feet into her shoes, grabbed her backpack and her suitcase. She hadn't unpacked anything yet. All she had to do was *go home.*

The woman at the counter who checked her in watched with

confused curiosity as Elena dropped her key cards into the return box. As soon as she walked through the automatic doors to the outside and into the humid night, Elena started to run. The wheels of her suitcase bounced along the seams in the sidewalk. Her car was around the corner of the hotel entrance and beneath a skyscraper-high streetlamp.

She unlocked the car with her key fob, opened the back, and threw in her suitcase and backpack.

And that's when the world went black.

Elena woke up disoriented. Groggy. A throbbing pain the only proof that she was alive.

She pried her eyes open against the pain, but all she saw was more darkness. Her body rocked back and forth in time with a rhythmic sound.

She was in a car.

Wait. *Vlad's* car.

How did she get here? What was going on?

The pain. Someone had hit her. Someone had snuck up behind her in the parking lot and hit her. She tried again to raise her hands to the spot on her scalp that hurt, but she couldn't move. Her wrists were taped in front of her body with something. Duct tape maybe?

She couldn't see who was driving. The outline of his eyes in the rearview mirror was all she could see from this angle in the back seat. Nothing about them were familiar. Elena strained to turn her head to see out the window where they were, but all she could see was the glare of lights as they passed by.

Think. She had to think. She could easily reach the door locks, but they were driving too fast for her to attempt an escape. Maybe she could distract him, force him off the road somehow. But she was as likely to die in that scenario as if she opened her door and rolled out.

Her eyes darted around the back seat. Why did Vlad keep such a clean car? There wasn't even a stray pen lying on the ground that she could use to stab someone if necessary.

"I know you're awake back there." Elena gasped and froze. The accent was Russian, but he spoke in English. "How is your head?"

"Who are you?" Elena rasped.

"I am sorry about hitting you. You surprised me. I didn't expect you to come out until the morning. Our plan was to take you on the way to the airport, so we had to improvise."

Dread turned her stomach to rot. *Calm, Elena. Stay calm. Keep him talking.* Her father's voice came out of nowhere in her imagination. "How long have I been out?"

"About five minutes. I was starting to worry."

Her stomach revolted at his fake concern.

"I found your phone in your backpack," he said, almost bored. "I tossed it in the parking lot before we left, so don't bother looking for it."

She swallowed her panic.

He laughed. "They were right about you. I did not think you would fall for it, but you are a lot like your father was. The promise of a big break was all it took to get him out of the house too."

Agony tore a hole in her chest. It was all a ruse, and she'd fallen for it. Is that how they got her father too? "You knew my father?"

"That's enough talking. You should save your strength. You'll need it later."

"Just tell me," she begged, ashamed of the way her voice gave away her fear. "I just need to know. What did you do to him? Where is his body?"

"Gone. That's all you need to know."

"No. Please tell me. Why can't you just tell me? You're going to kill me anyway. Did you kill him the night he disappeared?"

"Yes."

Grief, new and raw, ripped open all the old scars. A sob brought her bound hands to her mouth. All those days she waited for him in the hotel . . . he was already dead.

"He begged us to leave you alone," the man said. "It was actually kind of touching. He told us you knew nothing, that he never told you anything. But then you couldn't leave it alone, could you? You had to start digging just like him. I actually think he'd be proud of you in a weird way. He loved you. I don't know if that's any consolation, but he did."

Grief became an unbearable pain. Tears burned her eyes, clogged her throat, hacked her breathing. She opened her mouth to scream, but nothing came out but agonized air, a silent sob that ended with a violent cough.

Her father had begged for her protection. Before he died, he'd been thinking of her.

"Would you like some water?" the man asked.

"I don't want anything from you."

"I can understand that. Try to relax. We are almost there."

Be calm, Elena. Be calm. He father's voice came to her again. She tried to slow her breathing and rein in her thoughts. She had to think. She had to get out of here. He said they were almost there. So, they were still in Nashville. They had to be. If she'd only been unconscious for a few minutes, then they couldn't have gotten far. Maybe she could make a run for it as soon as he opened the door. It was her best option, but she would have to surprise him, maybe even overpower him, first. She had to be ready to pounce, but she had no idea which side he would open to get her out.

In the front seat, the man's phone rang. He laughed and hit the speaker button. "I assume this is for you."

A familiar voice filled the car and turned her blood to ice. "Hello, Elena. I hear you're not cooperating."

No. It couldn't be true.

"You really are too much like your father. He didn't know when to quit, and neither do you."

Not him. Not Yevgeny. He couldn't be part of this.

He chuckled. "I thought that by hiring you, I could keep an eye on you, but you were even further along than I ever dreamed you'd get. That's the sad irony of this. You're a hell of a good journalist, Elena. You could have had a wonderful career, but your fatal flaw was the same as his. You trusted the wrong people."

She wanted to scream, claw, spit, and fight, but she couldn't. Grief had stolen everything she had left . . .

"You were my father's friend."

"And that made it harder than you can ever know to have to stop him the way we did. But he got too close, just like you."

"Too close to *what*?"

"To unmasking me."

"You're Strazh." She was dizzy with the rush of rage.

"I am. Nice to meet you."

"You won't get away with this."

"I already have, Elena. More times than you know."

"You have daughters. How can you do the things you do and not see their faces every single time?"

"By not bothering myself with the details. I make money. That's all it is."

"Please," she choked. "I don't care what you do to me. Just, please, leave Vlad alone. He knew nothing about this. Okay? You have to believe me. I never told him anything. Please don't hurt him. Please."

Yevgeny laughed. Loud and openly, as if she'd just told the funniest joke in the world. "Do you want to know the last thing your father said?"

Snot and tears mixed together on her face.

"He said, *Don't hurt my little girl. She doesn't know anything.* You two are so alike."

She didn't try to fight or argue anymore. The pain this time was overwhelming.

"I promised him I would look after you. And I tried. I really tried. I've known all along where you were, Elena. Every step you've taken since that moment, I've known where you were. But you just couldn't leave things alone. You couldn't have just married that rich hockey player of yours and moved to America and lived a life as a bored hockey wife, could you? You just had to be as much of a pain in the ass as your father."

"What did you do to him?" she whispered.

"Does it matter?" Yevgeny paused. "I'm sorry, Elena. I really am."

He hung up.

Her father was dead. He had died trying to right the wrongs of the world, a noble cause, but he'd left her alone because of it. He'd left her alone with no details on what happened to him. What if she disappeared just like her father and Vlad never knew what happened to her? She had to get back to him. She wasn't going to leave Vlad with the same unanswered questions, the same guilt and grief, that she'd lived with for so many years. She wasn't going to let a fruitless quest steal what really mattered from her. Him. It had always been him. She'd just been too blind to see it.

She wasn't going to do that to Vlad. The cycle ended here. She had to find a way to escape.

Elena turned onto her side on the small seat to look around the car again for a weapon, *anything*.

"What're you doing back there?"

She adopted a pained voice. "Trying to get comfortable. My head hurts."

"It won't be much longer."

A chill stole over her body at the double meaning in his words. She shifted again.

And that's when she felt it.

In her front pocket.

The burner phone. *He hadn't found the burner phone.* Maybe he hadn't even thought to check. He would have been in a hurry to get her body into the car before anyone saw them.

Heart racing, her eyes darted to the rearview mirror. He was still staring at the road ahead, but if he so much as glanced back, he would see what she was doing.

Elena rolled onto her other side to hide her front from his view.

Facing away from him, she angled her hands toward her pocket and worked her two pointer fingers inside. It took several slippery tries with her sweat-soaked skin to ease the phone out inch by inch. It fell onto the seat with a quiet thud, but it might as well have been as loud as a gunshot. She held her breath for his reaction, but . . . nothing. She picked up the phone between her bound hands and pondered another problem. How was she going to hide the light from the screen when she turned it on? Faking a moan, she curled into a tight ball to surround the phone as she hit the home screen button.

It lit up, and she shoved it facedown on the seat.

"I really am sorry about your head," the man said. "I do not like to hit women."

Right. He just kidnapped them and trafficked them.

Elena eased the phone onto its side, cupping it close to her body. Fumbling, she found the button to turn down the brightness. Then she flipped the tiny button on the side to silence it.

Acting as fast as she could, she hit the icon for messages and thumbed in Vlad's number by memory. Another lesson from her father. Never rely on technology to remember phone numbers.

With fat, clumsy fingers, she typed a single word.

Sparrow.

Vlad clenched the phone in his hand. The word swam in his vision. Turned and twisted and floated as his brain tried to push it away. He sank against the island in his kitchen, and his crutches fell with a crash.

"What's wrong, man?" Colton looked down at the text message. "What is *sparrow*?"

Vlad's knees gave out. Colton wrapped his arms around Vlad's chest just in time. "Jesus. What the fuck. Vlad, what is going on?"

Vlad choked on his own voice. "Call the police."

"*What?*"

"Call the fucking police!"

"Why? What the fuck is going on?"

Vlad grabbed the front of Colton's shirt. "She's been taken. Elena has been kidnapped."

CHAPTER TWENTY-SIX

Elena curled into a ball and made a noise like she was crying.

"Please do not do that," the man said. "I cannot stand to hear a woman cry."

The sonofabitch. Men like him got off on making women cry. She was going to enjoy making him pay. With her body shielding the light and sound, she hit the button for 911 and then quickly muted it so he wouldn't hear the dispatcher answer. She just hoped the dispatcher could hear *them*.

Elena moaned again for effect. "Why are you doing this to me?"

"You know why," the man said.

"Just tell me where you're taking me."

"You'll see soon enough."

Sweat ran down her face. Could the dispatcher hear his answers or only her questions? "Why not just kill me when you had the chance? Why are you torturing me like this?"

"Because we need you alive for a while."

Elena made her voice wobbly and scared, which wasn't a stretch. She was terrified. "I need you to do something for me."

The man laughed. "Right."

"Will you at least tell my husband where my body is? Please. Do you know who my husband is? He's a very gentle man, and this will destroy him. His name is Vlad Konnikov. Do you know him? He's a hockey player, but he's not like most hockey players. He is sweet and kind, and it will destroy him if you kill me and leave him with no answers."

She glanced down at the phone. The dispatcher was still there. Still listening.

But in the front seat, so was someone else. His voice grew cold. "What are you doing?"

"I'm begging you to have mercy on my husband."

He suddenly jerked the wheel as he whipped his head around to look over his shoulder. "You bitch! Do you have a phone?"

"No—"

He jerked the wheel again, and this time she crashed onto the floor. The phone flew under the front seat, out of her reach.

All she had left was to scream. "My name is Elena Konnikova! I have been kidnapped! I am in my husband's car. A Cadillac Escalade, license plate NBT-413."

Another lesson from her father. Always know your license plate number.

The car rocked to the right as the man whipped off the road. Her face whacked against the floorboard of the back seat, sending spots before her eyes and blood into her mouth.

"Fuck!" The man beat his hands on the steering wheel. "You fucking bitch!"

Beneath his seat, the phone was facedown. She had no idea if the dispatcher heard her scream for help. The man suddenly threw open his door and got out of the car. Elena scrambled to sit up, but she was trapped between the seats. He stormed around to the passenger side, the side where her feet were. Good. She could struggle better that way. She could kick and make it impossible for him to pull her out of the car.

Elena drew her knees up.

He wrenched open the door and leaned in.

She kicked with all her strength.

Her feet connected with his face. There was a disgusting crunch as blood spurted from his nose. He stumbled backward, and Elena hoisted herself to a sitting position. He lunged for her again and managed to grab one of her ankles.

Elena screamed and kicked again as she twisted toward the front. She wrapped her bound arms around the console between the front seats and used the leverage to haul her body up. Her leg slipped from his grasp, and this time he fell.

Elena threw herself forward, scrambling into the front seat. The car was still running.

She looked over her shoulder as he lunged toward the open door. She bent and used both her hands to put the car into drive. Then, without looking, she jammed her foot on the gas pedal.

The SUV lurched, and Elena looked back just in time to see him fall again. With a jerk of the wheel, Elena hit the gas again and whipped out into traffic.

And right into the path of an oncoming car.

There was a scream. A crash. The crunch of metal on metal.

And the world went black again.

CHAPTER TWENTY-SEVEN

Vlad was going to be sick. He stumbled just in time to the bathroom and heaved into the toilet.

Colton came running. "Everyone's here, man. It's going to be okay. We're going to find her."

"It's my fault. I should have stayed here. I shouldn't have let her go."

Malcolm, Mack, Noah, and fucking Cheese Man crowded around the bathroom door. "It's not your fault," Mack said. "You couldn't have known."

Vlad sagged against the wall. His leg throbbed, but he barely felt it. "How could I just leave? Why didn't I *stay*?"

"Vlad! Get out here!" Michelle's voice was a high-pitched panic.

Malcolm and Mack each grabbed an arm, hauled him up, and helped him back into the hallway. Michelle stood at the front door.

"A cop is here," Michelle said, her hands coiled into a tense ball against her stomach. Neighbor Dog woofed and began to wag his tail.

Noah strode forward and opened the door. Just in time, Colton grabbed Neighbor Dog's collar to stop him from launching himself at the cop's chest as he walked in. The officer introduced himself as Lt. Zamir Hammadi.

"My wife," Vlad sobbed, fear turning his muscles to useless rubber.

"Sir, is your wife's name Elena Konnikova?"

Another sob broke free from his mouth. "Yes. Yes. Someone has taken her. She's a journalist and—"

"Sir, please listen to me. Your wife has been found."

His knees gave out, and once again, the guys had to grab him to keep him from falling. "Where? Is she okay? Is she hurt? Who had her?"

The officer raised a hand. "Sir, I need you to calm down so I can answer all your questions."

"Vlad, let him talk," Colton said. But even he was biting his nails.

"What I can tell you is that she was involved in a car accident—"

Vlad swayed again.

"—but her injuries do not appear life-threatening. She has been taken to Nashville Memorial."

Vlad looked at Colton, who was already digging his keys out of his pocket. "Let's go."

The officer sighed. "I'll drive you."

"The rest of us will follow," Colton said.

Vlad ignored the pain in his leg and ran to the police cruiser parked in the driveway. As soon as the doors were shut and belts buckled, Vlad turned his best defenseman face to the police officer and said, "Tell me everything you know."

The details made his stomach clench again, and he was afraid he'd have to lean out the window and puke on the way to the hospital. A man had taken her from the parking lot of a hotel where she'd just checked in. She'd managed to secretly call 911 after texting him, and dispatchers heard everything. Including when she saved herself. And when the car crashed.

"Your wife is incredibly brave," Lt. Hammadi said.

"I know," he groaned. And he'd tried to make her feel guilty for it. He'd told her she was chasing a ghost, a lost cause. He'd pushed her away and straight into their trap.

"Put your head between your legs, man," Lt. Hammadi said. Vlad must've had *gonna boot soon* written all over his face. He obeyed, and a calming hand squeezed his shoulder.

"She's okay. She's okay."

"She has to be. She's the best thing that ever happened to me."

"Make sure she knows it."

As they ate up the road, he vowed that he would. From this point forward, he would spend every minute of the rest of their lives making it up to her.

"The driver of the car has been arrested. That's all I know."

"He didn't do this alone. She was working on a story. There were other people."

"And investigators will find them. You just focus on your wife."

They sped into the ER bay, and Vlad was out the door before the car had barely stopped. Behind them, Colton's car screeched to a stop. He ran to catch up. "Everyone is behind me."

The officer joined him in a brisk jog. Which was good, because no one stopped them when they ran in. Vlad slammed his hands against the swinging automatic doors that stood between the waiting room and the ER beds. They eked open, and he swore at every millisecond it took before he could run through.

"Elena!" He shouted her name, and he ran. He ran because it was grand gesture, and he was going to drop dead if he didn't get to her.

He shouted again. "Elena!"

Ahead, a woman in a gown stepped out from behind a curtain. She had blood on her face and ice on her wrist.

Elena.

"*Vlad.*"

He ran toward her.

He tripped.

And fell at her feet.

CHAPTER TWENTY-EIGHT

It's all fun and games until you're flat on your back in an emergency room and your wife starts yelling at you in Russian.

Elena towered over him, hands on her hips, and a fierce look on her face. He'd never been so in love in his entire life.

"I cannot believe you," she shouted. "What are you doing? Were you *running*? Where are your crutches?"

"I— We always run for grand gesture," Vlad panted.

Colton winced as he offered a hand to help him up. "Dude, I may not speak Russian, but pissed-off wife is a universal language. I don't think she appreciated the grand gesture."

Vlad ignored the sharp pain in his leg as he stood. He didn't care. If he'd hurt it again, his leg would heal, and even if it didn't, he'd survive. But he wouldn't survive another day without Elena. Nearly losing her had put things in perspective rather quickly.

He hobbled toward his wife. His beautiful, smart, generous, brave wife. Elena's features softened, and her arms shot out just in case he fell again. He limped straight into her embrace, wrapped his arms around her, buried his face in her neck, and sobbed. He clung to her. Breathed her in. Kissed her neck and tasted the life-affirming salt of her sweat and tears.

"I was so scared," he choked. "I thought I lost you."

"I thought I lost you too. I'm so sorry, Vlad. I'm so sorry."

He pulled back and smoothed the hair from her face, rage pushing at his temples at the sight of blood on her skin. "I wasn't there, Elena." His voice was a snotty hiccup. "If I hadn't left, if I'd been there—"

"I'm glad you weren't, because they might have killed you on the spot."

He went cold at the factual, impassive tone of her voice. As if she were willing to risk her life to protect *him*. Vlad wiped his face and glowered. "You say that like any of this is *normal*."

"In my life, it kind of has been."

He shook his head. "I can't believe your father made you think that."

She curled her lips into a patient smile. "Vlad, I think you should sit down, because I need to say some things."

"*Now?*"

"Yes, now. I need you to hear me."

Vlad nodded reluctantly. He sat down, and she stepped between his legs. He had to look up to see her.

"You learn a lot about yourself when someone kidnaps you," she said.

"That isn't funny," he rasped. "How can you joke about any of this?"

She smoothed his sweat-soaked hair back from his forehead. "Because a macabre sense of humor is how journalists like my father and me process the horrific things we see."

"You are *not* like your father."

"But I am. In so many ways I am." She rested her hands on his shoulders. "He did a lot of things wrong. You were right about that. And I think you were also right that I've been desperate to make his absence in my life worth it."

"I shouldn't have said that. It was cruel."

"No, I needed to hear it. I couldn't see what I was doing to myself and to us. You helped me see that, and I will love you forever for it."

Her bottom lip trembled, so he gripped her hips and tugged her closer. She pressed a hand to the center of his chest. "But I need you to understand that this is part of who I am and will always be part of who I am. I am a journalist at heart, and I don't want to deny that part of me. Not when I know that I have a passion and a skill that can do good things in the world. I can't change who I am, but I can promise that I will be better. Better than him. Better than I have been. Better to *us*."

She curled her hands around his cheeks. "I will never put us at risk for the sake of a story. Ever. Because nothing is more important to me than you. I've been living with the ghost of my father for so long that it blinded me to everything else. To you. And *I* nearly lost *you*. And I'm so, so sorry, Vlad."

Her expression was a combination of tenderness and ferocity, and he realized with a jolt that it was uniquely *her*. Two mutually exclusive traits had somehow merged when the universe created this woman, and he'd never appreciated it, never saw it, until now. Until she stood before him with her gentle fingers on his face and her determination sparking like lightning in her eyes. For so long, he'd considered the two sides of her as separate beings at war with each other, and only one could win. But to truly love her, he had to love both sides of her. The nurturing woman who heated his blood and fed his soul with her poetry and passion. And the warrior woman who would likely give him heartburn but make him so damn proud with her crusades for the rest of his life.

Vlad turned into her touch and kissed her palm. Then he slid his own hands up her back and brought her flush against him. "I love you," he declared. "And if this is what you want to do, then I am behind you. Just promise me, *promise me*, that you will never shut me out. I want to be part of it all. Every ugly part of it. Don't hide anything from me, because you are part of me."

And then he kissed her, and she kissed him back. She kissed him like she knew how close they'd come to never kissing again. She kissed him with unrestrained passion and roaming hands and panted breaths. Like it was their first time and their last chance. She kissed him with his name on her lips, her heart in her eyes, with joy in every breath.

"It's going to be okay now, Lenochka," he whispered. "Everything is going to be okay."

A clearing throat brought them apart. Vlad looked around her body to see Colton peeking his head in through the curtain. "You know, just because none of us speak Russian doesn't mean we don't understand sex noises. You're shocking the staff."

Elena laughed and dropped her face to Vlad's shoulder. He hugged her tightly, hand palmed around the curve of her neck to hold her, safe and sound and secure.

"So, is it safe to come in now or what?" Colton asked.

"Go away," Vlad grumbled.

Elena laughed and turned around in his arms. "You can come in."

A single-file line walked through the curtain. Colton. Mack. Malcolm. Michelle. Claud. Noah. Cheese Man.

Cheese Man? Vlad glowered at Colton. "What is *he* doing here?"

"He's a friend of Elena's too."

"I was very worried," Cheese Man said. He reached for Elena's hand, probably to kiss it, the bastard. Vlad slid his arms around Elena's waist and pulled her against his chest in an unabashed possessive pose.

"Thank you for coming," Elena laughed, covering Vlad's hands with her own. "That was very kind of you."

Cheese Man pointed at Vlad. "You are a lucky man, my friend. I hope you recognize it."

Vlad kissed Elena's neck. "I do."

"Keep it PG, kids," Colton said. "You can't do the humping in here."

The aggressive scrape of the curtain rings heralded the arrival of a very annoyed ER doctor. "Folks, we can't have this many people in here. Just family."

Elena leaned into Vlad's chest. "This *is* our family."

"Damn straight, it is," Mack said.

"Well, there are too many of you. You can visit her when she's admitted to her own room."

Vlad tightened his hold on her waist. "You're admitting her?"

"Overnight for observation."

"Do I have a concussion?" Elena asked.

"Yes, but I cannot go into details with *all these people* here."

Colton snapped and pointed. "Point taken. We're leaving."

One by one, the guys stopped in front of Elena to kiss her cheek and pat Vlad on the shoulder. Except Cheese Man. He just waved before ducking out. Michelle gave her a long hug, and Claud just smiled. The doctor left, too, and said he'd be back in a few minutes to discuss the results of her CT scan.

Vlad turned Elena around his arms and then stood up on one leg. "You need to be in bed. A concussion is serious. I know these things."

He held her hand as she crawled onto the mattress. Then he draped the thin white blanket across her lap before sitting down in the small chair next to her bedside. Their hands laced next to her hip.

"I love you," she said, resting her head on the pillow.

"I love you too." He leaned forward and kissed her hand. "And I want us to have a real wedding."

"You do?"

He looked up in time to see a happy tear roll down her cheek. "Here in America, with all our friends and my parents. I want to wait for you as you walk down the aisle, and I want to kiss you in front of everyone, and I want my mother to read a poem."

"Sounds like you have it all planned out," she teased, another tear dripping onto the pillow.

"I've thought about it a lot."

Elena smiled. "I just have one request."

"Anything," Vlad said, using the pad of his thumb to wipe away her tear.

"Can Cheese Man cater it?"

EPILOGUE

One month later

Vlad thought it was torture when the guys were reading his words. That was nothing compared to this.

It had been three hours since Elena had taken his manuscript with her to bed with a stern order not to bother her until she was done. He'd set his rehab back a month with his fall in the hospital, so he'd used the time to his advantage. He took care of her as she recovered from her concussion, and he finished his damn book.

Taking care of Elena had been the harder part of the two. In the month since the incident, there had been FBI interviews and media attention and interest from literary agents who wanted to sign her to write a book about her experience and her investigation. The team's immigration attorneys were working to make sure they didn't violate any visa laws if she chose to do so, but it was low on Elena's priorities. She'd already vowed that any money offered for her story would immediately go to Marta and the other women Yevgeny and his goons had hurt. Marta was now safely hidden under federal protection while Gretchen represented her claim for asylum.

The assholes who'd taken Elena were in prison awaiting trial on charges that would ensure they never stepped foot outside a cell again. That didn't make Vlad any less worried, though. He'd upgraded his security system and hired a bodyguard for when she left the house without him. She'd tried to argue that issue, but one look at his face, and she'd backed down.

After all that, it should have been a breeze to have Elena read his book. It wasn't. He was dying. He lay on the couch and flipped through the channels as the hours ticked by. Finally, her soft footsteps padded down the stairs.

He couldn't see her face or her expression at first when she walked into the dark room. He zapped off the TV and sat up. "Well?"

Elena stepped into the light. Her eyes were puffy and red. "Vlad . . ." she breathed.

"Wh-what does that mean?" He gulped.

She crossed the room to the couch and curled up next to him. When she pressed her hand into his chest, his world tilted off its axis. It happened a lot with her. "Vlad, this is so, so good."

His heart leaped into this throat. "Are you lying to me?"

"No," she laughed. "Look at me."

He obeyed, but reluctantly.

"Why didn't you ever tell me you could write like this?"

"I don't know."

She rubbed a circle over his heart. "That soft part of you, the one that cries at animal shows and weddings, the one that studies poetry and kisses chickens . . . you've poured all of it into a story that made me cry and cheer and want to kiss you until you can't breathe."

He gulped again. "I like the kissing part of that."

She obliged. She straddled his lap, and their mouths met in a tangle of wild and unrestrained longing. It was a sloppy kiss, tender and fierce at once, just like her. This was the moment he'd read about so many times, but nothing he wrote in his own book would ever come close to capturing how this felt. The completeness of handing your whole heart to someone who gave hers back in return.

Vlad gripped her head and brought them brow to brow. "'My voice that is for you, the languid one and gentle . . .'"

She choked on an emotional noise, and her voice broke as she picked up the verse for "The Night," an ardent declaration about the burning fire of love, the poetry of passion, the rivers that ebb and flow between two lovers. Vlad stroked her velvet mouth with his tongue before pulling back and panting the final lines, written, it seemed, for them alone. "'My friend, my sweetest friend, I love—'"

But his throat clogged with a rising sob of joy, cutting off his voice. Elena kissed his nose, gently, sweetly, and took over for him, completing the promise with a fervent whisper against his lips. "'I love . . . I'm yours . . . I'm yours.'"

Promise Me

"Tony, you have to eat something."

He held the bandage at his side, where just a week ago, a Nazi bullet had torn a hole through him. He shoved the plate away with his other hand and stood. It had been a week since the rescue. A week since he'd been shot. A week since his last fleeting image of Anna standing above him, crying and screaming his name, before her blood splattered his face. And then the world went black.

Two days ago, the light returned when he'd woken up on this hospital ship headed for the U.S. with Jack sitting next to his bunk, an agonized and regretful look on his face. He hadn't left Tony alone since. As if they were bonded somehow in shared grief.

"You're not going to heal if you don't eat," Jack said, following with Tony's untouched tray. "I'm trying to help you."

"I don't want your goddamned help." He whipped around and knocked the tray from Jack's hands. Chipped beef and applesauce flew in every direction. Tony ignored the stab of pain in his side and grabbed Jack by the lapels of his hospital robe. "You were supposed to save her! Where the hell were you?"

"Do you honestly think I'm not as broken up about this as you are?"

"I don't care what you feel."

"*I'm* the reason she's gone. She saved my life, and I couldn't save hers. I have to live with that for the rest of my life. I loved her as much you did, Tony."

The sound of a high-pitched gasp brought them apart. A Red Cross nurse stood with her hand to her mouth, eyes wide and disbelieving. She took a tentative step toward them, blinked rapidly, and then spun around to run in the other direction.

"What the hell was that?" Jack asked, bending to pick up the tray Tony had knocked from his hands. "She looked at us like she'd seen a ghost."

Tony crouched. "We've all seen ghosts in this war."

An orderly came by with a mop and a bucket. Tony held his side as he stood and reached for the mop. "Let me do it. It's my mess."

"No, sir," the young man said. "This is my job. Yours is to get better. You go on and sit down. Both of you."

Tony hesitated but finally held out a hand to help Jack to his feet.

Another feminine gasp interrupted. They turned in unison. A woman stood alone by the small door, silhouetted against the light. A bandage was wrapped around the crown of her head.

She stepped forward on shaky steps.

Oh my God. *Anna*.

Tony felt his knees give way, and the orderly dropped the mop to quickly catch him. Next to him, Jack trembled from head to foot. How? How was she here? How was she on this ship? A million thoughts collided at once, but he couldn't focus on a single one except the fear that he was dreaming.

"Anna . . ." A man's voice groaned her name, and Tony had no idea if it came from him or Jack.

With a cry, Anna rushed forward and threw her arms around them both. Tony wrapped a single arm around her waist, still afraid that this was just a dream. But she felt real. She was warm.

"Anna . . . how?" That time it was Jack.

She held a hand to each of their cheeks and spoke as tears poured down her face. "I was rescued by a Red Cross unit and brought on board. There was so much confusion, and I was in and out of consciousness."

"You were shot," Tony choked. "I saw it."

"It grazed my scalp, that's all."

No. That couldn't be possible. Tony ran his hands up and down her body. "You're okay? I can't believe you're alive."

"Tony," she whispered.

A groan escaped his lips as he yanked her against him. "I thought I lost you."

Next to them, Jack shuffled his feet. Tony pulled away from Anna and watched in agony as she turned to him.

"Jack . . ."

A small, sad smile lifted the corners of his mouth. "It's okay, Anna." He leaned forward and kissed her forehead. "It's okay."

"I didn't mean to . . ." A sob broke off her voice.

"Didn't mean to fall in love again?" He looked at Tony. "You're a good man, Tony. I can't think of anyone else who could possibly deserve her."

Jack held out his hand, and Tony accepted it with a lump in his throat.

"Jack," Anna whispered.

He ran a knuckle down her jaw. "I'll always love you, Anna. But you belong with Tony." He wiped a hand across his cheek. "I'm going to give you two some time."

Tony couldn't move, couldn't speak. So, he did the only thing he could. He kissed her. In front of everyone. He wrapped his arms around her, ignored the twinge in his side, and held her as tightly as he'd ever held her. He was never letting her go.

"Anna . . ." Her name was the only word he could say. So, he said it over and over again. Chanted it like a sacred prayer.

"I'm here," she whispered, soothing him with her touch, her kisses. "Everything is going to be okay now."

"Promise me."

"I promise."

ACKNOWLEDGMENTS

When I created the lovable character the Russian in the first Bromance Book Club book, I never intended for him to get his own story one day. I owe a huge thank-you to all the readers, bloggers, and reviewers who sent me messages and tagged me on social media to say, "Please give this gentle giant his own book!" I listened, and I'm so glad I did. I hope I have done justice to the man you've all grown to love so much.

Huge thanks to my niece, Madison Kefferstan, a real athletic trainer who helped me research hockey injuries and rehab. Thanks for indulging all my questions, no matter how ridiculous. I can't wait to see where your career takes you! Also thank you to attorney Melissa Indish for your invaluable help in researching the complex and heartbreaking realities of the American immigration system. Any mistakes in either area are entirely my own!

As always, enormous thanks to my agent, Tara Gelsomino, for your hard work and enthusiastic belief in the Bromance boys. Equal gratitude to my editor, Kristine E. Swartz, who helped me work through several rewrites of this book to make sure the Russian's story was perfect and true to his character. And to the entire marketing, publicity, foreign rights, and sales teams at Berkley Romance—you are the best in the business.

Thank you to my friends—Meika Usher, Christina Mitchell, Alyssa Alexander, Victoria Solomon, Tamara Lush, Thien-Kim Lam, Erin King, Elizabeth Cole, G.G. Andrews, Deborah Wilde, Jennifer Seay, Amanda Gale, Jessica Arden . . . I couldn't do this without you.

And finally to my family. Thanks for putting up with me. You're the reason I do this.

Photo by Lauren Perry of Perrywinkle Photography

Lyssa Kay Adams read her first romance novel at a very young age when she swiped one from her grandmother's stash. After a long journalism career in which she had to write too many sad endings, she decided to return to the stories that guaranteed a happy ever after. Once described as "funny, adorable, and a wee bit heartbreaking," Lyssa's books feature women who always get the last word, men who aren't afraid to cry, and animals. Lots of animals. Lyssa writes full-time from her home in Michigan, where she lives with her sportswriter husband, her wickedly funny daughter, and a spoiled Maltese who likes to be rocked to sleep like a baby. When she's not writing, she's cooking or driving her daughter around from one sporting event to the next. Or rocking the dog.

Ready to find
your next great read?

Let us help.

Visit prh.com/nextread